Thou Son's Keeper

Rod Cole

Cole, Rod 1965-
Thou Son's Keeper: a novel/ by Rod Cole .-1ˢᵗ ed.

Summary: Thou Son's Keeper takes place in the late 1800's during a time when violence and brutality were considered at their worse. Donovan is a farmer married to Sidney, the woman of his dreams. They have one child together, a son, Sage. For a time their life is full of joy and bliss as Donavon enjoys and supports his family from the spoils of his land. Eventually, his life turns upside down when he and his family are brutalized by 5 outlaws.
The story begins 7 years later when Donovan tracks the last of the 5 outlaws to a small town, where he confronts the man in a saloon and kills him. Though Donovan is on the alert from the lawmen and prior enemies who pursue him, he is intent on returning to his son Sage. Upon his return, he is disheartened to find that his son is merely a broken down boy, afraid even to speak in his own voice. Donovan vows to end the cycle of violence. Yet, in his impatience with the local injustices, he seems to find himself in one violent situation after another, including mounting tension with the corrupt town sheriff and his narcissistic brother.

ISBN: 978-0-9989894-0-2
ISBN: 978-0-9989894-1-9

*This book is dedicated to my father, **Thomas** and my late father-in-law, **Clifton**. Two modern-day pioneers that made a difference, by paving the way, so that our families for generations to come could have better opportunities than they had for themselves.*

Hello Reader. *I'm so excited that you have selected this book as your next read. My hope as an author was to create an amazing story that would take you on an emotional journey from the first chapter to the last. I wanted to create characters and a story that you would care about. Though this book is Fiction, to me the characters and their stories are so true and so real. I hope you feel the same. After you finish the book, I would appreciate your* **feedback** *by rating this book. Hopefully, your feedback will help draw others to the book as well.*

To leave a review, please go here: Thou Son's Keeper: He thought he could leave his violent past behind and go home to his son...he was wrong

Thank you!

Rod Cole

The Soldier in You: *"An unhappy life can be delusional. You'll find that you are so much stronger, more successful, and have a hidden happiness that you didn't know you had." (Non-fiction)*

Table of Contents

Chapter 1

His horse trotted forward down the main road. The hooves clanked with each step. Donovan stared at the faces, looking for the one that seemed familiar. Searching for the one that he had traveled so far to find.

His horse passed the saloon, and Donovan looked inside the window. Inside someone was playing a song on the piano. It was loud and off-key every few notes or so. He could hear men's voices as they talked, shouted and laughed. There was a man's back to the window; he was sitting and playing cards with other men. Their faces were hidden from the glare of the window. He could see a lady dressed in red walking about, handing these men their drinks.

Donovan guided his horse to the trough just in front of the hotel. He climbed off as his horse dunked his head into the water trough. He reached over and patted the horse on the neck. The horse dripped water on Donovan's shirt as he craned his head around, and then he turned back to the trough gulping more water.

As the people walked passed him, Donovan again studied their faces looking for the one that was familiar. He recognized none. He grabbed his sleeping gear, and duffel bag from the saddle tossed them over his shoulder and headed into the hotel. He didn't bother to tie Fletcher to the post. The animal preferred to roam about of his own free will. If he were tied he would buck so that either the post would be destroyed, or his leather harness would tear as he attempted to break away.

The hotel had three floors. On the main level, there was a sitting area with a small foot table a couch and a couple of chairs. Next to the sitting area was the check-in counter. Behind the counter was a man, he was sitting at a desk reading a newspaper as his back was to Donovan.

"I need a room," Donovan said as he approached the counter.

The man turned to Donovan, hesitated and frowned. Donovan was not surprised by the man's reaction. He glanced at the reflection of himself in the wall mirror close by. On his head was a brown wide brim hat. He wore it low just above his eyes. He hadn't shaved in over a week, and his face was dirty from the six-day ride to reach this town. His red eyes displayed how much sleep he had gone without. He had on a long brown overcoat that hung down almost to his boots.

"Just a moment." He said. And he turned back to finish reading his newspaper.

"Now," Said Donovan. He was not in the mood for waiting around. He had just come off a lengthy travel, and he wanted to settle himself and to have a meal.

The man turned to Donovan glaring, but his expression soon changed when he met Donovan's unyielding gaze. The man seemed nervous as he stood from his chair, and approached the counter. He wiped his palms on his black pinstriped pants. "I don't want no trouble here," The man said. "The sheriff ain't too far away."

"A room," Donovan repeated. He wasn't asking. He was telling. He set his gaze upon the man, daring him to test his patience.

"How long you staying?" The man finally asked.

Donovan wasn't sure, but his stay would be short. If all went as planned he would be gone within a couple of days, but in his life things hardly ever went as planned.

"A week." He answered.

"I will need the money up front," Said the man.

He nodded and reached into the pocket of his coat, pulled out a leather pouch that fit into the palm of his hand, pulled out some coins and placed them on the counter. The man placed the coins in his pocket and shoved a guest book, and writing pen in front of him. The book had pages of names and dates from previous guests. Some entries just had marks, such as X's, or O's or some sort of line.

"Do you know how to write your name?" The man asked.

Donovan signed and dated the book, but knew better than to use his own name. The man reached behind the desk and pulled out a key. He handed it to Donovan.

"Your room's on the second floor, door twenty-one."

Reaching into his pocket he pulled out a folded sheet of paper and stared at it. There was a sketching of a man's face. His hair at the top, thick and combed back, and the length went no further than the base of his neck. The most distinguishing features was the man's high-bridged nose and deep-set eyes. Eyes that when witnessed in person left no doubt to the man's malicious intentions. The sketching didn't quite capture this effect. Though it was just a sketching, the likeness of the man was very photo like. The words on the poster read. ***Wanted dead or alive for murders. Reward***

$1,000. Nevin Odland was the name written under the face. He studied the picture wondering how much this man had actually changed since he last seen him. He tossed the picture on the counter and said to the man. "You recognize him?"

The man never looked down. Donovan knew because he watched the man's eyes. He always watched the eyes in particular. The eyes divulged so much about a man's intent. This man's eyes revealed that he was distrusting of Donovan.

"No." The man answered. "Never seen him."

"You didn't look."

"You a bounty hunter?"

"No."

"You a marshal or lawman of some sort?"

"No."

"Then why should I look?"

Donovan gazed at the man. "Because you don't want any trouble, remember?"

With sweat on his brow, the man said. "The sheriff is close by."

"Do you really think the sheriff can help you right now?" Said Donovan.

Donovan watched the man come to the same conclusion as his eyes finally dropped to the picture. Surprisingly the man studied the picture. Donovan had figured him to give it a glance and then deny recognizing the photo. But instead, the man said. "I've seen him."

"Where is he?"

"What is it that you want with him?"

Donovan pointed to the poster. "Did you read it?"

"Yeah, I read it."

"What did it say?"

The man dropped his eyes to the poster, and read it again.

"Out loud," Donovan instructed. "I want to hear you say it."

The man glanced up and with his sleeve wiped the sweat from his brow. "Please." He begged. "I don't want trouble. I just work here."

With his index finger, he tapped on the paper. "Just read it."

The man dropped his eyes again to the poster and fumbled through the words. Reading to this stranger with the dirty appearance and partially hidden face was frightening. As his eyes scanned the poster the words came out. "Want-ed dead...or...a-live...for... mur-ders."

"Murder," Donovan said almost in a whisper. He dropped his head. "He's a murderer and a rapist. There was five of them. All murderers and rapists. Now there's only one." Donovan leaned forward and grabbed the man by his shirt and pulled him in close. He took in the man's cologne and freshly bathed skin. The man was bracing himself against the counter. As he held the man, he took a moment to calm himself. And when he spoke his voice was calm as well. "Now where is he?"

The man told Donovan everything that he knew about Nevin Odland. He rambled on and on. He explained to Donovan that the man that he was looking for had been in town for several months. Nevin Odland stayed in the fancy hotel on the opposite side. He usually didn't come out until afternoon. And he spent most of his time in the saloon. Apparently, he played cards and he drank each night. And because he floundered his money, he had quite a reputation with the local ladies. He would buy them dresses or shoes and take them out for a nice dinner. And afterwards right up to his hotel room, where they would sometimes stay days on end, living off of room service. He had been known to have three ladies in his room at once.

As far as poker, Nevin Odland lost money almost each night, the man explained. He was a poor poker player and didn't know when to stop. But what made Odland stand out the most was the bodyguard that accompanied him. The bodyguard never said a word and never left Odland's side. He was armed with side pistols and sometimes a rifle. He stood about watching everyone. Even when a conversation was directed his way he did not respond. He was so quiet in fact that no one even knew his name. And Odland never spoke of him. The only conversation that Odland and the bodyguard displayed in public was when Odland pointed and instructed him to attack a threatening patron. And when the bodyguard was instructed to attack, he was ruthless. He would beat the offending patron to a pulp. Once a man had accused Odland of cheating with one of his rare winning hands. There was $1500 at stake. The player reached for his gun while yelling that Odland had cheated. His death was assured as the bodyguard unloaded two rounds in his chest. The man finally told Donovan that Odland would be in the saloon tonight.

Donovan released the man. The man pulled on his shirt in an attempt to straighten it out. He looked up at Donovan. "If you're not a bounty hunter, or a lawman, who are you?"

He paused for a moment. Sadness displayed on his face. He thought about how long he had been searching for Nevin Odland. Seven years. Seven long years. Could this finally be the end? Would he finally get his justice after so many years? Would Nevin Odland have the same fate as the other four? He grabbed the poster from the counter, folded it and stuffed it into his pocket. He turned from the counter and said. "I'm the man that's looking for Nevin Odland."

Chapter 2

Inside the hotel room was a twin bed, writing desk, a closet and lanterns scattered about. Donovan dropped his sleeping gear and duffel bag inside the closet.

He pulled off his coat and placed it on the back of the chair by the desk. Without the coat, Donovan was armed. Two shooters resting on his waist. In the small of his back tucked under his gun belt a knife. Even in his left boot was a two shooter.

He approached the window. There was traffic of horses and wagons up and down the main road. Two boys of fourteen or so walked down the street shoveling up horseshit. At the trough, Fletcher was gone. He didn't like to stay in one place too long. That horse had a mind of its own he thought. He sat on the bed and put his hands on his face. The traveling had its toll.

He thought of Sage. He would be fourteen this year. He wondered if the boy would remember him. After they buried Sidney. Donovan asked his parents to care for Sage while he was away. He was not intending to be away for more than a few months. Yet the months turned into years. Now seven years later he had yet to return. He didn't want it this way, but the way he lived, it had to be. Donovan leaned back and closed his eyes. Nevin Odland would have to wait.

The restaurant was called Lacey's. Inside there were empty tables, except for the two men sitting together by the window. They took notice when Donovan walked in. A lady approached him. Her gray and black hair was tied in a bun, and her face was pleasant.

She led him to the table in the back, and the two men watched Donovan as he walked passed them. She told him of the many different foods that they served and the prices. He ordered the steak, a side of corn-on-the-cob and a piece of cornbread. She smiled and informed him that it would be ready shortly.

The steak sizzled in its own juices and smelled wonderful. She waited until Donovan took his first bite. The meat was thick and pink, and the juice dripped on his chin. Unlike any meat that he had before, the steak had a hot spicy flavor. Almost as if it had been sautéed in hot sauce. A damn good steak he thought. He nodded his approval; she smiled and went back to the kitchen.

Throughout his meal, the two men at the window would periodically look back. Donovan ignored them. After a while, one of the men approached.

"You ain't from around here, are you boy?" He asked.

Donovan swallowed, wiped his mouth with the cloth napkin, and then looked up at the man. He was dressed in black, from his hat, his vest, pants and finally his boots. His hair was even black and slicked back.

"No," Donovan said.

"What's your business here?" The man in black asked.

Donovan didn't like the man's tone and didn't feel it necessary to explain his business. He had been approached this way before. It wasn't just his grimy appearance from his travels and his unshaven face that caused folks to react to him in this way.

"You the Sheriff?" He asked.

The man in black snorted a chuckled. "No, I ain't the sheriff." He pulled back the flap of his jacket exposing his holstered colt. "What's that got to do with anything, boy?" Afterwards, he turned to his partner grinning. And for a moment his partner grinned along with him. But as quick as the grin had come, it was replaced with astonishment. The man in black took notice of his partner's change and turned back to Donovan. When he did so, he had found Donovan was on his feet with his pistol pointed at his face.

"I should kill you," Donovan said. "You show your pistol, then you turn away. What kind of gunslinger are you?"

"I'm sorry...I didn't mean...nothing." The man in black tried to explain.

"Sure you did," Donovan said. "I knew after you saw me that you would come over."

"Please don't kill me?"

Donovan frowned. "When someone shows their pistols, I shoot them dead. I don't like threats. But today I'm here on separate matters. I can't be distracted by the likes of you and your foolishness. If you had caught me on a different day, you'd be dead already, along with your partner." Donovan cut his eyes at the man across the room. He was visibly shaken also. He paused for a long time. Finally, he said. "I'm going to let you go. But it ain't because I'm a good guy. I'm far from that. I don't care about you one way or the other. But if I see you again, I'll kill you. Both of you. I just ain't got time to deal with you right now."

The man in black nodded.

Donovan nodded in the direction of the door. "Go." This time the man in black did not take his eyes off of Donovan as he felt his way back toward the door. He bumped into a table and knocked over a chair.

Donovan finished his steak, paid the lady, and gave her a little extra for the service. She smiled and thanked him.

Chapter 3

Outside the restaurant, Donovan scanned the area. There were people in and out of the shops, horses and wagons up and down the main road, kids playing off to the side, and adults talking. A few stray dogs were wondering about, one had hurried just in front of him with its tongue out and eyes looking back at Donovan.

Fletcher was not around. Donovan had saved the corncob from his meal and wanted to give it to him. He didn't suppose someone had taken Fletcher, but usually, he would have seen him by now. Fletcher was hard to take or steal that is. Donovan was the only one that could ride Fletcher. If Fletcher didn't know you, or you weren't accompanied by Donovan, you didn't get on. If you tried he would buck you something terrible, and after that, if you didn't get the point, he would drop to the ground and roll over. And if you were stuck in that saddle, you rolled along with him, broken bones an all.

Once he had witnessed a man that had both his legs crushed because he couldn't get out of the saddle before Fletcher rolled over on him. The injured man laid on the ground, legs going this way and that, screaming. Lots of screaming. He was damn lucky that he was alive. But from the looks of his mangled legs, he would never walk again. Those that had witnessed the scene demanded that the crazy horse, as they called him to be shot. To Donovan, this man was attempting to steal his horse and had gotten what he had coming.

A crowd of twenty or more gathered around the man. He yelled to them. "Look at me! I'm cripple!"

The crowd went into an uproar. Someone started chanting, "Shoot the horse! Shoot the horse!" And before long the crowd was chanting in sync, "Shoot the horse! Shoot the horse!" A man stepped out with a rifle in hand and the crowd went silent. Donovan heard some laughter, and a voice shouted. "Shoot him, Bill!"

Bill looked around as if he had done something brilliant. Donovan watched him closely. Bill raised his rifle in the direction of Fletcher. Donovan pulled his pistol and shot Bill in both of his meaty thighs. Bill dropped the rifle and fell to the ground. He moaned as he rolled from side to side.

Donovan turned to the stunned crowd. "Anybody else want to shoot my horse?"

He reached into his pocket and pulled out the picture of Nevin Odland. He studied it. He had seen this picture hundreds of times. He memorized every line on his face, every strand of his hair, the deep-set eyes, and the creases across his face where the picture was folded. He stuffed the picture back into his pocket and headed for the saloon.

Donovan stood inside the doorway. The inside was larger than he thought. There were several small tables throughout. In the front toward the window were three card tables. At one of the card tables, some men were playing poker. The other two card tables were empty. A lady in a blue dress walked about serving drinks and refilling glasses. At the back of the saloon was a stairway that led to other rooms. And against the wall at the end of the bar was a piano.

He studied the faces in the room; none of them were Nevin Odland. It didn't matter it was still early.

Donovan took a seat at the bar. The bartender stared at Donovan and then approached him.

"We don't see too many niggers in here." Said the bartender. "We don't like our niggers drunk."

"A beer," Donovan said.

The two men stared at each other; finally, the bartender broke the silence. "I don't want no trouble from you." He reached behind the counter grabbed a glass and poured a beer. The foam spilled over the sides of the glass. He handed it to Donovan. "You pay me now." He said as he wiped his hands on his dirty apron.

Donovan tossed a coin on the bar and turned in his seat to have a better view of the room. He sipped his beer, as he waited.

Quite some time had passed of faces coming and going before Nevin Odland and his bodyguard finally walked in. At the time the saloon was half full of patrons and two of the card tables were occupied with four or five players on each. Some of the customers yelled Odland's name and cheered him when he entered. Odland grinned at the crowd, shook some hands and spoke with those that had approached him. His bodyguard, on the other hand, was not approached.

After Odland made his rounds with the crowd, he made his way over to the card tables. His bodyguard followed and stood behind him with his arms folded. A man patted Odland on the back and joked. "How much you gonna lose tonight Nevin?" All at the table laughed. Odland laughed with them, but his bodyguard was silent.

Donovan watched Odland. He had not changed much since he had last seen him. His once black hair now had streaks of gray. He was only a few pounds heavier and had a calmer relaxed look about him. But the deep-set eyes and the big nose were the same. It was the same man, but then it wasn't. He didn't seem like the ruthless killer that Donovan had known him to be.

Seeing the man so relaxed made Donovan angry. With all the evil destruction that he and his men had caused, he had no right to be relaxed or happy about anything.

The anger must have shown on his face for when he glanced at the bodyguard he found him looking right at him. He set the beer on the bar. After moments of locked eyes, the bodyguard marched over to Donovan.

He got in Donovan's face. His green eyes showed no emotion. He was just a professional doing his job. He was protecting Odland his boss. There was a holstered pistol on the left side of his waist. At this point, it didn't seem that he was going to use the pistol. He probably thought that he didn't need it. Besides Donovan was covered up, and appeared unarmed.

Folks took notice of the men and the room quieted. The card game behind them had halted and Odland watched the scene with familiarity.

"What you looking at nigger?" Said the bodyguard.

From behind the bar, the bartender spoke. "Is he bothering you, mister? You want me to throw him out?"

The bodyguard shook his head. "I'll take care of him."

"Make it fast." Said Odland. "We got us a game to finish."

The men at the table laughed.

"What you looking at boy?" Said the bodyguard.

Donovan stood to his feet and said. "I'm looking at you."

The bodyguard was taken aback by this man's lack of fear and nonchalant attitude. It was as if he was thinking to himself, didn't this man know that he was about to get the beating of his life? Didn't he know that he might be killed? He launched for Donovan but missed when Donovan stepped aside. He grabbed the bar instead. Before the bodyguard could turn around Donovan had swung a series of punches to the man's back. He went down on his knees cursing. But he was on his feet and launched again. This time Donovan didn't move. He kicked the man in the chest, which caused him to fall backward knocking over a table. The man stayed on his back and then climbed to his feet. He was disoriented. Donovan stepped forward and hit him across the face, and he went down like a stiff board.

All eyes were on Donovan and the unconscious bodyguard. Donovan cut his eyes at the bartender, as he did so the bartender moved to the other end of the room.

Donovan approached Odland at the card table.

"Remember me?" Said Donovan.

Odland studied Donovan's face and nodded. "Never seen you before."

Donovan removed his hat and tossed it on the card table. This time he saw the recognition on Odland's face. "How about now?" Donovan said.

"You're alive? You can't be alive."

"I'm alive. But your buddies aren't."

"That was you? One of those men was my brother."

Donovan slammed his fist on the table. The money and cards bounced. Some of the drinks fell over. Beer spilled on the table. The yellow liquid was spreading toward the ends. The smell of beer was in the air. Odland leaned back in his chair. "Am I supposed to feel sorry for you?! My wife is dead! I don't give a damn about you! All I know is you're the last one. After tonight I can put this nightmare behind me. I can finally go home to my son." Donovan paused. "Remember my son?" He didn't give Odland a chance to answer. "He was seven years old. He was just a boy. He's alive also. Just like me. You didn't kill him, you didn't kill me."

Odland stood to his feet, his hand near his pistol. Donovan pulled back his coat exposing his holstered pistol as well. Those at the card table scattered. Some jumped to the floor others ran for the nearest wall. Folks at the other tables ducked for cover as well and those close enough to the front door ran out. The bartender was on the floor behind the bar.

"That was a long time ago. I ain't the same as I was then." Said Odland.

"I ain't the same either." Said Donovan. "What you did changed me."

Odland reached into his coat pocket and pulled out a hand full of money. He tossed it on the table. "This is more than five thousand dollars. It's yours." Said Odland. "This won't bring your wife back, but maybe you and I can put all this behind us. My brother was everything to me."

Donovan was annoyed that Odland was cowardly bargaining for his life. This situation was beyond bargaining. Beyond forgiveness and turning the other cheek. So much had been sacrificed up to this point. Lives were lost. Not just Sidney and the four men that had killed her. There were others. Many others. Then there were those years that he had been away from his son. Time that he'll never get back. All of which because of Odland and what he had done.

"No." Said Donovan.

The two men stared at one another. Finally realizing that he had no choice, Odland went for his pistol. Donovan fired two explosive shots into the man's chest. The shots echoed within the saloon as if it were empty. Odland fell back over the chair. Some of the people screamed and ducked deeper behind the tables. Donovan stepped forward and stared at Odland. The unfired gun was still in his hand. His dead eyes staring upward. His chest bloodied. He reached into his pocket, pulled out the wanted poster and tossed it on Odland's body. He stared at Odland trying to savor the moment of his death. Oddly he felt nothing. He finally picked up his hat and the money off the table and headed out the door. Some of the people on the floor spread to move out of his path.

Donovan raised his fingers to his mouth and whistled. It was so loud that folks close by ducked for cover.

Down at the end of town, Donovan could see the Sheriff and his two deputies making their way on foot toward the saloon. They were far enough away that he was out of firing range of their pistols.

A cloud of dust appeared behind one of the buildings on the second cross street. Within moments Fletcher appeared cornering sharply onto the main road just in front of the sheriff and his deputies. They fell over each other trying to get out of the horse's path. A cloud of dust followed Fletcher as he raced toward Donovan with his hooves clumping on the road. When he reached Donovan he circled him and bobbed his head. Donovan rubbed Fletcher's neck to calm him. He reached into his pocket and gave him the corncob.

Donovan could barely see the Sheriff and his deputies through the dust that Fletcher had left behind. The men were waving the cloud away from their faces.

He leaped on Fletcher and yelled and the horse raced toward the other end of the town. When Donovan looked back he saw the lawmen running in the opposite direction to retrieve their horses. Fletcher raced down the main road leaving more dust in the air. The folks that Donovan passed were ducked behind wagons, horses, and inside the shops.

Just ahead Donovan saw a man in black. It was the man that he had seen earlier in the restaurant. The man wasn't running or hiding like the others. He stood watching Donovan as he approached. He had a grin on his face. Donovan pulled on the reins and Fletcher slid to a halt. The man's eyes gave himself away. He guided his horse over to the man and stopped just in front of him. The man grinned at Donovan, and at that point, Donovan pulled back his coat and rested the flap behind his pistol.

The smile eased off the man's face. Donovan watched the man retreat cowardly toward the shop behind him. "I warned you. You don't get another chance." Donovan pulled his pistol and fired a single shot. The man fell in the doorway. Only his legs were sticking out.

He glanced over his shoulder and he could see the lawmen making the first turn onto the main road. He yelled and Fletcher jumped forward racing once again toward the end of town.

After several hours, Donovan long past realized that the lawmen were no longer chasing him. Even so, he still wanted to get as much distance between them and him as possible. So he pushed Fletcher until they finally came across a stream for which they could drink and rest. He left Fletcher at the watercourse and sat with his back to an oak tree. The horse gulped the water, his coat was wet with sweat, and his nostrils flared wide with each breath. Donovan didn't like to push Fletcher this hard.

Countless stars filled the dark sky. Watching those beautiful stars through the tops of trees was his favorite past time. The crickets chirped somewhere among the trees. He thought about Sage. He hadn't seen him for such a long time. Now that justice had been served on all the men that killed his mother, it was time to go back. But what would be waiting for him? His stomach turned when he thought about it. It was finally time to go home.

Chapter 4

Donovan and Fletcher had been riding for a while. The sun was fading to the west and it would not be long before it was dark. A rabbit appeared through the brush about twenty feet away. Donovan tugged on the reins and Fletcher stopped. The rabbit was light brown with long high ears. His mouth worked quickly as it chewed on a plant. He pulled out his side pistol, aimed and fired.

He gathered some sticks and started a fire. When he was satisfied with the flame he grabbed the limp rabbit, skinned and gutted him. He stabbed a stick through the flesh and held it over the blaze. He watched as the animal's raw purple body turned brown and in some areas black from being too close to the heat. The meat sputtered and crackled from the direct contact with the flame.

It was a cooler night and the warm rays from the fire felt soothing on his hands and face. Wild rabbit was not his ideal choice of meat. He usually found it tough to chew, with an odd salty flavor. But it had been some time since his last meal, so the aroma at this moment was tantalizing. After the meal, he added more sticks to the fire and set up his sleeping blankets.

He watched the blaze dance as the breeze passed through and listened as Fletcher grazed and moved about just outside of camp. A few more days and he would be with his son. This was difficult to fathom after being away for such a long time. His ritual would change. He would no longer be living on the road, sleeping under trees, hunting his own food, and passing through one town after the next.

Maybe he could have a home, some property, just like when Sidney was alive. She had been deceased for over five years, and he still missed her. However, he was no longer the man that she had married. She probably would not like the man that he was now.

Donovan guided Fletcher onto the property sometime after dark. The house was a couple hundred yards out from the main road. Inside the two front windows, Donovan could see the reflection of the fireplace. He could also smell the burning wood coming from the fire stack on the roof. As he and Fletcher moved on, he noticed three other buildings. Buildings that was not present before. One seemed to be a chicken house. The other was a barn with huge double doors. And the last building looked as if it were another house, but hard to tell at this time of night.

He climbed off Fletcher and stepped onto the porch. The winds crashed into him. He ducked his head and held onto his hat. Moments later mists of rain dropped about.

There were voices inside, a man's and a woman's. He raised his gloved hand and knocked.

Inside, the curtain pulled back and a face pressed up against the window. Because of the poor lighting and raindrops on the glass, Donovan could not make out the face. He suspected that it was a man.

The face disappeared as the curtain closed. There was a tapping on the floor that worked from the window to the front door. A man's voice spoke from behind the door. "Who's there?"

Donovan listened through the wind noises. He did not recognize the voice.

"Who's there I say?" This time the voice was much louder.

Once again Donovan listened, and it still did not sound familiar to him. "Donovan." He answered reluctantly.

"Who you say?" Said the man's voice.

"Donovan." He repeated.

He heard the front door unlatch and then drag open. The lights from the doorway danced around his feet. The old man braced himself on his cane as he stepped onto the porch. He leaned forward trying to get a better view. "Donovan, is that you?"

The old man had gray shaggy hair, dark bags under his eyes, and a very thin frame that leaned against a homemade cane. He wore a tan button up shirt that was tucked into his brown pants that partially covered his bare feet.

"It's me," Donovan said.

Papa stepped forward lifting his cane as he reached to embrace his son. "My GOD. You're alive. My GOD." The two held each other tight.

Over Papa's shoulder, he saw an older woman appear in the doorway. She was short heavyset and her complexion was very dark. She wore a faded tan dress that covered her arms and legs and her hair was tucked in a blue scarf. Donovan stepped away from Papa and approached her. She pressed her hands against her face, and tears squeezed through her thick fingers. The old woman clinched her fist and shook them at the sky. "Thank ya, Jesus! Thank ya, Jesus! Thank ya, Jesus!

Donovan reached for her and held her. "Mama." He said. Her wet cheek pressed against his and she sobbed into his ear.

"You is home. Baby you is home now." She cried.

After a long embrace, Donovan tried to pull back so as to get a look at his mama but she refused to loosen her hold on him. Finally, she regained her composer and wiped her face with the back of her hands. Years later she had grayer hair, darker skin and was few pounds heavier. To Donovan, she was such a beautiful sight that he refused to take his eyes off of her.

Mama led Donovan inside and Papa followed closing the door as they entered. The house was warm and cozy. The fireplace provided plenty of heat and light throughout the room. Every few minutes the fire crackled and sizzled. The sounds of the wind and rain tapped the windows. To the right was a small kitchen area with an iron stove. Just off to the side where the family room and kitchen met was a long eating table. In the family room were two sitting chairs facing the fireplace. One was a rocking chair, the other was a plain chair. Both had blankets in each.

"You hungry, baby?" Asked Mama as she led Donovan over to the eating table.

Donovan nodded. "Yeah." He hadn't eaten since the rabbit two days earlier.

"You sit right here," she said pulling out a chair. "I'll fetch you some fried chicken and corn left from dinner."

Donovan seated himself in the chair at the table and as he did so his long brown coat opened exposing one of his side colts. Papa stared at the gun and when he finally looked up Donovan could see the worried expression on his face. Papa seated himself in the chair next to Donovan. He put his hand on Donovan's arm. "You in some kind of trouble son?" He asked.

Donovan looked him in the eyes. "No. Everything's fine." There was no point in worrying his Papa. But the truth was there were many folks that wanted him dead. Mostly relatives and friends of the men that he had killed. At first, Donovan was naïve. He thought that he could avenge his wife's murderers without consequence, but what he soon found was the dead men had family or friends that didn't care nothing about Donovan's murdered wife. All that they knew was that their family or friend laid dead in the street or a saloon with a bullet in the face or the chest. Unfortunately when these relatives and friends came after Donovan wanting vengeance they themselves suffered the same fate as their friend or relative before, laying also dead in the street with a bullet in the face. He then realized the violence doesn't stop with him it only grows. This cycle of vengeance never stopped. There was always someone out there wanting to take Donovan's life because of who he had killed. This is one of the reasons that it took Donovan this long to get back to his son. He couldn't bring this type of danger to him.

Mama came out of the kitchen area with a plate of chicken, corn, and a biscuit. She placed the plate on the table and invited Donovan to eat. She then sat in the chair across from him with elbows on the table and her hands clumped in front of her face. She studied Donovan as he ate. Sometimes she smiled and other times sadness blanked her face. The meal was wonderful. The chicken crust was brittle and crunched as he bit into it. The spicy flavor was not only in the crust but also deep in the meat. The biscuit was soft, buttery and moist, and the outer layer was flaky. He bit into both the chicken and the biscuit and savored the taste in his mouth. Unbelievable. He finished the last piece of biscuit then pushed his plate aside. "Thank you, Mama. That was real nice."

"You want more?" She asked.

"No. I'm fine." He said.

The sad face came back again as she stared at Donovan. He reached across and grabbed her hands. "You ok?"

She pulled his hands to her face and began to sob again. His hands became wet from her tears. Papa watched them. "I thought I would never see you again." She said. "And now you here with us. GOD sho is good to me."

Donovan didn't respond. He was here by his own free will, nothing more. One of the back doors creaked open. Without being noticed Donovan rested his hand next to his holstered colt. He was so used to folks attempting to kill him that he was alert to the sounds and movements within his surroundings. However, as his hand rested near his colt he seriously doubted that anyone coming out of that room would be looking to kill him. Even with this realization Donovan still kept his hand close to his colt.

Mama and Papa turned in their seats to face the back room. They could see that the door was ajar, but because of the dark background, the face in the crack could not be seen. "Come on out," said Mama. "We hears you. We knows you're there."

After a long moment, the back door finally pulled open and there stood a young boy staring at the floor. He was still hidden partially by the darkness of the room.

Mama smiled. "Don't be bashful. Come look who's here." The boy rocked side to side but he did not move, and he did not look up from the floor.

"It's ok baby. Come see who's here."

The boy hesitated then he came into the light and approached Mama. She put her arms around him to comfort him. Donovan stared at his son with deep affection and sadness. After all these years the sight of him was still hard to bear. Across the left side of his face was a long scar that climbed over his cheek just past his eyebrow. He was no longer the seven-year-old boy. He was fourteen. Donovan couldn't take his eyes off of him. He had waited so long for this moment. He was so big compared to the little boy that he remembered. He was so handsome. He looked just like his mother. She would be so proud.

"Do you know who this man is?" Mama said pointing to Donovan. The boy didn't respond.

She lifted his chin with her fingers. "It's ok Sage. You can look at him." He slowly raised his head and stared at Donovan, but only for a moment then stared back at the floor. "This here is ya Daddy," Mama said.

Sage showed no emotion or acknowledgment of what Mama had said. "You already know who he is, don't you Sage." Sage stood motionless. Mama smiled at him once more and reached over and hugged him. "Go fetch Uncle Miles." She said, and Sage headed to the front door.

Donovan watched his son as he exited. He was now as tall as Mama. It puzzled Donovan that the boy didn't seem to care one way or the other about his presence. Donovan couldn't blame him; it had been a long time since they had seen each other. He doubt if the boy even remembered him. If it wasn't for his scarred face, Donovan probably wouldn't have recognized Sage himself. However, his demeanor was odd. No self-esteem whatsoever. Afraid of the world. Donovan wasn't expecting this. What the hell happened to him? "How is he?" Donovan asked.

With his hand on his cane, Papa leaned back in his chair and sighed. "He's had some hard times. More than most young un's I guess." Said Papa. "I suppose he made no friends on account of how he looks and all. The younguns just won't have nothing to do with him. Sometimes grown folks got no sense around him either. Sometimes Sage is right there when they talks about how ugly he his." Papa nodded his head. "They think Sage got no feelings on account he don't talk much. But Sage got plenty of feelings."

The front door reopened and Sage came in with the wind and light rain. The rain sprayed the floor in the doorway. He turned his back to them and closed the door. He walked passed them staring only at the floor.

"Where's uncle Miles?" Mama asked.

Sage froze in mid-step. His voice was barely audible never looking up from the floor. "Be here in a minute." Sage went on to the back room and closed the door behind him.

What the hell happened to him? Donovan thought.

Chapter 5

The front door pulled open and the wind blew the rain onto the floor in the doorway. The wind swished as it pushed its way in. Donovan turned in his chair to see his older brother Miles. He was surprised how huge Miles was. He was much bigger than Donovan had remembered. His large body almost filled the entire doorway. His shirt soaked with rain clung to his body revealing the bulkiness of his shoulders, chest, and biceps. The sleeves on his shirt were rolled up to the elbow exposing his muscular forearms.

Miles rubbed the rain from his eyes and stared at Donovan with disbelief. The wind continued to swish behind him. "Donovan?" He questioned.

Donovan stood to his feet and Mama and Papa stood with him. "Yeah, it's me," Donovan said.

Miles blinked and rubbed his eyes. "How could this be?" He questioned.

Mama motioned Miles away from the doorway. "Come on in Miles. You lettin cold air in."

Without taking his eyes off Donovan he stepped away and closed the door. The swishing of the wind dropped to a low faint hum. He approached Donovan. With each step, his boots knocked against the planked floor. A trail of wet footprints temporarily stained the floor. Miles was slightly taller and definitely wider. He probably outweighed Donovan by fifty or more pounds. He studied Donovan. His face was drenched from the rain, with an expression of disbelief. "We thought you was dead." Said Miles.

"A part of me is dead," Donovan said.

Donovan watched as his brother continued to eye him. They were four years apart in age, and at one time they were close. But at that moment it was as if they were strangers. And judging from his brother's squinted dark eyes, maybe even enemies. "Where you been all these years?" Asked Miles. He seemed as if he didn't believe his own eyes.

Donovan was hesitant to answer this question. The last several years had been of violence, death, and pain. "All over," Donovan answered.

"You couldn't write or come by before now?" Asked Miles.

Papa interrupted. "Now Miles your brother just got here. Let him settle a bit before you ask him a bunch of questions."

Miles snorted, walked away and paced. His boots knocked. The wet footprints not as obvious. He came back though. This time he was in

Donovan's face. His warm breath blowing in his eyes. Donovan wasn't accustomed to allowing anyone to get in his face. This was usually signaled as a threat.

"Why come back after all this time?" Asked Miles.

"I'm here to see my son."

He sighed, blowing trickles of rainwater from his lips onto Donovan's face. "Your son?" He questioned. "Your son don't know you."

"That's why I'm here. To know my son."

"You're too late," said Miles. "He's fourteen. He don't need knowing now."

"That's enough Miles!" Said, Mama. "You let him be!"

Miles glanced at Mama who glared at him. He turned to Donovan. "Where you been all these years? We got the right to know."

Donovan knew that Miles was right. They did have the right to know. After all, they had been looking after and caring for his son. He was grateful. But what could he tell them? Not that he had tracked and killed one by one all the men that had killed his wife. All five of them. How he ignored some of their cries for mercy and shot them in the face. How even when they laid in the street or a saloon floor with their open unseeing eyes that he was not satisfied with their death. How he still felt incredibly empty because Sidney was still dead. And how he was often disappointed because killing those men did not take away the emptiness caused by her death. He could not tell them that in the process he had also killed other men. Men that had for various reasons tried to kill him and failed. He could not tell them that there were men at this moment that would kill him if they had the chance. The very men that would probably torture and kill his family if they had knowledge of them. And because of which, Donovan stayed away, refusing to bring this danger upon his family. There was nothing about his dreadful past that he could share. Though they probably suspected as much anyway. It only made sense, seeing how he left right after Sidney was murdered. But even so, what he did and how he lived, he could never speak of. He wanted to forget and start a new life. A new life with his son.

"You don't want to know where I've been." Said Donovan.

Miles seemed baffled. "We want to know."

"No," Donovan answered firmly.

"Then tell us why you left?" Asked Miles.

Donovan frowned. "You know why I left."

"I want you to tell me anyway." Demanded Miles.

"Maybe later." He said coolly.

Miles was furious and his wide eyes gave away his emotions. He grabbed Donovan by the lapels of his coat and was attempting to pull Donovan into him, but just as he reached, Donovan pivoted on his left foot facing the opposite direction, grabbed and threw the larger Miles over his shoulder onto the ground. Because Donovan never released his grip he actually landed on top of his brother. They were face to face. Donovan had reached for his colt.

"Donovan!" Mama yelled.

He stared at his brother laying beneath him, with the colt in his hand. He was ashamed as he watched his brother staring back at him. He stuffed the gun back into his holster and climbed to his feet. The room was silent except for the rain drumming onto the front windows and the wood crackling in the fireplace. Donovan walked over to the rain-splattered window and watched into the darkness.

Miles still on his back watched Donovan approach the window. Only then did he dare to move, and he rolled over climbing to his feet with Mama and Papa reaching to help him. They all watched Donovan. Mama whispered to Papa then went into one of the two back rooms and closed the door. Miles and Papa approached Donovan. "You need to go back to whatever hell you came from." Said Miles. His voice was sharp with anger. Miles stepped around so that Donovan could see him. "I ought to kill you for what you just did."

Donovan turned to his brother. "Have you ever killed a man before?" But he knew before he asked the question that his brother had not. The two stared at each other. Donovan watched his brother's expression change when he realized that Donovan had probably killed many men. Finally, Miles left the house without another word, and Donovan turned back to the dark window.

It was a settle hint, but he felt Miles understood the point. He was so used to men trying to kill him that when threatened he would defend himself. Something he had done over and over for the last few years. If Mama hadn't called his name, he might have killed his brother. It saddened Donovan to think that he almost killed his brother. But Miles had threatened to kill Donovan and he wanted to discourage his older brother from any type of retaliation against him. He wanted Miles to understand that if he was to do so, that brother or not, he would be killed.

In the reflection of the window, Donovan could see Papa leaning on his cane. "You gonna be alright son?" He asked

He reflected on the question for a moment. Alright? What did that even mean? Depending on what alright meant.

In the physical he was fine. He was alive. He had somehow managed to stay alive. He wondered how much time he had left though. One can only escape death so many times before it catches up to you.

But he wasn't alright. He wasn't alright with the death of Sidney. He missed her so much. But it wasn't just her death that hurt him so. It was how she died. He was there and he couldn't stop it. The horrible memories of that day have haunted him. Even at this moment.

"Yeah. I'm fine." Answered Donovan. "I won't be staying, I'm just passing through. I wanted to see my son is all."

Papa put a hand on Donovan's shoulder and squeezed. He was surprised how firm the old man's grip was. "Why just passing through?" Papa asked. "This is your home. We is your family."

Donovan thought this over for a moment. This wasn't his home; his home had been burned down by the men that killed his wife a few miles down the road. However, there was no denying this was his family and he missed them greatly. He thought of them often on many days and nights on his long travels. He wondered how they lived day to day.

"I made a mistake. I was hoping to be a part of Sage's life. But he's older. He don't have much use for me now." Said Donovan.

Papa sighed and leaned into the rain-splattered window, his nose almost touched the glass. He then turned his head to the back room that Mama had gone through earlier. When he was satisfied he turned his attention back to the dark window. He and Donovan stood listening to the many raindrops tap against the window.

"Sure glad of this rain." Said Papa. "Hadn't rained for over a month. Thought we was gonna have a dry spell. This gonna be mighty good for our crops." Papa turned and glanced at the back room again. The door was still closed. He then turned to Donovan. "Let's go on the porch and talk for a bit."

"It's raining." Said Donovan not concerned of himself getting wet, for he had slept in the rain on many nights, but he was concerned for his Papa who seemed more fragile. An old man in the rain could catch pneumonia and never have enough strength to recover.

Papa laughed. "A little rain not gonna hurt you, Donovan." And without waiting for an answer he adjusted himself on his cane and headed for the front door. Donovan followed knowing that his Papa wanted to talk with him without the presence of his Mama.

Outside on the wet porch, there were two wooden chairs. Papa sat in one and invited Donovan to sit in the other. Papa still holding onto his cane leaned back to relax. Donovan watched his father amused that he was sitting in the rain on a wet chair in a comfortable like position as if there was no rain. As if he was not getting soaked. He imitated his father and leaned back as well and gazed out into the fields as the rain fell.

"When you leaving?" Asked Papa.

"In the morning," Donovan said.

Papa sighed. "Where will you go?"

Donovan thought the question over as the rain splashed on him. He was already soaked and cold. He hadn't thought about where he would go. He didn't know. He only planned on coming here to see his son and nothing else. He had been on the road all these years, never staying one place longer than six months. He had never been anyplace that he could call home. He had never met anyone whom he could call a friend. He lived alone and traveled alone. His only companion was his horse, Fletcher. "I don't know. I guess back to where I came from." He said.

"And where is that?"

"All over," Donovan answered.

Papa leaned forward using his cane for support and turned to Donovan. His clothes soaked and his face serious. "Didn't think we would ever see you again. Thought you was dead. After a couple years went by and we didn't hear from you, just made sense you being dead. It took your Mama a long time to get over that." He said. "I've been with her forty years or more and I've never seen her in such pain when she thought you was dead. I can't stand to see her heart broken like that again. Stay a while. She's in there making up a bed and getting you some sleeping clothes."

"And Miles?"

"Don't worry about Miles none. I'll handle him." Papa said.

Donovan was bothered by this information that his Papa had told him about his mother. She was the last person in the world that he wanted to hurt. When he left he didn't stop to think that she would be affected in this way. It was just that he loved Sidney so much that when they killed her, nothing else mattered.

But his mother was special to him also. When he was a small boy he and his mother spent a lot of time together. They shared moments that boys and mothers didn't usually share together. Sometimes he would help his mother cook and prepare the family meals while Papa and Miles worked in the fields. Other times he would help her repair, create and sew entire outfits. Papa would sometimes scold Mama, accusing her of turning his youngest son into a sissy. But the opposite was actually true. Donovan was no sissy. He was as active and normal as any other small boy. He loved his mama is all and wanted to help her. His fondest memories were when he and his mama worked on family chores side by side, talking and laughing.

Pulling on his cane Papa managed to his feet. "We best be getting inside now. Mama's gonna be wondering about us."

Agreeing Donovan followed Papa into the house. They stood in the doorway dripping rainwater onto the floor. Mama had just come out of the back room holding a thick blanket and some sleeping clothes. She stared at them and then frowned. "What's this?" She asked. "Why is you all wet?"

Papa blurted a nervous laugh. "Me and Donovan needed some fresh air, so we went on the porch."

"In the rain!" She yelled. "That's a fool thing to do. You could catch yourself sick."

Papa gave her his best-confused look. "Guess I didn't think of that."

Mama stared at him as if she was reading his mind. Her expression on her face gave Donovan the impression that she didn't believe him. After over forty years of marriage, she knew him better than anyone. "You two get out of them wet clothes." She snapped. She then handed Donovan the blanket and sleeping outfit that she was holding. "This is your Papa's stuff. You can wear it tonight." She pointed to the first of two backdoors. "You can sleep in there with Sage. Your bedding is on the floor next to the wall. I'll come and see after you in a minute." She turned her attention to Papa. He was standing in a puddle on the floor that had dripped off of his clothes.

The light from the moon came through the window giving Donovan a clear view of the bedroom. Inside Sage was on his bed facing the opposite direction sound asleep. The plushy covers almost covered his head. Donovan was on the bedding on the floor with his back against the wall watching him. He had already changed into his Papa's old sleeping clothes that Mama had set out for him. He had been dreaming about this day, which seemed like all his life. He was finally with his son. That dreamed feeling that he thought of every night before he went to sleep did not come close to the actual reality of the situation that he was in now. He wanted to live in this moment as long as he possibly could. If possible he would stay in this position all night, watching.

There was a knock on the door. His mother poked her head in. "May I come in?" Donovan nodded. She entered and sat next to him on the bedding. She grabbed his hands and smiled and he smiled back. For the first time in years, Donovan had a reason to smile. And right now he was smiling at his mother's beautiful familiar face. "I sure missed you, Donovan." She said.

"I missed you too Mama."

"I came in here to ask you to do something with me." She paused looking for a reaction out of him. He gave none. "I want you to pray with me. I want you to give thanks to the LORD for your safe return." Again she paused looking for a reaction, but once again he had none. "Close your eyes baby." Mama closed her eyes but Donovan did not close his. Instead, he silently watched her. "LORD. Thank you for bringing my baby back to me safe. Thank you, LORD. Thank you." She stopped, and couldn't go on. She sobbed. "I guess that's all I have to say, amen." She opened her eyes waiting for Donovan to say amen, but he didn't. He remained silent. She smiled as she caressed his face. She then climbed to her feet using his shoulder to brace herself and headed to the door.

"Mama," Donovan called out.

"Yes, baby." She said as she turned in the doorway.

He waited a long moment as he stared at her. "I missed you." He finally said.

"I know baby. I missed you too."

Chapter 6

The three men on horseback rode single file down the pounded dirt path. The many hooves thumped against the road. Sheriff Landry was the man up front. He was tall and seemed too big for his horse. His long legs dangled freely on either side of the horse's belly. With his left hand he guided his horse, with the other he held a Winchester rifle.

The prisoner, Dale Gentry was on the second horse. His hands cuffed behind his back. A long rope went from the horn of his saddle to the horn of Sheriff Landry's saddle. His young face bruised and smeared with blood from his nose and mouth. Though he was not asleep his eyes were closed and the ride caused him to wince often from his injuries.

On the last horse was a small man named Gunther. He was the sheriff's younger brother and deputy. He was impeccably dressed in a burgundy sports jacket, matching slacks a white shirt and a string-like burgundy bow tie. Because of his appearance, he almost gave the impression of a young boy. However, the thick mustache that covered his grin and the deputy star across his chest eliminated some doubt that he was a child.

Without looking back Sheriff Landry yelled to his younger brother. "Are you paying attention, Gunther? We don't want no surprises."

A cocky smile lingered on Gunther's face. He rubbed the ivory handle of his holstered colt. He pulled it out and pointed it at the prisoner. "You don't need to worry Landry," he said. "I'll handle all surprises that come our way." He pulled the hammer back. The click was loud enough that the prisoner opened his eyes and turned toward him. His expression was of fear and exhaustion. Gunther laughed. "Should I just put this old boy out of his misery?" He yelled back to Landry.

Landry was not amused. Once again his younger brother was taking a serious situation lightly. This was a dangerous ride. The prisoner that they had captured had two other riders with him. Both riders had gotten away. To make matters worse neither Landry nor Gunther got close enough to identify them. The immediate danger was the slow pace in which they were forced to ride with the injured prisoner. This pace would give the riders a chance to catch up, hide and ambush the lawmen. And since the town was just a day away, the riders could arrive into town before them, blend among the town folks and attempt to kill them when they arrived. Landry was irritated that his brother didn't seem to understand this hazard.

"I'm not talking about him. I'm talking of the other riders." Answered Landry. "Keep an eye out. They could be hiding anywhere."

Gunther grinned under his thick mustache. "I know. I'm just saying if they show up, he'll be the first to go."

Landry sighed. He had seen this act before. His brother was trying to entertain himself by frightening the prisoner. He would point his gun, wave it and cock the trigger all in an attempt to frighten the prisoner or whoever provoked him. Luckily this prisoner showed some fear, or Gunther may have killed him.

As they rode on, Landry glanced at the sky. It would be dark before long and they had been traveling for two days. Another full day and they would reach the jailhouse. Each night they would set up camp and Landry and Gunther would take shifts sleeping while the other would sit just outside the campsite with a rifle in hand watching and listening for an ambush. None had been attempted. However, since they were so close to town Landry felt that it might be the riders last chance, so instead, he announced to Gunther that they would be traveling through the night. After Landry's broadcast, Gunther smiled when he heard the prisoner groan his disapproval.

As the sun went down and they were approaching darkness sheriff Landry was even more cautious. He didn't like traveling on the main road. He felt they were sitting ducks to anyone that wanted to harm them but he knew of no other way back to town. However, there was a chance that the two riders were far behind and had no intention of trying to rescue their friend. But deep down he knew this was not likely the case since they had not only captured their friend but also seized the three bags of money that was stolen from the bank two weeks before. For their own safety, he had to assume that the riders were close with the intent to kill.

Landry left nothing to chance. On several occasions, he would stop his horse and watch in the direction of which he saw some sort of disturbance. He would hold this position pointing his Winchester until he was assured that all was safe. Sometimes it was just a bird or squirrel leaping from limb to limb. Other times it was the breeze shaking leaves on low bushes. Either way, Landry didn't move until he was certain. On one occasion Landry left the prisoner and Gunther at the road to inspect a movement within a thicket of trees. Again it was just another rodent, but in light of the situation that they faced one couldn't be too careful, he thought. When he returned, he found that Gunther had knocked the prisoner off the horse, and he was laying on the road. Gunther smiled when he saw Landry returning.

"What happened to him?" Landry asked.

Gunther shrugged his shoulders. "I guess he fell off."

Landry frowned at his younger brother. "You knocked him off. You can put him back on." He said.

Landry, Gunther and the prisoner traveled all night. They were very cautious and as they rode without sleep. The men were exhausted, but they kept their course until they finally reached town by mid-morning.

They stopped at the outskirts of town and cautiously watched. This was a small town with only one main road straight down the middle. On one side of the main road were a hotel, restaurant, clothing store and a blacksmith shop. On the opposite side were a saloon, supply shop, barber and a bank. Down the middle at the end of the main road facing them was the jailhouse. The jailhouse was the only building that stood by itself.

Some folks were walking about the planked sidewalks and others were crossing the main street heading toward their individual destinations. Three wagons were parked at the supply store. Landry could see one man loading his wagon with bags of dried food. So heavy in fact that the man grunted when he lifted the sack into the back of his wagon. In front of the saloon, Landry counted five horses tied to the post. He tried to remember if those horses looked familiar to him. Normally he wouldn't have cared, but today these unfamiliar horses could mean two new strangers in town.

"What are we waiting for?" Gunther asked.

Landry sighed. How could Gunther be so careless? The two riders could be somewhere out there waiting. Waiting for the right moment to kill them, and rescue their friend then take back the bags of money. They didn't know what the riders looked like. They could easily hide unnoticed among the town folks. Landry wanted to study the environment before he moved forward. He wanted to make sure that no one seemed suspicious.

"I'm making sure is all," Answered Landry. "And you should be doing the same. We've come too far to ride into an ambush."

Gunther glanced at the town just ahead of them. "You worry too much Landry. We've been ambushed before and we've never gotten so much as a mark on us. If they want to come let them come. They'll die like the others."

Landry turned on his saddle to face Gunther. His expression was firm. "That don't mean nothing Gunther. You take too many chances. We ain't in no rush. We gonna take our time and make sure all is fine." He stared at his brother for a moment. Landry wasn't this careful because he was afraid for his own life. In truth, Landry had never met a man that he was afraid of and seriously doubted that there was a man alive anywhere that could scare him. The only fear that Landry felt was that his brother Gunther may be taken away from him. This is why he was so careful at this moment, for he did not want his cocky brother to be killed. He turned on his saddle and led them down the road toward the jailhouse.

Folks took notice of them with surprised glances. Some faces could be seen pressed against the windows while others could be seen wandering out of doorways to peek at them. Landry watched everyone. Whenever someone got close to them, Landry would stick out his large palm to signal the bystander to stop, and they would do so.

Shouts were heard among the men. "Did you get the money?" One man yelled.

Gunther was only too happy to pull the three moneybags off his saddle and wave them high in the air for the crowd to see. Some folks cheered at this causing Gunther to grin. Landry, on the other hand, was frowning. If the riders were somewhere in the crowd, this would certainly increase their urgency to retrieve the money before it was stored away safely at the jailhouse which was only a couple blocks away.

Sheriff Landry sighed. Now because of Gunther's actions, they would have to be even more careful. "Take your pistol out." He instructed to his younger brother. "And keep it pointed at the prisoner." Landry was hoping this would be a deterrent from anyone trying to get to the money.

Gunther pulled out his gun with a smile and pointed it at the prisoner's head. Some of the crowd cheered. One man yelled. "Shoot him!" Laughter was heard within the crowd.

Landry was annoyed with his brother for letting himself be distracted by the crowd. It was now more important than ever to stay focused and alert. This is where assassins could conceal themselves.

Landry took notice of a beautiful woman standing in the hotel entrance. Her arms were crossed as she leaned against the frame inside the doorway. She seemed uninvolved with the situation.

"Dr. Tracy!" Landry yelled to the woman.

Neither her expression nor pose changed when she looked up to acknowledge him.

"Meet me at the jailhouse. We have an injured man here." He instructed. She nodded.

When they reached the jailhouse Landry climbed off first with rifle in hand. He glanced over the area once more, again looking for suspicious men. He found nothing. Even so, he had to assume that the riders were out there somewhere or at the very least they would arrive soon wanting the money and the prisoner.

He nodded to Gunther, and he too then climbed off his horse. Landry noticed that Gunther did not look around for any gunman. He just assumed that all was well. Landry was disappointed; a lawman with a prisoner can never assume all is well, he must assume the opposite, expect the worst so as not to be caught off guard. A lawman that can be caught by surprise is usually a dead man.

"Take him inside." Instructed Landry as he continued to scan the area looking for a possible attack.

Gunther pulled the prisoner off the horse, letting him fall face down. The prisoner cried out. Gunther held up his hands in defense and grinned. "Ooops. That old boy just slipped through my fingers."

Landry was not amused.

Chapter 7

The morning sun shined through the bedroom window. Donovan rolled over and squinted as the bright light shone upon his face. He had fallen asleep after all. He turned to the bed next to the wall. Sage was gone.

"Morning baby," Mama said from the doorway. Donovan turned to her. She probably had been watching him for a while. Otherwise, he would have heard her approach.

"Morning Mama." He answered. "Where's Sage?"

Her eyes filled with joy as her thick hands covered her face. Watching her, Donovan realized how much he had missed her. "Sage is doing his chores. He's out there with Papa and Miles." She said. "Made you breakfast."

He thanked her and followed her to the eating table in the other room. She pointed to the plate. It consisted of ham, scrambled eggs, and a biscuit. "This is yours." She said.

"Where's yours?" He asked.

She smiled. "I ate already."

She then sat across from him and watched as he scooped and chewed his food.

Just before he had finished she leaned forward and asked. "Want more?"

He nodded. "No Mama. That was plenty."

"You get ya'self-changed." She said. "Then come sit with me on the porch for a bit."

On the porch, Donovan seated himself in the empty chair next to Mama. She grabbed his hand and smiled as her view wandered into the fields.

Donovan looked out as well. Not too far from them was Miles who was digging and overturning the land with a shovel. He was getting the land ready for spring planting, which was only a few weeks away. From what Donovan could tell he still had a lot of land left to turn.

Donovan turned his gaze to scan the property. To his left one hundred yards or so was a chicken coop. At the entrance was a knee-high wooden fence that made a nice size yard for the chickens to roam. Inside the fenced area, Papa and Sage had a bucket of feed and were tossing the feed about to the chickens that clucked and pecked the food at their feet. Not far from them was a fenced in pigpen. He counted about ten pigs rustling in the mud within the bordered area. Out ways were about seven cows walking about the grassy plains.

Papa took notice of them and waved. Mama laughed and waved back. Papa pulled Sage's sleeve and pointed toward Mama and Donovan. He tried to coax Sage to wave as well, but he would not turn around to face them. Papa tossed up his hands in a playful manner and then went back to feeding the chickens.

Further back behind the chicken coop was a barn. And to the right of this barn was another house. On the porch, a woman was leaning on the post looking in their direction. Her long hair and dress moved with the breezes like laundry on a clothesline.

"That's Maria. Miles's new wife." Said, Mama. "They been married almost a year now. They've got problems. But with the LORD's help, they'll work em out."

Taking notice of Donovan, Miles leaned on his shovel as he breathed heavily and watched. With the front of his shirt, he wiped the perspiration from his face. Gripping the shovel he headed toward them. Donovan felt Mama's hand tense within his, and then she released her hold and placed her hands within her lap.

Donovan studied Miles as he continued to walk toward the porch. His demeanor and facial expression were hostile. Donovan was in the habit of watching others, trying to get a feel if they were intending to attack or not.

He didn't know why Miles was coming in his direction with a shovel in hand. Maybe he wanted revenge for last night, or maybe he just wanted to intimidate Donovan. Truthfully Donovan didn't care one way or the other, a shovel as a weapon was not much of a threat. Over the years he had seen men use more dangerous weapons. However, this was his brother he reminded himself, and he didn't want his brother hurt.

He looked over at his mother and saw the stress on her face. This made him sad. He wondered how many times had she made that same face through the years when she believed him as dead. He reached and grabbed her hand. "Don't worry Mama." He said.

She turned to him with a gentle smile, but the stress was still obvious.

With the shovel in hand, Miles stopped in front of the porch.

"Get that shovel away!" Mama warned.

Miles was confused. "Why?"

"It's got dirt on it!" she snapped. "And I just swept this porch."

Miles shrugged.

Mama stood from her chair and pointed toward the field. "Get that dirty shovel away from my clean porch!"

Miles stared at her; he was startled by her reaction. But she did not turn away. Finally, he tossed the shovel aside. Only then did she relax and sit back into the chair. Even though she was no longer looking at Miles he was still watching her, baffled. She ignored him.

Turning his attention to his younger brother, Miles leaned forward placing one foot on the porch, then he caught himself as he looked down at his dirty boot. He quickly looked up at his mother expecting another scolding, but none was given. He then turned to Donovan. "How long you staying?" He asked.

"Don't know." Said Donovan. "Why you ask?"

"If you're staying a bit we could use another hand."

"Doing what?"

"The fields." Said Miles. "I'm the only one that works them. Papa can't with his bum leg, and Mama's not strong enough, besides we need her in the kitchen."

Donovan had not done fieldwork since his late wife Sidney was alive. In those days, to support his family, he worked the fields from sunup to sundown; as he was certain that Miles did now. However, that was a long time ago, and much had changed since then. With the bounty money that he had collected over the years, and the money he had taken from Nevin Odland if he chose he would not need to work to support himself for years to come. But it wasn't that he was against fieldwork or any honest work for that matter. It was more because he had not seen his son in such a long time, and fieldwork required great hours and he was sure that this would diminish any small chance that he might have to develop a relationship with his son. "No." He said. "I won't be doing fieldwork."

Miles was at a loss. "You'll need to earn your keep around here." He said. "I won't be supporting you with my back and sweat."

"My money is my keep." Said Donovan. "I'll buy what's needed. But I won't be joining you in the fields."

"You got something against fieldwork?"

"I've got nothing against the work. I want to spend what little time I may have with my son."

Miles thought this over and then nodded. "We need supplies." He said. "Papa's riding into town tomorrow. You can ride with him. You can pay for your share."

"I'll just give him the money." Said Donovan. "It's not necessary for me to ride with him."

"On account of his bum leg, he'll need you to help load the wagon. I would go myself, but the travel time would take me more than half a day away from the fields, and I've still lots of work to do before spring."

After killing Nevin Odland and the man in black, no town within a state or two would be safe for Donovan to visit. Nevin's bodyguard and the local lawmen might be searching for him. These past few months of his travels he had avoided the towns so as not to leave a trail of his whereabouts. As it were now, because he had avoided human contact, they had no clue of the direction that Donovan was headed. In truth, he would probably be a few more months before his searchers would give up. But even then he would never truly be out of harm's way. The day would come, as it usually did when someone would recognize him. Usually, he wore his wide brim hat low over his face so that folks would not easily identify him. But sometimes this was not enough.

"I'll ride with Papa."

"Good." Said Miles. He picked up his shovel and headed back to the fields.

Mama's hand relaxed inside of his. "Papa could use your help." She said.

"I reckon so." Said Donovan. He was uneasy about his decision to go into town.

After Miles had left, Maria stepped off her porch and started in their direction. When she reached them Donovan could see the playful childlike manner about her. She had dark long stringy hair. Her dress had flower patches all about. Her bare feet were small with perfect toes.

"Hi." She said as she approached them eyeing only Donovan. Donovan nodded. "Is this the one that I've been hearing about Mama?" She asked.

"This here is my youngest boy, Donovan," Mama said without looking in her direction.

"He sure is pretty." She said as she smiled at Donovan. She extended her hand to his. "I'm Maria."

He grabbed her hand and squeezed it. "I'm Donovan."

"Nice to meet you, Donovan." She twisted side to side with a playful smile. "So you're Miles's younger brother."

"Yeah." Said Donovan.

"He don't like you much." She said with a giggle.

"No, I guess he don't."

"And why is that Donovan?"

Donovan was quiet for a moment. He didn't like people asking him a lot of questions, especially someone he had just met. "You need to ask him." He said.

Maria laughed as she turned to watch Miles in the distance digging and turning the land. "Miles don't talk much. All he do is work." She turned back to Donovan. The smile eased off her face. "He never takes a day off." She turned in Miles's direction again. "He don't care about nothing but his work."

"But he's a good provider." Said Mama from her chair. "Papa can't provide no more on account of his bad leg. So it's all on Miles. And he don't never complain. He just do what needs to be done. There's a many women out there who wants a hard working man like Miles. We all should be grateful."

Shamefully Maria looked down at her little feet, and then came back up to meet Mama's eyes. "I didn't mean nothing by that Mama. I just wish that I matter to him is all."

"You do matter child." Responded Mama. "We all do. That's why he work so hard."

Maria wanted to change the subject, so she turned to Donovan. "Your horse ran off this morning. I saw him run into the woods. Ain't seen him since."

"He's not far," Donovan said.

"I went looking and didn't see him."

"He's out there." He said.

"How you know?"

"He don't go far, he likes to stay close to me."

Maria turned toward the woods. After a moment she said. "Well, he's gone now."

Donovan put his fingers to his mouth and blew an ear-splitting whistle. A startled Maria ducked and turned to him. "What are you doing?" She said trying to catch her breath.

He stood from his chair and pointed. "He'll be coming soon."

"Who?" Maria said as she turned to look.

"Fletcher, my horse."

The horse's snicker was heard somewhere in the woods. Then the brown horse was seen as it raced out of the woods at full speed toward the house.

"Oh my gosh, look at him go." Said Maria.

Papa and Sage took notice of the horse racing across the field. Even Miles leaned on his shovel so as to watch the massive horse gallop pass him.

When the horse neared them Maria stepped onto the porch and stood behind Donovan. "Make him stop!" She yelled.

Donovan stepped off the porch to greet the horse. It seemed as if the horse would collide into him, but instead, he circled around Donovan keeping his immense head low. He patted the horse on his neck and the horse snickered and excitedly bobbed his head up and down.

Mama and Maria watched them from the porch, Miles from the field, and Papa from the chicken coup. Sage was the only one who seemed not to be interested.

"I thought that horse was gonna kill you." Said Maria from the porch.

Donovan rubbed the horse's neck. "I told you he wasn't far."

"I believe you now." She said. She then stepped to the edge of the porch. "Is he dangerous?"

"He can be if you try to ride him. But as long as I'm around Fletcher ain't gonna hurt, nobody."

She stepped off the porch and cautiously approached Donovan and his horse. She reached for the horse's lower neck and rubbed. She smiled. "He likes me." She said.

"That's good, cause he don't like everybody," Donovan said.

Mama watched them in silence from her chair.

After few minutes with the horse, Donovan reached for the duffel bag around the horn of the saddle and dropped it to the ground. He unbuckled the saddle under the horse's massive belly, and strained as pulled it off and dropped it to the ground with a thud. He reached around the horse's neck and pulled over Fletcher's head a large leather bag that was supported by a long thick drawstring. He swatted the horse on the rear, and Fletcher trotted away in the direction that he had come.

"Where's he going?" Maria asked.

Donovan shrugged. "The woods I guess."

Donovan turned to Mama at the porch. He held up the duffel bag. "These are my worn clothes." He said. "Where can I wash them?"

"I'll wash them, baby." She said as she reached for the bag, but Donovan held on. For the past few years, he had been totally independent not needing anyone to help him with the cooking or his laundry. The last thing that he wanted was to be a burden to his mother.

"I'll do it, Mama. Just need to know where is all." He said.

Her face was saddened. So he released the bag, and she smiled.

Chapter 8

The river was just over three miles from the house. Donovan remembered many days when he and his childhood friends would come here to fish, swim or just sit around and talk. The only time they would bathe in this river was in the spring and summer when the water was tolerable. During any other season, the water would be much too cold.

In the winter when Donovan was a child, he and Miles would grab two-buckets each and head for the river and bring back water for bathing. Then the whole family would take turns sharing the recycled water. Since Donovan was the youngest he was usually the last to bathe, and the tub of water was always at its filthiest by then.

Donovan stripped out of his clothes at the river's bank and stepped into the cold water. He had the soap, which his mother had given to him in one hand. He left his pistols in the riverbank. Though it was early spring, the water was still cold, and it took his body a few minutes to adjust to the temperature. Once he adapted to the water, Donovan washed himself with the bar of soap. It felt good to be clean again.

After he had finished washing, he dropped into the water so that the river line came up to his chin. He thought how fortunate he had been. With all that he had been through within the past few years, he was damn grateful to be alive right now. In actuality, he thought he would never survive long enough to one day be able to see his son again let alone his mother and the rest of his family.

He winced as he thought of Sage. Donovan wondered what sort of life Sage had lived for all these years. He didn't like to think of Sage in the way he was now, with his scarred face and meek existence.

Donovan felt the pressure of rage in his chest rise as he thought of what they did to that little boy. Sage was helpless, and they injured him and left him for dead.

The pressure then turned into sadness and despair. He wasn't sure how to handle these feelings of grief. Anger he could handle, for over the years he had learned to control his anger to a point. But pain and despair was an emotion that seemed impossible to control.

Still low in the river, he closed his eyes, trying to clear his mind of all thoughts, of all the horrible memories of his past. He particularly tried to clear the memories of his son and past wife.

There was a movement within the trees beyond the river. It was slight but he heard it nonetheless. He did not want to draw attention to himself, so he opened his eyes and dropped lower into the water so that only his eyes and nose were above the river line. He looked in the direction that he thought the noise had come from. He did not see anything. Though nothing could be seen, Donovan trusted his ears, without a doubt he had heard something. But what he heard he could not verify. It could be anything, the wind, an animal, kids, a fisherman, his enemies, anything.

He looked toward the bank where he had left his pistols. He had floated too far from them. He looked around thinking of an escape route. Many thoughts quickly came to mind, depending on what he faced. If it were one man with a pistol, he could swim to the other side of the river and escape on the opposite bank. However, if the man had a rifle, he most likely would float downstream low in the water for a mile or so, and then climb out at the opposite bank if the opportunity presented itself. If it were several armed men, without his weapons he would not survive.

After a lengthy wait of hearing and seeing nothing else, Donovan attempted to appear casual as he swam toward his guns on the riverbank. As he did so he continued to carefully monitor for more possible movements. He stayed low in the water as he reached for his pistols. He stepped out of the water pointing his pistols in the direction that he had originally heard the movement. He waited for a long time.

After a while, he finally saw another movement within the thick bushes to his left. The motion was so slight that if he hadn't been looking directly at the hedge he would have missed it. He pointed his guns as he moved toward the brush. When he was less than a few feet away he pulled the hammer back on both pistols. They clicked, which was enough warning for anyone close by that they were going to be killed.

"Donovan!" The woman's voice called out. "It's me, Maria." She said as she stepped out from behind the shrub with her head turned away and palms outstretched as if this were enough to shield herself from incoming bullets.

Donovan kept his gun pointed for he was confused by her presence. "What are you doing here?" He asked.

"Are you gonna shoot me, Donovan?" Her tone was now playful, and her hands that were previously used for defense were now comfortably at her sides. She faced him directly and smiled. Her eyes scanned his nude body.

Donovan finally lowered his pistols and crisscrossed them below his waist to cover himself. "Who else is with you?" He asked.

"No one." She said smiling. "Just me and you."

"Why are you here?"

"I wanted to talk."

"I'm not much of a talker." Said Donovan.

She playfully twisted her dress from side to side. "Miles ain't much of a talker either. Unless he's talking to his Papa about business stuff." The smile vanished, and she appeared off to the side. "I didn't just come to talk." Her playful mannerism did not exist for the moment. "Do you think I'm pretty Donovan?"

"What does it matter what I think. You're married to my brother."

"Your brother don't like you none."

"That don't matter, he's still kin."

"Most people think I'm beautiful. That's why I ain't got no friends. All the women folks are jealous of me. They talk about me behind my back. And if they catch they husband looking at me, sometimes them wives slap em in the face. I try to be nice and talk with the women folks, but they just ignores me and walks away."

She paused to make sure that he was listening and then decided to continue. "The only people that will talk to me are the men folks." She displayed a playful smile. Then she grabbed the rim of her dress and lifted it to her chin so that her nakedness was exposed. "Do you think I'm beautiful?" She asked him again while holding up her dress for him.

Donovan could not bring himself to turn from her slender uncovered body. She had caught him off guard and she knew this from his hypnotic state.

"Yes." Said Donovan as calmly as he could. "I think you're beautiful."

"Good." She said as she dropped her dress. "I think you're beautiful too." She turned and skipped into to the woods.

Donovan wondered of her intentions as he watched her disappear behind the trees.

Chapter 9

The restaurant was empty; the last couple from the breakfast hour had just left. Alfred brought the dirty dishes to the back. When he returned the two men standing inside the doorway surprised him. "Hello, senor." He said in his Spanish accent, trying to get back his composure.

Neither of the men responded which caused Alfred to be uneasy of them. Both men stood in the doorway looking the restaurant over. The men had not shaven for weeks and looked as if they had not bathed for just as long. The shorter man on the right was heavy almost fat. His partially bald scalp glistened with drops of sweat and dirt. The other man was of average weight and height with short black oily hair, and long black sideburns down his cheeks. He had an impatient nature about him.

The man with the sideburns walked over to the window table and seated himself. The other man stared at Alfred and then approached him as if a cat stalking an unknown prey.

"Hello," Alfred said again, his voice uncertain.

The bald man looked past him into the back room. He then stared hard at Alfred, and Alfred had to look away. "Do I scare you boy?"

Alfred nodded.

The bald man smiled, but it wasn't a friendly smile. "You alone?" He asked.

Alfred nodded.

"Who else is with you?"

Alfred hesitated he didn't want to answer this question. The man continued to stare at him, and Alfred folded under his glare. "My wife Sofia is here." He said with regret.

"Anyone else?"

Alfred nodded again.

"Where is she?"

He looked over his shoulder. "She's in the kitchen, in back."

"Call her out." Instructed the bald man.

"Why senor? She's very busy."

The bald man glared at Alfred until he finally gave in and called to Sofia in Spanish.

The bald man grabbed Alfred's arm and squeezed. "Speak English." He said.

After a few moments of waiting Sofia did not come.

"Call her again." Instructed the bald man.

Alfred called to her again, and when Sofia came out she displayed a frown. "Why is it you call me so much?" She scolded.

Alfred pointed to the man. "He wants to see you."

Sofia turned to the bald man and smiled graciously. "What is it that you need, senor?" She said.

The bald man eyed her from head to toe. Even with the food-stained apron, her black gritty hair, and her sweat-beaded forehead she was quite attractive. He turned to Alfred. "How much for her?"

He tried to appear calm, but he could not believe his ears. "Pardon me, senor?" He asked.

The bald man reached into his pocket and pulled out some bills. He pointed to Sofia. "How much for one night with the woman?"

Alfred turned to Sofia to see her expression. She had none. No expression of surprise, or anger, or even embarrassment, nothing. He then turned his attention back to the bald man. He ignored the money that the bald man was trying to hand to him. "Senor, this is my wife, you cannot buy her."

With the money in hand, the bald man gawked at Alfred. This time Alfred did not turn away. Sofia stepped forward and grabbed the money from the bald man's hand. She passed through the bills quickly as she counted. She smiled, "You think I'm beautiful, senor?"

The man smiled. "You are indeed, beautiful."

She turned to her husband. "It's been a long time since anyone say I am beautiful." She then turned back to the bald man. "And you are willing to pay for me, senor?"

"I am." He said.

She waved the money in front of him. "How much will you pay?"

Alfred began to protest, and she shushed him.

"Whatever it takes." He said.

She smiled and then handed the money back to him. "I'm not for sale, senor. I'm not a whore. This is a restaurant, not a whorehouse. We have good food here. You eat or you go." Her voice was firm through her smile. She gently stroked his chin. "Thank you for the compliment. Now sit, and Alfred will bring you some food."

The bald man stuffed the money into his pocket and headed over to the table with his partner. Alfred glared at the bald man's back, and then he turned to glare at his wife who had already disappeared into the back room.

"We've got strangers in town." Said Alfred to Sheriff Landry as he placed the basket of hot food on the desk.

Sheriff Landry was leaning against the window as he faced Alfred. His brother Gunther was in the corner pulling his side pistols at an imaginary criminal.

"Damn I'm fast," Gunther said with his famous grin. He turned and pulled the pistols and pointed them at Alfred. "You see that?" He said to Alfred who had put his hands up to protect his face. Gunther found this act amusing and then warned. "Putting them hands up ain't gonna help you none. If I wanted you dead, you'd be dead." He then put the guns back in their holsters. "Just be glad I likes you some."

Alfred nodded. "Thank you, senor." He unfastened the red and white cloth in the basket, releasing the steam. "My Sofia made you fresh stew. It has beef and some vegetables, there's bread too. It's very good."

Sheriff Landry ate his stew and bread at the window. Gunther, on the other hand, stood at the bars facing the prisoner, chomping his food to antagonize him. "Hmm, this is good." He would say after each bite. When he finished the bowl he went to the basket and grabbed two pieces of cornbread. Once again he approached the jail. He ate the first piece and licked his fingers afterwards. Holding up the second piece he asked. "You want this?" The prisoner nodded. Gunther raised the bread to his lips spat on it, and then tossed it into the cell. The prisoner looked up with angry eyes and then brought his foot down, crushing the bread to crumbs.

Gunther laughed. "I guess he ain't hungry enough."

"Stop with the games, Gunther. Let's get to business." Said sheriff Landry. He turned to Alfred. "Tell us about these two men in your restaurant."

Alfred reached for Sheriff Landry's empty bowl and placed it in the basket. "They ain't too friendly is what I know. One of em is plain spiteful. They've been sit-in at the window all day, like they watching for someone."

"All day?" Sheriff Landry questioned.

"Since this morning after my breakfast rush." Responded Alfred. "They're there now."

"What are they doing?" Asked Landry.

"Far as I can tell, just looking out the window."

"What do they talk of?" Asked Landry.

"I don't hear much. They get quiet when I come around."

"What makes you think these sons of bitches is spiteful?" Asked Gunther as he inspected his pistol.

"It's how they look at you." Said, Alfred. "They've got mean eyes. They like to stare at folks. I asked one of em when he was leaving. He didn't answer. He just stared at me with those eyes."

"That's it." Laughed Gunther. "Hell, you afraid of half the folks in this town."

Alfred nodded. "These men are different senor, Gunther. Some men come to restaurant, they talk a lot, they have big tales of some of the awful things they've done. Sometimes they talk of men they've killed. I think most of their talk are lies. But these men are different. They don't talk, they don't have big stories, they just sit and watch." He paused for a moment. "The men like these in my restaurant now, are the most dangerous. These types of men have given Sheriff Landry and Deputy Gunther the most trouble."

There was silence between them. Gunther was no longer smiling.

Landry patted Alfred on the back. "You did us fine Alfred. Let us know if anything new comes about."

Alfred politely nodded and headed for the front door. "My Sofia will come later with supper." Said, Alfred, as he closed the door.

Laundry turned to the prisoner in the jail. He was lying on the bench facing the wall. "I think those men are lookin for that man in the jail."

Gunther nodded. "I think so too."

The prisoner rolled over in his bed and grinned at them. Gunther cut his eyes at him. "I'll give that son of bitch something to grin at."

"Relax Gunther, you'll get your chance." Responded the Sheriff.

Chapter 10

It was early the next morning and Donovan reached under the bed and pulled out his knife, two pistols, and a short caliber. He placed each firearm on the bed and inspected them. A simple ritual he had done each morning for the past several years. His pistols were his lifeblood, and he had to make sure they were in working order and loaded. Though he had not fired his pistols in several weeks, he still checked, and sometimes rechecked. He didn't leave anything to chance. This knowing gave him his mental edge. It gave him calmness during the encounters that he faced.

Donovan was still in his sleeping clothes when he stepped onto the porch. The wood porch was cold on the soles of his feet. The morning air was crisp, but the sun gave a hint of a warm day ahead. Mama and Sage were watching Papa guide the horses and wagon out of the barn. Their dressy attire surprised him. Mama was wearing a nice brown dress and a straw hat with the fabric brim to match the color of her dress. This reminded Donovan of when he was a youngster, and his mother would dress up on Sunday for church service. His son Sage was also well dressed in his blue overalls, white shirt, and black boots.

She looked Donovan over. "You not dressed baby. We'll be leaving in a bit. Papa's bringing the wagon around now."

"We?" Donovan asked.

Mama smiled. "Me and Sage is going too. We decided on that this morning."

"Me and Papa don't need any help." He said.

"Oh, no child. I'm too old for that. I hadn't been in town for a time. I figure on seeing some old friends is all."

He watched as Papa guided the wagon to the porch, "Whoa!" He yelled as he pulled on the reins, and the grinding from under the wheels had stopped. Papa laughed as he observed Sage. "Ain't you something to see." He said. "All dressed up like a little man."

Sage eyed the ground in silence. Mama straightened the straps on his overalls. "Papa just paid you a mighty fine compliment. What you gonna say, baby?"

Sage uncomfortably twisted, and then said in a whisper. "Thank...you."

Papa nodded and turned to Donovan. "We bouts ready to go, son, you needs to get yourself changed?"

Because of his enemies, Donovan was uneasy about riding into town with his father. He often didn't suspect an enemy until they made their move.   But they paid with their lives. But he paid as well with injuries of his own. If these men were to find out that Donovan had a family. They would come after them. He gritted his teeth. He would not let that happen. "I've got some things to do," said Donovan. "I'll meet you in town."

"What you got to do?" Papa asked.

"I need to tend to Fletcher."

"Fletcher?" Papa questioned.

"My horse," Donovan said.

Papa nodded. "We'll wait on ya."

"No need, I'll just meet you."

"Can it wait till we gets back?"

"No," Donovan said. "Fletcher don't wait on nobody."

Papa looked intently at Donovan. "That don't make no sense. He just a horse. How long you planning to be?" Asked Papa.

Fletcher was more than a horse he was family.   Not only that Fletcher had saved Donovan's life many times. Too many in fact to count. Because of his speed, Donovan's pursuers could not even dream of catching him. Because of Fletcher's loyalty, Donovan could call and count on him at any moment. All he had to do was whistle, and the massive horse would arrive. Never did he not show. Never was he slow to approach. It didn't matter of the danger.   Fletcher always showed. Donovan would climb on, and away they raced.   His endurance was endless.   He would run and run until Donovan was safe and out of harm's way.   It was as if the great animal understood that Donovan's life was at stake. He loved this animal. But Donovan didn't need to tend to Fletcher. The massive animal tended to himself. He found his own food and water. Roamed about of his own free will. This was just an excuse so that he didn't have to ride into town with his folks. He wanted to arrive later, scope out the people, and if all seemed okay, he would help his papa.   If he suspected anyone, he would move on. He wasn't going to bring danger upon his family.

"An hour or so." He answered.

Papa nodded. "That'll be fine. That'll give me and Mama a chance to visit some old friends I guess."

Donovan helped Mama and Sage into the seat of wagon while Papa grabbed their hands and pulled them up. Donovan watched as the wagon let by two horses pulled away.

After some time had passed Donovan again stepped out onto the porch. This time Maria was in the fields trying to get Miles's attention. He dug hard into the soil, there were rolls and rolls of turned earth behind him. She followed him and he ignored her. From what Mama had said, Miles didn't stop working unless to get water or food. She tried to kiss him; he pushed her away. She stood back, slipped out of her dress and stood in front of him. He didn't even look at her. He again pushed her aside. She picked up her dress and was taken aback to see that Donovan was watching her. She smiled at him, tossed the dress on the ground and headed for her house. She looked back to see if he was watching, to her delight he was. When she arrived at her porch, she turned to him one last time and then disappeared into the house.

He glanced at Miles, his back was to him and he had no idea that Donovan had been watching them. He put his fingers to his lips and whistled. He heard Fletcher whinnying from somewhere in the woods.

It was early afternoon, and the men had been in the restaurant since that morning. The bald heavy man, Lee Fatkin and his partner with the greasy black hair and long sideburns Dylan Stocklin, sat at the end table by the restaurant window. They both viewed periodically out the window and talked low amongst each other. Whenever Alfred would walk by their conversation would cease. Sometimes Fatkin would glare at Alfred until he scattered away. Stocklin raised the cup to his lips and sipped his coffee. He spoke as he lowered the cup. "You think we did right coming back here?"

"Don't see as we had much of a choice." Said Fatkin.

"You think anybody knows us, is what I'm saying?"

Fatkin looked around the half-filled restaurant. Three of the tables were occupied. None of the folks seemed to take notice of them. He nodded. "Nobody knows us here."

Stocklin sighed before he took another sip. "You sure he came back here?" He asked.

"Where else could he be?" Said Fatkin in more of a statement than a question.

"He could be long gone with our money." Stocklin shot back.

"Not Dale. We've known him since he was a youngster. He ain't like that."

"Then where the hell is he with our money?"

"I told you already." Said Fatkin. "I think he got himself caught by the sheriff and his deputy? It's our own fault. We didn't expect such an odd pair to come after us. They probably followed us a ways. And when you and me left camp to scout the area, that's when they grabbed Dale and the money." Said Fatkin.

"I don't know about that." Responded Stocklin. "Dale couldn't be caught by the likes of those two."

"Well something happened to him, and this is the best I can figure. He wouldn't just run off unless he got a good reason."

"How we gonna find out if they got him?" Asked Stocklin.

Fatkin leaned back in his chair. "That's what I don't know. We just gonna have to sit about for a while until we figures that out."

Stocklin nodded in Alfred's direction who was speaking to a young couple as he poured water into their glasses. "Why don't we ask him?'

"No, this would cause him to be suspicious of us."

"He's already suspicious."

"No, he's fearful, not suspicious. Our faces were covered that day, he suspects nothing. If we were to ask of him about Dale and those lawmen, then he would know we had something to do with the bank."

"What if we're wrong and Dale's not here?"

Fatkin looked around to make sure no one was in hearing range. His face was serious as he leaned forward, Stocklin leaned forward to meet him. "You're right, we're taking a big chance coming back like this. If Dale betrayed us and ran off with our money, I promise you we'll find and kill him. But if he got himself caught by those peculiar lawmen... we got no choice, we gonna have to get him out."

"What about our money?"

Fatkin frowned. "You know we ain't leaving without that money."

Chapter 11

At a casual trot, Donovan and Fletcher reached the outskirts of town. Donovan thought back to when he was a child, and he couldn't remember this town being this small. Admittedly the town had grown since he had left seven years before. He spotted a few new buildings, but the town was still considered small compared to the other places that he had traveled.

Donovan was comforted to observe that a number of patrons wondering about weren't all that much. He saw folks on the planked sidewalks talking. Others were seen inside the shop's window shopping. Horses and wagons were spread about loosely alongside the main road. Donovan spotted Papa and his wagon backed up to the supply shop. He was conversing with a couple of men dressed in overalls. He did not see Mama or Sage.

The supply shop was where he had first noticed Sidney. At that time he had caught a glimpse of her through the window. He was taken aback by her beauty. She had long wavy black hair and gorgeous dark eyes. He even remembered the sky blue dress that she wore that day. When she finally came out she was pleasantly startled to find that Donovan had been watching her. Six months later they were married. Ten years later she was dead. He lowered his head. After all these years it was still hard to bare.

He guided Fletcher down the main road. His head was tilted downward, and his large brown hat shielded much of his face. Though Donovan did not want to attract attention to himself, as a newcomer this was sometimes difficult.

As he neared Papa, Donovan noticed that the two men leaning against the restaurant wall were watching him. One of the men was rather large with a partially baldhead and some facial hair, and the other was medium height with short black hair and long dark sideburns. The large bald man appeared to have hostility in his glare. As Fletcher moved closer Donovan studied their faces for a long time. But he did not recognize either one.

Papa seemed as if he was going to wave, and then decided against it. Maybe he sensed that the men were watching Donovan as well. Donovan nodded and continued on down the road.

He guided Fletcher along and then turned in front of the gun shop. He climbed off his horse and glanced at the two men once more. At this time the bald man had stepped into the street and was watching Donovan.

The bald man's actions were odd but not enough for Donovan to react. Not now anyway. He wasn't motivated by violence anymore. All the men that had killed Sidney were dead. Donovan stepped into the gun shop.

Fatkin remained along the roadside as he watched the colored man enter the gun shop. He headed back toward his partner.

"What's the interest with the colored man?" Asked Stocklin.

"I know him. I don't know his name, but I know him all the same."

"Where bouts?"

"A couple years back in a saloon." Answered Fatkin. "He shot the man next to me. Blew his head off, and then said something about the man had killed his wife."

"That's a good reason to kill somebody, but what's that got to do with you?"

Fatkin leaned against the side of the restaurant. "Nothing." He said.

The gun shop was poorly lit. Some daylight shined through the small front windows and the one lantern at the back of the store gave off very little light. He stood at the entrance for a moment to allow his eyes to adjust. The smell of gunpowder was strong. It always was in these types of places. A well-dressed man in a visor and wire-framed glasses was bent behind the glass counter, which displayed various pistols of many makes and sizes. He peeked over and frowned when he saw Donovan. He rose up with contempt. Donovan approached him. The man continued to stare, but Donovan was looking behind him at the rows of boxed bullets. The lantern near the back provided just enough light

Donovan pointed. "I'll take five boxes of 44's."

The man frowned. "What does a nigger need with five boxes of bullets?"

Donovan glared. "Just get them."

The man smirked when he said. "Them bullets ain't for sale. Not to niggers anyway."

Donovan watched the man, they were about the same height except the man was wider and stocky. He had a confident grin to match his strong physique. He leaned forward across the counter and pointed to the door. "Now get!"

Unfortunately, the man had positioned himself close enough for Donovan to grab his throat. The man gagged and pawed, but Donovan did not release his grip. Finally, Donovan released his hold and the man collapsed to the floor. He clutched his throat and wheezed for air. Donovan leaned over the counter and watched the man. He tried to yell for help, but his voice was hoarse, and could not be heard by anyone.

Donovan waited for the man's breathing to become regular, then he pointed to the wall. "I'll take those boxes of .44's."

The man palmed his throat. After a while, he managed to his feet and grabbed the boxes of .44's and set them on the counter. "Here, take them all." He said in a harsh whisper. "You can have it. Just get the hell out of my shop."

Donovan reached into his pocket and pulled out his pouch. He tossed some bills on the counter. "I'm not a thief." He said.

Gunther was inside the jail and poked at the prisoner who was lying on the cot. "Get up," Gunther commanded.

The prisoner was not responsive to Gunther's commands. After he kicked the cot, Gunther pulled out his pistol and pointed it at the prisoner's head. "This is the last time I'm gonna tell you, boy. The next sound you'll hear is the gunshot in your head."

The prisoner opened his eyes and moaned. He pulled himself up, but his shoulders dropped forward and his arms hung limp. "Water." He begged.

Gunther smiled and turned to his brother who had been watching them with his rifle within reach on the desk. He then turned back to the prisoner. "Well hell, we done gave you a cup of water yesterday. We ain't giving you anymore."

The prisoner fell back on the wall "Please deputy. I's mighty thirsty."

The deputy thought it over, then approached the wooden bucket of water outside the jail. He raised the ladle and poured the water into a tin cup, and walked back into the jail. The prisoner's eyes opened wide as he watched the deputy. He reminded Gunther of a dog that he once had that would wait patiently for him to toss food scraps from the table. Gunther smiled and tossed up the tin cup consuming the water. He sighed. "That's good water."

The prisoner began to sob. Gunther smiled again. "I guess you ain't got much to grin about now, do you boy?" Gunther leaned in close. "This is just the beginning. You thought me and the sheriff was a couple of country boys. Thought you could just ride in our small town and steal from our bank, and that would be the end of it. Well, it ain't the end boy, it's the beginning. You don't know us around these parts. Me and the sheriff got us a reputation around here. You ain't the only one that tried to hold up that bank. We've caught a many of folks for that. But you were sporting that little grin yesterday. Me and the sheriff figures you got it too good around here. So we worked things out, so you don't have too much to grin about anymore. And when your friends come looking for you…well me and the sheriff got some surprises for them too."

"Get on with it, Gunther." Ordered the Sheriff from his desk. "We ain't got much time."

Gunther pointed his pistol at the prisoner's face. "Take off your clothes. Shorts and all."

"What?" Said the prisoner as if he thought he had misunderstood.

"You heard me."

"Why?"

"Because you gonna be more presentable for our little walk."

Gunther grinned as he watched the prisoner stare at him with confused eyes. Gunther then turned to his impatient brother and smiled to him as well, but the serious Landry did not return the smile.

Papa was standing at the wagon waiting for Donovan. Earlier he had seen him go into the gun shop. He thought it was odd that Donovan had passed him up. He wondered if Donovan was in some sort of danger. He hadn't seen his youngest son for such a long time that he didn't know much about him. He thought back to the night when Donovan had arrived at the house. His coat opened, exposing his shooting pistols. Why would he need those types of guns?

His wife, Mama as he affectionately called her, was making her way down the planked sidewalk, leading Sage by the hand. He had been calling her Mama since their first child was born thirty-six years ago. It was their way of teaching the newborn how to talk their names. She called him Papa as well.

"What's on your mind?" She asked when she approached.

"Just waiting on Donovan is all." He answered.

"He ain't here yet? He about do by now."

He sighed. "He'll be here soon enough, Mama. Did you see your church folks?"

Her eyes brightened, as he knew they would. "Oh yes. I saw the Bakers and the Jacobs. God has blessed them as he has blessed us." She said with her eyes closed and her hands clamped together.

Papa nodded as he looked down the street waiting for Donovan to come out of the gun shop. He didn't want to tell Mama just yet that

Donovan was in town, in case he decided for whatever reason not to come to them.

As he was peering down the street, what he saw shocked him, along with many others that were watching. He stepped away from the wagon to get a better view. Outside the jailhouse, a naked man was chained to the post that supported the roof of the overhang. Even from this distance, the man looked to be weak as he sat on the sidewalk with his back leaning against the post.

More folks were taking notice of the man. Some of the more curious was stepping into the street to get a better view. Papa figured the man was one of the men that had robbed the bank a few weeks back. Papa had heard from some of his friends that three men had actually robbed the bank, and two of them were still at large.

He saw some folks pointing to an object that was just out of reach of the man's feet. Papa stared at the object for a moment, and then came to realize that it was three bank bags, probably full of money. Probably the very bags that were stolen from the bank a few weeks back. He nodded his head in disbelief, the actions of the sheriff and the deputy seemed to have no limits.

Papa guessed the chained man and the bank bags were bait. The lawmen were taunting the two bank robbers that were still at large. If they were around you can bet the two lawmen were watching the money. Anyone that was foolish enough to attempt to take that money would be killed before they got the bags off the ground.

Mama stood behind Papa with Sage's hand in hers. "We better go we don't need to get mixed up in some trouble."

Looking around Papa wondered, did the sheriff and deputy suspect the other bank robbers to be in town, or were they just hoping. "I reckon you're right. We'll come back another day. No telling what that crazy sheriff and his deputy are up to. Don't need to be around some mess."

He helped Mama and Sage into the seat of the wagon and was just about to climb in himself when he noticed the two men outside of the restaurant across the street. He watched the bald man lean forward and squint his eyes to get a better look at what was going on. He tapped his partner on the chest and pointed down the street.

Papa heard the man with the sideburns say. "What the hell is going on down there?"

The men watched the scene for a long moment ducking and squinting to get a better view. "Don't know." Answered the man with the sideburns. He finally made his way over to his horse and pulled out an eyepiece. He looked through the eyepiece. "Got dammit! It's Dale. They got Dale…and our money."

He handed the eyepiece to the bald man. "Where the fuck is his clothes. They took his fucking clothes." He took a breath. "I told you he got himself caught. He never ran off with the money. He never ran off with nothin. We gonna get him out of there."

"When?"

"Now."

"They're expecting us."

"I don't much care bout that. Dale don't look like he have much time left." Said the bald man. "He's damn near dead. We gotta fetch him a doctor."

"We gonna have to kill them, two lawmen, first."

"That's what I'm planning. Gonna need us a couple of shields."

The two men turned to Papa who was watching them. They walked over to him. The bald man pointed down the street. "What's going on down there?" He tried to come across as casual and friendly as he could.

Papa shifted on his cane, come to think of it, he had noticed them when he had first backed his wagon to the supply shop. He was not fooled by their friendly mannerism for he felt it was forced. As he watched the bald man, he now remembered that he had seen him studying Donovan earlier. At the time he didn't think much of it, but now he wondered if these men were the reason that Donovan had chosen to ride on.

"I ain't got nothing to say to you, mister," Papa said.

The reaction of Papa caught the bald man by surprise. His friendly manner vanished as he and his partner glared at Papa. "Come again?" He said.

"We was just leaving." Said Papa softening his tone some.

The men glanced at each other. Finally, the bald man smiled showing his yellow teeth. It was a wide smile almost on the verge of a laugh. He pointed to Mama in the wagon. "This here your wife?" He asked.

Papa didn't answer.

The bald man and his partner again glanced at each other.

A backhand struck Papa in the face knocking him to the ground. When he looked up he saw the man with the sideburns standing over him. He could hear Mama crying from the wagon. The man with the sideburns grabbed and pulled him to his feet. "When we ask you a question boy, we expects an answer." He said.

Papa could hear Mama crying.

Pointing, the bald man asked. "Is that your wife?"

Again Papa gave no answer.

Another backhand knocked him to the ground. He heard Mama yell. "Oh Jesus no!"

This time Papa was flat on his back looking up at the man with the sideburns who had just struck him again. He grabbed Papa and jerked him to his feet once again, holding him close, face to face, nose to nose. His bitter breath filled Papa's nostrils.

"Is that your wife?' He asked again.

Turning his head, Papa spat the blood from his lips. "What does it matter to you?"

"It doesn't." He raised his hand yet again, but this time he did not strike.

"I is his wife!" Mama cried out from the wagon seat. "Now you let him be!"

The bald man looked up at her. "You come on down here."

"Just leave us be. We ain't bothering nobody." Mama said.

"Don't make me come get you." The bald man threatened.

Mama didn't move. The bald man frowned and took steps toward the wagon, but yelled out when Papa's cane struck him across the back of his head. The man with the sideburns snatched the cane from Papa. He raised it high and hit Papa across the chest. Papa let out a hollow scream.

Mama cried. "Please let my man be! Please let him be!"

Sage was also upset, he was moaning as he rocked back and forth. "Don't kill my Papa." He whispered. Mama grabbed him and held him.

The men were becoming impatient. The man with the sideburns pulled out his pistol and pointed it at Papa. At that moment Mama blurted out. "Oh Jesus no, don't kill him!"

The bald man turned his gun to Mama and yelled. "Shut the fuck up!" Mama quieted, with her face buried in her hands. Sage was again rocking and moaning.

The men looked around, at the moment there were no witnesses. Most folks were at the end of the street watching Dale and the moneybags. It seemed for the moment they were alone with the Negro couple.

Sideburns grabbed Papa and pulled him in close. The gun was pointed at his chest. "Don't make me kill you, old man." He said. "You do what I say, and you'll be alright. We going for a walk, and your misses is comin with us."

Papa turned to the man and said. "My misses ain't coming with us."

The man with the sideburns frowned as he put his pistol on Papa's cheek. He pushed the gun into his meat. "Come again?"

"This is between me and you. My missus ain't got nothin to do with it." Said Papa. "You fixin to use us to get that money. She's old, she'll slow you down."

The men stared at him as they thought it over. Finally, they decided against taking the old lady. The man with the sideburns pulled on Papa's arm. He dropped the gun to Papa's chest. "You do as I say, or when this is over, I'll kill you, then I'll kill your missus."

Papa nodded.

The bald man glared at Mama. "You make so much as a whimper, and I'll kill him." With her hands, she cupped her mouth to mute any sound that may escape her lips.

The men led Papa off to the side of the street. The man with the sideburns was closest to him with his left hand gripping Papa's arm, and in his right hand, the pistol pointed at Papa's side. The bald man was a few steps away, with his pistol resting against his leg. The men watched in all directions as they moved unnoticed down the street.

Papa glimpsed up ahead at the gun shop. He saw the door open, and Donovan stepped out. He looked to be carrying many small boxes, so many in fact that it took both of his hands to carry them to his horse, which was waiting just outside the shop.

He looked at the men, they didn't seem to notice Donovan or maybe they didn't care at the moment. They were focused only on the bags of money and those around it. Even if they got to that money, the sheriff and his deputy would kill them Papa thought. The problem was that they would probably kill Papa as well. Once he remembered witnessing an innocent man shot deliberately by the deputy, so that he would have a better angle for shooting the man that he was after. Of course afterward, the deputy claimed it was an accident. No one believed him.

He had figured by now, that the men that were walking alongside him, where the two at-large bank robbers. The sheriff's trap had worked, for it lured them back for the money and their friend. He wanted to warn the men, tell them that they would not survive the sheriff and his deputy. He wanted to tell them that the sheriff and his deputy were probably watching them at this moment. He wanted to warn them, but not to save them, he didn't give a damn about them, but he only wanted to save himself. But he said nothing, for they would not have listened anyway.

But there was another reason why he did not warn the men. He wanted them dead. He wanted them dead for putting a pistol in his wife's face, the woman he had loved with all his heart for over forty years. He wanted them dead for beating him as she watched helplessly. He wanted them dead for causing her the pain from watching them walk her husband down the street with a pistol pointed at his side. He wanted them dead even if it meant that he would die along with them.

He watched Donovan slap his horse on the rear, and the horse took off full speed toward them. The men stopped as the horse raced by, leaving clouds of dust behind. The men even turned to watch the horse race by. When they turned back around they were surprised to see Donovan walking toward them. The bald man raised his pistol from his leg and pointed in Donovan's direction. The other man still kept his gun pointed at Papa's side.

The men did not move as they watched Donovan approach them.

"That's far enough." Said the bald man. His gun was extended and aimed at Donovan's chest.

Chapter 12

Donovan stepped out of the gun shop, his hands were crammed with several boxes of bullets. His hat was low over his face. He saw the crowd forming around the naked man that was handcuffed to the post at the jailhouse.

Up ahead he saw the men guiding Papa down the street. One had their pistol on him. He stuffed the boxes of bullets into a leather pouch that was strapped to the saddle. He thought about reaching for the rifle in the saddle. But he was too far away, and the men with the guns were too close to Papa.

He walked around and slapped Fletcher on the rear. Fletcher took off knowing he had Donovan's permission to run wild. Donovan blocked him so that he would run in the direction of Papa and the two men.

After Fletcher took off, Donovan moved toward Papa and the men with him. His stomach turned. His worst nightmare had come true. One of his enemies had finally got to his family. There was no one to blame but himself. He was becoming soft and careless in his attempts to avoid violence and bloodshed. He should have confronted those men earlier when they seemed to have recognized him. If he had his papa wouldn't be in danger right now.

But how did they know that he and Papa were kin? Did they catch on to their slight interaction earlier? Donovan only nodded and Papa barely raised his hand in a half attempt to wave. But even from this, one couldn't possibly assume that they were family. He studied the men as he moved toward them. Admittedly he still didn't recognize them. But he didn't always recognize his enemies.

Fletcher ran with such astonishing speed that the men had to turn to observe. Most people couldn't resist watching the horse when he raced by them. When the dust settled and the men were no longer distracted by Fletcher, Donovan was upon them.

"That's far enough." Said the bald man. His gun was extended at Donovan.

Donovan stopped. He was as close as he needed to be. He focused on Papa, analyzing the dark bruises on his face and the blood on his lips. He frowned.

He studied their faces as they studied his. He still did not recognize them. "Do I know you?" Donovan asked.

"I don't reckon we know each other." Answered the bald man. "Don't know too many niggers, but I've seen you around nonetheless. I was there when you shot that man in the saloon couple years back. A white man at that."

"I don't remember you," Donovan said.

"Maybe." Said the bald man. "But I remember you. You chased that man into the saloon. He was begging for someone to help him. No one had time before you got to him. I was so close to him that some of his blood got on me. I heard you say something about your wife. That he killed her or something."

Donovan remembered the incident, but he still didn't recognize this bald man. "A friend of yours?" Donovan asked.

"No, just a man in the saloon. Didn't know him before that day." The bald man paused for a moment. "Did he kill your wife?"

"Donovan nodded. "That's right."

Strangely the bald man was sympathetic. "That explains why you killed him. Half the town was looking for you. Especially him being a white man an all. I was just passing through, so I didn't stick around. I figured they had caught and hung you by now. Then I sees you earlier, and I couldn't believe my eyes. I had to get a closer look." The bald man took a nervous breath. "How did you get away?"

Donovan nodded toward the direction that Fletcher had raced by. "My horse."

The bald man nodded. "I can see that. What brings you our way?"

"Me and this old man know each other. Seems to me you got him against his will." Said Donovan.

The bald man nodded toward the jailhouse. "You see that man down there?"

Donovan nodded. "I've seen him."

"He's a friend of mine. Been friends since we was youngsters. We're fixin to get him out."

Donovan glanced at Papa. Though he had blood on his lips, and a bruised face, his eyes were brave and defiant. His papa reminded him of a captured soldier that was being escorted to his execution.

"What's that got to do with this old man?" Said Donovan.

"He's going to help us." Said the bald man.

"He's not." Said Donovan. "You'll help your friend without the old man."

The bald man frowned. "Can't do that. But you can move along. I got no quarrel with you."

"I got no quarrel with you either." Said Donovan. I'm more than tired of bloodshed. I figure there's got to be a better way than men just killing each other. I understand your situation, maybe better than you do. My wife was killed a few years ago. I killed every man that had anything to do with it. But now I'm done killing. You do what you got to do, but without the old man."

The men studied Donovan. The man with the sideburns leaned forward and turned his gun on Donovan. "Is that right? Well, you're in no position to talk about killing. Maybe I'll just kill you." Sideburns pointed at the jailhouse. "Since you care so much for the old man, you can join us. You can help us get that money and free our partner." Said Sideburns.

The bald man smiled at Donovan. "You see what happens when you don't mind your business."

Sideburns pointed. "Let's go."

Papa was about to take a step but saw that Donovan didn't move. Donovan was eyeing him. "What happened to your face?' He asked.

Papa thought this was a strange question to ask in a time like this, when both their lives were at stake. All Donovan's actions to this point were strange to him anyway. He saw Donovan send his horse running. Then he walked right over to them. He had to have seen the men and their guns. But he came anyway. And now with their guns pointed at Donovan, he was asking him about his bruised face. He almost didn't answer the question, but he could see that Donovan wasn't moving until he got an answer.

"I was beaten." He said under his breath.

"Let's go." Sideburns commanded. Donovan ignored him. His next question to Papa surprised him even more.

"Which one?"

At first, Papa found it very odd that in the midst of the current situation Donovan would even want to know which man had hit him. But as he looked into his son's eyes, he came to realize what Donovan was planning to do. He was certain that underneath Donovan's coat he had two side pistols. Until now he didn't quite understand why he needed such armory, but from listening it turns out that Donovan had killed all of the men that had killed his wife Sidney. He was certain that he was going attempt to kill these two men as well.

Sideburns nudged Donovan with his pistol. "Enough talk, let's go."

Donovan once again refused the command and glanced at Mama and Sage on the wagon about fifty yards away. "Did they harm them?"

"No," Papa whispered.

"Sideburns lost patients with Donovan and tried to backhand Donovan with his pistol. But Donovan was the quicker, and pulled out both his pistols and fired his first shot into the bald man's face, who also got off single shot, which hit Donovan in the shoulder. The impact of the bullet forced Donovan to lose his balance, but before he hit the ground he managed to get off two rounds into the chest of sideburns. Sideburns fell on his back.

Donovan struggled to his feet. The bald man's eyes were open wide with death. The man with the sideburns was still breathing; but his eyes were closed. Donovan pointed his pistol at his head. "Hey," Donovan said.

Sideburns opened his eyes.

"This is for beating my Papa," Donovan said.

A moment later Sideburns laid dead with a bullet in his forehead.

Behind him, Donovan could hear the screams of the crowd down the street. He dropped the empty shells from the chambers and reloaded.

Papa watched him in disbelief. "You're gonna need a doctor."

The blood was starting to trickle from the shoulder. "It's not bad enough for a doctor." He said as he stuffed the pistols back into their holsters. He looked behind; some of the crowd were making their way toward him but stopped when he turned to them.

He put his fingers to his lips and whistled for Fletcher.

Papa was stunned as he eyed the dead men. He couldn't believe that Donovan had pulled this off. It happened so fast that he didn't realize what had happened until it was over. He watched his son who seemed unfazed. From his demeanor, he had obviously been in this type of situation before.

"You should be dead." Said Papa. "Both of us should be dead."

Donovan nodded. "I reckon we got a lucky break."

Papa grabbed Donovan by the arm. "I appreciates what you done for me. Those men was going to get me killed."

Donovan turned to the dead men on the ground. "I didn't want it to end this way. They left me no choice."

Papa turned to Mama. She was still on the wagon with Sage. Her hands were covering her face. "We best go tend to your mama. After what you just did, she probably about to have a heart attack."

Chapter 13

Dr. Tracy saw the incident from her hotel window on the second floor. It all happened so fast and with certainty. She first witnessed one of the strange men slapping Papa to the ground. At that point, Dr. Tracy knew Papa was in danger. She could not comprehend why any man would want to beat Papa. Papa was a decent man; she had known him and his wife for the past two years when she had first arrived in this town. She called him Papa, not because he was like a father to her, but because this was how he had introduced himself.

The pressure of panic was in her chest as she ran down the stairs of the hotel. By the time she reached the front door, both the men were pointing their pistols at Papa as they led him down the street. She froze and watched them. She thought of fetching the Sheriff, but she would have to pass the men to do so. She didn't feel this could be done without bringing attention to herself.

The massive horse raced passed, and they all watched. Then the dark man with the long brown coat approached them. She watched them point their pistols at him. And within a blink of an eye, the dark man fired his pistols. In her twenty-eight years of life, she had never seen a man draw his pistols while another man's pistols were pointed at him. When the dark man fell to the ground she figured him to be dead.

Dr. Tracy stepped into the street. She watched him wondering if he would hurt her. Not knowing she approached them anyway.

As she walked across the street toward the scene she felt uncomfortable when she realized the dark man had been watching her. Though his pistols were tucked away she could still smell the gunpowder in the air.

She looked at the first man. His eyes open, his face with no expression and a bloody wound on his left cheek. She glanced at the dark man who was still watching her. She waved her black hair behind her shoulders and then approached the other man. He was also dead with a bullet wound to the chest and forehead just between his eyes. The chest area on the second man was quite bloody. An indication that this man did not die right away.

Knowing the dark man was still watching her she walked over to Papa who was standing next to him. She touched his face, guiding it from side to side to view all the wounds. Papa moaned as she did so.

"I don't think it's broken. I'll look again later." She stepped back to get a full view of Papa's body. "Do you hurt anywhere else?"

Papa nodded. "Just my face."

Tracy looked at Sage and Mama on the wagon about five yards or so out. Sage was rocking back and forth moaning. Tracy locked eyes on him, smiled as she put her finger to her lips and said. "Shhhh."

Sage quieted immediately.

She turned to the dark man. His gaze was not hostile, nor friendly. Her eyes dropped down to his wounded left shoulder. The blood was soaking his coat. She wondered why this man had helped Papa.

"I need to look at that." She said.

"Who are you?' Asked the dark man. His voice was calm and low-key.

"They call me Dr. Tracy." She raised her eyes to meet his. "And you are?"

He hesitated for he wasn't accustomed to giving out his name. "Donovan." He finally said.

She glanced at Papa and then Mama and Sage on the wagon. "I've known these good folks for two years now. They're like family to me. It would have been a shame if that ended today." She turned to Donovan again. "Nowadays people don't care much for one another. Thank you for what you done."

Donovan nodded as he watched her black wavy hair swayed from the wind, like the tail of an air kite that he had seen once. As she stood in front of him, he realized that she was almost as tall as he was. She had on a button up shirt and some trousers that fit snuggly around her shapely hips. Her face was brown with freckles on either side of her nose.

Her voice was a continuous monotone with no peaks. So much in fact that listening to her eased his mind of the present situation. His breathing was now calm and for the first time since the shooting he looked at his shoulder and felt the ache when he saw the blood. He then turned to Dr. Tracy and said. "No need to thank me." He looked behind Tracy toward the jailhouse. Folks were spread out leaving the street clear. Some were pointing in their direction. The door of the jailhouse pulled open and out stepped a large man with a rifle in hand and behind him a small man.

Tracy looked over her shoulder. After she saw the sheriff and the deputy she turned to him and said. "Don't challenge them."

"Why would I challenge them?"

"Because they may provoke you to do so, especially the small one. They are brothers and very protective of one another. If you make a move toward any of them you're as good as dead."

"Why would they provoke me? I acted in self-defense."

Tracy glared at him. "You strategically assassinated those men." She looked over her shoulder, the sheriff and deputy had just stepped off the sidewalk in front of the jailhouse and were headed in their direction. She turned to Donovan. "I'm not judging, they deserved it. They beat Papa and was planning on killing him." She paused for a moment. "But these men coming down the street you cannot kill?"

Her sincere dark eyes mesmerized him. So much so that he felt he could trust her.

"She's right." Said Papa. "These men aren't ones to fool with. They're gonna want to know what happened. You tell them that these men tried to take you as a hostage to get the money and you killed them. Maybe they'll let you go home."

"Maybe?" Donovan questioned.

"Maybe," Tracy added. "If they don't like you, you'll be going to jail tonight. Or worse they'll kill you if you give them a reason."

Donovan turned to Tracy as he asked. "Why do you take the time to warn me of these men?"

Tracy looked over her shoulder to see the position of the lawmen, they were half the distance away. She turned back to Donovan. "I tell you this because you saved Papa's life, and Papa is family to me. These men are dangerous. And they will kill you. Do not do anything foolish. You will not survive."

Donovan frowned and then said with certainty. "I'll do as you say…but I won't go to jail. That I can promise you."

Tracy stepped to the side and they waited as the sheriff and the deputy made their way to them.

The Sheriff and his deputy stopped at the first dead man. Without a word, they glanced at Papa, Tracy, and Donovan. Then they walked over to the other dead man.

"This son of a bitch is dead too." Said the deputy. He turned to Donovan. "This oh boy done killed both these men."

Donovan was silent. The lawmen approached, stopping a few feet from the three. Donovan watched them as they watched him. The sheriff was probably the biggest man that Donovan had ever seen. His only weapon was the rifle, which he casually carried.

The deputy, on the other hand, was a complete contrast to the sheriff. Considering they were brothers they seemed odd together. The deputy was short and stocky. He was no taller than Sage. His black boots shined to perfection matching his dark suit and bow tie. On his waist, he holstered two six shooters. He did not appear to be as relaxed as the sheriff, instead, his face and body were rigid and tense, ready to react or overreact at any moment.

The lawmen studied Donovan as he studied them. Finally, Papa broke the silence. "Sheriff, Deputy," Papa said as he nodded a greeting.

The sheriff nodded to Papa. The deputy ignored him, still focusing on Donovan.

"What happened here?" Asked the Sheriff.

Dr. Tracy spoke. "You almost got these two killed." She grabbed Papa's face and turned it exposing the bruises. "This is what they done to him. They beat him." She pointed to Donovan's wounded shoulder. "They shot him."

The sheriff looked at Dr. Tracy. "How you figure this was our doing?"

Tracy frowned. "They were friends of that man you got tied up at the jail. They was looking to free him and get the money. They figured to take a couple of hostages."

The sheriff turned to Donovan. "And how is that those men are dead now?"

Donovan remained silent.

Gunther stepped forward. "The sheriff asked you a question boy."

Donovan turned to the deputy. "You know what happened."

The deputy's eyebrows raised. He was surprised by the injured man's response. "How you figure?" He said.

"You were in the window watching. I saw you. And you saw us."

Gunther tried to take another step closer to Donovan, but the sheriff lifted his arm to the deputy's chest. "Relax Gunther." He said. He turned to Donovan. "Haven't seen you around here before. What's your name?"

He hesitated for a long moment before he answered. "Donovan." He finally said.

"Donovan what?" Asked the deputy.

Giving his first name was rare, but giving his last name never happened. "Just Donovan." He said.

The deputy reached down and rubbed the pearl handle of one of his side pistols. "I asked you a question boy, you best answer it."

Donovan's eyes dropped down to the Deputy's hand, which was at the ready to draw position. He glanced up looking into the Deputy's eyes. He tried to hide his agitation. The deputy had noticed and was pleased by the reaction.

"What's your story on what happened here?" Asked the deputy as he continued to eye Donovan.

He lowered his head, with the brim of his hat hiding his face, and then he raised his head looking the deputy in the eyes. "I reckon it's as the doctor said. These two men tried to take us hostage. I reckon they was planning on shooting us. Now they're dead."

"I don't believe you boy." Said, Gunther, as he rubbed his bushy mustache. "I think you're lying. I think you gonna spend a couple days in jail until we figured out what happened here." A grin lingered on Gunter's face. He was pleased with himself.

Donovan lowered his head as if defeated, once again hiding his face. This time he even raised his hand to his forehead to give the appearance of frustration or attempting to wipe away sweat that was none existent. As he raised his head, he had simultaneously with his other hand tucked his coat behind his pistol. Donovan stared at the deputy, his face angry and his eyes alert. "I won't be going to jail deputy." The strong tone of his voice gave the impression that Donovan meant his words. The lawmen and the others had no doubt that Donovan was prepared to fight or die. It was only moments earlier that he had shot and killed two men that were prepared to kill him.

Donovan could tell by the Deputy's expression that he was not expecting to be challenged in this way. For a moment the Deputy looked confused, but he gained his composure. "Think about it son. I'm the law. I don't want to have to kill you." Warned Gunther.

"You've already made your mind about me. What does it matter now?" The two men eyed each other with their hands resting on their guns. Some of the town's people were watching the scene from a safe distance. Mama put her hands to her face and the tears fell out of her eyes. She looked at the sky and said a prayer. Papa was shaking his head from side to side. He couldn't believe what was happening. It was over now. Donovan would be killed, Papa thought.

Surprisingly the sheriff sidestepped as he attempted to block Donovan's view of his brother. He then stepped forward standing face to face with Donovan. The sheriff's expression was serious. His rifle still pointed off to the side. The man was so tall that Donovan had to raise his chin high to look him in the eyes.

"I'm sheriff Landry, and this man behind me is my brother deputy Gunther." Gunther stepped aside after the introduction. Some of the deputy's anger had departed. "I just stopped him from killing you." Said the sheriff.

Donovan did not respond.

"Don't you have respect for the law?" Landry's voice was firm and had a hint of irritation. "Don't you have respect for these badges?" He tapped the badge on his chest.

"It depends who's wearing it." Answered Donovan.

Donovan and the Sheriff locked eyes.

"You're right we saw everything from the window. These men robbed our bank about four weeks ago. We didn't get to look at none of them. But we caught the one that we got tied to the post a week or so ago. We figured we would use him and the money we found on him as bait to draw the other two in. When we saw them walking down the street with Papa, we figured we would wait until they got close to the jail, then we would arrest or kill them, depending on what kind of fight they put up. Since we never saw these bank robbers, we had to wait until they made a move for the money or their partner. But then you stepped in and they never made it."

Landry glanced down at Donovan's exposed side pistol. "You're pretty good with them pistols. I've maybe seen eight men as quick as you. One is my deputy behind me. The other seven, well they're dead. Me and the deputy faced them all and killed them all."

He paused and watched Donovan's eyes dropped down to the sheriff's unarmed waist. "I know what you're thinking." Said the Sheriff. "You're wondering why I don't wear a pistol. Well, the truth is I really don't have much use for one. The only time I wear my pistols is if I'm serious about killing somebody. Besides Gunther here is all the protection I need. If anyone makes a move on me, he'll kill them in a blink of an eye." The two men continued to stare at each other. "I'm the law in this town and this is my town. Everybody will respect the law in this town. They will respect me, they will respect my deputy."

Donovan displayed no visible emotion as he made his way over to Fletcher. He patted the horse and then climbed on.

The lawmen stood firm as if they were daring Donovan to make a move for his pistols.

He turned to the Sheriff. "Some of the lawmen I've come across ain't too lawful. Some I've found don't protect their citizens. I find that some hide behind their badges like cowards. I respect the man, not the badge. " He pulled the reins on his horse and jerked forward, and they galloped away.

Give me your rifle!" Yelled Gunther. "This son of a bitch is gonna die!" The sheriff handed him the gun.

"On my signal." Instructed the sheriff.

Gunther raised the rifle to his face and took careful aim. "Tell me when." He said.

Landry watched Donovan race down the street. Mama cried silently from the seat of the wagon. Papa walked over to the wagon and tried to comfort her by reaching for her hand. Once again Sage rocked back and forth moaning. Dr. Tracy seemed uneasy as she watched Donovan near closer to the edge of town but still in range of the rifle.

"Tell me when Landry." Said Gunther still looking down the barrel. "He'll be out of range soon."

Landry thought about it as he continued to watch the horse race further away.

"Let him go." He finally answered. "We don't want him like this."

Gunther dropped the barrel down and laughed. He turned to the nervous crowd on hand. "That lucky son of a bitch almost lost his life."

Landry turned to Papa and Mama for a moment. Without a word he turned on his heel and headed back to the jailhouse. Gunther turned to the bystanders, smiled and then followed after the Sheriff.

Dr. Tracy walked over to Mama who was still crying, she put her arms around her. "Are you alright?" She asked.

"We is fine," Mama said. "We just thanking the Lord we is alive."

Dr. Tracy looked down the road where Donovan and his horse had gone. They were no longer in sight. She wondered if she would see him again.

Still gazing along the road Dr. Tracy asked. "Why did that stranger help you, Mama?"

"That was no stranger, child. That there was my youngest son. The Lord brought him back to us." Said, Mama.

A surprised Dr. Tracy said. "I didn't know you had another son."

"I never mentioned him before cause we thought he was dead. Haven't seen him in years. He's Sage's daddy."

Dr. Tracy turned to Sage who was still sitting on the wagon. He was rocking back and forth as Mama held him close. She then looked over her shoulder to see Landry and Gunther stepping onto the porch of the jailhouse. They walked by the prisoner tied to the post. He was laid out on the street unconscious. She knew the young man would not be allowed food or water and would be dead within a few days.

She turned to Mama. "Donovan gonna need our help. We gonna have to get that bullet out of him."

Chapter 14

By the time Donovan had reached the house his wounded shoulder was numb, and the left side of his coat was wet with blood. He felt light-headed as he arrived slumped over the horse's neck.

Miles was in the fields working with his back to Donovan. Donovan led Fletcher to the porch and slid off. He held onto the horse's reins to keep from falling on his face. He pulled a leather pouch off the horse's neck and stumbled through the front door.

The house was quiet and empty. Within the fireplace, the fire had long been burned out, but he was grateful that there was at least wood inside. He reached into his leather pouch and pulled out some matches. He placed the straw from the foot of the fireplace on top of the previously burned log. He lit the match and a flame came alive. When the fire was large enough, he placed a log from the stack outside the fireplace onto the flame. Within minutes the blaze engulfed the log. He placed his knife into the flame. He watched until the long blade gleamed hot orange. He eased out of his coat and shirt and tossed them on the floor.

His shoulder was wet with blood. There was a hole where the bullet had planted itself. When he moved his arm he could see blood ooze out.

Donovan's chest was a graveyard of scars. Several raised circles were evidence that he had been shot. There were more across his back and shoulders. Crossways on his forearms and stomach were long continuous scars where he had been cut. Deep welts dominated his chest, stomach, and back, which were caused by a bullwhip.

Donovan reached into the fire and pulled out the glowing knife. He held it close to his face and felt the heat from it. What he had to do next he regretted deeply. He took a deep breath and then put the hot knife into the wound. His flesh sizzled, and then it was black.

Everything was moving so slowly. He tried to run but he could only walk, his movements were in slow motion. Just up ahead was a woman. He couldn't make out who she was, but she was headed toward him. She also moved in slow motion, her stride was long. With each long step, her arms extended far from her body to match her lengthy stride. As she came closer he could see that she was smiling at him. He stopped and waited for her. He felt himself smiling as well. He was happy to see her, but who was she. As she stepped closer to him he studied her face. She was beautiful. Her hair was black and long and flowed back as she walked forward so slowly in his direction. Her lips were naturally pink and full as she smiled at him. Her eyes were dark brown and cracked slightly at the sides of her face to absorb her wonderful smile. "You are so beautiful." He tried to say, but his mouth would not open to speak. He could only smile.

When she reached him she stood before him and gazed at him endlessly, smiling. Her head tilted sideways as she stretched to caress his face. When she touched him, he felt his happiness change to sadness, and the smile drifted from his face. As his smile changed so did hers. She seemed to mirror his expression as her smile disappeared. "What's the matter?" He tried to say but again the words would not come.

In slow motion, her hand reached for the pistols on his waist. He grabbed them as she did. She pulled and he pulled but neither one would release the guns. She looked into his eyes and smiled once more. And again he felt himself smiling. "I know you." He tried to say. "I know who you are." At that moment she moved forward and kissed him. He released his pistols to her. She caressed his face as she continued to smile at him. She then turned on her heel and in slow motion went the way she had come. He waited for her to look back, but she never did. Soon she was out of view. "Sidney. Sidney don't leave. Sidney don't leave me. I love you Sidney don't go."

"Who is Sidney?" Asked Dr. Tracy. They were in Sage's room; Donovan's eyes were closed as he lay in the bed. Beads of sweat formed on his forehead. His head twisted from side to side as he moaned. Dr. Tracy and Mama stood on either side of the bed watching him. Two hours previously they had found Donovan on the floor unconscious with his knife in hand. They grabbed Miles from the field, and he carried Donovan into Sage's room. After that, it took Dr. Tracy just over twenty minutes to remove the bullet from Donovan's shoulder. However that was two hours ago, and he was still unconscious.

"Sidney is his wife." Said, Mama.

"His wife?"

"Yeah. He used to be married, but she's dead now. Been dead a long time. More than Seven years she's been gone. He took her death pretty bad. We all did I guess. She was a mighty fine woman."

She stared at Donovan's face and watched him as he moaned. "Seven years is a long time." She said.

Tracy placed the back of her hand to his moist forehead. "He has a fever. We'll need to cool him down a bit." She reached for the towel on the table and dipped it into the basin of water. She squeezed the excess water into the bowl and placed it on Donovan's moist forehead.

"Is he gonna be alright?" Asked Mama. "He don't look too good."

"He'll be fine Mama." She assured her. "He lost some blood so he'll be weak for a day or so. Just make sure when he wakes, he gets plenty of water, and if he runs a fever put a damp towel on his head."

A couple days had passed before Donovan was sitting up in the bed. His shoulder was extremely sore, and he could barely move it. Not only could he not move his shoulder, but any type of movement or shift in the bed caused his shoulder extreme pain. Once he tried to get out of bed to walk about but shifting his weight to do so caused distress to his shoulder. So he was instead forced to lay back down with no more attempts for movement. On another occasion, he had a coughing spell. The jerking of the coughing about killed him with agony, he thought. The more he tried to stop coughing, the more he needed to cough and painfully did so.

Mama would come in from time to time, and give him water and blot his forehead with a moist towel. It wasn't until the third day that she actually brought him food. At first, the pain was so great that Donovan didn't think much about food. But now on his third day in bed, he noticed his stomach ached from hunger, as the pain in his shoulder was more bearable.

On this day Mama brought Donovan a plate of fried chicken, sweet ash potatoes and a slice of cornbread. She helped him balance the plate on his lap. She smiled when he was finished and then took his empty plate back to the kitchen.

On the fourth day, Dr. Tracy showed.

"How you feeling?" She asked. Donovan found her not to be friendly or unfriendly. She was neutral.

He raised himself to a sitting position. "I'm in a lot of pain. But it seems to be getting better." He said with a grunt.

She cautioned. "The pain will probably be for a few more days."

Donovan frowned. "I reckon so."

The only expressional change on Tracy's face was her twisted mouth. And Donovan didn't have any idea what that meant.

"Mama wanted me to keep a watch over you for a few days. You look to be doing fine. My only concern was when you didn't wake up for as long as you did. We figure you was out for a half a day or so."

Tracy stepped closer to the bed and leaned forward as she reached for the covers, and pulled them down just enough to expose his bandaged shoulder. "This is going to hurt a little." She warned.

She pulled the white dressing off of his shoulder. It was sticking to parts of the wound that had healed itself to the dressing. He made a face when she tugged on the cloth, opening the wound once more to trickles of blood.

She inspected his wound by pulling and pinching his meat. Donovan made faces of discomfort as she did so.

While she was inspecting his wound he was inspecting her. She was fine looking. Her wavy hair was black just past her shoulders. She had thick full lips, small dark eyes and thick nose to match. Her clothes were different from what most women wore. Most women preferred long dresses. She instead had on trousers and a button up shirt. The pants fit snuggly around her waist so as to expose her shapely hips. Her shirt was close-fitting enough that Donovan did not have to guess the shape of her breasts.

She pulled out a fresh cloth from her bag and rewrapped his shoulder. "It's healing fine. I see no sign of an infection."

Donovan liked the sound of her voice. It was a low tone but it was easy to hear. The tone in her voice varied only slightly as she spoke. "That's good to hear." He answered.

"Do you always try to doctor yourself?" She asked.

"Sometimes."

She watched him for a moment; he saw the concern in her eyes. She reached over and slowly pulled down his blanket to expose the scars on his chest. "What happened to you?" She asked as she rubbed her hands across his scars. "Were you in the war?"

Donovan was quiet for a moment. She stared at him waiting for his answer. He never spoke of his personal life, but at the moment he could not resist her. "Yes, I was in a war. But it wasn't the war between the North and South."

Her expression was puzzled. She didn't understand. "I wasn't aware that there was another war. What war were you in?"

Donovan hesitated for another moment then decided to answer briefly. "It was my own personal war."

"Did you win?"

"No. I didn't win. I lost everything." Donovan leaned back into the bed and became withdrawn. All the energy seemed to escape from his body. He pulled the covers up to his neck. "I'm tired. I need some rest." He said. Dr. Tracy nodded and then left the room.

Mama was in the kitchen pulling the feathers off the chicken that Papa had brought in for her to prepare for dinner. Dr. Tracy closed the bedroom door and sat in the chair at the table. She wondered what Donovan meant when he said. 'My own personal war.'

Mama put the chicken on the counter and wiped her hands on her apron. "How is he?" She asked.

"He's fine." Said Dr. Tracy. His shoulder will be sore for awhile, but he doesn't have an infection."

Mama put her hands to her face. "Thank the Lord for that." She watched Dr. Tracy. Mama sat in the chair across from her. She leaned closer to Dr. Tracy. "What's wrong child?"

"Your son has been through a lot." Said Dr. Tracy. "I've never seen anything like it. He's been shot and stabbed, and he's been beaten something terrible." Mama placed her hand on Dr. Tracy's shoulder. "But the worst is not the wounds on his body, but the wounds on his soul. What on earth happened to him?"

"I don't know child. I ain't seen him for years. I don't know much about him now. He's not like he used to be."

"What was Donovan like before?"

Mama thought it over. "He was happy. Now he don't seem happy to me."

"Do you think he's dangerous?" Asked Dr. Tracy.

She nodded her head. "I suppose he is. But not with us, not his family."

Tracy stood behind Mama and put her arms around her thick waist. "You're a good woman, Mama. I love you and don't want you hurt."

Mama smiled. "Nobody is going to hurt me, child. You staying for dinner?"

"Yes, I am."

Chapter 15

Donovan reached for his pants and shirt. When he was dressed he stepped into the hall. Mama, Papa, Sage, Maria and Dr. Tracy were seated at the table. Mama pointed to the chair next to Maria. "That be your place, Donovan." She said.

"What about Miles?" He asked.

"Don't you worry none about Miles. He's still working. He'll be with us later." Said, Mama.

He seated himself next to Maria. Across the way, he could see that Sage and Dr. Tracy were holding hands underneath the table.

Not only did it smell delicious, but the fried chicken, baked ham, biscuits, and corn looked appetizing as well. In all those years on the road, he had almost forgotten how tasty his Mama's cooking was.

"Let's bow our heads and give thanks to the Lord," Mama said.

They grabbed hands around the table. "Lord," said Mama leading the prayer. "We thank you for the food we is bouts to eat. We thank you for all the lessons in life that you teach us. We think you for your protection." She glanced at Donovan. His head was not bowed nor were his eyes closed. She smiled. "And we thank you for Donovan's safe return. Amen." She finished.

All chimed Amen except for Donovan who remained silent.

Mama watched him as he reached into the breadbasket that was passed around. She wondered what type of life had he lived for the past few years. She wondered if Dr. Tracy was right about him being dangerous. She noticed that Dr. Tracy was also watching Donovan. She caught Mama's eye and turned to her plate.

During their meal, the only noise that was heard was the smacking of lips as they chewed their food, and the groans suggesting that the food was quite appetizing. Papa broke the silence when he leaned back in his chair and said. "That was a mighty fine meal, Mama."

More compliments of the meal echoed around the table. Mama smiled graciously.

He glanced across at Sage. There was life in him, and yet he was lifeless. The young boy displayed no emotion, as he continued to pick at the food from his plate. Donovan blamed himself and believed that if he had been a part of Sage's life, he would be different now.

Donovan sensed the joy within the room and was engaged in light conversations around the table. This social setting was different for him. Over the years he had grown accustomed to being alone as well as eating alone. He caught Tracy smiling at him, but when their eyes met she turned away.

Donovan came to realize for the first time in such a long time that he did not have any worries of any kind. He felt no pain from great loss from his past and was not anxious that someone wanted him dead. For this brief moment, he was free to enjoy his family. He glanced at Sage again. He wished he and Sage had some sort of relationship. As of now, they didn't say a word to one another, nor did he as much as look in Donovan's direction.

Donovan thought back to when he was his son's age. As a child, he was so much different from Sage, for he was a high-spirited boy and was always getting into trouble of some sort. He was an extrovert and never missed a chance to strike up a conversation with people. The other kids his age at that time loved hanging around him. He was like their group leader. They would often consult with him before they did anything that was fun or adventurous.

Donovan looked across the table and once again he found that Tracy was watching him. This time she didn't look away.

What a beautiful woman. Not since Sidney had he ever considered the beauty of another woman. He was curious about her. He wanted to get to know her, but not just on the physical level, he wanted to know who she was.

The front door opened and the wind from outside rushed in nearly blowing out the small flames on the lamps located in the corners of the main room and the candles on the table. Even the flame in the fireplace moved about wildly in an attempt not to be suffocated. Miles looked exhausted. His clothes were wet with sweat and soiled from the fields. His eyes not focused as if he had been walking in his sleep. His body in the doorway blocked the wind and the fires were once again calm. He stumbled into to the room as if he was drunk, but he was merely exhausted. Sometimes he could barely walk home.

"You hungry Miles?" Asked Mama. She was obviously concerned. She knew he had worked hard that day.

Miles grunted, which meant yes. Mama loaded an empty plate. The mood of the dinner had changed since Miles had arrived. The table was silent and there were no longer shared smiles among them.

With plate in hand Miles glanced at all the food that Mama had prepared. "What's all this?" He asked.

"I was in a cooking mood," Mama said.

Miles nodded toward Donavan. "Is all this for him?"

She ignored the question. "Sit down Miles, and eat. You've got to be hungry by now.

He nodded and moved to the empty chair by his wife Maria. He closed his eyes in prayer, and then quickly chomped away his food. "This is real fine, Mama. You did yourself real fine."

"That's good child, I'm glad you like," Mama said.

"It's more than good." Miles shot back.

Mama nodded as she smiled.

After a while Miles turned his attention back to Donovan. "You look much better than you did the other day. Wasn't sure you were going to make it. Papa said you had run into some trouble in town. He said if it weren't for you he be dead. He said those men had their guns pointed right at you." Miles paused. "How did you do it?"

Donovan barely looked up from his plate. "You can't really know how these things are going to turn out Miles. We could of just as easily died out there. We was just lucky this time."

"Papa says you is a gunslinger of some sort." Responded Miles.

"I'm no gunslinger." Said Donovan. "I've seen the likes of a few and I ain't nothing like them. I've seen them kill for no reason. I've once seen an unarmed man shot for stepping on a gunslingers boots. The man was with his family. This made no difference to the gunslinger. He shot that man dead in front of his wife and son." Donovan remembered the painful expression of the boy moments after he had watched his father murdered. He remembered the horrendous cries of the wife when she fell on top of her husband and tried to shake life back into him.

Dr. Tracy reached across the table and touched his hand. "Then what happened?"

He looked up at her and realized that he had lost himself in that day. "I watched that boy seeing his Pa dead. All that pain right on his face. It shouldn't have happened. The gunslinger was talking and waving his gun as if he had done something grand." He looked up at Dr. Tracy. "I took another look at the dead man. I shouldn't of, but I did. I looked at his eyes and the blood on him. That man was no more than a husband, a father, and he wasn't even armed. He wasn't going to hurt nobody. Just shot down for sport I guess. So I called that gunslinger out and unloaded my pistols on him. He never even got his gun out. Maybe he was too drunk. When that boy cried on me afterwards, I knew I did right by them."

Dr. Tracy had pulled back her hand and placed it in her lap. He wondered if he had told them too much. But he had to explain that he was not a gunslinger. He didn't kill people senselessly.

He glanced around the table at the others. No one would meet his eyes, not even Miles. And then Papa turned to him. "I just realized after listening to you some that you have been through a lot in the last seven years. I'm mighty lucky to be alive right now. "If it wasn't for you Donovan I wouldn't be sitting here right now with you folks enjoying this meal enjoying my family." Papa pulled out a handkerchief from his pocket and dabbed his eyes. Donovan had never seen his father cry before.

Papa took a drink from his glass. "Watching you I realize a couple of things. First thing is you not the same man we once knew, and that makes me sad some. It seems life has changed you. The second thing is you're a man that folks should be afraid of. But that being said I can say that I'm not afraid of you son." Papa looked around the table. "And neither should any of you. We is family. That's all that matters is that we is family."

Donovan took in what his Papa had just said and knew he was right. The last seven years had changed him. Not the seven years itself, but the fact that they had killed Sydney. That kind of loss can destroy a man. He hadn't been the same since. Though those men are dead for their crimes, it still didn't change what they done to Sydney. He spent many sleepless nights trying to understand why it happened. She never hurt anyone, and never did anyone wrong that he could remember. Everyone loved Sydney. He loved Sydney.

Even so there something wrong about killing another man regardless of the reason. Taking a man's life was strange. There was the endless blood and unseeing eyes that had no life when moments before he had been walking, eating, talking. Ending a man's life didn't change the past. Even worse the pain of their acts didn't go away. Actually, the act itself left Donovan feeling empty inside. But this didn't stop him from killing the rest of them. After all, they still had killed his wife.

He looked at Dr. Tracy; she didn't return his gaze. Their moment was over he guessed. He figured hearing about killing another man would turn any woman away.

Donovan turned to Papa. "Most of what you say about me is true. But I'm no danger to this family. Never will be."

Donovan excused himself and grabbed his coat from the other room.

Mama rubbed her hands on her apron. "Where you going, Donovan?"

I'll be back Mama. Going for a walk is all."

She glanced toward the rattling window. "But it's mighty windy."

"I don't mind the wind." He pulled open the front door and stepped out.

Sage made his way to the window. Mama placed her thick hands on his shoulders. They both stared out, listening to the wind thump against the window. "Don't worry baby, he'll be back. He just walking off that good food I made."

Chapter 16

Dr. Tracy and Mama were in the kitchen side by side washing the dirty dinner dishes. Mama washed in one bucket and Tracy rinsed in another. Papa faced the fireplace as he sat in his favorite chair. The warm orange light from the flame glowed on his face. Sage was not present for he had not long ago excused himself and was in his room.

Tracy had dried her last dish and placed it on top of the others in a raised shelf nearby. She removed her apron and placed it on an empty peg on the wall.

"Thank you for the fine dinner Mama. I do need to get back now." Said Tracy

"It's late child. Maybe you should stay the night." Said, Mama.

Tracy smiled. "You know I'm not gonna do that. I'll be fine."

Mama nodded in agreement and then went to the family room and nudged Papa.

"Dr. Tracy's leaving now. She gonna need her horse."

Papa turned in his chair to view Tracy who was standing in the kitchen. He then pulled his watch from his breast pocket. "It's after ten. There's no point in leaving now. Maybe you could stay this time." He said."

Mama turned to Tracy waiting for her answer.

"No," Tracy said politely. "I'll be fine."

Papa moaned. "Well, I'll ride you home then."

"No." Said Tracy. "That's not necessary. I can ride myself home."

Tracy was silently stubborn, and if she made up her mind there was no changing it. She would never fuss or raise her voice. She would instead politely resist until the other person gave up. Sometimes folks would be misled by her politeness, assuming that they would change her mind, however, in the end, they always found out different.

Papa leaned on his cane as he stood to his feet. "Since we can't change your mind, I reckon I'll fetch your horse."

Papa stepped onto the porch as Mama and Tracy waited for him to arrive with the horse. He stood at the edge of the porch and watched out into the blackness. He could only see just a few feet ahead, so he waited until his eyes adjusted to the darkness.

"What ya doing Papa?" Said Donovan from one of the chairs.

"Damn!" Yelled Papa as he jumped. "I didn't figure you to be out here. You damn near scared the mess out of me boy."

"Didn't mean to startle you. Just wanted you to know I was here is all."

Papa sighed as he eased over to the empty chair. "What you doing out here all alone Donovan?"

"Thinking and watching the stars." He said.

"Is everything alright with you?"

"All is fine. I'm just used to being alone is all. And the stars seem to take my mind off my troubles I guess."

Papa looked up at the dark sky. "I reckon so. We all got our share of troubles."

Donovan turned to him. "I figured you to be in bed by now."

"I would be, but Dr. Tracy is leaving so I'm fetching her horse."

"You riding her home?"

He sighed. "No. She don't want no company, and she won't stay the night either. She never does. Don't want to be a burden I guess."

The two men were quiet for a moment. "You want me to fetch her horse?" Asked Donovan.

"Much obliged if you would."

Donovan stepped off the porch and headed for the barn across the way. Papa heard a loud whistle then a few moments later he saw Fletcher racing into the barn.

Finally, Donovan came out of the barn riding Fletcher and leading Tracy's horse.

As he approached, Mama and Tracy stepped out of the house. Tracy stepped forward. "What are you doing Donovan?" She asked.

"I'll be riding you back." He said calmly.

"That's not necessary." She said. "I can take care of myself."

"I'm not doubting that. These roads at night can be dangerous though."

"Because I'm a woman?"

"Because you're alone. I've seen some terrible things these past few years. Some I wish I could forget. The night can be dangerous, especially when you're alone. On my travels, I've seen men, women and sometimes families lying just off the road dead. Most of the time they were robbed of all their belongings, including the clothes on their backs. I wouldn't even let my brother ride on those dark roads alone. I'll be riding with you." It was no suggestion, and his words were final. There was, however, no authoritative tone in his voice, and he wasn't even offensive in his approach, but they all knew he meant what he said, and no one questioned him, not even Tracy.

With that Tracy climbed onto her horse. Her horse was a dark brown and white Mustang. The horse's face was brown and the body was mixed with brown and white splotches. It looked more like an extra large Dalmatian dog than a horse. The Mustang was not nearly as large and powerful as Fletcher and stood at least a full head shorter.

From her saddle, Tracy turned to Donovan. "After you drop me off you'll be riding back alone. Aren't these roads dangerous for you as well?"

Donovan nodded. "I reckon so." He then pulled back his coat exposing his side pistol. "But as long as I have my pistols the danger goes both ways."

The horses trotted down the dirt road. On either side of the road sometimes deep into the pasture they would pass one house after another. As Tracy glanced at the dark windows, she felt safe knowing that Donovan was just a few steps behind. Even though she had always put up a fuss about riding home alone, she always felt uncomfortable and unsafe doing so. She had always known how dangerous the night could be, and she had heard some awful stories about what had happened to some people traveling alone at night. Especially women, but she had pride and didn't want to be a burden to anyone. So she never stayed the night anywhere, and she never let anyone ride her home. Even when she was on a house call, which was at least twice a week, her patient's loved ones would offer to ride her home, but Tracy would always refuse. Yet each time she passed a dark house alongside the road she usually felt a strong sense of loneliness and abandonment. There was no one on these dark roads but her.

As they continued down the road to the left on a high branch Tracy saw an owl twisting his head to watch them. She smiled. For the first time in a while, she was not alone on these dark roads. Tonight she would let Donovan do all the worrying. As she thought about it, she knew that Donovan would not have been persuaded otherwise.

They had been riding for more than halfway before Donovan finally spoke. "How much do I owe you?" He asked.

Tracy turned on her saddle to face him. "What?"

"How much do I owe you for taking that bullet out of me?"

Tracy frowned. "Is this why you're here now? Because you feel you owe me?"

"No. I'm here because I want to be. I have cash." Said Donovan. "What do I owe you for your service."

Tracy laughed. "My service." She repeated. "You don't owe me anything."

"I have cash," Donovan said again.

"Your folks have taken care of your debt."

"How?"

"They feed me whenever I show up. Your mother helps me to wash and mend my clothes. And your son Sage accompanies me when I take my walks into the woods. Your folks are like family to me."

Tracy slowed her horse so that she was even with Donovan's. He was faced forward with his head slightly down, and his hat was just over his eyes. She could not see his face. "Donovan." She called. He tilted his head up and his face came into view. "Why are you doing this?"

"Doing what?" He said.

"Why are you riding me home? You don't have to do this."

"I'm not doing it because I have to."

"Then why?"

"It's not safe, I told you already."

"That's only part of your reason." She said. "You don't know me. Why do you care if it's safe or not."

There was a long pause as the horses trotted side by side. Tracy waited for an answer. He finally glanced in her direction. "Maybe I know you enough." He said.

Tracy was finally satisfied with his answer and turned away letting Donovan off the hook. They rode on in silence until they reached the outskirts of the town. They could hear voices and laughter within the saloon, but for the most part, the town was asleep.

"Thank you." Said, Tracy, as she turned her horse toward Donovan. "I'll be fine now."

Donovan glanced at her and then looked toward the town. He saw the lights glaring through the saloon windows and the front entrance. At that moment he heard loud laughter and someone yelling inside. He turned to Tracy. Her black wavy hair rested on her shoulders, her dark brown eyes looked back at him.

"Where's your home?" He asked.

She pointed to the hotel on the other side of the saloon. It was two stories high and three windows across. "I live on the top floor. I've been living there for two years now."

Someone stumbled out of the saloon entrance, he fell face down. Two men quickly followed. They watched the man on the ground and laughed at him. They then pulled him up and dragged him back into the saloon. Donovan turned his attention back to Tracy. "Do you want me to ride you to your hotel?" He asked. His expression was serious and concerned.

"No." She said. "That won't be necessary." For a moment she watched the ground. He continued to look at her, and finally, her eyes rose to meet his. "This is not a safe place for you."

"I know." He said.

"This is as far as I want you to take me. The sheriff is most likely standing at his window waiting for my return. He watches for me each night that I'm out. He stands in that dark window and waits. You don't even know he's there unless he comes out. Sometimes he scares me. If he sees me with you, he'll come out. And you'll be dead. Just like the others."

Donovan nodded. "I'm not looking for any trouble. I've had a lifetime of that. I've long been tired of it." He paused for a moment. "What is this sheriff to you?"

"He's nothing to me."

Donovan was hesitant to ask this next question. "Can I see you again?"

"If you like." She said.

"When?"

Tracy smiled. "Soon."

Donovan nodded. "I'll watch you from here. Once you reach your hotel, I'll leave."

With that, she agreed and positioned her horse toward the hotel and nudged forward. Donovan was hidden in the darkness of the outer edge of town as he watched. She rode forward and not once did she look back. There was more laughter and loud voices from the saloon. The double doors flung open and the three men that came out earlier stumbled out on drunken legs. One of the men stumbled into Tracy's horse. He bounced off the horse and fell on his back.

Lying on his back he cursed. Tracy watched as the other two men helped him to his feet. The man that fell glared at Tracy with drunken angry eyes. "Watch it you black winch!" He shouted with his whiskey breath. He shifted his weight back and forth trying to maintain his balance.

She nudged her horse forward in an attempt to ignore the man's comments. This angered one of the men. He released his friend leaving the other to hold him alone. He chased the horse and grabbed the reins. "Where do you think you're going?" He said almost with a laugh. He pulled the horse back to the drunkest man.

"What do you have to say for yourself?" Said the drunkest man still swaying but leaning on the other man. Tracy said nothing.

This seemed to anger the man holding the reins. "Get off the horse." He said through his smile with a firm tone. Tracy, however, did not move. The man holding the reins became visibly irritated. "Who do you think you are?" He said. "Trying to act like you is a proper lady. You ain't nothing but a nigger winch. Get off that damn horse."

Tracy ignored his command and remained on her horse. The man's face became distorted with anger as he reached and pulled her from the horse. She fell to the ground with a thump. Almost before she hit the ground two gunshots were heard from the darkness outside of town.

The first bullet hit the man in his arm. The man swung around from the impact. Before he could recover the second hit him in the thigh. The man went down screaming.

After the shooting, the other two men became sober quick. They moved toward their friend crouching low so as to not be a target as well. Said the tallest one. "Shut your mouth." The injured man's shouts quieted, but his breathing and panting were still loud.

Tracy did a quick visual over the man on the ground. The shirt on his arm was wet with blood. The man's thigh, which he was clutching seemed to cause him the most pain, was also wet with blood. After her visual inspection, she came to the conclusion that the man's injuries were not life-threatening. However, he would be in a lot of pain for a long time to come.

"Wrap his arm tight above the wound. That'll stop the bleeding." Said Tracy. "Elevate his leg and head, and keep talking to him. Ask him questions about his name and where he lives. Otherwise, he may go into shock. If he gets warm take off his clothes. If he gets cold put more clothes on him. That should hold him until Dr. Solimen arrives. If he's in town that is."

The men looked back at her with worried faces.

She looked over her shoulder in the direction where she had left Donovan. She wondered if he was still there. Tracy grabbed the reins on the horse and led him to the barn behind the hotel. When she returned, the injured man was lying in the street, with his buddies at his side. The men looked at her as if they wanted her to help. But she looked away. If she thought the man was going to die, then she would not have hesitated. But she could see from this view that he was not in danger, but instead only in great pain.

Those that had watched the scene from the saloon had finally come out. Some of them were looking about ducking low just in case they were targets also. One of the men was telling another saloon member his side of the story of what he thought had just happened and stopped in mid-sentence when he saw Tracy and watched her with apprehension. As she stepped onto the hotel porch she glanced over at the dark window of the jailhouse. She thought she saw movement.

Chapter 17

Inside her hotel room, she peeked out of the small window. The crowd around the injured drunk man was larger now. Sheriff Landry and Deputy Gunther were now amongst the people below. The drunk men were telling the Sheriff their interpretation of what had happened. She pulled the curtain back and seated herself on the bed. She was tired and wanted to change into her sleeping clothes, but because of what had happened, the Sheriff would be visiting soon to question her.

Sitting on the edge of the bed, her shoulder drooped forward, and her head rested in the palm of her hands. She closed her eyes and thought about Donovan. She wondered about the type of man he was. He seemed distant and hurt, and yet at times, he seemed caring. She did not expect him to offer to ride her home. And though in the past she had refused all that wanted to do so, she did not refuse him.

Tracy had not been with many men. She didn't have the desire to be with a man. The only man that she had the desire to be with was her father Dr. William Brown as he was called. Although her desire with him was not of a sexual nature. When she was a small child she remembered how hard he worked. He would be with patients on house calls sometimes nearly all day, and then at night he would sit up at his desk and read his medical books by the lantern light half the night. He worked hard. The only time she could really get his attention was at dinnertime, and that was only an hour or so, during which all of his three children would compete for their father's attention. He would listen to each of them patiently as if he had all the time in the world. But at the end of dinner, he was either on the road on his way to another house call or back to his desk reading his medical books.

At those times when her father was reading his medical books, Tracy and her two older brothers knew better than to bother him. If he were disturbed during that time he would become very angry, blowing a sigh from his lips and then displaying a frown on his long thin face. The only person allowed to bother him during this time was her mother, and even she was a little apprehensive about disturbing him. Sometimes her mother would come out and check up on him in the middle of the night. He would sometimes be sound asleep, head down between the pages of his books. She used to wake him and begged him to come to bed, but he would only awaken so as to read and study some more. So she decided it was best to let him sleep on his desk, then at least he would get a good night sleep.

Tracy lifted her head out of her hands and smiled as she thought of her family. She was twenty-eight years of age and was not married. Some women frowned at this. Sometimes they would talk to her with pity and promise her that she would find a man one day to marry. They would promise her that someone out there would want her. "You're still pretty they would say. There's still time." She would smile politely as she listened to the sympathetic women, but the truth was she was not concerned about marriage. If it happened and she was as happy as her mother was with her father, great. But if marriage did not come her way, that was fine too. It wasn't that she didn't have chances. There had been men interested, but she wasn't interested in them. She was never rude, always polite, always let them down easy, and in many of those times remained friends afterward.

There was a hard knock on the door. Tracy pulled the front door open. Sheriff Landry smiled as he stepped in. He was so tall that he had to duck his head under the entryway.

"Hello, little lady." Said, Landry, as he walked under the door. She closed the door behind him. "I understand you was in a little trouble tonight. You alright?"

His demeanor was friendly and jovial. Too friendly Tracy thought, but that's how he usually was with her. She knew different. She knew about the other side of him. The side when you crossed him he would either kill you or make you miserable. He was that way with everyone except his brother, Deputy Gunther. Some people were fooled at first by his polite demeanor, and they would attempt to cross him misjudging his politeness for weakness. He would never forget this person's misreading his character. If one didn't do anything to warrant a killing, then each time he encountered that person he would at least give them a horrible frown. If later this one individual came to him for some help of the law, he would refuse them. Even if some time had passed after the incident, he still would not help them. Sometimes he would harass them with surprise visits in the middle of the night and force the whole family to stand out in the cold while he and Gunther searched for valuables. He being the law, there wasn't anything that could be done. Some would try to retaliate but they never lived. Some would try to leave town but he and his brother would find them and bring them back, and then treat them twice as horrible and visit them twice as often. Sometimes even burn down their houses depending how much he disliked them.

"I'm fine," Tracy said.

Landry walked around the room glancing at her stained wallpaper. Then he walked over to the window, boots knocking on the wooden plank floor. He pulled the curtain back just enough to peek out. He spoke as he viewed out the window. "What happened out there?"

"A drunk man wasn't watching where he was going and stumbled into my horse."

The sheriff was still at the window, the tone in his voice serious. "Then what?"

"Then his buddy pulled me off my horse."

Landry turned from the window and looked at her. "Then what?"

"Then someone shot him."

"Who shot him?" Asked Landry.

"I don't know." Said Tracy. "It was dark."

Landry turned toward the window and stared out again. Tracy sat at her desk near the wall. Finally, Landry broke the silence. "I don't understand why someone would be shooting at those drunks. It don't make no sense to me." Tracy sat silently at her desk. Landry turned from the window to face her. "Where were you coming from this late?"

This question had caught her off guard. She tried to keep her composure and hide her surprise, but she wasn't sure if she had pulled it off. She had known Landry for two years now, and he had frequently arrived at her hotel at late hours. Sometimes he would greet her before she entered the hotel. And sometimes he would even come up to her room. And at those times they would just talk. Mostly about the weather, and sometimes they would talk about her patients, but this was the first time that he questioned her on her whereabouts.

"I was at Mama's house." She answered.

"What was going on at Mama's house?"

"She invited me to dinner. Then we sat on the porch and talked a bit. I guess I lost track of time."

"Why is someone out there looking out for you?" He asked.

"Don't know." She said evenly.

"Someone said the shot came from the woods." Said, Landry, as he observed her. "On your way back did you pass anybody in the woods close to town?"

Tracy nodded. "No Landry I did not."

Sheriff Landry stared at her for another moment, then he stood to his feet, and his boots clanked on the floor as he walked past her to the front door. He pulled it open, then turned to her. "I'm glad you're okay." He said as he ducked under the doorway and closed the door behind him.

She sat at her desk for a while. She wondered what this visit was really about. She wondered what he really knew. Did he know about Donovan? The Sheriff was hard to read and yet she felt that he was giving her hints that he suspected something.

When she first arrived at this town, the sheriff had taken an immediate liking to her. A few times he hinted that he wanted to court her but she had always been able to avoid his mild advances. However, they remained friends. Sometimes it was hard to avoid his advances. The longer she had known Landry, the more dangerous she found that he was. Though she never let her fear be known she was afraid of him. Everyone was afraid of Landry. The first impression of him was that he was very nice and maybe overly cordial to people. He would walk the wooden sidewalks waving to all that he saw, and stopped every now and then to small talk with a few about their families as if he really cared. He did not realize it, but he came across as insincere. He would ask them questions and then hardly let them finish before he quickly moved on to the next person to ask them the very same question. Landry was not polished in his approach with people and he seemed to be very detached when socializing. Yet people took the time to talk with him, and many times they would seek him out in the public places and greet him with overly friendly handshakes and wide smiles.

Even though Tracy was afraid of him, her relationship was honest. She did not pretend to laugh at his jokes. She did not seek him out and give overzealous greetings.

She walked over to the window. It was about three in the morning, and the night air felt good on her face. The injured drunk man and his buddies were gone. The saloon was black, and quiet for it was closed. At the end of town, she watched the jailhouse. It was dark as well. However, Landry liked to stand at the window unnoticed and watch the town. His town as he usually called it. It was eerie sometimes. She wondered how late he stood in that window. He seemed to always be there. He would be there from morning to late afternoon it seemed.

What puzzled her the most was that Landry picked and chose his battles carefully. At first, she didn't understand the logic in his decisions. A fistfight would break out in the street, sometimes in front of the jailhouse and he would observe from his window leaving the fighters to work out their own differences. When it was over either one or both of the men would be on the ground with faces bruised, eyes blackened, teeth knocked out, clothes torn and bloody. Only then would Landry come to investigate. He would tower over the injured men, and then lecture them about fighting in his streets and how their injuries were punishment enough and then he would send them on their way.

Sometimes a gunfight would breakout. Landry would watch from his window and wait until the shooting stopped. Then he and Gunther would walk around the dead bodies. If anyone was left alive he and his brother would arrest them. Maybe make them stay in jail for a week or two. Sometimes if the individual were badly wounded, he would send them out of town with no medical attention. If they were too injured to ride he would leave them in the streets and let them die. He would give strict orders for no one to help them in any way. Not even family members were allowed to help the injured if Landry gave his orders. Sometimes men would lay in the middle of the street bloody, for days before they died. Horses and wagons were forced to ride around them.

Tracy found that Landry became directly involved in the violent events of town if his brother was somehow drawn in. Landry didn't take any chances with his brother. He didn't wait to watch from the window. He was immediately on the street or in the bar when he saw or heard his brother was involved, and at that point, he was on the verge of madness some thought as they watched him.

One time, in particular, came to Tracy's mind. It was mid-afternoon, the sun was high and hot in the middle of July. The day was Saturday on the town's busiest day of the week. The sides of the main road were packed with wagons and horses. Many people were in the shops buying supplies and lingering about, while others were loitering and socializing on the wooden sidewalks outside. Landry was in his usual place in front of the window watching everyone.

Landry had noticed some sort of commotion coming from the saloon. People were running from the front entrance ducking with their hands over their heads for protection. At this site, Landry became concerned for his brother who was in the saloon. However, this didn't necessarily mean that Gunther was in any danger, for Gunther himself could have caused the commotion and chased the patrons out.

Nonetheless, he grabbed his holster belt with his two six-shooters as he stepped out the door. When he reached the saloon he could hear men arguing. One of the voices he immediately recognized to be his brother Gunther. When he carefully entered he was horrified to witness Gunther on one side of the saloon arguing with five armed and hostile men on the other side.

Landry eyed the room. Most of the people in the saloon had cleared out. The only people left were the bartender who stood behind the bar with a nervous expression, and next to him was the town whore who had on a red dress cut low exposing the tops of her breast. A couple of older men that couldn't get away were cowering under the tables. Some folks watched the scene through the two front windows, crouching low to shield in case some bullets went flying.

The five men were standing across the room with their hands by their sides next to their guns. One man in particular on the end closes to Landry had an expression of rage. Landry eyed him for a moment.

He walked over to Gunther, not taking his eyes off the five men, particularly the hostile one on the end. "What's this all about?" He asked the room.

"Welcome to the party Landry." Said Gunther in his signature playful tone.

His brother's playful demeanor at this time seemed to irritate him. Gunther had gotten himself into a life and death situation and was treating it as if it were a game of some sort.

"What's going on here?" Landry asked again. His long arms were resting at his side, next to his pistols.

"These men don't like me much." Said Gunther behind his grin. "They say I talk too much."

"You damn right you talk too much you short son of a bitch!" Yelled the angriest man at the end. He had a thin build and dark brown hair with bangs that laid on his forehead. He looked as if he had not shaven for a week or so. "I paid good money for that whore over there." He nodded his head to the lady in red behind the bar. "We was about to go to a room when that son of a bitch takes her from me and starts dancing with her. After a couple minutes I walk up to them and I said I paid for the whore and she's coming with me. He starts laughing. He asks me how much I pay for her? I tell him. He pulls some money out of his pocket and tosses at my feet and tells me to go get another whore, she's with him now. Everybody starts laughing. Well nobody's laughing now."

"But he's still got that stupid smirk on his face." Said another man at the other end as he pointed to Gunther. He was larger than the first man, had a potbelly, a full beard, and mustache. His brown hair was beginning to bald up front. He had a few strands of hair at the end of his forehead separated from the body of his hair. "We're gonna take the smirk off his face."

Landry leaned toward Gunther not taking his eyes off the five men. His voice was low so that only Gunther could hear. "Take that grin off your face." Gunther frowned. Landry continued. "When this is over you and I gonna have a long talk."

Gunther nodded.

Landry was angry with his brother for putting himself in this situation. If he hadn't come along, his brother would have had no chance against these five armed men. He wondered what his brother was thinking when he provoked these men.

Landry spoke to the men across the room. "You have two choices." He said. His voice was firm with authority. "You drop your belts or you die."

The five men started talking amongst themselves. They looked over the short cocky man, and then the tall awkward-looking man, they smiled to each other. Finally, the thin one on the end spoke. "We ain't going to no jail. We ain't done nothing."

"You threaten a lawman. That ain't allowed in my town."

"He ain't no lawman." Said the thin man. "He ain't nothing but a little runt."

There was a long pause as the men stared at each other.

Finally, Landry spoke. "I guess you made your decision." The word *decision* being the signal for Gunther to pull his pistols and kill. Almost as quick as the eye could blink Landry had pulled out his pistols in either hand and fired shots into the three men on the end. Even as the men lay on the floor with the appearance of death Landry still fired one last shot into each of them. The three on the ground still had their guns in their holsters, and their eyes were wide with surprise and death.

Gunther had pulled out both his guns simultaneously and shot both his men as well. The first man didn't even get his gun out before he dropped to the ground dead. The last man managed to get his gun out of his holster and fire a single shot to the ground before he took a bullet to the chest and face. Gunther yelled in celebration of his victory. "Ohhh weee! Did you see that! Got damn I'm good!"

Landry was quiet; he did not share in his brother's celebration. He looked over the bodies carefully to make sure they were dead, he didn't want one to sit up and shoot them. Once he had seen a man that was shot and believed to be dead sit up minutes later and kill the very man that had shot him earlier. And a couple hours later that man then died himself.

The five men were definitely dead, Landry concluded. He walked past Gunther who was still celebrating and headed for the front door. Without looking back or slowing down. "Meet me at the jail now." His voice was tense with anger. Then he pushed the door open and stepped outside. The crowd outside was quiet. They quickly moved out of his way when he walked through them.

After his older brother's words, the celebration in him was gone. Gunther bowed his head in defeat. Then he turned and went out to the crowd. They cheered him and patted him on the back. He grinned at them. He pulled his pistol out and waved it in the air in celebration. "Them men in there didn't stand a chance." The crowd laughed and cheered. "I tried to tell them how good I am, but they figured since I was outnumbered they had a chance." He turned and faced the front door of the saloon, pointing his gun. "I guess they was wrong." Then he turned to the cheering crowd that had gathered tight around him, and pushed his way through them and headed for the jail to meet his brother.

A few days later Landry had come to Tracy's hotel room to talk about how foolish he thought Gunther was to pick a fight with the five armed men. He mentioned to her that he thought one day Gunther was gonna get himself killed. He had said that if he hadn't have shown up when he did Gunther would have died that night. He told her that his brother was his only family and he didn't know how he would go on without him. She had never seen the Sheriff in such a vulnerable state before. And she had witnessed this similar state a few more times afterward when Landry became concerned about his brother's reckless behavior. That was over a year ago.

Tracy changed into her sleeping clothes, which was just a long white gown that rested just above her ankles. She blew out the lanterns around the room and laid in her bed with her hands by her sides. She was tired. It had been a long night, and she had a busy day tomorrow with her patients. Just before she closed her eyes she thought about Donovan. She thought about his demeanor. He was very quiet yet unafraid. He was so serious never smiling never laughing. Was he in some sort of emotional pain and kept it concealed or was he just dangerous. She thought about the way he gunned down those men a few days before that was going to kill Papa. She thought about him laying in bed unconscious after he attempted to doctor himself when he was shot in the shoulder. She thought about all the nasty deep scars on his body and wondered what type a hell had he been through and what type of hell did he bring upon others. She thought about his horse and how he would come to Donovan when he whistled. And she also thought about the man outside the saloon that he had shot just a few hours earlier. She thought about their ride into town together. They didn't say much to one another but it felt right. She felt comfortable and safe with him. It was as if she had known Donavan before. She never felt this way about any man except her father. She smiled. Her father. She closed her eyes and just before she fell into a sleep, she remembered how Donovan looked at her when he first laid his dark brown eyes on her. He seemed to be in a trance.

She wondered if Donovan was home by now. She wondered if he was thinking of her at this moment while she was thinking of him.

Chapter 18

The rifle blared as Donovan fired two shots into the drunk man. The loud rifle could have easily given away his position, so he guided Fletcher around through the woods but stayed close to the limits of town keeping Tracy and the drunken men within his view. He watched as Tracy led her horse around the back to the stables and then later returned as more interested onlookers stood about watching the scene. Without incidence, she went into the hotel.

Even after she was inside the hotel he waited and watched to make sure that no one had followed her. He was relieved that no one did, for he would have had to come out into the open and charge the hotel.

He watched as more folks gathered around the wounded drunk man. Donovan was surprised however not to see the sheriff and his deputy, seeing as how the jailhouse was only a few blocks from the scene.

He stuffed his rifle into the side pouch on Fletcher and pulled the reins to turn the horse in the direction to the house. Donovan guided Fletcher through the woods about thirty yards away from the main road, just in case someone was looking for the shooter.

When he finally reached the house he could see the flickering of the light from the fireplace glowing in the window. He guided Fletcher to the barn so as he could remove the saddle, then he slapped him on the rear and sent him racing into the woods.

When he stepped onto the front porch he heard the locking latch pull up and then the front door cracked open. The warm heat from inside touched him as he watched Mama's dark face fill the doorway. She stepped back and pulled the door open.

"Is everything all right?" She asked.

Donovan nodded as he walked through the door. "All is fine Mama."

Mama closed the door and then walked behind Donovan as he sat in one of the chairs in front of the fireplace. She sat in her chair next to him. "It's after three, why is you getting back so late? Did you run into trouble?"

Donovan slumped back in his chair and watched the blaze as it cracked within the fireplace. He nodded. "We just took our time is all." He turned to her. "You've been waiting up all this time?"

She smiled as the reflection of the orange fire glowed upon her face, and then she reached for his hand. "I was waiting up for you." She said.

His stomach turned at this. He thought about what his papa had said a few nights before when he had first arrived. He said his Mama had been praying every night for his return. Each night for seven years she had been waiting and hoping for him to walk through the front door. There was no excuse for him leaving and hurting his family in the way that he did. He should have told them the truth on why he was leaving.

He looked into her eyes and squeezed her hand. "I wish I didn't hurt you like I did." He said.

She frowned. "Nonsense, you ain't hurt nobody." She said.

"I should have told you why I was leaving."

She released his hand and turned to the fireplace. She swallowed. "I already knew why you was leaving. I hated them men for what they did to your wife and your son. I hated them for what they did to you. I wanted them men punished." Mama covered her face with her hands and sobbed for a moment.

Donovan reached over to touch her leg. "Sorry, Mama." He said.

She turned to him with a scowl. "You ain't got nothing to be sorry for. You remembers that. I'm not crying because of nothing you done. I'm crying because of what they done to you and your family. I'm crying because of what they done to me. I'm crying because of what they done to all of us. It hurts so bad when folks you love so much are done wrong, like the way they done you and your family. I wish that all that was done to your family was done to me instead, maybe then it wouldn't hurt as bad."

He turned to the fire. He closed his eyes. He could feel her hand inside of his again. Her touch was comforting to him. At this moment he needed her touch. "I'm gonna do right by Sage."

"That would be nice. " Said, Mama. "That boy needs you right now."

"I need him too." Said Donovan.

Mama sat with Donovan until he was asleep. She covered him with a blanket and placed another log in the flame. She stared at him for a moment. She then left his side and went into her room and closed the door.

The next morning Donovan was still in the chair asleep. The blanket covered him high on his shoulders, and the fire had long past burned out. Nothing left but cold crisp black ashes.

Standing across from Donovan was Sage. He did not make a sound nor did he make any movements, as he watched. It was more like he was studying Donovan. He had been standing there unnoticed for a few minutes before the sound of the bedroom door jarred open. He turned and saw Mama coming out. When she saw him standing in front of Donovan it caught her by surprise, but she smiled reassuring him. He turned away to get one last look at this strange man who claimed that he was his father. Donovan's now open eyes had surprised him. He immediately dropped his glance to the floor and walked toward the front door and out. Donovan cranked his head as he watched the little boy exit the house; Mama continued to watch the scene from the doorway.

"I never seen him do that before." She said

"Do what?" Asked Donovan from his chair.

"I never seen him get up that close on somebody. He don't like being close to folks. That makes him uneasy. I wonder what he was thinking about." She said and then headed to the kitchen.

"Where's he going all dressed up? Asked Donovan.

"He got school." Said, Mama. "He learning to read and write. He been going about a year now.

Donovan pulled the blanket off and folded it. He then walked into the kitchen and stood next to Mama and watched her as she made breakfast. She was making biscuits.

"How long have you known Tracy?" He asked.

"Oh…about two years I guess."

There was a pause. "What's she like?"

She blurted a laugh and looked at him with surprised. "What's she like?" She repeated. "She's a real nice person. She cares a lot about folks. And Sage just loves her to death." She then looked at Donovan. "What do you think of her?"

Donovan took a breath. "I don't know, Mama. I don't know what to think of her." He decided to change the subject. "Where's Sage's school house?"

"It's a few miles down the road. It's off in the woods kind of hidden."

The schoolhouse was painted white with a large bell on top of the roof that was embedded within a small roof of its own. The school was just off the road about half mile into the woods. The property around the school was surrounded by flat grassy terrain. Just outside the grasslands were thick healthy trees and bushes. In the yard around the school, there were several short tree stumps showing signs that the builders had cut down trees to clear out the land for the yard. This particular school was also used as a church each Sunday.

From outside through the open window a man's voice could be heard. The voice was low and patient, as it taught and lectured. Sometimes the voice would speak with excitement and other times it would stay low in monotone.

In the classroom, a thin man with a gray suit and dark bow tie was at the front of the class. To his students of twenty-three, his name was Mr. Bowmen. With one hand he frequently pointed his long pointer stick to the chalkboard and in his other hand with the chalk, he would write quickly and violently on the board often breaking the chalk onto the floor. When the chalk dropped to the floor he would inspect it while lecturing, not missing a beat. If it were usable he would hang onto it. If the chalk were too small he would kick it across the room. The bottom of his shirtsleeve and hand were powdered with chalk dust.

The class behind him was a good mixture of boys and girls. The boys wore trousers and white shirts. The girls wore dark dresses, mostly blue or brown. Mr. Bowmen had previously met with all the parents and had convinced them that education was important and should be taken seriously. The first step would be the children's attire. At first, some of the parents didn't agree. However, he had gone to a four-year University and had received a bachelor degree in education, therefore he knew what was best for the children. His tone was arrogant and he used his educated vocabulary as a method to intimidate the uneducated and unsure parents to give in to his demands.

When Mama and Papa first heard about this teacher a year back, they wanted to enroll Sage into the new school. At that time Mr. Bowmen looked at Sage for a long time seeming to give the matter careful consideration.

He then eyed them over the top of his wire frame glasses. "There's no hope for this boy. I'm afraid he doesn't have the intelligence to learn to read nor write."

Mama and Papa displayed hurt and disappointed expressions.

"Don't be offended." He continued. "This is just my professional opinion as an educator. I've been doing this a long time now. I know what I see. And in all my years of teaching, I have never been wrong about this."

Mama was drawn almost to tears. "What do you see in this boy?"

"Well." Bowmen laughed. "Forgive me. Some things are better not said." He leaned back in his chair and watched them.

"I see," Mama said clutching her purse in her lap. She then looked away under Bowmen's gaze. He then turned to Papa who was calm and seemed unfazed by Bowmen's comments.

"My you're a quiet one. I'm curious about you. What's your take on the matter at hand?" Bowmen said as he stared at Papa.

Papa nodded as he dropped his eyes to the floor pretending to give this careful thought. When he felt it was a long enough pause he looked up and locked onto Bowmen's eyes.

"My thoughts is this sir. Folks tell us you is a smart man. You got your schooling from a University. I don't know nothing about Universities but I hear it was one of the best."

"You heard right." Said, Bowmen, as he leaned forward on his desk. "A University is where I graduated. I sweated blood there. That experience changed my life." He paused as if going back in time. "It wasn't the best University, but it was a good one."

Papa respectfully waited until Bowmen was finished. "Yes, sir. I guess I wouldn't know about that. Me and Mama have been thinking a long time about Sage's education. We've talked to many folks about what to do. We talked to Mr. Jones the owner of the wood shop. We've talked to Mrs. Docker the preacher's wife. And Mr. Sullivan, the local barber. All of them have their youngons in your school."

"That's right." Bowmen said. "And what did they say?"

Papa's eyes locked on him. "They said that you was the only one who could learn this boy to read and write. I guess you ain't as good as they thought. Next time I see them I'll tell them such."

"Wait a minute." Said, Bowmen. "What kind of game are you playing old man?"

Said Papa. "I'm not playing no games, sir."

The two men continued to stare at each other. Finally, Bowmen broke the silence. "Alright, I'll teach him. But I can't promise you he'll learn. Colored boys aren't good learners."

"Yes, sir." Said Papa.

On the way home in the wagon, Mama leaned up close to Papa. She was so happy that Sage was going to learn how to read and write. But most of all she was proud of Papa for making it happen.

Mr. Bowmen's students consisted of thirteen boys and ten girls. All the students were white with the exception of Sage who was the only colored. Mr. Bowmen seated Sage in the back in the corner away from the rest of the class. Sage liked his seating arrangement for he didn't feel comfortable being amongst his classmates.

Mr. Bowmen didn't pay Sage much attention. Most of the time ignoring him completely as if he was a fixture of some sort. Sage didn't learn much his first few months as he only watched and listened silently from his quiet corner. Many times the other students were called on by Mr.

Bowmen to read out loud and to participate in the class learning, but Sage was not called on. This did not bother him, for his skill level was well below his classmates, and he did not want to draw attention to himself as dumb. Sometimes during the lectures, some of the students would glance back at him making faces of disgust.

Sage disliked recess the most. During recess was when he felt alienated as he separated himself on a tree stump away from the rest of the class, and watched silently as the kids ran, screamed and laughed together. This was a time when all the school kids would play outside on the trampled down grass. Sometimes the kids would yell out to each other about him. "Look at that dumb nigger over there?" They would say. "He's ugly. What happened to him?" Another would say.

Sage watched helplessly as his classmates delivered one painful blow after another in his direction.

When he arrived home, Mama would smile at him excitingly. "How was your day at school, baby?"

Sage would always nod and answer. "Fine."

Mama would then hug him. "That's good baby. That's good."

Sage didn't have the heart to tell Mama the truth about how he was treated, and how he wished he wasn't in the school, and how at times he felt like a ghost, except at recess, where he felt pain and humiliation. Since it seemed that Mama was the only one that believed in him, he didn't want to disappoint her by not going to school. Besides he was there when Papa got him into the school. It was a difficult matter; he could not quit now, especially after his Papa had convinced Mr. Bowmen to take him in as a student. Too many people involved now. Too many people would be hurt if he quit. So he ignored his own pain and humiliation and went to school.

He and Mama would spend much time together doing chores side by side. They cooked together, mended and made clothes together. And sometimes at night before he went to bed, he and Mama would sit by the warm fireplace, and Sage would read to her from the light of the fire. As he would read from his books, she never took her eyes off of him. Sometimes tears would come down her face. Often she became so excited that she reached over and kissed him on the cheek and blurted. "Oh, Sage I'm so proud of you. You gonna be the smartest person in the family." Those words from Mama meant everything to Sage.

Yet if she saw the way Bowmen and the other students had treated him, she would not be so proud. If she knew how much more learned the other students were compared to him, she would be very disappointed. The other students read much better, and they could do math, sometimes in their

heads without writing the problem down. Sage hardly knew math at all.
Not only was he a poor student, but Mr. Bowmen never collected homework
from Sage as he did with the other students. So Sage never did homework.

Mama was so excited about Sage's progress that she and Papa
surprised Sage by picking him up after school one day. The school kids all
raced out of the school screaming and yelling as if the school was on fire.
Some of them ran between Mama and Papa practically knocking them over.
One boy, Joshua Killeen yelled out as he bumped into Papa. "Watch it, or
else!" He threatened then ran down the road with the rest of the kids.

"That boy needs his ass beat." Said Papa to Mama.

"I know." Said, Mama. "But you ain't the one to do it. Besides his
papa ain't got no sense." Papa nodded and they continued to wait by the
wagon. Sage finally came out. He was the last one. He learned earlier not
to leave at the same time as the others or they would pick on him for sport.

He was surprised to see Mama and Papa. Mama had one of her
famous apple pies in her hand wrapped in a white cloth.

"This here pie is for Mr. Bowmen. Me and Papa want to thank him
for learning you." She said.

Sage didn't know what to say. He wanted to stop them but didn't
know how. The charade was over. They would find out now that for the
past few months Sage was a poor student. Mama's heart would be broken,
and therefore his.

Inside the school, Mama handed the pie to Mr. Bowmen. He looked
surprised. "What's this?" He said as he reached for the pie.

"We appreciates you learning Sage is all."

Bowmen glanced at the pie, and then at Sage. "Well, I…"

"He doing real fine." Interrupted Mama. "Sometimes he read to us
and he read real good."

"Really." Said Bowmen surprised, again looking at Sage. "Well…"

"Them folks was right about you." Said Papa. "You can learn
anybody."

"Well…" Started Mr. Bowmen

"You don't need to say nothing." Said, Mama. And with that, she
grabbed Sage's hand and headed for the door. Papa tipped his hat to Mr.
Bowmen and followed her.

After Mama and Papa's visit things changed for Sage. Bowmen
started taking interest in him by watching him more closely and sometimes
asking him to participate in class discussions. Sometimes Mr. Bowmen
would test Sage's reading skills by asking him to stay during recess and to
read aloud to him. Other times he would ask Sage to skip recess to perform

math problems or just to write on the board. Sage enjoyed staying with Mr. Bowmen versus going outside with the other kids that would either ignore him or pick on him.

Bowmen taught his last lesson on the board and dismissed the worn out kids to go home for the evening. Sage sat at his desk pretending to pack until he was sure he had given a safe distance between himself and his schoolmates.

He walked about a mile before he heard a rustling noise in the thick bush behind him. When he turned to see what it was, he was knocked to the ground on his back.

"Gotcha!" Yelled Joshua Killeen as he stood over Sage. "I gotcha good that time." He laughed. And at that moment two of his friends stepped out from behind the bushes as well. One was Billy Pudgy a dark-haired boy with light orange freckles. The other was Danny Claire, a boy with thin red hair that wrapped around his head like a bowl, and very white skin, like snow.

They all pointed and laughed. "Look how scared he is." Said Joshua.

"Oh my gosh." Said Billy pointing to Sage. "Look how he's shaking."

Sage was shaking from fear; he was alone with these boys and no one was out here to protect him. He started moaning in a rhythmic tone rocking his body back and forth.

"What's he doing?" Asked Danny.

"He's crying." Answered Billy.

"No. He ain't crying. He just making animal sounds. But he'll be crying soon." Said Joshua. And with that, he stepped over Sage and slugged him in the face. The moaning ceased as Sage's face filled with pain and he became dazed. But no tears.

This made Joshua angry. "You think you're tough? You don't cry?" He then slugged Sage in the face again. Sage moaned once more from the blow but that was it. He was in more pain and that punch nearly knocked him unconscious, but no tears.

The three boys looked at each other. "What kind of animal is he?" Said Danny.

"He's the worst kind, a nigger. Let's get him." Yelled Joshua in frustration and the others followed his lead as he stepped to Sage and began kicking him. Sage moaned with each blow but no tears.

This enraged Joshua but he and the boys were getting tired. They leaned over Sage breathing in and out deeply.

"He still ain't crying, Joshua." Said Billy in between deep breaths.

"I know!" Snapped Joshua.

Sage ached all over. He was in so much pain that he didn't think he would make it home. He coughed violently then rolled over and vomited making a hacking noise as it came up.

The boys stepped back and cursed him. And then left the scene in disgust.

Sage rolled over grunting in pain.

He headed home and with each step the pain throbbed in his body and face. When he finally reached the property he collapsed.

Miles was the first to spot him. He picked him up and carried him to the house.

Mama's face was distorted with anguish as she instructed Miles. "Take him inside, put him in his bed, I'll look after him there."

Mama leaned over Sage. "Let's take a look at you." She grabbed his chin and turned his head. His right eye and cheek were swollen. "Who did this to you?"

Sage did not answer.

Mama looked him over. "Where else do you hurt?"

"My side."

"Let's look at it." She pulled up his shirt. Sage moaned. When she saw his purple side she immediately stood to her feet. "Who did this?!" She yelled. "What devil did this to you? And I want to know now!"

Sage's eyes became wide. He had never seen his grandma this angry before. Even though he knew she wasn't angry with him, he still felt very uneasy.

"Who Sage? Who?"

Sage was silent.

"Fine, then tomorrow I will go up to the school house and I'll find out who done this. And when I finds out I'm gonna take those kids to their mama's house and tell them what they done to you."

"No!" Yelled Sage.

"And why not?"

Sage hesitated for a long time, and Mama waited patiently. Finally, he spoke. "Because they'll beat you like they beat me."

Mama's face turned angry. "I don't care about none of that. This ain't right. A child should be able to go to school without getting beat. Tomorrow I is going up there and finds out who done this to you."

Sage grabbed her arm. "No Mama. You don't know them like I do. They'll hurt you."

"I don't care about that. This needs to stop."

"You can't!"

"Look at you, Sage. Look at what they done to you. Them boys ain't gonna get away with doing you like this. Them boys ain't gonna hurt my baby no more." She said as she raised her hands to her face and cried.

A movement was heard in the hallway, and Donovan stepped inside the doorway and approached Sage. Sage watched Donovan's face tighten with anger. Donovan then pulled back the covers and lifted Sage's shirt exposing his bare bruised ribs.

Sage studied Donovan's face wondering what he was thinking.

Donovan turned to Mama. "This boy's fourteen now. He's almost a man. He don't need his grandma fighting for him. He's got to fight for himself."

Mama glared at him. "How's he gonna do that? There's more of them than him."

"That's not for you to figure out. He's got to figure his own way."

Mama thought about it and then said. "This ain't right. A boy ought not to have to go through this. Tomorrow I'm going to the school to find out who these boys is. Then I'm going to talk some sense into them. And if I need to I'll talk some sense into their folks."

Donovan sighed, and then he unbuttoned the front of his shirt and pulled it off exposing the nasty scars on his bare chest, back, and forearms. Deep nasty scars proving that he had been shot, whipped and stabbed on many occasions. Mama placed her fingers over her mouth and Sage couldn't stop the tears from flowing out his eyes and down his cheek. Even though he hardly knew this man, he still felt a strong connection of some sort to him. Maybe because this man claimed to be his father. Or maybe because this man's tortured body showed that he had been through so much suffering. Maybe because this man's tortured body demonstrated exactly how Sage felt on the inside about himself. He felt scared and tortured from the many negative experiences that he had with children and adults alike. Not so much from weapons or physical confrontations like Donovan, but more from name calling and being excluded and treated as if he didn't exist.

"You see these wounds, Sage?" Donovan asked.

Sage hesitated for a moment and then nodded.

"I shouldn't be alive now but I am. Somehow I survived. I reckon most of us walking around has survived somehow. I reckon you'll do the same."

Sage studied Donovan's body looking over each of the many wounds as if reliving in his mind what he thought happened. Finally, he looked

down at himself and pointed to his purple ribs. "I reckon I'll survive too."
He said.

"I reckon you will." Said Donovan. And then Donovan turned and
left the room. Sage's eyes followed him. Then he looked up at Mama who
still had her hands on her face. He could tell by her expression that she
changed her mind and decided against going to the school.

Chapter 19

Outside on the front porch, Papa and his best friend Corwin were seated in the wooden chairs. Corwin was in his early sixty's and looked fit for his age. He had a full head of kinky hair with sprinkles of gray throughout. His clothes were neatly ironed giving the impression that he had just bought them from the clothes shop. Even as Corwin sat in the chair talking with Papa there was an arrogance about him. His head was always high with pride like a soldier standing at attention for his superiors. Corwin chewed on a long straw twig and pulled it from his mouth when he spoke.

"Sheriff ain't too happy these days. Folks say he upset on the count of that fellow shooting up them robbers a few days back. Sheriff thinks he got no respect for the law." Said Corwin.

"Those men put a gun to me. They was gonna kill me until that fellow stepped in." Said Papa.

"Uh huh." Said Corwin pulling out the twig. "That's powerful lucky that stranger helping you in all. Lord knows the Sheriff didn't do nothing.

Papa leaned against the back of his chair. "What people saying about this fellow?"

"Not much. No one seen him since that day. Folks think maybe he just passing through." He laughed. "I'll tell you what, the Sheriff and the Deputy looking for him."

Papa cut his eyes toward Corwin. "Why you say that?"

"Cause they been asking around. Nobody knows what he looks like." Corwin laughed again. "They didn't get close enough to find out. I guess they didn't want to get shot."

"I guess not." Said Papa.

Corwin sat up in his chair and looked off into the distance. Papa turned and looked in the same direction. Across the way on his horse riding at a trot was Donovan. He was moving toward them. Corwin pointed his twig. "Who's that there?" He asked.

"That's my youngest boy Donovan. He's back home now."

With a confused expression, Corwin turned to Papa. "You have a youngest boy?" He questioned.

"Sure do." Said Papa. "I would have told you except we thought he was dead. He Sage's daddy."

Corwin stared back into the field and stood from his chair. "I'll be damn. That's Sage's daddy?"

Papa stood from his chair as well. "That's him."

"How long he been gone?"

"About seven years." Said Papa.

Corwin slapped his leg. "Ohh wee, that's a long time. Where's he been?"

Donovan was moving closer toward them but still far from hearing range.

"Don't know." Answered Papa. "He don't want to talk about it, and I'm not asking."

The two men quieted as they watched Donovan approach the porch. Corwin was trying to get a good look at him. Donovan didn't seem to notice. He climbed off his horse, slapped it on the rear and the horse bolted full speed across the field leaving a cloud of dust behind.

"That's a fast horse you got there mister." Said, Corwin, as he watched the horse race away.

Donovan glanced up at the stranger. He didn't answer but instead nodded, then stepped onto the porch. Corwin continued to stare at him.

"Donovan this is Corwin, our neighbor." Said Papa.

With a wide grin, Corwin reached out his hand. "How do you do?" However, Donovan didn't take his hand. Finally, Corwin dropped his hand and his smile.

"Do I know you?" Asked Donovan.

"No sir." Said Corwin. "You don't know me. And I don't know you."

Donovan eyed the old man for a moment, then he walked past him and headed inside the house.

The two men were quiet.

"I best be leaving now." Said Corwin. "Walk with me, Sam." Sam was Papa's birth name; however, most folks called him by his nickname, which was Papa. Nonetheless, for whatever reason Corwin was one of the few folks that chose to use his birth name instead.

Papa grabbed his cane next to his chair and the two men walked side by side into the field. When they were far enough away from the house Corwin spoke. His tone was serious and his face was concerned. "I've seen your youngest son before." Both men stopped and faced each other.

"When?" Asked Papa.

"It was before I met you. Just before I moved my family to this town. About four years ago I guess."

"I'm listening." Said Papa.

Corwin was no longer displaying his self-assured demeanor as he had done a few minutes earlier. He tossed the twig on the ground and was quiet thinking about what he was going to say. Papa leaned on his cane and watched him.

"I remember it like it just happened." Said, Corwin, as he glanced around to make sure no one was close by. "You're the only friend I got." He said. "Nobody in this town cares for me much. Sometimes I'm not sure if my old lady and my three daughters like me."

"Well, you brought most of that on yourself." Said Papa. "You don't treat people right."

Corwin agreed. "I guess." He said. "I know when I tell my stories sometimes I add a little bit for entertainment. You know. Sometimes I'll put a twist on it to keep it interesting. But what I'm about to tell you happened exactly the way I'm gonna tell you." He faced Papa waiting for his response.

Papa nodded.

"I was in the town of Munford. It was just over five years ago, just before we moved to this town. The old lady had just had our third child. Her labor was hard so she was bedridden for a few days. She was in so much pain that she sent me to town to get some medicine from the doctor. I'll never forget. It was a Saturday afternoon, and it was hot that day. The town was full of people, most were shopping for supplies for the upcoming winter, some were drinking. Lots of newcomers just passing through. Some of them were making a lot of noise, yelling and screaming and such." Corwin laughed. "Some were even shooting their pistols in the air." Corwin rubbed his chin in thought. "I was minding my business and just came out of the Doctors office, when I noticed the whole town was quiet. Not a sound. Folks were packed together on both sides of the road, inside the hotel, the saloon, and the supply shop. Some folks was hiding behind wagons and horses. I've never seen nothing like it. It didn't take long before I knew why." Corwin paused again to collect his thoughts. Papa watched him as he leaned forward on his cane. Corwin continued. "About fifty yards out I saw three men standing in the middle of the road. They were yelling curse words that no woman and child should be hearing. I recognized one of em. He was the one shooting his pistols at the sky earlier. But just in front of me, maybe fifteen feet out was another man standing by himself. He was dressed in all brown and I remember his hat was so big that I could hardly see his face. He wasn't saying nothing. He was just watching those three men yelling at him." He looked at Papa.

"Go on Corwin. I'm listening."

Corwin nodded. "The three men kept yelling and the one man with the hat just waited. I thought to myself this boy gonna die. Then something strange happened. Another man stepped out and stood with the three men. Now there was four against the one man." Corwin nodded his head in disbelief. "I couldn't believe it. And the one man with the hat didn't move. He just watched as the four men cursed at him something terrible. Then one of the four men reached for his pistol, and I dove to the ground. I covered my head and heard nothing but gunfire. It was loud. But it didn't last but a few seconds. I stayed down until the shots stopped. When I rolled over. I couldn't believe my eyes. All the men including the one man with the hat were on the ground all bloody. But the man with the hat was the only one moving and all the other men were dead. He laid there with a pistol in each hand. Then he rolled over and climbed to his feet. He had blood all on him. He looked around. No one came near him. The way he was swaying I figured him to drop dead in that street."

Corwin paused and then continued. "The bloody man standing in front was Donovan."

"Donovan," Papa repeated. "Are you sure?"

Corwin nodded. "I'm sure."

"What makes you think so?"

"Because the man I saw had a horse."

"A horse?" Papa questioned.

"This was no ordinary horse. It was one of them smart horses. The kind that when you whistled it would come a running. And that's just what happened. The bloody man whistled and that horse came a running from nowhere. Then he climbed on the horse all slumped over and raced out of town. And I ain't seen him since until now. The way that man was shot up, I figured him to be as good as dead."

"That doesn't mean he was Donovan."

Corwin pointed to the horse that was pasturing nearby. "You see that horse there."

Papa nodded.

"That's the horse I saw on that day. I remember it like it just happened."

The two men were quiet.

"What was the fight about?" Asked Papa.

"Don't know. Folks claimed they knew one another from somewhere."

Papa leaned on his cane and grabbed Corwin on the arm with his free hand.

"What's this?" Corwin said as he tried to tug away, however, Papa didn't release his grip, the one he was famous for.

He looked into Corwin's eyes. "Listen to me, Corwin. You're right we are best friends and I'm your only friend. You trust me and I trust you. It's been like that with us for years. So as my best friend I trust you not to tell a soul of what you just told me. Not even your wife."

"Why?"

"Because this info could get Donovan killed. And if that happens I'm not sure my wife could handle that."

"Okay Sam, just you and me will know about this."

At that Papa released him and had a worried look on his face. "Damn." He said.

Chapter 20

Just before dawn, Maria walked about lighting the lanterns and candles. Fully dressed in his work clothes Miles was seated at the table. He watched her in silence as she moved from one candle to another.

Maria approached him from behind and brushed the tips of her fingers across the back of his neck. "Most men would love to have a wife as beautiful as me. You got it so good Miles and you don't even know it."

"You're the one that's got it good," Miles said. "I make a good living for you and everyone else around here. It don't matter if it's raining or snowing. I'm in those fields providing for all of us."

Maria made her way around and sat in the chair across from him. She reached affectionately for his hands. But as she did so he leaned back so as to avoid her. She instead placed her hands on her lap.

"I know you do Miles." She admitted. "You're a good provider. No one could say different. It's just you spend all your time in those fields. I just want some of your time is all. With all your work I don't see much of you. And when I do see you, you're too tired for good company."

Miles sat quietly as he listened to her. Maybe she was finally getting through to him.

"I have to provide for this family. Without me, we won't survive." He said

"We more than survive Miles. We live well. We live better than some of the white folks I know. I just want some of your time is all. Maybe you could take a Sunday off. Or maybe take off an afternoon so that we could walk or something. Maybe you could stay in bed one morning just holding and making love to me."

"I need to stay on top of my work. We may be doing all right now, but it wouldn't take much for that to change. If I was to take time off, then the next season we would suffer. Maybe even starve. I won't take that chance."

"Not a lot of time Miles. Just every now and then for me, your wife."

Miles stood to his feet. "I can't-do it. I have too many folks counting on me."

Maria stood as well. She was trying to stay calm. "What about me Miles. I need you too. I need you to be my husband."

"I am your husband. I provide for you."

"You hardly ever touch me." She paused as the tears came down. "Last night I cried all night after you didn't want me."

Miles watched her as if he was going to say something but then decided against it and pushed past her and headed out into the dark fields.

The coldness of the morning slipped in and chilled her skin. She crossed her arms and squeezed herself for warmth. She sat quietly thinking about what Miles had just done. She hated him. He was none responsive to her needs. He didn't appreciate her at all. She doubted that he even loved her. At least he didn't treat her as if he loved her.

This marriage was not what she had thought it would be. It's been a difficult marriage almost from day one. For one thing, Miles was a terrible lover. He didn't know anything about a woman's body and how to please her. He didn't know how to touch her so as to bring her pleasure. His touch was rough and quick. He did more grabbing than touching. She wanted him to take his time to caress her body, to enjoy her body. Sometimes she would guide his hands teaching him how to touch her, but he never listened.

Also, he didn't know how to move his body when they made love. He would enter her abruptly and with a few quick thrusts, he climaxed within minutes. Maria would beg him to slow down and take his time, but he was not responsive to her suggestions.

Not long after they were married she found that Miles worked all the time. She noticed that he only took short breaks to drink water or to eat a meal. Watching him she found it hard to believe that a man could work this hard.

What shocked Maria the most was that Miles not only worked this grueling schedule during the week, but he also worked this difficult schedule on Saturday and Sunday as well. This was too much she thought. It was not necessary for him to work this hard. With this schedule, he had no time for her at all. And even with the little time that he had she could see that he was much too exhausted and cranky to be around.

She thought for a moment about all that Miles had given her. She had a husband that could provide for her. She had a roof over her head and food in her belly. He provided her with more than just a roof, she lived in a nice house. Not a house by rich white folks standards, but a nice house nonetheless. She also had access to money when needed. If she wanted to take some money to buy some nice clothes at the clothing store, she was free to do so. They weren't living in hard times and struggling like many Negroes living in town. And this was mainly due to Miles extreme work ethic.

She decided after careful consideration that she would appreciate Miles for the man that he was and not for the man that she wanted him to be. On this day Maria decided that she would surprise him by making him breakfast. She would bring it to him in the fields to show him how she appreciated him for how hard he worked to support the families. The problem was that she didn't know much about cooking. Mama did all of the cooking on the property. Sometimes Maria would watch, but she didn't pay much attention to how Mama prepared her recipes.

Maria went to the chicken house outside in search of some eggs. She had never been in the chicken yard before and she didn't know what to expect. When she entered the yard she stood in the doorway near the chickens. Some were clucking in alarm, however, most sat quietly in their hay nests. She watched them for a long time trying to guess which chicken would be the safest to gather eggs from. None of them seemed safe to her. And to top it off there was so many of them. She figured maybe fifty. She lifted her lantern high so that she could see the light spread about the chickens. Some were walking about the dirt floor, approaching her probably looking for food, which she did not have.

Maria stood in the gateway afraid and not wanting to provoke the chickens to come after her. She remembered watching on many occasions from the safety of her porch, the chickens charge Sage and Papa while pecking at their legs. Sometimes Papa would strike back by kicking or swinging his cane at them.

One chicken, in particular, seemed to take notice of Maria. The chicken was all white except the head, which was black. The small head moved back and forth in a quick jerking motion. Its beady black eyes glowed as Maria shined the lantern in its direction. With its head jerking the chicken clucked from the end of the yard, then started walking in Maria's direction. She quickly looked around searching for some sort of weapon to use. She found nothing except for more chickens. She cautiously moved back as the chicken moved closer in her direction. When the chicken was a few feet from her, it violently flapped its wings and clucked loudly as it charged her. Maria screamed and kicked, but missed and the heavy chicken crashed into her legs. At impact, Maria screamed again and ran to the other side of the yard.

She wasn't injured, but the weight of the chicken made her think that this animal could possibly harm her. The black-headed chicken stood in front of the gate, which made Maria feel trapped. The chicken started to approach her again. This time Maria moved out of range to the other side of the chicken house. The chicken stopped in mid-step and then decided to ignore her. Maria was relieved. She then shined her lantern on one of the quiet chickens sitting on the hay. She used the bright lantern to push it away, then she jumped back almost falling over when the chicken leaped, clucking and flapping its wings. At that moment she grabbed the warm eggs and ran out the barn.

Inside the house, she pulled out a black skillet that Mama had given to her when she and Miles were first married. This is so much fun, why didn't she do this sooner she thought. She promised herself that she would get up early every morning and cook for Miles. She would be the wife that he wanted.

When she finished the biscuit she turned it over and placed it on the plate next to the eggs. The side up on the biscuit was cooked golden brown just right. The side down was black for she had cooked it too long. Maybe Miles would not notice. She wanted to taste this magnificent breakfast but decided not to, for this was Miles's breakfast. She hesitated for a moment admiring the beauty of the yellow egg next to the golden brown biscuit. Her first breakfast.

Maria peeked out the window. The sun was beginning to rise in the east, birds were chirping in the nearby trees. Papa was already up and was headed toward the chicken house with a can of feed in hand. She could see Mama sitting on the porch in her rocking chair and Miles in the fields.

She grabbed the plate and headed out the front door towards where Miles was working. When she approached him his back was to her. She could already see the sweat starting to work its way down his shirt. By nightfall, his entire shirt will be soaked.

"Miles." She said softly as if a mother gently waking up her child. He did not hear her. "Miles." She repeated in the same motherly tone but raising her voice a notch or two. "I made you some breakfast."

Miles stopped and turned in her direction. His face was of irritation, he did not like to be disturbed while he worked. He looked at the plate but said nothing.

Maria held the plate out. "I made you some breakfast." She said in the same calm tone as before. He dropped the hoe by his side and reached for the plate with both hands. She watched him, smiling. She turned to look at Mama who was leaning forward in her chair watching them. Maria waved. Mama hesitated and then waved back. Maria then turned and watched Miles as he dipped his fork into the eggs and scooped a bite. He chewed for a moment and then made an abnormal face as he turned his head and spat to the ground.

Maria was concerned. "What's the matter?" She asked.

"Them eggs don't taste too good."

"Oh." Said Maria. She was hurt. "Try the biscuit then."

Miles reached for the biscuit. He looked it over.

"It's burnt." He said.

"Not all of it." She said

Miles groaned then took a bite. After a moment, he made another awful face and started coughing and choking. He then turned his head and spat to the ground again. Maria watched him in shock.

"Damn. That is the worst cooking I have ever had." And with that, he tossed the remaining biscuit across the yard into a small group of chickens. "I bet they don't even eat it." He blurted more to himself. Maria was speechless. "Can't you do nothing?" He added then picked up the hoe and went back to work.

Maria just stood there devastated not saying a word. She turned to the chickens and watched them. She desperately hoped that they would eat the biscuit. After a moment they did. She felt a little relieved; at least the chickens would eat it she thought. Then she turned to Mama who was still sitting on the porch. At that moment she pulled herself out of her chair and went inside the house. Maria turned to Miles again. The tears welled in her eyes.

Without thinking without knowing she found herself on Miles's back screaming, hitting, kicking, and scratching. She called him a bastard and every other name that she could think of. Maria had absolutely no control of what she was doing and did not come to realize what she had done until Miles pulled her off and tossed her to the ground. When she tried to get up, he stepped forward and slapped her down. Her face rang with pain. She palmed her face and began sobbing.

Miles stood over her towering; he pointed his finger in anger. "You just better watch yourself. I had about enough of you." He eyed her a moment longer before returning to work.

She laid on the ground crying. Rejection had always been a part of life for Maria. People have never seemed to like her. It was always the same. When people first meet her they were usually friendly toward her, but after some time her new friends would soon abandon her. Most times she wasn't even sure why people responded to her in this way. After a while, she found it difficult to take the initiative to make new friends, for she could never keep their interest.

At times it was very lonely for her. When she first met people she tried very hard to impress them. Too hard maybe. Whenever they talked about something exciting that they had accomplished she would try to top them with an even more exciting story. This seemed to strain the relationship and soon her new friends just avoided her. It would hurt her the most when her ex-friends made new friends and were getting along with them very well. It would hurt sitting off to the side watching them all laughing, playing and talking together. It was so lonely.

Her mother died when she was seven, so she had no one to turn to. If her mother were alive maybe things would have been different. She could have asked her mother how to make friends and keep them. If she lost a friend she could cry to her mother and tell her about her loneliness and pain. Even if she had no friends, at least she would have her mother.

Maria rolled over and climbed to her feet. As she watched him she tightened her fist with anger. She tempted to jump on his back again but decided against it. He didn't even notice her watching him. He was an easy target. However, he was still much larger and stronger than she was. She would once again be no match. She turned and headed toward the house.

Inside the house, she cleaned herself and changed into a nice light blue dress with large white dots all about. The collar of the dress was a large white flap. The dress dropped down almost touching her pretty white shoes. She then sat in front of the mirror combed out her hair, and she looked at herself. She was beautiful with black hair that rested behind her back down to her waist. She leaned forward, the only part of her that may not be considered attractive was the small bruise on her cheek where Miles had slapped her.

As she appeared at the bruise, she became angry again. Her face tightened with a frown. "That son of a bitch." She said to herself as she stepped away from the mirror.

She walked onto the front porch and watched Miles for a moment. He did not look up. As beautiful as she looked right now he did not even notice her. With that Maria stepped off the porch and headed to the barn. She saddled the smaller brown horse.

Miles looked up briefly as she came out, but he did nothing else except return to his work. She tugged on the reins and headed toward town. If he had just said something to her or maybe even looked at her for a moment longer she would have climbed off her horse and headed back toward the house. Yet Miles barely acknowledged her as usual. Too busy, too unfeeling. Now she was headed to town. She would visit a friend. A male friend.

Chapter 21

Gunther faced the wall next to the empty jail. Sweat beaded upon his forehead and his sleeves were rolled up to his elbows. His black bow tie laid across the desk next to him. His shiny black boots were behind the desk for he stood barefooted.

He stood still trying to bring his heavy breathing under control. When his breathing had finally slowed he again looked forward toward the wall. His face was serious with concentration. He quickly reached down and pulled out his pistol on his right side and pulled the trigger as he pointed it at the wall. The gun-clicked empty it wasn't loaded. He stuffed the gun back into its holster and paused for a moment to concentrate again before he pulled out the gun on his left side and pulled the trigger as he pointed it at the wall as well. He stuffed the pistol back into the holster and concentrated again as he stared towards the wall at his imaginary bandit of some sort, then pulled out both guns simultaneously and clicked the empty guns as he pointed them at the wall.

Gunther would practice this ritual with his pistols each day. He was convinced that he was one of best gunmen around, and to maintain this status he practiced and honed his skills daily. Even as good as Gunther felt that he was, his older brother Landry was still quicker to the draw and more efficient when hitting his target. When he was a child he used to watch his older brother practice for hours a day, shooting skillfully with either hand. Now his older brother hardly practiced at all, and even so, there wasn't a gunman around who could take him. Gunther had asked his brother on one occasion why he didn't practice as much anymore? And his older brother responded by saying. "I can't get any better than I am now. And I've practiced so much that it's all instinct now. I don't even have to think about pulling my pistol, it just happens."

As far as Gunther could remember, he and Landry grew up in an orphanage. He didn't know his Mama and Papa but from what he had heard they were very poor. So much, in fact, they decided that they could not afford to keep all of their eight children. From what Gunther understood his parents had decided to let two of the eight children go to an orphanage across the state line. He and his older brother Landry were the chosen ones.

At that time Gunther was just barely one year of age and Landry was seven. What made this story strange to Gunther was that he almost understood why his parents chose to give him away, for he was the youngest and probably the most troublesome. However, it did not make sense to him why his older brother Landry was chosen for this orphanage. From what Gunther understood Landry was not one of the youngest children, he was somewhere in the middle. Not only that but at seven years Landry was big and strong for his age. He looked more like a teenager than a seven-year-old. Gunther felt that Landry should have been viewed as valuable and would have been helpful working the land and doing chores around the house for his parents.

On many nights Gunther and his older brother had discussed why they felt their parents would choose Landry for the orphanage. After several years he and Landry came to the conclusion that maybe their parent's motives were one of two. First, maybe they realized how close the two siblings were with one another, even at such a young age they didn't have the heart to separate them. This made sense because Gunther and his older brother Landry were very close to one another since the beginning when Gunther was first born. The second reason could have been that since Gunther was so young, his parents wanted to send one of his older brothers with him to the orphanage for some sort of protection. And as Gunther thought back, his older brother had done plenty protecting over the years.

The orphanage was a difficult way to grow up. Mr. Locus owned the orphanage farm and he had about thirty other unwanted kids that lived on his ten-acre ranch. Locus was a thin man with wire-framed glasses and a bald head except for the short hair around his ears and base of his neck. He usually wore a vest with a chained watched attached within the breast pocket. He was typically very grumpy and yelled a lot. He was strict with discipline. When he gave an order he expected it to be followed without complaint. In his back pocket, he carried a fresh cut switch just in case one of the kids needed on the spot discipline. Locus worked the kids hard. He would get them up just before the sun peeked over the trees and worked them until noon, which was lunchtime. After lunch Locus's wife would teach the kids reading and writing for a couple of hours. When she was finished she then would turn them over to Mr. Locus and more work would be completed until the sun started to come down. After the long day, the kids were free to do as they wished. At this time some of the kids that still had energy would play games, like hide and seek, or chase. Some of the other kids would just sit under trees and rest. Others would go to their sleeping bunks and not come out until the next morning when Mr. Locus called them out again, and then the long day would start all over.

The kids at the orphanage ranged from all ages, toddlers to young teenagers. Once the kids reached about seventeen or eighteen they were forced to leave. None of the kids were allowed in Mr. Locus's house, therefore they slept in one of the two small lodges behind the house. The boys of age four and older slept in one lodge, and the girls and the toddlers slept in the other lodge.

Inside the lodges were two rolls of small beds leaned against either wall. Each of the two rolls had eight beds across. All the beds had two blankets and one pillow.

Though Gunther was small for his age, he was very sure of his physical abilities, and on many occasions didn't get along with some of the other boys. Sometimes he would get into physical confrontations with the older and bigger boys, and they would hardly fight back. And the reason being wasn't so much because Gunther was strong for his size or because he was considered tough for his young age. It was more because his older and large brother Landry was always watching and very protective of his younger brother. All the boys knew that if you fought with Gunther then later you would be fighting with Landry as well. And at age sixteen Landry wasn't one to fight with. At this age, Landry was almost as big and strong as most grown men, and even they wouldn't be foolish enough to get into a fight with him.

There was one boy in particular who was also sixteen at the time, did not get along with Gunther. His name was Josh Demin. Not only was Josh Landry's age, but he also had the same tough reputation as Landry. The difference being, Landry never bullied or bothered anyone unless they provoked him by threatening himself or his brother. On one occasion an incident in town added to Landry's reputation and stayed with those that knew him for all the days of their lives.

On this day Landry, Gunther and a couple of the orphanage boys accompanied Mr. Locus into town to purchase supplies for the farm. Mr. Locus stood on the sidewalk and watched the four boys as they went in and out of the shop with arms full of supplies and loaded them onto the wagon.

Mr. Locus saw one of the boys struggling to carry the extra heavy load and decided to rush to help the boy before he hurt himself or dropped the supplies. While doing so he accidentally collided with another man and they both hit the ground. Mr. Locus climbed to his feet first and apologized as he reached to help the other man to his feet. But this man did not except his helpful hand and jumped up with a frown. Mr. Locus again attempted to apologize for the accident, but the man clearly did not accept. And while the man was yelling obscenities he managed to sneak in a wild punch to Mr. Locus which sent him soaring flat on his back. The orphanage boys watched the scene with disbelief.

Mr. Locus rubbed his chin and moaned as he lay on his back. The man then walked to Mr. Locus, grabbed him by his jacket and jerked him to his feet so that they were face to face, and yelled more obscenities. He cocked his arm back to hit Mr. Locus again but was stopped when Landry grabbed his arm from behind, swung the man around and then hit him square in the face. Blood squirted out from the man's nose as he stiffened like a board and went down.

Gunther looked at the unconscious man's bloody nose. It was purple and twisted slightly to the side from the powerful punch. "I think he got himself a broken nose." He said.

After which Mr. Locus and Landry became friendlier. Landry was the only one that was allowed inside the house. Often they were seen together chatting and sometimes even laughing. Mr. Locus referred to Landry as his right-hand man and told him that he could stay as long as he wished.

Josh, on the other hand, bullied freely without the need of an excuse to be provoked. At meal times, seconds weren't allowed, so if he wanted extra food he would take it from another boy's plate. If the boy refused to give any part of his meal, Josh would then take all the boy's food and leave the boy with nothing, or he would just knock the plate of food into the dirt, which meant the boy would get nothing as well. Sometimes a boy would complain to Mr. Locus, but when he asked if anyone witnessed this, all the other boys would deny out of fear that Josh would retaliate on them.

Josh and Landry didn't get along and they would have arguments from time to time, sometimes just short of a physical bout. But on those occasions, it seemed that Josh would back away not wanting to test his strength with Landry's. Yet he and Gunther, on the other hand, would mix words and get into shoving matches. Josh seemed to know better than to take this any further than a harmless shove.

Gunther knowing that Josh was afraid of his older brother would test Josh often. On many occasions, he would humiliate Josh in front of the other kids by calling him silly names, which usually caused laughter amongst the young bystanders. As time went on it became obvious that Josh was becoming irritated with Gunther's lack of fear and respect. Sometimes Gunther would catch Josh glaring at him, and at those times he would grin until Josh turned away. Once he even yelled, "What ya lookin at beaver?!" The kids close by laughed. Beaver was the nickname that Gunther had given Josh because his teeth seemed to be so large for his mouth. Josh was taken aback by his new nickname.

None of the other kids were brave enough to use this nickname in public. But in private when they referred to Josh they would use his nickname, Beaver. Sometimes in the fields, Gunther would greet Josh with a "Hi Beaver." And as usual those nearby would laugh. Once at dinner Gunther yelled across the table. "Hey, Beaver! Pass the bread!" Again more laughter from everyone, except Landry that is.

Landry never found Gunther's antics humorous. On many occasions in private, he warned his younger brother of the danger of teasing a person like Josh. "One day you may push him too far," Landry warned. However, Gunther ignored his brother's counsel.

Even though Josh did not retaliate against Gunther, he did, however, take all his aggression out on the other boys. Those that laughed or even smiled at his expense, paid dearly later. Over time he became more vicious with his attacks. He would do things such as knock over their food and then smash it into the floor with his boots. Sometimes he would make the other boy get down on the floor and lick up the spilled food like a dog. Once he even made a crying boy bark as he licked the floor clean. All that watched were in shock and fear.

On another occasion he made one of the bashful boys take off his clothes and march naked into the girl's lodge, and he told the boy to stay there until he yelled ten times "I'm lonely! I'm lonely!" There was so much screaming and hollering from the girl's lodge that Mr. Locus finally came out of his house in time to see the naked boy running back to the boy's lodge.

Mr. Locus ran into the boy's lodge yelling. "What the devil is going on in here?!" He turned to the little sobbing naked boy who was now getting dressed. "What the devil are you doing boy?!"

The boy was too afraid of Josh to tell Mr. Locus how he was forced to go into the girl's lodge naked. Instead, he just sobbed.

Mr. Locus turned to the rest of the boys in the room and demanded to know what was going on. Gunther stepped forward. He pointed to the smug Josh across the room. "He made him do it." He said.

Mr. Locus turned to Josh. "Is this true? You made this boy do such an offensive act?"

"He's lying!" Shouted Josh.

Mr. Locus turned to the crying boy. "You've never been any trouble before. Why would you do such a foolish act? That's not like you at all."

Gunther spoke again. "Because Josh told him that if he didn't he would beat him."

"You liar!" Josh yelled. "I said nothin to him!"

"Quiet!" Instructed Mr. Locus. He then turned to Josh. "You've been nothing but trouble since you came here. I don't know if I believe you.

If I find out you threatened this boy, you'll deal with me." He said as he pulled the long switch from out the back of his pants and pointed it to Josh.

Mr. Locus turned to face the other boys. Anyone else here knows what happened?

After a long pause, Landry spoke from the back. "I do." He said. "Gunther tells the truth. Josh made him do it."

Then the other boys spoke up one by one admitting that Josh threatened him to go to the girl's lodge. Some of the boys told Mr. Locus other stories of how Josh had done them wrong in the past. They told him how they were afraid to speak up because Josh would punish them for it. Mr. Locus listened to them all, and then assured all the boys that Josh would not harm them anymore, he would make sure of it.

He turned to Josh and pointed to the door with his switch. "Outside." He ordered. "You've caused enough trouble around here. It will end today."

All the boys followed as Josh and Mr. Locus went into the yard. Mr. Locus pointed to a post that he wanted Josh to grab onto. He instructed Josh to pull down his pants. He did so. Then Mr. Locus lectured for a couple of minutes about right and wrong and the rules of his home. And he instructed Josh that if he were to continue to stay here, he would follow all the rules. And finally, he demanded that Josh never lay another hand on any of the boys or the consequences would be immense.

After the lecture, he raised his switch and came down on Josh's naked hide about twenty times. Josh yelled OUCH! After each blow. After the whipping Josh pulled up his pants and sneered at Gunther who of course was smiling at him.

After the incident, Josh and Gunther didn't say much to each other. They would sometimes pass each other but wouldn't so much as look at one another. Some of the boys were afraid at first about speaking out against Josh. They felt that if Mr. Locus weren't around he would lash out against them for tattling. But he never did. Not only that but after the whipping, he mostly kept to himself. Even at meal times he would take his food outside and eat alone.

One night during the middle of the week, Gunther walked into the lodge accompanied with two of his buddies. It was after midnight and most of the boys were already asleep. His older brother used to wait up for him, and then give lectures about the dangers of being out so late, and how he needed to get more rest. However, Landry grew tired of his ignored warnings and allowed his younger brother to stroll in at his will.

The two boys that were with him separated and headed to their beds as Gunther headed to Landry's bed. Gunther would climb in his brother's bed from time to time if he had been awakened from a bad dream, or if he was ill. However by morning before the others were awake, he would slip back into his own bed.

Usually, Landry didn't pay much attention when his brother climbed into his bed, but on this night for whatever reason he took notice.

"Gunther," Landry whispered. "You alright?"

It was a while before Gunther answered. "I ain't feeling good. Just want to lay here for a bit." The tone in Gunther's voice was shaky.

"Did you have another dream?"

"No. Just ain't feeling good. That's all."

Gunther felt the bed shake as his older brother sat up. Within the darkness, Landry moved off the bed. He listened to Landry make his way over to the wall, grab the lantern and bring it back to the bed. He heard the match strike against the box, then saw the flame of the lantern light up around him.

The lantern moved to Gunther's face, exposing his black eyes, bruised forehead, bloodied and split lips.

"What happened to you?" He asked with panic in his voice

Gunther was barely audible. "I'm tired. I wanna sleep."

Landry felt the weight of his brother's head on his shoulder as he leaned into him. He reached over and patted his younger brother on the back in an attempt to comfort him.

I'm okay Landry. It's not as bad as it looks."

Landry's voice was hardly audible. "Who did this to you?"

"I don't want no trouble, Landry."

"You let me worry about that. Who did this?" Demanded Landry. For a moment he almost broke down but composed himself.

"What will you do if I tell you?"

"You let me worry about that." Said Landry. I ain't gonna ask again. Who did this?'

He knew his older brother would not stop until he had the answer to his question. Landry was like that; if he wanted information from his younger brother he would persist until he got it. The only reason Gunther hesitated now was because his brother under the right circumstances had a powerful temper. In most situations, his older brother was low-key and very easy going. But when it came to protecting his younger brother he could be very aggressive and ruthless. Sometimes it was uncomfortable watching him in those situations. At those moments it seemed that nothing could stop him from his rage.

"Promise me, Landry, if I tell you, you'll think about it before you do anything."

"What's to think about?"

As far as Gunther was concerned there was a lot for his brother to think about. He had never been beaten like this before, and if his older brother overreacted, which he most certainly would, he could be taken out of the orphanage and sent to prison or even hanged, and they would never be together again.

"I don't want to be apart because of this. All I have is you." Said Gunther. "If they take you away I'll be alone."

Landry dropped his head, and when he came back up his eyes met Gunther's. "Alright." He whispered.

Gunther knew his older brother's words to be true. They had a strong trust and neither would lie to the other.

"It was Josh." Said, Gunther, as he grabbed onto his brother's arm so that he would not leave his side.

Lifting the lantern Landry pointed it toward Josh's empty bed across the room. He had not yet returned.

"Anyone else?" Asked Landry.

"Just him." Said Gunther.

Landry shined the lantern back on Gunther. "For the next few days, you don't leave my side."

Gunther nodded. "What you gonna do?"

Landry dropped his head. "I'm gonna think this through as I promised."

After a few days went by Josh came to realize that Landry wasn't going to retaliate against him for what he had done to his brother. With this realization, he became more confident and bold around Landry and the rest of the boys. He started his old antics again with the taking of the boy's food and shoving some of them around. He would even say harsh words to Landry and Gunther as he passed them, but neither one responded to him.

His older brother's calmness and control surprised Gunther. He had never seen him use such restraint in this type of situation before. It was strange watching him in this manner. On a couple occasions, Mr. Locus tried to corner Gunther demanding to know what had happened to his face. Each time Gunther told him that he accidentally ran into a tree while playing chase. Mr. Locus didn't seem to believe this.

Three weeks after the incident with Josh, Gunther was awakened in the middle of the night by Landry.

"Let's go," Landry whispered.

He didn't ask questions as he rubbed his eyes and rolled out of bed. He didn't need to change into his clothes for Landry had requested the night before for him to sleep in his clothes. There was a duffel bag underneath his bed, already packed with all of his belongings. He grabbed the duffel bag and followed Landry as they made their way through the Lodge. Gunther stopped when he reached Josh's bed. The light from the moon shined through the window upon his face. His skin was gray, his unseeing eyes open, his expression was of fear and panic. Josh was dead. His older brother later told him that he had choked him with his bare hands.

When they reached outside, one of Mr. Locus's horses was tied to a tree nearby. They climbed on board and rode into the night never to return to the orphanage again.

Back in the jailhouse Gunther grew tired of drawing his pistols and placed both guns on top of the desk, he then sat in the chair behind the desk. He felt good about his practice session. Each day he felt himself getting slightly better than the weeks and months before. He felt there weren't many out there who could outgun him. He leaned back in the chair with his bare feet on the desk. Fresh sweat poured down his face.

There was a knock on the door. He reached for one of his pistols and pointed it.

"Who's there?" He said. The front door opened and Maria peeked in. She paused in the doorway when she saw the gun pointed at her. Gunther laughed and then placed the gun back on the desk. He stepped around to greet her. "Well looky here. If it ain't Maria? To what do I owe this pleasant visit?"

"I was in town, and thought I would come by and see how you was doing." She said in her playful tone.

The two hugged. "You know me. I'm doing just fine." Gunther stepped back and looked Maria over. "Ooh Wee. That sure is a pretty dress."

Maria laughed and then spun around to model it for him. "You really like it?"

Gunther rubbed his mustache. "I more than like it." He said. "I love it."

She smiled. "My husband didn't even notice me this morning."

"Then he's a fool."

Maria looked down at her feet. "He's a good man I guess. He works mighty hard though."

"How does he treat you?" Asked Gunther.

"Most the time he don't even know I'm around. All he do is work."

Gunther appeared to be disappointed. "You're kidding me. How could he not notice a pretty thing like you?"

Maria glanced up at him. "Maybe he don't think I'm so pretty."

He stepped closer to her and reached and pulled on her hair. "Don't you understand? Everything about you is pretty." "Your hair." He caressed her cheeks. "Your face." He stepped back and looked her over again. "All of you."

She smiled at him. He rubbed his mustache as he continued to look her over. "Do me a favor doll."

"Anything Gunther." She answered eagerly.

"Take off your dress. I want to see how beautiful you are."

She tried to control her smirk but she couldn't. She hesitated as she twisted her body side to side. "Gunther you know I'm married now. Those days are over between us."

Gunther became visibly upset but managed to calm himself. "I don't give a damn about that." He then walked around the desk and leaned back in the chair. "Why you here Maria?"

She approached the desk and leaned forward. She pointed to her face. "See my face. He hit me this morning."

Gunther leaned forward to get a closer look. "You want me to lock him up?"

"No." She said.

"Then what?"

"I want you to hit him like he hit me."

Gunther leaned back and thought it over. "It don't look like he hit you too hard. Besides what happens between a man and his woman is his business. There's nothing I can do for you."

There was an awkward pause before Maria made her way around the desk and stood before him. "What if I was to take off my dress, would you change your mind?"

Gunther pulled on his mustache. "It depends on what you do when the dress is off."

Maria smiled as she unbuttoned the front of her dress and let it slide to the floor. He watched her taking in every curve. His eyes slowly moved up and down taking in the magnificent view of her thin shapely legs, round wide hips, flat stomach, and her small round breasts.

He rubbed his mustache. "Turn around doll. Let me look at all of you." Maria turned and Gunther stared at her shapely calves, the backs of her silky thighs, her round well-formed buttocks, and her smooth bare back and shoulders. She then turned to face him again.

Gunther climbed to his feet and approached her. "I damn near forgot how beautiful you are." He reached with both hands to caress each full breast. He lifted them to feel their weight. She closed her eyes as he fondled her. He then kissed her on the neck and worked his way to her lips. "If you was my wife, I would work only after I had made love to you. I would only sleep after I had made love to you."

Almost before he finished his words she kissed him. Quickly she removed his clothes. He led her to the back room to his bed. When they were finished they laid still, both wet with sweat and exhausted.

Gunther turned toward Maria. "I'll make a visit to your husband tomorrow. I'll make sure he don't hit you again."

Maria smiled and closed her eyes.

Chapter 22

It was late morning, and the sun was towering and warm. The wild birds were flying from tree to tree, chasing butterflies and small insects. Miles again was in the fields, and his wife Maria watched from her chair on the front porch of their house. Papa and Sage were outside the chicken coup throwing feed for the many chickens that were clucking about.

Mama and Donovan were seated on the porch of her home as well and watched everyone. She hummed a tune as she reached for his hand and squeezed it. "Sure is nice out here." She said.

Donovan nodded in agreement.

She sighed. "I guess I should be tending to our lunch soon."

"I reckon so," Donovan answered.

She sat and hummed for a few more moments before she finally went into the house.

He continued to sit on the porch and trying to remember when he had last felt this relaxed and at ease. He had to always be alert and knowing of his surroundings. His survival depended upon this. It was an art form in fact. He had to appear to be relaxed so as not to draw attention to himself, but at the same time, he observed all that he could. This type of strategy spared his life many times.

In the distance, Donovan saw two men approaching the property on horses. They were the two lawmen that he had run into the following week. He was unarmed, so he left the porch.

Once inside the house, he went into the back bedroom to retrieve his weapons. When he reentered to the main room, he found Mama already at the window looking out. She turned to him. Her expression was uneasy.

She looked down at his two side pistols. "Why you got them pistols?"

"I don't trust them strangers riding up." He answered.

She frowned. "Them men ain't strangers. They be Sheriff Landry and Deputy Gunther." She said. Then she turned back to the window. Donovan stood next to her and did the same.

Sheriff Landry and his brother Deputy Gunther rode silently side by side as they approached the property. Landry did not agree with his brother taking this trip. He felt the Negro family had never been any trouble to them in the past, and he didn't think it was necessary to visit with them now.

Gunther insisted that they do so because he claimed that the Negro Miles beat his wife.

Landry questioned Gunther on this. "Why would we care if that Negro man beat his Negro wife? That's not our business."

Gunther then responded by explaining that Maria had come to him asking for his protection.

Landry frowned at this, then blatantly asked. "When she came to you for your help, did she lay in your bed?"

The wide grin on Gunther's face betrayed him. Landry was not surprised that his younger brother had another married woman in his bed. Women were one of his passions. He had many women friends as he called them that lay in his bed. It didn't matter to Gunther if they were married or single. He laid down with whomever he wanted.

Gunther was not always discrete with the wives, which would cause tension between him and their husbands. This didn't bother Gunther because he seemed to always be looking for confrontation. On a couple of occasions, he had pulled out his pistol and pointed it at an irate husband's head so that they would get the message not to retaliate against him. Once however, he had to kill an enraged husband after he was caught in the man's bed with the man's wife.

How Gunther told it to Landry was that the husband was supposed to be out of town for a few days, yet the husband returned earlier than expected and walked in on Gunther and his wife when they were in the bed. The husband was so angry that he went into the other room to fetch his shotgun. When he came back, Gunther shot and killed him.

Most of the men were terrified of Gunther, and even though they suspected that he was having a relationship with their wives they were apprehensive about confronting him. They had heard about or seen firsthand too many situations when the deputy either threatened folks with his pistols or flat out killed them for whatever reason he could justify with his law.

Out of fear was the only reason most of the married women would agree to have a relationship with the deputy. If a woman refused him he would take this very personal, and would sometimes retaliate against their family members. Mostly focusing on the husband with surprise visits, and threatening jail time for made-up charges, or sometimes occasional beatings at the deputy's whim.

After such treatment of their husbands, the women would give into the deputy's demand for a relationship. Most of the time the relationships were private and discreet, but at other times they were not. This would mostly depend on the deputy's disposition, and how he felt about the husband involved. If he didn't like the husband, then the relationship with the man's wife was in the open. So much so that he would actually go to the man's house and demand him to leave, while he led his spouse into the bedroom.

Landry had warned his deputy many times of the danger of having an association with another man's wife, but Gunther dismissed this warning, claiming that the men were too fearful to be of danger to him.

They guided their horse onto the farm and headed to the porch where Maria was sitting and watching them. She stood to greet them. Her face was worried.

"Howdy boys, what brings you about these parts?"

Gunther laughed. "Did you forget already? It was just yesterday when you was begging me to visit. You said Miles hit you."

Her smile was uneasy. "Things is better between us now."

"Oh," Gunther said as he turned to look at Landry, who had no expression. Then he turned back to Maria. "Well nobody told us, and we're here now."

"I changed my mind, Gunther," Maria said.

Gunther smiled. "Really. Well, it ain't that easy. Me and Landry been on the road for more than an hour. We didn't ride all that way for nothing."

"What do you want from me?" She asked.

He pulled on his mustache. "Me and you can go in the house for a bit. After we're done inside, then me and Landry will leave."

The sheriff spoke up. "That's not necessary Gunther."

"It's necessary. She's wasted our time. I didn't come up here for nothing." Said Gunther.

Maria looked passed the two lawmen to observe Miles watching them. "I can't, my husband's standing right there."

Gunther looked over his shoulder to view Miles, then turned back to Maria. "That's not my problem doll. Make a choice. You and me, or me and him."

The sheriff spoke up again. "That's enough Gunther."

He turned to his brother. "I'll handle this Landry. Back off."

The sheriff frowned but said no more.

"Why do you have to be like this Gunther? Can't we just forget about it?"

The deputy shook his head. "There ain't gonna be no forgetten. What's it gonna be little lady?"

In the yard, Miles dropped his hoe and started walking toward the lawmen.

"He's coming," Maria said.

"You make a choice then, or I'll make it for you." Said the deputy.

She thought it over as Miles made his way across the field. Her husband would not tolerate her being with another man, but how would he react, Maria could not guess. She originally went to Gunther because she felt he would appreciate her. Initially, she wanted from him what her husband was not capable of giving. Before she married Miles she had laid in the deputy's bed several times. Once when she suggested marriage to the deputy he laughed at her. He told her that he was not in love with her and would never marry a Negro woman.

"You talk with him." She said. "Do as you came to."

As Miles approached, the deputy climbed off his horse.

"What's going on here sheriff?" Asked Miles.

The sheriff pointed to his deputy. "You'll need to talk with Gunther on that."

Miles then turned to the deputy. "What is it, deputy?"

The deputy cranked his head to look at the much taller and larger Miles. "Maria tells me you hit her."

Maria watched as Miles turned to her for, then he turned again to face the deputy.

"When did she tell you this?" He asked.

"Yesterday." Answered the deputy.

Miles took a breath and sighed. "We was fighting out here in the yard. Nothing serious though."

Gunther laughed. "Nothing serious? A man not ought to beat his wife. To me that's serious. As big as you is, you could of killed her."

She could see Miles becoming impatient with this. "I didn't beat her. Look at her. She's fine." He said.

The deputy smiled easily. "When I saw her she had a bruise."

"Well, we've worked it out since then deputy. All is forgotten now." Said Miles.

He frowned. "I ain't forgot." Said the deputy.

Maria felt her inside turn when she saw the surprise on her husband's face.

"What do you mean deputy?" Asked Miles

The deputy took a step closer to Miles and had to swing high so as to hit him in the face. The surprised Miles took a step back adsorbing the blow. Soon afterward blood started dripping out of his nose. He leaned his head forward as the blood dripped to the ground.

It was an odd moment for Maria watching her husband get hit like this. Even as the blow connected, Miles never made a sound. Not even a grunt as the blood dripped from his nose.

Stepping forward the deputy took another swing, this time hitting Mile in the throat. He clutched his throat as he struggled for air.

The sheriff watched from the saddle of his horse.

Maria began to sob. "Please deputy. That's enough."

The deputy turned on her, grabbed her by the hair, and pulled her into him. "You're the reason I'm here in the first place. When I think it's enough, you'll know, because I'll be gone." He then shoved her to the porch.

"Leave her alone!" Miles yelled while gasping for his breath.

The deputy turned to him and smiled.

Mama and Donovan watched from the window. When Mama saw the deputy hit her oldest son she stepped away from the window with her hands in her mouth. "Oh Lord no." She cried. When the deputy hit her son again, she turned away not able to watch the beating anymore. "Why is he beaten, my boy?" She cried.

"Don't know," Donovan said. "But I'll find out."

He headed for the door but was surprised when Mama grabbed his arm.

"You can't go out there." She said. "Them men will kill you."

"If I don't they might kill Miles."

"Don't you understand, they is lawmen. There's nothing you can do to help him. You'll just make it worse and get yourself killed." She sobbed. "Then I'll be without both my sons."

While pondering his mother's request, Donovan approached the window to look out once more. Miles was down on his side, as the deputy repeatedly kicked him. As he watched his face became tight with anger. He didn't know of the intentions of the lawmen. Were they going to kill him by beating him to death, or were they roughing him up as some sort of punishment?

He turned to his mother and she looked back at him with her wet tearful face. Her pain was his pain, and his stomach ached to see her this way. The more he thought about the two lawmen the angrier he became. They had caused the suffering of his mother, which in turn caused him, anguish as well. If it weren't for his consideration of his mother's wishes, he would have already been at his brother's side with pistols drawn.

"They're still beating him, Mama." He said.

She burst into tears again. "We can't-do nothing about that. We just have to pray is all. And leave it in the Lord's hands."

Donovan approached her, squeezing the tops of her shoulders. "I can't-do that. This is how Sidney died. Can't let the same be done to my brother."

"After what happened last week, when they sees you with them pistols, that'll be all the excuse they'll need to kill you. Leave them pistols with me. Take away their reason for killing."

"These pistols are the reason I'm still around after all these years."

"These lawmen may be plum down mean, but they is reasonable. They ain't gonna kill you unless you give them a reason." She said.

"Then what's their reason for beating Miles?"

"Don't know," she said. "But I suppose they have one."

Walking without his pistol was like being in public naked. It was just something Donovan didn't do. However, the pistols on his waist would be perceived as a threat to the lawmen. And if the lawmen were threatened then they would most definitely draw their weapons, which would result in a shootout, and the outcome could be death either for Donovan, his brother or the lawmen.

He slipped off his gun belt and dropped it to the floor. "If I don't come back, I want Sage to have all my possessions."

She nodded. "I'll pray for you."

Donovan frowned. "Don't need your prayer. My pistols would have done me fine." He said.

When he stepped out of the house the large man on the horse noticed him first. He bent low to say something to the deputy, and then the deputy looked up to watch Donovan as he headed their way. He was still too far away to hear their words, but their stiff body language told him that the lawmen were surprised and uncomfortable as they talked amongst each other.

The Sheriff pulled out the rifle from the horse's saddle, climbed down and stood next to the deputy.

As Donovan moved toward them he was fearful of confronting two armed men without his pistols at his side for protection. Though he carried a small pistol inside his boot and a knife that was concealed in his rear belt in the small of his back, he still felt no relief because these small weapons were meant for close range. He reminded himself that his goal was to be a distraction so that the deputy would stop beating his brother, which had been achieved when they witnessed him step away from the house.

As he got closer, he turned his attention to the deputy who was standing over Miles. The two men stared at each other. If Mama had not taken Donovan's pistols, the deputy would be dead now. But there was still hope. If he could get close enough, he would gut the deputy with his knife.

The sheriff spoke from behind the deputy. "Didn't think we would see you again. Thought you was just passing through."

Donovan turned to him. "I was, but I changed my mind." He said.

The sheriff eyed Donovan searching for weapons. Afterwards, he seemed satisfied. "I suppose it's no coincidence you being here an all."

Donovan nodded.

"And last week in town, that was no coincidence either, was it?"

"It wasn't," Donovan answered.

"Who are these people to you?" The sheriff asked.

"My family." He said.

"I figured as much." Said the sheriff.

"This man is my brother." Said Donovan.

Gunther blurted out. "I don't give a damn who he is, he broke the law."

"And what law is that?" Donovan demanded.

The deputy was taken aback by Donovan's bold tone. He stepped around Miles and approached him. "Watch your tone boy."

"You don't have a reason," Donovan said. "You make up reasons to suit your law. I've seen it before."

"You saying I'm dishonest." Said Gunther.

"Calm down Gunther." Said the sheriff.

"Dishonest is too good a word for you. You're more of a liar." Said Donovan.

"The hell with you!" Gunther yelled. He then took a swing that just missed Donovan's face as he stepped aside.

The deputy seemed surprised that he had missed, but recuperated by attempting to swing another punch. But Donovan stepped to the side in the opposite direction, which caused the deputy to miss again.

Frowning and breathing heavily, the deputy stared at Donovan, who stared back. Yelling the deputy charged Donovan swinging a fury of punches. This time Donovan held his position as he raised his arms to block each and every punch. The deputy stopped, for none of his punches made its mark.

"You son of a bitch!" He yelled, then he pulled out his pistol and pointed it at Donovan. "Let's see how you dodge bullets."

Donovan debated on reaching for his knife, but with the gun now pointed at his face the odds for success were impossible. To do such an act he would need a distraction, and the deputy was too focused to be distracted. So instead accepted the realization that over the years he had cheated death many times, and this would be the time that death would finally catch him.

"Gunther!" Yelled the sheriff. "Our business is done here."

He continued to point the pistol, with his hand shaking. Donovan was surprised that the sheriff had ordered the deputy to back down, but didn't believe that the deputy would actually do so.

"Now!" Commanded the sheriff. "We've done what we came to do, it's over."

The deputy lowered his gun but refused to put it back into its holster. Instead, he rested it against his thigh. The deputy backed away until he reached his horse, then he climbed on. To Donovan, the deputy seemed undecided about the sheriff's last command.

The sheriff stepped forward with the rifle across his chest. "I don't like you much, and neither does my deputy. You're gonna have to go."

Donovan did not respond.

The sheriff continued. "Because ya mama and papa are decent folks, I'm giving you two weeks with them. After that, I want you gone. And I don't wanna see you again."

"And if I'm not gone?" Asked Donovan.

Puzzled by Donovan's question. "If you're not gone in two weeks, I'll kill you."

Again Donovan did not respond but wished at this moment that he had his pistols.

The sheriff backed away until he reached his horse, and then climbed on. He eyed Donovan before he turned his horse around, and galloped off the property, with his deputy just behind him.

Donovan reached for his brother and pulled him to his feet. His chin was wet with the blood from his nose, and he stood awkwardly leaning to his left from his injured ribs.

"I think he was gonna kill me." Said Miles as he leaned on Donovan for support.

Miles looked up at Maria when she reached for his other arm. "Why did you send them here?"

She didn't know what to say, so she said nothing.

Donovan frowned and she looked away.

Donovan saw Mama, Papa, and Sage walking toward them. Mama burst into tears when she witnessed her injured son. She had never seen him this battered before. "Oh Miles, why would they beat you like this?"

Miles turned to Maria. "Ask her. She knows why."

Mama turned to Maria and said. "I've always known you to be no good."

Maria glanced at all the hostile faces. Even little Sages face was unfriendly. "I didn't want all this to happen." She then left them and went into the house alone.

"Get him to the house," Mama said.

Miles resisted. "I've got work to do."

"You can't work like this Miles." Insisted Papa. "Missing a half day ain't gonna hurt nothin."

Miles was led away to the house where Mama was able to check him over.

Chapter 23

It was after two in the morning when Tracy arrived in her hotel room. She was exhausted, for she had just helped Mary Jane a newlywed mother deliver her first baby. The mother was in labor for several hours, and when the baby finally came, the umbilical cord was wrapped around its neck. Tracy was doubtful that the baby would survive, for she struggled to pull the baby out while unwrapping the umbilical cord. When the head of the baby appeared, its skin was dark purple, and it was not breathing.

After she unwrapped the umbilical cord, she placed her mouth over the baby's face and sucked the liquids from its airways. Within moments the baby desperately took in its first breath and then screamed its first cry.

After the baby was born the young father begged Tracy to stay the night, but she refused insisting on sleeping in her own bed.

She flopped on her bed, too tired to even change her clothes that were stained with the mother's afterbirth. On her back, she closed her eyes. Her father came to mind. She wondered how he maintained his exhausting schedule as a doctor for all those years. How did he sustain his freshness when sometimes he hardly slept at all?

As a child, she once asked him. "Why do you work so hard?"

And he responded with. "I work hard because lives depend on it." He then stroked her little chin and said. "I hope someone shows my family the same consideration when it's needed."

She dozed off as she thought of him.

Later that night Tracy opened her eyes to the darkness. She lay listening for noises within her room, but there was only silence. She closed her eyes again but nearly jumped out of bed when she heard the knock on the door.

Now alert she sat up in her bed and watched the door. Some time went by before another knock thundered across the room. Managing to her feet she approached the door and leaned on it. "Who's there?"

"It's me." Said Landry from behind the door.

She unlocked the door, pulled it open, and then sat down on her bed. Landry ducked under the doorway as he stepped in.

"It's late." She said.

The moon's reflection provided some light, but not enough. He pulled some matches from his pocket and lit the lantern on the desk. The rays of the lantern replaced the blackness. Tracy was on the edge of the bed with her head down and eyes closed.

"I need to talk with you." He said.

"What about?"

Landry sat next to her, the bed sank from his heavyweight, which caused Tracy to fall into him. Opening her eyes she adjusted herself on the bed.

Landry smiled. She rubbed her eyes and sleepily looked around the room.

"Where was you tonight?" He asked.

"Delivering a baby."

He tried to sound excited. "Whose baby?"

"Mary Ann Miller. She had a little girl." She said.

Landry nodded. "Oh." He said. "I hope all went well."

"It did."

There was more silence between them as they both gazed at the floor. Finally, Landry spoke. "Me and Gunther stopped at Mama's property today."

It now made sense why Landry was visiting her at such a late hour. At this moment she felt herself in danger as the fear of her situation filled her stomach. If he went to Mama's house, did he run into Donovan? And if so what became of this meeting? And why was he here now?

Maintaining her composure she turned to him. "And what happened?"

He studied her as if he was trying to somehow read her thoughts. "Donovan was there." He said.

Under his gaze, she turned away.

"Did you know he was there?" He asked.

"I did." She admitted, knowing the truthful approach would be the only safe route in this situation. For he trusted her, and the consequences of that broken confidence would be great. And in her evaluation of the situation, she felt strongly that he was already aware of her knowledge of Donovan's whereabouts. His questioning of her was more for confirmation.

After giving this more thought, she began to convince herself that she had not really done anything wrong. She knew of Donovan's whereabouts, but that shouldn't be offensive to Landry. However, it was strange of him visiting her at such a late hour. Maybe something happened.

After she calmed herself, she asked. "What's this about Landry?"

He sighed. "Why didn't you tell me about him?"

"What is there to tell, Landry?" She asked. "He is of no importance to me."

"Since that day in town, we've been looking for him." He said.

"Why?"

"Because he's dangerous."

"Dangerous how?" She asked.

He watched her. She might have gone too far. She tried to replay in her mind how she sounded when she asked the last question. Tracy hoped that she did not come across as defensive.

"How well do you know him?" Asked Landry.

Tracy looked away, she felt off guard. It was no secret that Landry had feelings for Tracy, and wanted to initiate a relationship with her. However, Tracy was not interested in a romantic courtship with him and had been able to avoid his advances. If Landry suspected that she had feelings for Donovan or any other man for that matter, then Tracy and the man she cared for would be in danger. The sheriff was a jealous man and would not tolerate Tracy choosing another man other than himself. Especially after she had put him off for the past two years.

"I don't know him at all." She said.

Once again he studied her. "How did you come to know he was at the house?"

"I saw him there." She said. "Last week when I was visiting Mama, he was there."

"And you didn't think to tell me this?"

"I didn't know you was looking for him." She said. "I'm not in the law business. I don't worry about such things. My patients are my worry. If I had known you were interested I would have told you." She said.

As if he understood, Landry nodded. Tracy was relieved.

But then he asked. "Did you treat him?"

As if she didn't understand the question, she stared at him.

He went on to explain. "Last week he took a bullet in the shoulder. Did you help him?"

Again she looked away, how would she answer this question. What did he already know? Was he only seeking confirmation again? Landry was difficult to read. If she answered differently than what he had already known, then he would become suspicious of her. Then the mistrust would seep in and further probing would be done.

Turning to him again she answered. "Yes, I helped him." Tracy became afraid again when he frowned. "If I had known, Landry I wouldn't have. You must believe me."

Disappointed he looked at the floor. "I figured as much." He admitted. "You couldn't have known about this man. I suspect many folks wouldn't."

She was curious of what Landry suspected about Donovan. What did he know about him that she didn't?

"What kind of man is he Landry?" She asked.

"Dangerous." He said.

She hesitated before she asked her next question. "Forgive me, Landry, I'm not in your law business. I don't know people as you do. What makes you suspect this Donovan to be dangerous?"

He seemed surprised by her question and stood to his feet. He paced in front of her. This time she did go too far. She wished that she could take the question back.

"You seem interested in this Donovan fella." He said as he faced her.

"Only because of you." She said. "You're focused on this man as if he's done something to you, and I'm just trying to understand what."

His face and body relaxed as he nodded as if he understood again. "It's Gunther." He admitted. "I'm afraid for Gunther."

Now it all made sense to Tracy. Gunther was Landry's brother, his only family, and he loved him dearly. Landry had admitted to Tracy on many occasions that his brother's reckless ways would one day get him killed. He feared the day of finding his brother dead in the street with a bullet in his face because he had crossed the wrong person. The Sheriff was troubled that Donovan could possibly be a threat to his brother.

"Gunther hates him," Landry said. "He wants to square off with him. But I gave him orders to stay away. This Donovan is not one for him to take on alone."

"Why? How is this Donovan different from the men you've come across before."

The bed sunk as Landry sat back down next to Tracy. "His eyes." Said Landry. "You can know about a man through his eyes. Some men's eyes are playful and fun, others have sadness and pain, some have sickness, some men just got plain mean eyes. And most men that come across me and Gunther have fear in their eyes. But the eyes of this Donovan are dead. I can't read them. Personally, I've never come across eyes like that." He paused. "Except maybe yours Tracy. I can't read your eyes either."

Tracy thought she understood partly of what Landry was saying about Donovan's eyes. They were different, but to her, they didn't appear dead or unreadable as Landry claimed. When she looked into Donovan's eyes she clearly saw a glimpse of his pain and despair. Through the image of his eyes, she did not dare try to envision the great anguish that he must have survived over the years. And even if she had known Donovan from now to the end of her life, she would probably never know of the experiences that brought on his pain, for he seemed to be reserved to a fault, and would never talk of these experiences.

Landry was right to suspect Donovan to be a dangerous man. All the scars embedded on his body convinced her as much. Judging from his wounded body, Tracy figured that emotionally he had to be just as wounded. Yet Landry would not know this for he was not present to see his injured body.

Landry's judgment was based on witnessing Donovan face an impossible situation last week. Two armed men with their pistols pointed at him, and somehow Donovan managed to kill both of them. Most men if not all would have never even attempted to reach for their holstered pistols when two armed men already had theirs out. The chance for survival would be impossible. And yet Donovan survived, with new scars on his body and soul to mark another battle.

But what probably troubled Landry the most was that on the day of the shooting, Donovan refused to back down from his brother Gunther the deputy, who was also stubborn in these situations.

She found herself thinking of Donovan often since she had first met him last week. She thought of his face, and how serious it was, hardly ever smiling, maybe lost within his own endless thoughts. He could have been reliving the experiences of his past that were tormented with sorrow. Or maybe he was just lonely. As she thought of him she remembered that he did not laugh at all. If he found something to be amusing he would nod and smile. But no sounds of laughter came from his lips. She wondered what would Donovan find amusing. So much she wanted and needed to know about this man.

"What are you thinking about?" Said Landry, interrupting her thoughts.

"Nothing." She said. "Just listening is all."

"I gave him two weeks." He said. "I told him if he's not gone in two weeks, he's as good as dead."

She was relieved that for the moment Donovan was safe. "You've never done that before."

"Done what?"

"Give a man you don't like so much time. You and your brother usually run them out that day." She said. "Sometimes you just kill them on the spot."

"True, but them men deserved to die. I knew they would come back later to kill us. This Donovan is different than those men; he came upon us today without his weapons. I figure he's not planning to kill anybody unless they is planning on killing him. And this is why he's dangerous to my brother. Twice Gunther has made it clear that he wants him dead. This is why I gave Gunther orders to stay away from the house, to stay away from Donovan. If he runs into Donovan under no circumstances is he to challenge him. Besides Mama and Papa are good folks, and they ain't never caused me and Gunther no trouble. Mama makes us apple pies and cooks for us from time to time. I figures I at least owe her some time with her son. But after the two weeks, he ain't ever coming back."

"Why does Gunther hate Donovan so?" She asked.

"Forgive me Tracy, but he doesn't like colored folks. And he especially don't like a colored man that ain't afraid of him."

Tracy nodded in understanding. "Will Gunther stay away from him?"

Landry thought it over. "I've made myself very clear to him. He won't go against my words. He knows better."

All was quiet as the small fire from the lantern flickered and fought to smother some of the darkness within the room.

"I hope I didn't make a mistake Tracy. I'm thinking we should have run Donovan out today. Two weeks is a long time. A lot can happen between now and then. My brother is all I have. Nothing can happen to him…Nothing." He said.

She listened. He turned to her. Fighting the urge Tracy did not look away. Landry leaned forward. "I care about you too." He said. And then he kissed her, and she returned the kiss and then pulled away.

Tracy tried to spare Landry's rejected feelings by coming across kindheartedly. "I don't want a relationship, Landry. We've talked about this before." She finished.

"I've been more than patient, Tracy. How long do you want me to wait? Most men would have given up by now." Tracy was silent. Landry continued. "Is it because of who I am? Because I'm a white man?"

Again Tracy was silent as she looked at the floor. The bed shifted as Landry made his way to his feet. His face was rigid as he watched her. "I'm good to you Tracy, and I've given you plenty of time to decide about us. Most men wouldn't be this patient." He said. Landry turned and headed to the front door, he pulled it open, but before he stepped through he turned again to her. She watched him. "By now most folks know how I feel about you. Don't make a fool of me. You know me well enough that I don't take lightly to being made a fool of." He then ducked under the door and closed it behind him.

Tracy blew out the flame in the lantern and then slipped back into her bed. She wondered how much longer could she hold Landry off. She didn't want a relationship with him, but not because he was a white man, but more because of the type of man that he was. She found him to be temperamental, callous, brutal, and most important she was afraid of him.

Within the darkness of her room, she closed her eyes and once again thought of Donovan. She was saddened, for in two weeks time, he would be out of her life forever.

Chapter 24

Maria had packed a few days worth of clothes. She loaded the bag into the wagon. Because of the mistreatment from Miles and his family, she thought it would be best to leave for a while. Since she hadn't seen her father in over six months, she decided to pay him a visit and to stay with him until the situation calmed itself. Traveling by wagon it would almost be a full three-hour ride until she arrived at her father's place.

Since the incident with the lawmen yesterday, no one would respond to any of her attempts to reconcile. On a few occasions, she tried to speak with Mama but was only disappointed when Mama silently avoided her by going into the house. Rejected and alone Maria would turn and walk that long awkward journey back to her porch. When Papa was nearby, she on two occasions attempted to strike up a conversation with him but was surprised when he did not even acknowledge her presence. It was as if she was a ghost trying to communicate to the living, but the living could not see or hear her.

Rightly so her husband Miles was the most hostile. Not only did he not speak with her, but he would sometimes stop in the middle of his work and stare at her with his resentful eyes. Many of those times he would not turn away until she looked away, or went back into the house.

The loneliness of her situation sunk in the most when she found that she was not invited to eat dinner at Mama's house. Maria instead sat alone in her own house while her husband and the rest of the family ate and enjoyed a wonderful family meal that Mama had prepared for them just across the way. Since she and Miles were first married a year ago, Maria could not recall a single day that she and her husband did not eat dinner together at his Mama's house. Until now that is.

Maria climbed into the wagon and looked out across the field. Mama was on her porch in the chair looking the opposite direction, obviously to avoid Maria. She turned to her husband, who was steadily overturning the land with his shovel. The ground crunched when the shovel hit its mark. His shirt, arms, and face were wet with his sweat. Watching Miles unnoticed for a long time, she wanted to cry. She was not even gone yet, and already she terribly missed him. How could she hurt someone she loved so much? She should have never confided in the deputy, and most importantly she should have never laid in that awful man's bed. If Miles were to ever find out about her and the deputy's night together, he would most definitely end their marriage. Somehow she had to make things right with her husband, but for now, they needed time away from each other. Hopefully, it wouldn't be too much time.

When Maria finally arrived at her father's house, for the most part, it was just how she had remembered it six months earlier. The house was a small run down shack with two rooms. The outside was worn, faded and cracked by years of weather. Opened wide and dangling freely was the front door, it did not have a latch to hold it in place. In this house, the nonexistent glass windows were replaced by moveable shutters, which were all open at this time.

The condition of the surrounding land was just as run down as the house itself. In between the very sparse patches of corn, tomatoes, and potatoes, thick beds of weeds were growing. So much in fact that in some areas it was hard to know where the weeds and the crops were separate. Even the chickens close by were sparse in numbers. Maria counted three of the skinniest chickens she had ever seen. As she continued to look around, the inside of her stomach churned with sadness. Miles was right, she should be grateful that he worked so hard to support his family.

When Maria walked through the open front door, the awful smells instantly filled her nostrils. Some of which seemed like urine, feces and spoiled food. She covered her nose and mouth with her hand and placed her suitcase on the dirt-soiled floor.

She called out. "Daddy...Daddy are you here?" She waited for an answer. There was none. She stepped into the front room. The sun through the open shutters provided enough light for her to a see pile of dirty dishes and pans on the table. One of the chairs under the table was turned over on its side. There were small piles of dirt scattered about the floor from the winds blowing through the open front door. Even in the corner by the stove, she noticed some tumbleweeds.

Maria stepped deeper into the small house. "Daddy. It's me, Maria." Again she stood quietly listening. And again there was no response. Less than a step away she heard tiny feet scatter across the floor and disappear somewhere in the wall. A mouse she thought.

At the back of the room, there was a stained brown curtain that hung from the ceiling and spread from one side of the wall to the other. She had no doubt that her father was behind that curtain. But what she was not certain of was his condition. Was he alive or dead?

Standing behind the sheet she hesitated before she finally reached up and pulled it back exposing the unknown. She was relieved to find her father there. The smell was strongest in this room, which was barely large enough to house the small bed for which he now slept.

Maria jerked the curtain back to the wall. The rays from the open shutters and front doorway gleamed on her father. He appeared lifeless, his skin was tight on his bones; she guessed he was no more than a hundred pounds, which was thin for a man that was over six feet. His once black face had a pale whitish tone, and his gray kinky hair was matted and grimy. She sobbed at the sight of his pitiful state.

With his eyes closed, he moaned from his bed. "Who's there?" His voice was dry and almost inaudible.

Quickly she answered. "It's me, Maria."

Her father tried to laugh with excitement, but instead, he hacked an awful cough straight from his gut.

"Don't talk," Maria instructed. "I'm here now. I'm gonna take care of you." She glanced around the filthy house, wondering where to start in such a mess. She was going to have to clean up and get rid of the smells, which seemed to be everywhere. She would need to change and wash her father's clothes and bed, for the strongest of the smells were on him. Her father must have been too weak to move, for his bed smelled atrociously of urine and feces. Or he had just given up on life. Maria turned her head and vomited on the floor.

Forcing herself she again stared at her father in his weak incoherent state. She wondered if there was anything that could be done for him. Were these his final minutes in life? After watching him for a long time, she decided that if it was his time, she could at least make him comfortable. Her first priority would be to get him, water and food. She wondered when was the last time he had either. Then she would clean him, his clothes and the house.

"I'll be back daddy. I'm gonna get you some water. Then I'm gonna fix you something to eat." He didn't answer.

With that, she went into the small kitchen area and grabbed the large empty aluminum pale with its long handle. Then she climbed into her wagon and rode it to the river less than a mile away. Once she reached the river, she dipped the pale into the water and scooped it fully. On her way back she spilled about one-third of the water from the bumpy ride. Inside the house, she lit the iron stove and placed the aluminum bucket of water on top. Once the water had boiled for a bit to remove the bacteria, she then set the bucket aside and dipped a tin cup into the hot water and set it aside to cool.

Once it cooled she carefully carried the water to her father, and slowly poured it into his mouth. At first, he choked, coughed and spluttered the water on the front of her dress. But she patiently continued on, until all was gone. Then she went back to the kitchen and scooped up another cup. In all, she made five trips. Just from the water alone, she could see that her father's demeanor was changing. Though his eyes remained closed, he seemed to be more alert.

Next, she went to the yard and grabbed one of the skinny chickens and wrung its neck. She was surprised how easy it was to kill. Maybe because the chickens were smaller and weaker than the ones at home, and therefore she was not intimidated by them. She cut the guts out and laid them over a tree to dry out. Then she pulled the stiff feathers off its yellow bumpy skin, and then hung the chicken over the tree to dry out as well.

While the chicken dried on the tree, Maria gathered some wood and some large rocks nearby. She placed the rocks in a small circle and then placed the wood inside the rocks. She then sprinkled dry twigs on top of the wood and set a match to it. Within minutes a small fire erupted. When the fire was large enough Maria found a spear like stick and stabbed it through the chicken. She then sat on ground and extended the chicken over the flame. For less than an hour, Maria maintained this position, switching hands every so often after the weight of the chicken became unbearable. When the chicken was finally finished she set it on top of one the of rocks and shook her hands of their aches.

Once the chicken had cooled Maria carried it into the house, to the back room where her father was. She pulled tiny pieces off and fed him by hand. He chewed and moaned with pleasure. It sounded more like a low hum. While she fed him she was surprised to see him gaining his strength. His eyes were now open, and his dark skin was changing to its original tone. After gulping almost the entire chicken by himself, her father was ready to talk.

"How's my girl?" He asked.

"I've been better, Daddy. I don't like to see you this way." There was a moment of silence as Maria fought her tears. She continued. "What happened to you? How did things get so bad?"

He reached his hand out and she grabbed it. "I'm getting old now. I don't got much to live for these days. I just want to leave this world."

The tears flowed down her face. "Why do you feel this way?"

"I've felt this way ever since your mama died when you was a young on. But I had to stay strong to take care of you. But you is all grown and married now. Don't need me no more. And I'm too sick to take care of myself now."

"What you sick with daddy?"

"Don't know, I ain't seen no doctor. I just knows I'm sick with something."

"Why ain't you seen no doctor if you is sick?"

"I'm too sick to fetch one."

"I'll fetch one, I'll get Dr. Tracy."

He waved his hand weakly. "No. It's too late for that. A doctor can't help me now…Besides this world is hard and cruel, I'm ready to leave it."

Maria was quiet for a long time as she watched him. Against her father's wishes she could fetch Dr. Tracy, but by the time she returned a few hours later he could be dead. And she selfishly wanted to spend his last minutes with him. As she watched him, she couldn't help but feel partly responsible for his condition. If she had visited him sooner and more often, maybe his poor health would have been avoided. The guilt escalated when she realized that the only reason she was visiting her father now was because she was fighting with her husband and his family, otherwise who knows when she was planning to visit him.

It wasn't that she didn't love her father, for she loved him dearly, and she knew that he loved her, but her father was not good at expressing his feelings, and most of the time when they were together they hardly spoke at all. There wasn't any anger or tension between them, they both just went about their own business trying to stay out of one another's way. This was the main reason she hardly ever visited her father. Because of how she was raised by him, she didn't have an emotional attachment to him and therefore didn't think that he needed her around.

But now watching him suffer, she realized that she had misjudged him, and she would not leave his side. "Daddy, why don't you come home with me?" She asked.

"No, I don't want to be a burden to you and your new husband."

"You wouldn't be. And we have an extra room you could use."

"What about your husband? How would he feel about this?"

"I'm his wife." She said. "He would want me to be happy. And you staying with us would make me happy."

From his bed, he thought it over. "Are you sure about this?" He asked.

"I'm sure." She answered. "I'll get you cleaned up, and then I'll clean up this place, and we'll be gone the day after tomorrow."

She felt warm inside as she watched the slight grin on her father's face.

"Good." He said, and then he went to sleep.

Chapter 25

Donovan stood on the porch looking out into the fields, as his older brother Miles worked vigorously. The early morning air was chilled, but the sunrise was combating the cold with some warmth of its own. This was his eleventh day with his family, and during this time he had come to respect Miles for his work ethic. The only time that he witnessed Miles pause for a break was at lunchtime, or when he needed water. Other than those times, Miles worked that land none stop until there was no more light in the sky. Donovan seriously believed that if Miles could see through the darkness, he would probably work the land well into the night.

Behind him the door creaked open, Donovan turned and it was Mama. Even though he was a long ways away from any danger, he was still apprehensive about noises from behind.

"Breakfast is ready baby." She said.

He turned away and watched out into the fields again. "Thank you, Mama. I'll be right in." He said. "What about Miles?"

"Miles will come when he's ready. He don't like to be bothered when he's working." She then went back into the house.

Unnoticed Donovan continued to watch his brother as he dug hard into the land and turned it over. His movements were steady and rhythmic, never slowing or speeding at any moment. Watching him one could get the impression that he would never get tired.

Donovan glanced around the land it was about fifteen acres in all. In the past few days since he had first arrived, he watched Miles work and turn this land, getting it ready for spring planting. Just looking around he could see that there was only a small section of land left that needed to be turned, and by the end of the day, Miles would have finally completed this, leaving none of the land untouched.

As Donovan watched Miles he couldn't help but feel some guilt for being absent and not working alongside his brother for all those years. He felt that he should have stayed and helped his brother support the family. Yet at that time seven years ago he made a decision, a decision that changed his life. His choice was to either stay with his family, his son or to go after the men that raped and murdered his beloved wife Sidney. At the time Donovan didn't feel that his choice would be such a sacrifice to his family or his son because he didn't think he would be gone for more than a few months at the most. For whatever reason, it didn't cross his mind, that he could possibly be killed and never to return. However, after he had been wounded on many occasions, he soon realized that the odds of him coming back to his family or his son were not likely. And yet seven years later, he had somehow survived and made it back. Even though it appeared that he was safe at this moment, he actually was not safe, and probably would never be again. He had many enemies. Most of which if they could, would shoot him in the back.

When Donovan stepped into the house the fried ham and bacon filled his nostrils. Mama, Papa, and Sage were already seated at the table waiting for him. Donovan seated himself in the chair directly across from Sage. He noticed that Sage avoided him by looking intently at his plate. Mama closed her eyes as she lowered her head, "Let us pray." She said.

Papa and Sage followed Mama's lead as they also lowered their heads and closed their eyes, but Donovan did not. And no one expected him to do so because they soon realized that he would never lower his head or close his eyes for prayer.

After Mama finished thanking the Lord for their meal, and the safety of her family she opened her eyes and smiled at Donovan, then they all began to eat. At breakfast, Mama and Papa discussed the chores that would need to be completed for the day. It was agreed that along with her usual cooking, Mama would also need to do laundry, which she did once a week. Papa's chores would consist of going to the river to fetch Mama some water so that she could wash the dirty clothes. This was done when the well water out front was low. Papa would also help Sage feed the chickens and plant various vegetable seeds where Miles had previously turned and softened the soil.

Donovan and Sage ate in silence as Mama and Papa talked further about their chores for the day.

"Maybe I can help," Donovan said.

Mama frowned. "Oh, no child. You ain't got to help us none. Besides the sheriff only gave you two weeks with us. We don't want you to spend that time working, you need to rest yourself before you have to go." After this statement, she sadly looked down at her empty plate. "I guess after that we won't see you no more." She paused for a long time. "I wish the sheriff wasn't like that. But if he wants you to go, you have to go. What a shame, you just got here and we hadn't had time to enjoy you." She raised her head and smiled at Donovan. "At least my prayers was answered. You is still alive and Sage finally got to see his daddy."

Papa agreed. "The sheriff and his deputy are dangerous men. They've killed many men over the years. It's a shame that they has it out for you like that. I just can't figure it, I'm just glad they didn't kill you. It's best you not go into town at all if they sees you they may change their minds and cut your time short."

Donovan nodded his understanding of the situation. However, he had not decided if he were leaving or not. As a matter of fact, until now he hadn't given it much thought. His main thoughts have been on how he could develop a relationship with his son. Whether the sheriff and his deputy wanted him to leave town was of no importance to him. If Donovan felt it necessary to leave then he would do so, but if he felt that he wanted to stay then he would stay. He didn't spend all those years away from his son, just to come back so that he could be run off again. He in all those years had accomplished what he felt was needed, which was to hunt down and kill all the men that murdered and raped his wife, his son's mother. However, now he had a different purpose. He was going to reestablish and develop a relationship with his son. He was just as determined to accomplish this as he was on finding and executing his wife's attackers.

His anger escalated as he thought about the sheriff and his deputy threatening him to leave town, to leave his son. If he had had his pistols on him that day, he would have made it clear to the lawmen that he was staying, and if they disagreed they could settle it at that moment with their pistols. Since he was not armed he did what only made sense, he backed down, for the moment anyway.

Donovan thought about his dilemma further. Was violence the only solution with the lawmen? He was greatly tired of this warfare. It was an endless black hole. He would kill a man, and that man would have family or friends that would come after him seeking revenge. So he would then have to kill them in self-defense, and yet they would also have family or friends that would want retribution as well. This cycle of bloodshed and vengeance seemed to never end. Knowing what he knew now about the atrocities of bloodshed, the cycle of vengeance and that these acts would keep him away from his son for so many years, he might not have made the choice to go after those men that assaulted his family. Instead, he would have remained a peaceful farmer like his brother Miles and would have established a solid bond with his son Sage.

His son he thought. Somehow he had to establish a friendship with his son. As of now, they didn't have a relationship, hardly talking at all to one another. It was sometimes awkward to be in his son's presence. He could sense how uncomfortable his son was around him. At a time in Donovan's younger life, some considered him a master when dealing with folks and maintaining friendships. It was in those earlier days that many folks young and old would take time out of their day to visit with Donovan. He couldn't walk through town, or into a shop without someone grabbing him for a quick chat. All too well sometimes folks would even, drop by the house to visit with him. Donovan remembered how angry Papa use to get when these folks would stop by keeping his youngest boy from his chores. If the visitors stayed too long Papa would eventually send them on their way. In those days he had an easy way with people. He trusted all and he liked all. Even if a friend had done him wrong, he didn't take it personally. He would instead try to understand their point of view of why they acted as they did. Then in his mind, all was forgotten.

That all changed when they took Sidney from him. He had felt no greater pain of loss than on that horrendous day. So much suffering in fact, that he believed that he would not overcome the burden of this torment, and he himself would die shortly from the grief alone. Maybe the only reason he was able to survive his wife's death, was because of deep inside, he knew he would find every man responsible for her demise and bring them to justice, his own personal justice.

He trusted no one and had no friends. Over the past several years in his travels he had met maybe two people that he considered trustworthy, and yet he still did not establish a friendship with them. His only purpose was to get information from them in order to continue his search for the killers. This isolated approach with people could create a problem for him and Sage. Especially since Sage himself seemed to be secluded from folks as well.

For a moment Donovan watched his son across from him, looking down at his empty plate. He was much more isolated than Donovan ever was. Even though Donovan was inaccessible much of the time, he was still very aware of his surroundings. When folks walked by, he looked them in the eye, when he ate his meals he looked about to see who was in the environment. When folks spoke to him he would speak back. And when he needed information he didn't hesitate to ask someone. This type of approach, not only helped him find the killers but also helped him survive all these years. The way Sage was now, he could not survive on his own. Though he was only fourteen years old, these habits would carry over to his adulthood and he would be killed or tormented for appearing helpless and weak.

Thinking back to the lawmen, was there a way to handle the situation without bloodshed? By far he wasn't defenseless to the lawmen, and he could care less what they demanded of him. However, he was home now with his son and he wanted to get out of this cycle of violence. At the end of the two weeks, if he was to face the lawmen and possibly shoot them down, he most likely wouldn't be able to stay in town, for a posse would be looking to hang him for his crime. This wouldn't do him and Sage's relationship any good. No telling when he would be able to come back to visit him.

He could possibly leave before the two-week period and take his son with him, but most likely Sage would not want to come, for Donovan was still a stranger to him. And even if Sage did come, what kind of life could Donovan provide for him? There were many folks out there that wanted him dead, and as it were Donovan was constantly on the alert for a potential attack. It wasn't safe for Sage to be in the middle of all this.

Also, Donovan didn't underestimate these two lawmen. He viewed them as dangerous, and it was very possible that he could be killed by them. Anytime one faced another man with a pistol in hand let alone two men, he was risking his life. But at the same time, the lawmen would also be risking their lives if they faced Donovan. A face-off would not be a good outcome for either participant.

After the numerous gun battles and various injuries, his intuition strongly informed him that the end of his existence was approaching. It was not reasonable to believe that one could continue over time, to put themselves in numerous life and death situations and survive every time.

Sage was safest where he was now, which was with his grandparents. However, his goal was the same, he needed to establish a relationship with his son. He had just less than two weeks to decide on what course of action if any to take with the lawmen. This would be plenty of time to come to a decision.

"I have money," Donovan said. "I can help in that way."

Mama reached and grabbed his hand. "No child, you keep your money. You'll need that for traveling."

"I have more than I need Mama. I can give you some."

Mama shook her head. "No…you keep your money."

Donovan nodded for she wasn't going to change her mind. She was stubborn on this. However, if the time came that he decided to leave, he would place the money in a location where he was sure they would find it. He looked at Sage again who was still looking down at his plate. The sheriff's threat was a reminder to Donovan that he didn't have much time with his son. Not because of the two weeks that they gave him, but because Donovan knew in his heart that one of his enemies would find and kill him.

"Sage," Donovan called to his son. Sage looked up in surprise. The strange man across from him had called his name. He looked back down at his plate. "What chores are you doing today?" He asked.

Sage was quiet until finally, he answered with. "Feed some chickens." He said.

Donovan continued to watch his son. He was irritated that his son would not raise his eyes to him. "Sage, I want you to look at me." He said and waited until his son did so. Sage raised his eyes to look at this strange man who claimed to be his father. Donovan continued, "When folks are talking, you need to look at them." Sage nodded uncomfortably at the man.

Donovan leaned closer to Sage as he locked eyes on him. "I know I'm a stranger to you, but I'm gonna ask you something." Sage nodded and Donovan continued. "I'm your father, but I know you don't see me as such since I ain't been around, but I want to make a go at being friends with you."

Sage looked down at his plate as he thought it over. He then raised his eyes to meet Donovan's. He cleared his throat. "I don't have friends." He admitted and turned to his plate to avoid the strange man's reaction.

Donovan sighed. "I don't have friends either," he said. "It's been a long time since I've had one. Sometimes it's just better that way."

Sage looked up. It was hard for him to believe that a man as handsome and brave as this stranger didn't have a friend. One would think that friends would come easily for him. Sage, on the other hand, understood all too well why he didn't have friends. There were a few reasons, but the main reason was because of how he appeared. He had a wicked scar across the left side of his face over his eye. On his neck, chin, and upper chest, his skin was raised and rubber-like. From the fire, Mama had told him. But she never gave him the details, except that it happened when he was very young.

Sage eyed his plate. "I'm too ugly to have friends." He said, and for a long moment, there was silence. When he finally looked up the strange man's eyes were locked on him. He could see a hint of anger or sadness in the man's expression. At that instant, he was fearful of the stranger.

The strange man leaned forward to get closer, but Sage out of a moment of fear sat back in his chair. Donovan grabbed his shirt and pulled him over the table so that they could smell the breakfast on each other's breath.

Sage grunted in surprise and then started his customary moaning which was brought on by fear. "Don't hurt me." He gasped.

Papa stood and grabbed Donovan's extended arm. "What are you doing?"

"I'm not gonna hurt him." He said. "We're gonna have our first father to son talk, and I want him close enough to hear every word."

Still holding steady Papa said. "You needs to tell him that. In these last few days, he's seen you do some curious things, he's a little troubled by you right now. Hell, we all are." Papa then released his grip and sat back in his chair. "First you show up after we thought you was dead. Then you gun down those men in town. Then the other day with the sheriff and his brother. And not to mention you almost killed your brother a few days back."

Donovan nodded his understanding and then continued to Sage. "I'm not going to hurt you. I would hurt myself before I hurt you. I just want to talk." Sage nodded and Donovan continued. "Whatever you want to say to me, just say it. I won't judge you." Again Sage nodded, and Donovan went on. "I'm your father, but since I haven't been much of a father, you can call me Donovan."

Sage was terrified when the strange man first grabbed him, but he soon came to realize the man's approach was too mild and slow to have the intention of doing any harm. He felt it odd to hear this man claim to be his father. There had to be a mistake. It was not believable that he was the offspring of a man of this stature. This man was brave, Sage was a coward, this man was strong, Sage was weak, this man was confident, Sage was timid, this man was handsome, and Sage was ugly. There was no match from what Sage could see.

While up close he studied the man's face to see if he could see a hint of his own. Nothing. Of course, his grandmother had always said that he looked more like his mother than his father.

"Don-o-van." Said Sage slowly only repeating what the strange man had asked to be called.

Donovan nodded. "This is what I want you to know." He paused to make sure he had Sages complete attention. "I've traveled across this country for many years, and I've come across many folks. What I've found is that most men walking this land is ugly in one way or another. Some are ugly on the outside; others are ugly on the inside. A man that's ugly on the inside is the most evil you can come across. He'll hurt you, your family and anyone close to you. Because he's ugly on the inside many times you won't know about him until it's too late."

Sage cleared his throat and spoke. "Then what?"

Donovan released the boy and leaned back. "Sometimes the people you care most about end up dead. Other times they hurt you so much that you wish you was dead. Unless you ugly on the inside, you ain't got nothing to be ashamed of."

He thought about what Donovan was saying. His eyes were locked on Donovan's face not wanting to turn away. He clung to every word because he felt they directly affected him. There weren't many days that went by that he didn't sometimes wish he were dead. And maybe for the first time in his life, he felt some relief about his circumstances. He was ugly and there was no changing that, but he was ugly on the outside not the inside like the evil people that Donovan was talking about. He was so grateful to realize this new information that he found it difficult to fight his urge to weep with relief. Sage watched Donovan as he stared at the floor. He wondered what Donovan was thinking about.

After a long silent pause, Donovan finally looked up. His face was slightly tense but calmed as he stared back at Sage. "I'm gonna help you with the chickens. Maybe we can talk a bit." Said Donovan.

"What we gonna talk about?" Asked Sage. Normally Sage wouldn't ask such a question of an adult or anyone for that matter, but Donovan had said he could say whatever came to his mind, and what came to his mind was what they would talk about?

"Don't know," Said Donovan. "I reckon whatever comes to mind."

"What If I ain't got nothing to say?" Asked Sage.

"Maybe I'll have something to say."

"What if you ain't got nothing to say either?"

"Then we won't worry much about talking I guess."

Sage thought this over. "If none of us is talking, is that okay?"

"Yes."

Sage was relieved and stood to his feet and walked around the table to where Donovan was sitting. He looked Donovan in the eyes. "You ready."

Donovan nodded. "I reckon so."

And Sage led the way as Donovan followed him out the front door.

Almost unnoticed Mama and Papa quietly watched the unusual conversion between Donovan and Sage. To them, this exchange was unusual because they were surprised by Sage's forthcoming behavior, for they had never witnessed him do this with anyone, not even themselves. Even after the two had left the house to go feed the chickens and maybe talk as they called it, Mama and Papa remained at the table dumbfounded watching the front door where Sage and Donovan had just exited.

Chapter 26

Donovan followed Sage across the field toward the chicken yard. He stood back as Sage opened the door to the chicken dwelling and watched as the chickens began to flow out into the fenced area. As the chickens came out, Sage reached into the aluminum bucket that he held and tossed out a handful of feed about the yard. The chickens snatched up the supplies in a jerk like motion. After a few tossed handfuls the chickens were clustered at Sage's feet competing for more rations.

Sage turned to Donovan who was leaning against the fence that enclosed the chickens. "You wanna try?" He asked.

He was satisfied with just watching Sage work his way around the frantic chickens. Since he had not seen his son for years, every act and movement that he performed was amazing to him. To Donovan, it was like watching your first-born smile for the first time, or say his first words or walk his first steps.

Donovan nodded and Sage walked over and handed him the pail.

Donovan walked over to the chickens and set the pail of feed between them, and then walked back toward Sage, leaving the many chickens to fight to get inside the pail.

"How's that?" Asked Donovan.

For a moment Sage watched the chickens fighting and leaping on top of one another to get inside the pail.

"That's not how you do it." Sage finally admitted.

"Why not?" Donovan asked.

"Some of the chickens aren't getting fed. And they're gonna knock that pail over wasting the food."

Donovan was challenging Sage to come out of his shell. So Donovan tried to provoke a reaction from him by placing the pail in between the chickens to cause a mini-frenzy. He was hoping that this would encourage Sage to protest against the act. He was surprised and pleased when Sage did so.

"Then how do I do it, Sage?" Donovan asked.

Blinking Sage looked back at him. He was a little surprised by the firmness in Donovan's voice, however, he understood what Donovan wanted from him. For whatever reason, he was expected to explain in detail how to feed these chickens. So he walked over to the pail, pushed away the chickens, and brought it back to Donovan.

He demonstrated to Donovan by first putting his hand into the pail and scooping out a fistful of feed. "Take out this much," he said. "And toss it about all the chickens." Sage then demonstrated by releasing the feed onto the dirt in front of a group of three that had separated themselves from the main bunch. Sage turned to Donovan. "You walk about all of them tossing their food here and there so that they all get their fair share."

Donovan nodded and Sage continued.

"Then you watch to see which chickens ain't gettin no food. Sometimes the big ones won't let the others get none. That's when you shoo the big ones away so that the smaller ones can eat too."

Donovan was delighted with his son, but he did not reveal so. His demeanor was composed as he said. "That's what I wanted to know."

Sage noticed that Donovan's voice seemed to have a hint of content. Maybe Donovan was pleased with him; it was difficult to know with this man.

After feeding the chickens as Sage had been instructed, Donovan led him over to the front of the house and then said. "I want you to meet my friend."

Sage squinted for he was puzzled. "I thought you didn't have no friends."

"I have one." Said Donovan.

"What if he don't wanna meet me?"

"He will."

Sage was not comfortable with the likely meeting of this friend. His encounters with people were usually not pleasant. Most people didn't feel comfortable around him because of his scarred face and disfigured forearms and hands.

"Maybe I shouldn't." Said Sage

Donovan could see Sage going back into his defense and he was a little irritated with him. "Why not?" He asked.

He looked up and said. "Because he won't like me. Nobody does."

The annoyed expression on Donovan's face caused Sage to again become uncomfortable. "I don't give a damn who likes you, and neither should you," Donovan said. "What's there not to like about you?" He asked.

Sage watched the ground as Donovan waited for his answer, but Sage gave none.

Donovan continued. "I know why folks don't like me, I've done some awful things. But I can't figure why folks wouldn't like you none."

"Because I'm ugly." Sage finally admitted.

Donovan frowned. "I thought we talked of this already. We all is ugly in one way or another."

Sage looked up at Donovan. "Ain't nobody as ugly as me."

It hurt Donovan to hear his son talk about himself in this way. He felt responsible. If he had not been away for all these years, his son would feel different about himself. He was out there fighting a violent crusade against the men that murdered his wife. As much as he wanted and needed to capture and kill those men, he understood that decision to be a mistake. He should have instead stayed with his son, so as to help him fight his own battles.

Looking at Sage Donovan made a silent promise to his son that no matter what happened in his own life, he would never leave him again. And somehow he was going to help Sage overcome his demons.

He eyed Sage with an unfeeling gaze. "You're not as ugly as you think you are." With that Donovan walked behind Sage with his hands firmly on his shoulders. He pointed towards the woods. "My friend's out there. You see him?"

Sage leaned forward and squinted. But he saw nothing in those woods. "Don't see nothing."

"He's there," Donovan said. "You just can't see him."

After a moment of looking into the woods, Sage was impatient. "There ain't nobody there."

Donovan stepped around so that he and Sage were side by side. "I'll call him." He then raised his fingers to his lips and whistled loudly. So loud that Sage instinctively hunched his shoulders and lowered his head as if this would censor his ears.

The horse snickered in the distance from somewhere within the woods.

"Here he comes," Donovan announced.

With anticipation, Sage stared into the woods where he thought he had heard the horse. He was relieved to realize that Donovan's friend was only an animal and not a human. For an animal would not pass judgment on his unpleasant appearance.

Though Sage did not yet see the horse, he could faintly hear the fast hooves pounding against the terrain somewhere inside the woods. After a moment of waiting and listening, the massive horse finally appeared on the edge of the wooded area and leaped out into view.

The horse was still a great distance away, but it was gaining as it raced at such a high-speed across the meadow in their direction. A cloud of dust followed the animal as its blurred hooves pounded the land. The horse was half the distance away now, and Sage realized that this animal was headed directly toward them. Panic tumbled in his stomach. He had serious reservations that this animal would not change pace or direction until it trampled them to their deaths.

He tried to step back, but Donovan sidestepped and blocked him.

"Don't move. He won't hurt you." He said.

"I'm scared!" Sage cried.

"You'll be fine."

"I'm scared!"

"Don't move." Said Donovan.

Sage was more than scared he was terrified. His legs were shaking and he could hear himself moaning. He wanted to run, but his shaky legs and Donovan's firm grip on his shoulder did not allow him to do so. He peeked up at Donovan, his face was calm and his stance was sure. That brief view of the self-confident Donovan gave him some reassurance of the situation, but not enough. Sage turned in the direction of the horse. It was much closer now. Within seconds it would be right upon them.

"Make him stop!" Sage yelled.

"It's too late," Donovan said.

And then the massive horse was upon them, and without slowing, it did a quick full circle around them kicking up clouds of dirt so thick that Sage could hardly see Donovan who was just beside him. He closed his eyes as he coughed and choked on the thick dust. When he finally opened his eyes, he about peed his pants when he saw the enormous muzzle of the horse that was bent low so that it was only a foot away from his face. The nostrils of the horse flared and noisily puffed out its warm breath. He grunted and tried again to step back, but Donovan was still behind him with his hand securely on his shoulder.

"It's okay Sage," Donovan said attempting to reassure him. "He's not gonna hurt you. He's just curious about you is all."

"He's big." He whispered in his attempt not to excite the animal.

Donovan laughed. "I reckon he is. But he won't hurt you."

Though Donovan's assurance of the situation did calm Sage to some extent, he found Donovan's laugh to be unexpected. The chuckle itself was not offensive for it was short, soft and somewhat non-emotional. However, he had never within the week since Donovan first arrived, heard or seen him laugh about anything. He had probably only seen Donovan smile once, and even then it wasn't much of a smile. At that time his mouth curled up slightly, but neither his eyes nor his face displayed an expression of bliss.

Donovan reached for the horse's mane and rubbed. "He wants you to do this." He said to Sage. "You try."

This was the largest horse that Sage had ever set his eyes on. The horse was overwhelming in size and power. The muscles on the chest, front legs, and rear legs were highly developed and pressed tightly against its short coat exposing protruding veins throughout its body. The underbelly was oversized containing massive guts. It was amazing that an animal this immense could move with such speed.

He felt the fear inside himself, but he did not want to disappoint Donovan, so he reached for the horse's mane. And as he did so the horse jerked his head up to the sky and snorted. Sage reacted by leaping back and tripped over himself until he fell to the ground face down. When he peered over his shoulder, he could see Donovan's extended hand in an attempt to help him to his feet. Sage studied Donovan's expression looking for a hint of disappointment but was relieved to witness none. He placed his hand inside of Donovan's and was pulled to his feet.

"Try again," Donovan instructed. "But this time slow. He doesn't know you yet, so you'll have to take your time or you'll spook him again."

This time he cautiously raised his hand to the fine hairs on the horse's neck. And as he did so he found that the horse did not react this time. Even on the horse's neckline, he could feel the curved muscle underneath the skin. At one point the horse lowered his head and appeared to be watching Sage with one of his side eyes.

"Fletcher seems to like you." Said Donovan. "I knew he would."

Sage smiled for it felt good to be liked; even if it was from a horse. The kids at school didn't like him, and they told him each time they encountered him. They would all play games, laughing and having fun together, while Sage sat in solitary watching and yearning to participate with them. The adults that he would come across from time to time, consulted about him as if he couldn't understand them. They all had similar comments about how peculiar of a boy he was, or how unsightly he appeared. They talked of Sage never finding anyone to love and to wed him. The thought that he would be isolated his entire life tormented him the most.

Donovan watched as Sage rubbed Fletcher's neck. Surprisingly the boy was in good spirits. This was the first time he had witnessed the boy interested in anything. He had hardly even heard the boy speak until this day. He was pleased that Sage was at least taking a liking to Fletcher.

Grabbing the reins Donovan leaped and swung his leg over on the horse's bare back. He leaned toward Sage with his hand out. "Let's ride." He said.

With Donovan on top, the horse seemed even more towering than before. And Sage didn't feel safe riding a horse this large, let alone without even a saddle for support. But he knew by Donovan's determined expression he would not easily convince him otherwise. So he grabbed Donovan's hand and held on as he was lifted onto the horse's backside.

"Hold on to me," Donovan instructed, and Sage grabbed Donovan's waist. The powerful horse shifted on its legs, and without a saddle for support, Sage felt as if he could easily slide off. At that point, he braced himself against Donovan for better balance. Pulling on the reins Donovan turned the horse around and then nudged forward. Though it was only a simple step for a horse, the jerkiness of that first step caused Sage to fall into Donovan.

"I'm gonna fall!" Said Sage.

"Then hold on." Said, Donovan, as he continued to guide the horse forward.

Sage was uneasy with Donovan's lack of understanding of his situation. This was his first time on a horse, let alone a horse this enormous. If he were to fall from this height he would surely break some bones. He eyed the back of Donovan's head. "I'm gonna fall," Sage repeated. But this time he was less convincing than before.

As the horse moved on, Donovan glance back at Sage. He then turned his attention forward as they continued on the terrain toward the barn. There was no point in saying anything else, for it was apparent that Donovan was not going to halt.

Mama and Papa were about one hundred yards off to the side throwing seeds into the grooves that Miles had dug a few days earlier. They watched Donovan and Sage ride past them. At one point Sage looked over to them only to see the awkward expressions on their faces. They noticed that he was hiding a grin as he abruptly faced the other way.

Puzzled, Mama asked. "What's Sage doing on that big horse?"

"Don't know, but I ain't never seen him that proud before." Said Papa.

Donovan guided the horse into the barn. Even though the time of day was late morning and the sun was high in the sky, the interior of the barn was still dimmed. He guided the horse to a sidewall by one of the windows. Donovan then eased his leg over and stepped down, and then he reached up and helped Sage do the same.

The saddle and the thick blanket were on the tossed hay next to the wall. First Donovan put the blanket on top of Fletcher's back. Then he grabbed the saddle and struggled a bit as he set it on top of the blanket, on the horse's back. He ducked underneath the horse and buckled the saddle tight. He then walked over to the window again and kicked at the loose hay. He then reached down and pulled out the rifle. He brought it back to the horse and set it inside the pouch attached to the saddle. With a quick leap, Donovan was in the saddle and then turned to Sage with his hand out.

He nudged forward and guided Fletcher toward the lighted doorway, and then into the open prairie. When Donovan looked over his shoulder he could see Mama and Papa standing side-by-side watching them again. Mama waved. Donovan raised his hand, and Sage-imitating Donovan did the same.

At a slow pace for Sage's sake, Donovan guided Fletcher into the woods. As they moved along the trampled down path Donovan monitored closely all movement and sounds within the forest. Though Donovan believed that he and Sage were safe from his enemies he was still cautious. He did not have his shooting pistols because Mama did not approve of his weapons. Donovan realized that witnessing a man with two shooting pistols on either side of his waist was probably very intimidating. Even if it were family doing so. So he instead decided to bring his rifle. He figured the rifle would not alarm her as much, for it was attached to the horse and not to him, as his pistols would have been. A rifle would not be as effective as a pistol if Donovan needed to get to it quickly, but it was better than having nothing at all for protection, and it was more useful for long-range targets. In truthfulness, he was more concerned with defending his son than himself.

As they continued on down the path in between the trees Donovan couldn't help but feel a little anxious to know that if an incident did arise he would be responsible for his son's life as well as his own.

After a short time of riding, Donovan and Sage reached the river. Donovan lowered Sage to the ground, climbed off himself, and then reached for his rifle and set it on the ground next to a nearby tree. He then patted Fletcher on his hind side, and they both watched as he trotted to the river, and then dropped his head to gulp some river water. Once Fletcher was done drinking he made his way further down the bank but stayed within their sights. Donovan and Sage then seated themselves under a nearby tree.

Sage watched the horse upstream grazing over some long grass. Finally, he said. "You say this horse is your friend?"

Donovan nodded. "Fletcher is my only friend."

"How can that horse be your friend, he don't even talk?"

Donovan turned to Sage. "A friend is not someone you just talk with. Besides Fletcher talks with his body, not with his tongue. If he's excited about something, he'll bob his head up and down. If he's afraid, he'll snort and twist his ears back. If he likes you he'll move his ears forward and bring his head close to you." Donovan turned to the river that flowed and crashed noisily against the nearby bank. "If you watch folks long enough you'll find that they talk with their bodies as well."

"What makes Fletcher a friend to you?" Asked Sage.

Donovan still watching the flowing river had a serious expression and then he turned his gaze to Sage. "A friend is someone you can count on when you need help. Someone you can trust who would never betray you. Someone that would risk their life to keep you safe. Someone who would take your secrets to the grave never sharing them with anyone. A friend is someone who accepts you as you are whether you're good or bad." Donovan was quiet for a moment as he thought about how his horse Fletcher on many, many occasions lived up to this definition of a friend.

Sage swallowed, he had remembered earlier when Donovan had mentioned that he wanted to be Sage's friend. A friend of Donovan is not something one could take lightly, for he had strict expectations. So rigid in fact, Sage wondered if he could actually live up to them.

Donovan turned his gaze back to the river, and as he did so he could feel that Sage was watching him. He picked up a flat rock and flung it into the water, it hopped the surface three times before it finally sunk.

Sage cleared his throat and then spoke. "Are you sure you're my father?"

Donovan nodded. "I am."

"What makes you sure? Maybe you've made a mistake."

He turned to Sage. "I watched your mother give birth to you. I raised you until you were nearly seven years of age. There's no mistake."

Sage was satisfied for the moment, but then he turned to Donovan again. "Do you remember my Mother?"

He looked at the flowing river for a long time before he barely got it out. "I remember her."

"What do you remember?" Asked Sage.

Without a word, Donovan got up and walked over to the bank. Sage watched him for minute and then joined him at his side.

"I remember everything about her," Donovan said.

He could tell that Donovan was struggling with the questions about his mother; it was obvious that he loved her a lot. Since Sage was only seven when she passed away, he only had vague memories of her. There was so much more that Sage wanted to know about her, and Mama and Papa would rarely discuss his mother with him.

"What was she like?" Asked Sage.

As the water continued to flow and slap against the bank Donovan observed. It was such a long pause that Sage figured Donovan was not going to answer any more questions about his mother. But then Donovan finally said.

"She was beautiful, Sage. She was the most beautiful woman I had ever met, and even to this day I have not set eyes on a more beautiful woman." He turned to Sage. "And you look just like her." He then turned back to the river. "She cared deeply for others. She would help mothers deliver their babies. She even cared for the sick neighbors from time to time. Sometimes she would stay with them all night just to comfort them. At those times when she was gone, it was just you and me." A slight smile lingered on Donovan's face. "Your mother didn't trust me. She always gave me strict instructions of how to take care of you when she was gone. And when she came back, sometimes days later she would fuss on how I didn't follow her instructions."

Sage smiled. "Did my mother fuss a lot?"

Donovan nodded. "Only at me."

Sage laughed. "You loved her a lot didn't you?"

Donovan was quiet for a long time. His expression was of sorrow. "I loved her with everything I had. And she loved us both very much."

This time Sage watched the river. After a few moments, he finally asked. "What happened to her?"

Donovan turned to him, surprised that he had asked this question. He thought that by now Sage would have known about his mother. He thought that by now Mama or Papa would have explained the situation to him. Did he really want to be the one to share such information with this young fourteen-year-old? It was obvious that no one had told the boy anything about his mother. Sage had every right to know the truth about her.

"She was killed." Said Donovan.

"How did it happen?" Asked Sage.

Watching Sage's none expressive disposition, he came to the conclusion that Sage was not surprised with this information.

"She was killed by some men," Donovan said, not wanting to give out too much of the details.

Again Sage did not seem surprised by this information. "And what happened to those men?" He asked.

Studying Sage's none expressive demeanor Donovan said. "They're dead."

"All of them?" Sage asked.

Taken aback by Sage's question Donovan didn't answer for a moment. He was beginning to realize that Sage knew more than he let on to know. "All of them are dead," Donovan answered.

With a hint of relief, Sage seemed to be satisfied with the new or confirmed information about his mother. He did not ask another question.

Donovan whistled for Fletcher and he and Sage hopped on and rode back to the house.

Chapter 27

It was late in the afternoon when Donovan and Sage returned home. They were on the outskirts of the property hidden among the thick trees when Donovan had pulled on the reins and Fletcher stopped. Cautiously Donovan looked around. First, he studied Miles who was digging hard and turning over the last section of soil. From what Donovan could see, his demeanor was the same as always, he was heavily involved in his work and took notice of nothing else around him.

Not far from Miles, walked Papa along the grooved land strategically dropping seeds. He too did not display out of the ordinary behavior from what Donovan could see. Donovan then turned his attention to the porch. He could see Mama and another woman sitting there conversing with one another. From this distance, he could not make out the other woman.

He watched all of them because he had to be certain that it was safe before he rode out into the open with his son. Donovan did not want to risk an ambush. Not that his enemies would find him here, for he seriously doubted that they could. But he felt that one of the reasons that he had survived for this long was because he never let his guard down, even when he thought he was probably safe.

The reason he watched his family was if they had any distress in their routine, then most likely they presently had an unfriendly visitor or one had come through. But judging by their ordinary demeanor neither was the case.

Even though all seemed routine with his family, Donovan still turned his attention to the surrounding forest on the outer edge of the property. His eyes moved along the trees and bushes searching for anyone possibly watching the property or even watching him and his son as they sat on Fletcher.

He saw nothing. Donovan was not naïve. He understood all too well that even though the sheriff and the deputy gave him two weeks' notice to leave town, they could easily change their minds and come after him sooner, before the deadline. So each day he stayed, the more dangerous this situation could become. The lawmen would either confront him face to face in the open, or they would hide and wait to ambush him. What Donovan knew for sure was that if he decided to leave town, he would do so not because of the lawmen, but only because he had failed in his attempt for a relationship with his son.

Once Donovan felt that all was secure, he guided Fletcher into the open onto the property. At a slow trot Donovan guided Fletcher toward the barn, and as he did so his eyes continued to search the edge of the property for any signs of danger. But he suspected nothing. As Fletcher guided them closer to the barn, he soon came to realize that the other lady on the porch with Mama was Dr. Tracy.

Inside the barn, Donovan lowered Sage to the ground and then climbed off as well. He then removed the saddle and rifle from Fletcher and slapped him on his rear, which sent him trotting out of the barn entrance. Donovan looked down at Sage. Some fatherly pride came about as he could see that the boy's demeanor had changed somewhat. The boy seemed more comfortable in his presence. Instead of Sage's eyes darting around and searching for the ground, he looked right at Donovan, anticipating.

Donovan felt this was a moment to say something to the boy. "You did good today." He said.

Sage smiled as he looked away embarrassed. This was a huge compliment coming from a man like Donovan. He thought about what Mama had taught him to say when he was paid a compliment. And this compliment that Donovan had just given him was the best one he had ever received. "Thank…you." He said as his eyes again found Donovan's.

Donovan nodded and then led Sage through the barn entrance. They walked side by side as they headed toward the front porch where Mama and Dr. Tracy were sitting. As they approached, Mama and Dr. Tracy stood to their feet.

"Well, you two have been gone for quite some time." Said, Mama. "I was wondering if you was gonna make it to dinner."

"Did you see me on the horse?" Sage asked excitedly.

"We sure did." Answered Mama as she stepped from the porch to greet them.

Dr. Tracy watched them with a slight grin on her face. Donovan glanced at her, and she avoided his eyes by watching Mama and Sage converse.

"His name is Fletcher, and he likes me."

"Fletcher?" Mama repeated. "That big ole horse has a name?"

"Sure does." Answered Sage with even more excitement.

Mama reached over and embraced Sage as she usually did when she greeted him. But this time he surprised her. In the past whenever he was hugged or touched by her or anyone, he would remain limp with his hands by his sides. This time Sage reached around her waist and squeezed her.

"Well," Said Mama. " What did I do to deserve such attention?"

Sage released her and shrugged. "Nothing."

Mama looked at him strangely. There was something else different about him. "Sage…In all the years that I've raised you, I don't believe I've ever heard you talk this much."

Sage ignored her and turned his attention to Dr. Tracy. "Hi, Dr.Tracy."

Dr. Tracy stepped off the porch and approached him. She placed her hands on his head and affectionately rubbed. "I don't believe I've ever heard you say my name before. Would you say it for me one more time?"

Sage looked around. They were all waiting for him to perform. "Maybe later." He said.

"Alright, maybe later." Dr. Tracy said in her calm soothing voice.

Grandma squeezed Sage one last time. "Why don't you see if Papa needs help before we sits down for dinner."

Sage nodded and then headed out into the fields. All the heads turned to watch him.

Mama turned to Donovan. "My, he's had quite the day with you, hasn't he?"

"We just went for a ride is all." Said Donovan.

"I've never seen him like this before. It's like he's a normal boy." Said, Mama.

"He is a normal boy." Said Donovan. "He just ain't got no confidence because of how folks treat him."

Mama nodded in agreement and then said. "How's your shoulder?"

"It's fine."

"Well, I want Dr. Tracy to look it over."

Donovan glanced at Dr. Tracy, who was already watching him. Her long wavy black hair was pulled back from her shoulders. And her soft brown eyes were so soothing that he wondered what they would look like closer, as in just before a kiss. He turned back to Mama. "That's fine." He said.

"Good," Mama said. She turned to Dr. Tracy. "Dr. Tracy, will you please look over Donovan just before dinner?"

Dr. Tracy nodded. "Sure Mama."

"And I hope you'll be our guest for dinner tonight." Suggested Mama.

Dr. Tracy glanced at Donovan. "Of course." She answered.

"Good," Said Mama. "I'll go finish up dinner, it'll be ready before long." With that, she headed up the stairs and into the house.

There was a moment of uncomfortable silence between Donovan and Dr. Tracy. Donovan spoke first. "How have you been?"

"Fine." She said. "I wasn't sure if you would still be here."

"I wasn't sure either. I'm not used to staying in one place so long."

"And why is that?"

"It just works out that way, I guess." He said.

She looked at him wondering, and then said. "Let's look at your shoulder." She led him over to the porch steps and seated herself, and then she watched him sit beside her.

"I need you to pull down your shirt so that I can look at it."

Donovan unbuttoned the front of his shirt and pulled it down just over the wounded shoulder. Covering the wound was a clean white bandage.

Dr. Tracy inspected the bandage. "I see you've been changing this. That's good. This will help prevent an infection."

"I changed it this morning." He said. "This wound is not that bad, I've had worse. But Mama has never seen such a wound and she's worried. So I promised her that I would change the wrappings twice each day. Sometimes if she asks I'll show them to her."

Dr. Tracy pulled off the wrap and inspected the wound. It was still raw in some areas, but she could see that it was scabbing in others. The scabbing meant no infection. If an infection was caught early it could be cured, but if not then the only option for survival would be an amputation. However, Donovan was wounded in the shoulder, and a shoulder could not be amputated. So his only option would be death.

Dr. Tracy reached into the black bag that hung from her shoulder and pulled out a clean piece of white cloth and a small bottle of clear liquid. "This is going to sting a bit." She announced. "But it will help prevent an infection."

"What is it?"

"It's rubbing alcohol."

Donovan nodded. "I don't need that."

"You don't need?" Dr. Tracy questioned. "This will help with an infection."

"My shoulder's not infected, I'm fine."

She frowned at him. And after she watched him for a moment the frown eased off of her face and was replaced by compassion. "You're afraid aren't you?"

"Afraid of what?"

"Of pain." She said. "I said this was going to sting, and now you can't go through with it."

Donovan became indignant which was out of character for his usual none emotional demeanor. "There's not much I'm afraid of."

This change in Donovan's character amused her. She did not expect to see a different side in Donovan's reserved personality. She decided to provoke him further. "If I had known that you were going to react this way, I wouldn't have told you what was in the bottle." Afterwards, she watched him with no expression and he watched her with irritation. But she did not look away, for she was enjoying herself.

"You don't know me." He said. "You don't know what I've been through. You don't know what I'm afraid of." His tone was serious, like a confession, a self-confession.

Dr. Tracy's tone became serious as well. "And what have you been through Donovan?"

He did not answer the question.

She reached over and pulled his shirt off of his shoulder so that it dropped to his waist. She stared at the many-welted wounds across his chest and stomach. She dragged her fingers across a long welted scar on his chest. She recognized this to be a knife wound. By the darkness of the scar, she could tell it penetrated deeply. "What happened here?"

Donovan looked down at himself, where her fingers touched his skin. "I was cut."

"Were you afraid?"

Donovan looked into her brown eyes. She did not look away. He was trying to read her. What did she want? Could she be trusted with something as fragile as his feelings, his personal thoughts, his past? "At first, but then I wasn't."

"What changed you so that you wasn't afraid?"

"I became angry. Very angry."

"Then what happened?"

Donovan squinted, he was visibly uncomfortable with the subject. But he liked Dr. Tracy, and he wanted her to know up front what he was like. "I killed him. I took his knife away and killed him with it."

"Because he cut you?"

"No. Because he tried to kill me."

"Why did he want to kill you?"

Donovan looked away. "It's a long story. And not one I want to tell."

"Why not Donovan? I would like to hear it."

He turned to her once more and looked into her brown eyes. It would be too easy to tell her everything about himself. She was so beautiful and so easy to talk to. Did he really think that he had a chance with a woman such as this? A few years ago maybe, but that was before his graphic past. He would only be fooling himself if he were to believe so now. Maybe this was a form of manipulation. Maybe she had been manipulating men with her beautiful looks all of her life. "Why do you want to know?'

Now she looked away. "Maybe I want to know what type of man you are."

"Why does it matter?"

She turned to him once more. "You remind me of someone I once knew. Someone I care very much about. Someone I hope to see again one day."

"And who is this person?"

She paused as if she did not want to disclose the person's identity. "Calvin Johnson. Dr. Calvin Johnson, my father."

Donovan watched her. He could see that she wasn't trying to manipulate him. She was genuinely sincere in her interest in him and bringing up her father brought up some painful memories for her. "Is your father dead?"

"I'm not sure. I think he's alive. I haven't seen him for almost three years. We ran into some trouble a couple years back. My father was one of the town doctors. He was the only Negro doctor in town. He was good. He was so good that some of the white folks called on him as their doctor. That didn't go over well with some of the white doctors and some of the white folks. But my father helped whoever needed help. He said a life is a life, it didn't matter what color they was." She paused and looked at Donovan, she had his full attention. "One night some white folks came to our door and begged my father to help their son. When my father got there, the boy was almost dead. The young boy was playing with his father's pistol and accidentally shot himself. My father told us later that the boy had shot himself in the chest. He knew right away that the boy was moments from death. He told the white folks that there wasn't nothing that could be done for the boy except for to make him as comfortable as possible. Not long afterwards the boy was dead. The boy's father was highly upset and threatened to kill my father. Somehow my father talked him out of it. But the next day, there was a large group of white men at our house, including the dead boy's father." Dr. Tracy paused to collect her thoughts. Donovan continued to watch her. "They broke into our beautiful house and took all my mama's good furniture and smashed it to pieces. Then they took out their torches and burned our house to the ground. My two brothers tried to stop them, but they were shot in their heads. They told my father he had until sun up to get out of town. Then they were going to hunt him down and kill him. We had nothing to pack because everything we owned was burned up in the house. The only thing we had was our clothes on our backs, and our horse and wagon. We left."

There was another moment of silence as Donovan took in the story. "Where's your family now?"

"I'm not sure. My father was afraid that those men would catch up with him and kill us all. So he dropped me off in this town with some money that he had left over, and told me that he would come back for me in three years." Dr. Tracy let out a long sigh. "The end of the three years will be coming up this next month. I hope they come for me."

"And if they don't come?'

"I'll find them. I'll leave this town and find them. I think about them every day. In my heart, I think they're okay." She turned to Donovan. "You're the only one that knows that part of me. And I expect you to share it with no one."

He sat in silence thinking over what Dr. Tracy had just told him.

Inside the house, the kitchen table looked wonderful. It was loaded down with chicken, some pork roast, broiled corncob and ash sweet potatoes. Just about everyone was seated at the table except for Maria. And during dinner, her name was never mentioned. Mama and Papa sat on the opposite long ends of the table so that they faced each other. Donovan and Sage sat next to each other on one end, and Dr. Tracy and Miles sat across from them on the opposite end. Mama had them all hold hands as she said grace. When she was finished they all greedily dug in. At first, no one did much talking. All concentrated as they served themselves the delicious foods. Once the food was served the smacking of lips as they chewed their food was a compliment to Mama.

Even Sage's demeanor was different. He was more confident for he didn't sit with his head low, his eyes met all that looked his way. He even talked a bit, which was mostly out of character for him. But generally, he would chat with Donovan. Sometimes it seemed as if they were alone and that no one else was in the room with them.

Mama glanced around the table and was delighted by all the happy faces around her. Even little Sage was happy which she thought would never be possible. And her youngest son Donovan was home, after being gone for such a long time. That was a miracle in itself. If only it could be like this for the rest of her life. But she knew in her heart that it was not possible. Life was not that simple. With that last thought, sadness blanked her soul like a dark cloud on a stormy day.

"What's the matter, Mama?" Asked Papa who had been watching her. She waved her hand at him. "Nothing, just happy is all."

Papa knew her better than that, but now wasn't the time to discuss it. He would talk with her again that night when they were alone.

After dinner Miles and Donovan exchanged friendly glances and then Miles headed home. Sage smiled at his father and then announced to everyone that he was ready to go back to school tomorrow, and then he headed to his room. Papa once again seated himself in front of the warm fireplace and was asleep within minutes. Dr. Tracy offered to help Mama cleanup, but Mama politely refused, for she knew that it was late and that Dr. Tracy should be heading home soon.

Mama turned to Donovan who was gazing out the front window. "Donovan, will you ride Dr. Tracy home, she'll be leaving soon?"

He turned from the window to look at Dr. Tracy. "As long as you're fine with it."

Pretending to think it over, Dr. Tracy finally said. "I'm fine with it."

Smiling slightly Donovan said. "I'll get Fletcher." And then he headed out the door.

Chapter 28

The hooves of their horses clumped against the dirt road. The occasional sounds of small animals just beyond the pathway were heard.

Donovan spoke. "What made you become a doctor?"

"I'm not really a Doctor. Folks just think I'm one."

"Why would they think that?" He asked.

"Because I save lives, help the sick, and deliver babies. I do what doctors do, except I never went to school for it. I learned everything that I know from my father. When he went to see his patients, many times I would go with him. I even read his medical books."

Donovan nodded as if he understood, and they continued to ride on in silence for some time before Tracy spoke again. "What about you Donovan?"

"Me?" He asked.

"You know about me, and I know nothing of you. What about you?"

Donovan thought it over and then asked hesitantly. "What do you want to know Tracy?"

"Tell me about Sidney." She asked.

Donovan was somewhat puzzled by her request. "How do you know about Sidney?"

"I heard you call her name when you were sleeping." She added.

Donovan was quiet for such a long time that Tracy was fearful. She knew that she had chosen a topic that was much too personal for him to discuss. She was disappointed in herself, why did she have to pick his deceased wife for their first major conversation about him. She should have waited until they were better acquainted before she pried into a question about his late wife. Tracy could not deny that she was interested in this man and wanted to know more about him. But the problem was, that he was such a quiet and secretive man, and shared nothing about his life. Even his own family didn't know about him.

"Sidney was my wife." He finally answered.

Not only was Tracy relieved, but she was also surprised, for she thought that he would withdraw and not speak at all for the remainder of the trip. "What happened to her?" She asked.

Again Donovan was quiet before he finally said. "She was murdered. She's been gone about seven years now."

Tracy nodded. "What was she like Donovan?"

"It's hard to talk about." He said sadly.

"You can talk with me."

Donovan studied her trying to decide whether to trust her or not. "I don't know where to begin."

"Just say what comes to mind."

The horses rode on side by side for another half mile while Donovan collected his thoughts. In the past years since Sidney's death, he had never talked about her with anyone. He had never even mentioned her name. Her memories were much too personal to share with others, and the loss of her was still great in his heart. He was uneasy for even considering discussing Sidney with Tracy, a woman he barely knew.

He began this way. "By nature, Sidney was a very caring person. Not only did she care for and take care of her own family, but she also cared for and tended to other families as well. During those times when Sidney got word of a friend or neighbor that was sick, she would actually pack some food, rush over and sometimes if needed stay the night. Most of the time I did not approve of Sidney staying overnight away from me and Sage, but she was very stubborn on these matters and would not be persuaded otherwise.

"When I pushed the issue by insisting that she stay home, she would in return tighten her face, point her finger and claim that I was being selfish, and then she would stomp out of the house. When she returned the next day I usually found that her resentment for me did not subside in the slightest. In fact, on those unpleasant nights, she would immediately start her disciplinary procedures. Sidney would announce to me that I was not allowed to touch or make love to her for at least a month or so. She went on to explain that I was selfish, and she was not going to share her body or love with a selfish man. So after numerous episodes of this, I finally grew tired of the punishment, and let Sidney go to her sick friends without further protest.

"Sage at this time was just a toddler, so when she anticipated staying overnight she would give me detailed instructions on how to care for him while she was away. Caring for the toddler was not an easy task for me. At that time I was a farmer and spent most of my time in the fields. Sage was then small and full of energy and sometimes I would lose track of him. And unfortunately, that was when Sidney would arrive home. At those moments she would march up to me and demand to know of the whereabouts of our son. I would turn to Sidney and shrug my shoulders apologetically and admit that I didn't know. She would then cut her eyes and stomp away only to find the boy less than a minute later eating dirt or sitting in cow shit.

"Even though I seemed to get fussed a lot by Sidney, I loved her almost more than life itself, and without a doubt, I knew that she shared the same love for me. We enjoyed each other's company immensely. Sunday was our favorite time together. This was when we would talk to one another all day, and sometimes late into the night. These times were special to Sidney because she felt the excitement of courting all over again.

"Because of the enormous trust and love we shared for one another, lovemaking was always amazing. Each time I made love to Sidney, it was as if I were making love to her for the first time. We would take our time exploring each other's bodies and enjoying the pleasures of our touches, caresses, and kisses.

"Some people disapproved of our type of relationship. Folks did not understand my so-called lack of discipline with my wife. They felt that I gave her too much freedom. She was allowed to come and go as she pleased, and if she was upset with me, she did not hesitate to chastise me, even in front of others. And I never made an effort to rebuke her. Sometimes I would even smile afterward because I thought it was humorous. And then she would scold me further for not taking her seriously. So I'd would apologize of all things."

On many occasions, Donovan was told that his marriage would fail because he was too weak to discipline his wife. Once he was even told that his lack of discipline confused his woman because she didn't know if she married a man or another woman. This kind of talk among some folks upset Donovan, but he loved Sidney and did not believe it was his right to treat her in the suggested manner. He felt that she was her own person and that she could make her own decision of how she wanted to conduct herself. Her strong sense of independence was one of the main reasons that he fell in love with her. Why would that change just because they were married? He refused to give into the societal pressures. From what Donovan could tell he and Sidney were the happiest couple that they knew.

Though Donovan did not approve of Sidney running to her friends and neighbors when they were sick, he equally did not like it when her friends came to her aid when she was sick. At that time the house would be crowded with chatty women. All would bring a dish of food, and as many women that could fit in the bedroom would be gathered around Sidney's bed, holding her wrist, patting her head and asking over and over, "How ya feeling?" It was so crowded in the house that Donovan and Sage sometimes would be forced to sleep outside.

Once Donovan was so fed up that he demanded that all the chatty women leave his house immediately, and he added that if they didn't leave at once he would throw them out. And that's when they all congregated together, chatting and threatening as they used their many bodies to force him to leave instead. What was most annoying for Donovan was that he knew that Sidney never had anything more serious than the common flu.

Not only did Sidney insist on helping her sick friends, but she was also adamant about riding into town alone. She was firm when she advised Donovan that she was not in any danger because she would only go into town during the morning and would return by early afternoon. And she added that most of the folks in town knew of her, and therefore would protect her if necessary. However, it didn't matter what Sidney's argument was, Donovan did not give in on this demand. He was so uncompromising on his stance that twice Sidney had actually got up before Donovan had awakened, and sneaked off to town alone. But when she returned after her first time, she was highly surprised on how furious Donovan was. She had not known that it was possible for him to get this enraged. Though she knew he would not harm her, she couldn't help but be afraid of him. When she had pulled up to the property in the wagon, he was not in the fields working as he had usually done at that time of day. He and Sage were instead on the porch waiting for her to return.

Donovan watched her until she had guided the wagon to the porch and stopped. Sage sat on Donovan's lap and made no attempt to greet his mother as he had done when she returned from her many trips previously. Donovan then lifted Sage and set him to the side and instructed him to stay put. And Sage did just that. Donovan then stepped off the porch to approach Sidney. When he reached her he eyed her. She could see that his face was angry and disappointed. He placed his hands around her shoulders and lifted her off the ground so that they were eye to eye. He then said in a voice that she almost didn't recognize. "You got folks laughing at me because you do damn well what you please. Folks say I'm weak cause you chastise me in front of others. None of that matters to me, but when I ask you to do something for your own safety, I expect for you to abide. A woman going into town alone is foolishness. If something were to happen to you, then Sage and me would suffer because of it. Don't put us in that situation again." He glared at her, and then he set her on the ground and walked away. He was so upset that he didn't speak to her for two days. She thought he would never get over it.

Even though she knew that Donovan would be highly upset, it didn't discourage Sidney from sneaking into town again nearly five years later. Her intention was to leave before Donovan got up and return by early afternoon. She figured Donovan would be furious again, but like the time before, within a couple of days, he would have forgotten all about it.

When Donovan got up that morning he was troubled to find that Sidney was not in the house. He stepped onto the porch and called out to her, but there was no answer. He then walked to the barn to see if her horse and wagon were present, and they were gone as well.

Now the question in Donovan's mind was where did she go? Either she went to visit one of her many friends or she went into town. He seriously doubted that she would go into town after he had made his concern for her safety so clear. Most likely she was with a friend in need. However, it concerned him that she did not tell him where she was going. It was as if she didn't want him to know of her whereabouts. And the last time that he didn't know of Sidney's whereabouts, he had found out later that she had gone to town.

Donovan told himself not to worry about Sidney's well-being, for she would be back soon enough as usual. But unfortunately, she didn't make it back until well after dark. It was so late that Donovan was just about to pack up Sage and go searching for her when she finally pulled onto the property in her wagon.

At first, when he saw her he was very angry. But after he saw her bruised face, black eye and her split lips he froze from disbelief. Even her dress was covered with dirt and was ripped. As he approached the wagon, he could also see dried blood on her face and clothing. Her eyes were sad and red as if she had been crying for hours. He had never seen her in such a gruesome state before.

"What the hell happened to you!?" He yelled out in a panic.

She stepped off the wagon and collapsed into his arms as she sobbed. "Oh, Donovan I'm so sorry." She said. "I should have listened to you."

He squeezed her and then said in her ear. "Did you go to town?"

She nodded.

He released his hold and stepped away from her. "Why Sidney?" She did not answer and began to cry again. His expression was of agony and anger as he watched her. "What happened to you, Sidney?"

She wiped her face with the end of her dress and said. "I fell off the wagon."

Donovan seemed somewhat relieved by her exclamation but glared as if he did not believe her. He had never known her to fall off the wagon before. And her bruises and the torn dress didn't seem to match the injuries that would come from falling from a wagon. "How did it happen?" He asked.

"The wheel hit a large rock and I fell off."

Donovan thought this over. It all made sense except for one thing. "Why is that you're just now getting home?" He asked. "It's almost midnight."

Sidney seemed stunned by the question, but she was quick to answer. "I was afraid to get back on the wagon, so I sat under a tree and closed my eyes. When I awoke it was dark."

Donovan again eyed Sidney. He was angry and disappointed that she would put herself in that type of situation after he warned her previously not to do so. But now wasn't the time for expressing these emotions.

A few days had passed and Sidney's bruises and cuts seemed to be healing, but emotionally she seemed to be getting worse. She was very quiet and withdrawn. She seemed to always be in a dream-like state. Sometimes she would break down and start crying for what seemed like no reason at all. When Donovan confronted her and asked why she was so upset, she would respond by saying it was a woman thing and he wouldn't understand.

What Donovan found most troubling was that two weeks after the wagon accident not one of Sidney's reliable friends had come to visit her. Usually when word got out that Sidney was sick or injured, what seemed like the whole town of women would be at his house trying to help her. Even her regular friends who could be counted on to come at least once a week never showed.

In his mind, Donovan began to question Sidney's story about the wagon accident. He was wondering if the accident actually occurred. Even odder, was when Donovan explained to Sidney that he would be riding into town for some supplies, she became hysterical and begged him not to go. So he delayed his trip for a day or so until finally in the early morning when she was asleep he tiptoed out.

When he did arrive into town, he found the behavior of some of the folks that he knew peculiar. They seemed to be watching him. And when he turned to acknowledge them with a nod or a smile, they would look the other way, in what seemed like a shameful manner Donovan thought.

Donovan parked his wagon in front of the shop called Polly's Store. Inside the shop were various supplies such as field tools, flour, sugar, various candies, shoes, and some clothes for both men and women. Behind the counter were Mr. Polly and his wife Mrs. Polly. Mr. Polly was short and plump, with a thick mustache and a balding head. His wife was slightly shorter with her black and gray hair tied in a tight bun. Both wore long white aprons over the tops of their clothes. Donovan smiled and nodded as he walked passed them, but he noticed that they both had troubled expressions on their faces.

From the aisles, Donovan picked up a couple of field hoes, some work overalls, farming boots and a sack of flour. He carried them all to the counter and set them down in front of Mr. and Mrs. Polly. They seemed awkward as they stood behind the counter. It was as if they didn't recognize Donovan, and Donovan had known these folks since he was a child.

As Mr. and Mrs. Polly handled the items on the counter, Donovan watched them. He then glanced around. At the moment he and the Polly's were the only ones in the store. He leaned slightly over the counter and waited until he had Mr. Polly's attention. "What's going on around here?" He asked.

Mr. Polly shrugged. "What do you mean?"

"Why are folks acting so curious?"

"Like who?" Asked Mr. Polly.

"Like you." Said Donovan. "You and your wife haven't spoken since I walked in. I've been coming in your store since I was a youngun. I have never known you to be short on words."

Mr. Polly and his wife exchanged glances. Then he nodded to her, and she left the room so that they could be alone. Donovan heard the back door shut where the Polly's slept.

"How's Sidney?" Mr. Polly blurted.

"Sidney's fine." Said Donovan wondering what Mr. Polly knew of Sidney's accident if there was, in fact, an accident at all.

Mr. Polly was relieved. "So she's safe?"

Donovan nodded wondering what he meant by this question. "Yes, why do you ask?"

"When she was last here me and Mrs. Polly was worried sick about her."

"Why, what happened?"

Mr. Polly stared at Donovan confused. "Didn't Sidney tell you?"

"She told me something, but I don't think it was the truth," Donovan said.

"What did she tell you?"

"She said she fell off her wagon."

Mr. Polly thought it over. "It could have happened, she was in a hurry to get home."

"What happened that she was in such a hurry?" Donovan asked.

"Maybe Sidney should tell you." Said Mr. Polly.

Donovan frowned. "I want you to tell me."

Mr. Polly took a deep breath and then began. "When Sidney came into town she was very friendly and happy and spent most of her time talking with some of her lady friends. You know how she likes to visit and all." His voice was serious and businesslike. "I guess the whole time she was talking, these men were watching her. There were five in all. After watching Sidney for a spell, one of the men crossed the street and walked right up to her. He started talking to Sidney, and she was friendly at first. But all of a sudden she yelled at the man and slapped him across his face."

"Why was she upset with the man?" Asked Donovan.

"The man had offered her money to lay in his bed." Answered Mr. Polly. "But after he got slapped, he went back across the street to be with the other men. They all had scowls on their faces as if they had been slapped by Sidney as well. The whole time that Sidney was in town those five men watched her. Sidney pretended as if she didn't notice, but she was very nervous about the situation. She even asked several of the townsfolk if they would accompany her home." Mr. Polly clutched his fist and dropped his head in anger. "But they all refused." He finished. "They were all afraid. She even went to the sheriff…he refused her as well."

As Mr. Polly paused Donovan looked at him with disbelief. Sidney had never told him any of this. He was beginning to fear the worst while hoping that it was true that Sidney injuries were just from falling off the wagon. His heart pounded as he listened.

Mr. Polly went on. "It was just sooner than dark before she finally came into our shop. Me and Mrs. Polly could see that something was troubling her. When my wife asked, Sidney told us what I had just told you. And when we looked out the window, we could see those five men across the street waiting for her, just as she said they were. We told her that she could stay with us for the night. And she graciously accepted our offer. So I locked all the doors, blew out the lanterns and put the closed sign in the window. I wanted to make it clear to those men that no one was leaving this shop tonight. After a couple of hours, the men were finally gone. Sidney was relieved and was ready to go home. Me and Mrs. Polly insisted that she at least stay until morning. But she refused our invitation. She claimed that she had to get home."

"What time was that?" Donovan asked.

"It was just after nine."

If Sidney had left town around nine, then she should have arrived at about ten or so. But she didn't get home until well after midnight, an extra two hours longer than what it should have normally taken her. Was it true that Sidney had fallen off the wagon and decided to sleep for a while, or did something else happen?

Mr. Polly went on. "Sidney finally climbed into her wagon outside the store and me and Mrs. Polly watched her leave." Mr. Polly dropped his head with sadness. "But then not more than ten minutes later we saw those five men race by our window on their horses. They were headed in the same direction as Sidney had gone. They must have been hiding and waiting all along."

Donovan was sick to his stomach. He feared the worst for his wife. Her torn clothes, the blood, her bruised face, the split lip. It all made sense and yet he tried to convince himself that it didn't, maybe she did actually fall off the wagon.

Donovan leaned forward. "What happened to Sidney?"

Mr. Polly looked surprised. "Don't know. You said she was fine."

"She's not fine." Said Donovan sadly. "Something happened." Donovan walked over to the window. "Those five men, are they here now?"

Mr. Polly looked out the window alongside Donovan. "I don't see them."

"When's the last time you've seen them?"

Mr. Polly paused before he answered. He wasn't thinking over the question, he was hesitating the answer. "Yesterday. I've seen them each day since, except today."

Donovan frowned. "How could these people turn their backs on her after all she's done for them?"

Mr. Polly frowned as well. "Don't know, me and Mrs. Polly was wondering the same thing."

Both men gazed out the window. Finally, Donovan turned to Mr. Polly. "Thank you for what you done. You saved Sidney's life."

Mr. Polly nodded. "We could have done more."

"You did enough." Said Donovan. "Her friends could have done more. The sheriff could have done more, but you and Mrs. Polly did enough."

It took Donovan just under an hour to ride home, and during that time he was burdened heavily with thoughts of Sidney. Did she actually fall off the wagon, or did those five men catch up to her? And why hadn't she mentioned those men? Some crucial unanswered questions that Sidney will need to explain.

When Donovan finally arrived at the house he was stunned to see five horses tied to his porch. Normally because of Sidney's popularity, Donovan would not have given those horses a second thought. But Donovan had never seen these horses before. And now after what Mr. Polly had just told him, he was suspicious. He guided the wagon right up to the house. He leaped off the wagon, ran across the porch and barged through the front door. But he was stopped cold with a pistol pointed to the side of his face. The man with the pistol had shoulder length dark brown hair that looked almost black. His thin face was dirty and had not been shaven for at least a week.

"We watched you ride in. So we got real quiet like. Didn't figure you to be back this early." Said the man with the pistol.

Donovan glanced around. There were two other men in the room with them. Both men had their guns pointed at him as well. Both men were similar in appearance with the dirty unshaven faces. One man was medium weight and height with short brown hair. The other man was taller and heavier than most and displayed the evilest set of eyes that Donovan had ever seen. As Donovan viewed at those evil eyes he had come to realize that this man was probably capable of all wickedness known to man. And he had just at that moment come to grasp the danger that he and his family were in.

"Where's my family?" Donovan demanded.

The man with the evil eyes walked up to Donovan and pointed his gun just underneath Donovan's left eye. "Sit your ass down."

But Donovan stood firm. "Where's my family?"

The man with the evil eyes used his thumb to cock the hammer on his pistol, and then he nudged it into Donovan's cheek. "Not gonna tell you again, boy."

Being that he was not armed and these three men were, Donovan felt that he had no choice but to comply. But he so badly needed to know if his family was safe or not. If they were, in fact, safe, then his family would need him alive after this was all over to help them get through the horror of it all. But if they weren't alive, then there was no point in Donovan cooperating with these thugs. His own life would not matter to him at that point. He would put his own life in jeopardy just to get at one of them.

Donovan eased himself into the armless chair close by. The man with the evil eyes then turned to the man by the wall with the short hair. "Make yourself useful and go fetch the rope off my horse."

The man with short hair was slow moving, but he finally left the wall, went out the front door, and then came back with a long rope in hand.

"Tie him good." Instructed evil eyes.

And the man with the short hair did just that. He tied Donovan's hands behind his back and his legs to the front legs of the chair. And then finally he tied his torso to the base of the chair. Donovan was tied so tight that he felt claustrophobic and struggled to catch his breath.

Once Donovan was tied, the three appeared to relax. Evil eyes and the man with the short hair placed their guns back into their holsters. However, the first man with the gun kept his in hand.

"That was easy." Said the man with the gun.

"It's not over yet," Said evil eyes. "We just beginning." He then turned to one of the closed bedroom doors and yelled. "Nevin! Bring that boy out here!"

One of the back doors opened and out came the younger Nevin Odland with the seven-year-old Sage by his side. Sage was silent and terrified. "What do you want with him?" Asked Nevin.

"Just stand there and hush!" Snapped evil eyes. He then turned to Donovan. "The boy is safe. And if you want to keep it that way you best not be any trouble to us. We'll be gone soon enough."

Donovan was tied to the chair as tight as one could physically be tied. So tight in fact that he couldn't even move. So he wondered how they could possibly think that he was in any position to cause trouble. Even though Sage seemed greatly afraid at the moment, Donovan was relieved to know that he was safe. Now he wondered about Sidney. Where was she?

"Where's my wife?" Demanded Donovan.

"You mean the lovely Sidney." Answered evil eyes.

Donovan was stunned that evil eyes knew his wife's name.

"She's busy right now." Said evil eyes with an obnoxious grin. This was followed by sniggles and light laughter from the men in the room.

Donovan stared hard at the giggling men and then yelled from his chair. "Where is she!?"

Evil eyes turned to Nevin. "Take the kid back in the room."

Nevin led Sage back into the room and closed the door.

Evil eyes walked over to the other door and said with a smile. "She's in here." He then pushed the door open. Just within view on her back on the bed was Sidney. And in between her naked thighs pumping inside of her was the fifth man. Donovan screamed! Which startled both the fifth man and Sidney who were not aware that the door had been opened. She looked at Donovan helplessly and cried. The fifth man cursed as he climbed off of Sidney and slammed the door shut.

Donovan screamed again and struggled desperately to get out of the chair. He rocked it until it fell over. Then he screamed some more as he struggled, but the tight ropes did not give.

Donovan finally quieted when evil eyes approached him. He dropped to one knee to get close to Donovan. He smiled as he said. "The week before last when we came across your Sidney, she put up quite a fight." Evil eyes blurted a laugh. "She's a tough winch. We had to rough her up a bit before she would open her legs for us. But she did finally and it was worth the fight. But today we're disappointed. She didn't even fight us. It kind of took the fun out of it."

Donovan screamed again, and this time he yelled over and over. "I'm gonna kill you! I'm gonna kill you all!"

Evil eyes stood to his feet and viciously kicked Donovan in the head several times before he was unconscious and silent. When Donovan came to, he found that he was tied to a large tree. His arms were extended around the trunk of the tree while his wrists were tied tightly to one another on the other side. After a short struggle, Donovan found that his feet were tied around the tree as well. In fact, he was tied so snuggly that his feet didn't even touch the ground. As Donovan became more conscious he found that his predicament was even worse. He realized that he was also completely nude, and his genitals squashed against the rough scratchy bark of the tree.

Just behind him, he heard a swooshing sound followed by a loud cracking noise, and then he felt the deep stinging sensation across his left shoulder and down his back. The pain was so unbearable that he yelled out. It felt as though his skin and meat had been sliced open to the bone. Another swooshing sound cut through the air, Donovan tried to brace himself. The whip cracked loudly as it cut into his back, and again he screamed. This scream was louder than the one before. It sounded as if it had come from the depths of his soul, the depths of his pain, the depths of hell.

Over and over the whip cracked into the air before it sliced through Donovan's flesh. The whipping was endless as it sliced up and down his shoulder blades, back, and legs. He tried to look over his shoulder to see which one of the five men was whipping him. But his vision was limited for the man stood directly behind him. Before long his screams were compiled into tortured cries. He was ashamed of himself. He did not want to give these men the satisfaction of witnessing him weep.

The whipping kept coming and coming creating new wounds while crossing over old wounds. After a while, it became apparent to Donovan that these men weren't just whipping him, but they were killing him. Then all went black.

When Donovan became conscious he was lying face down on the ground. He could hear many rushed and panicked voices around him. He tried to move, but was not able to, for the pain along his backside was too great.

"He's coming around." Said a man's voice.

Donovan tried to focus. He could see that he was only a few feet from the tree that he was tied to earlier.

"Oh thank you JESUS." Said Mama's voice. He strained hard to lift his head to face her.

Beside him, she was on her knees. "You gonna be okay. Mama gonna take care of you." She cried.

He shifted his eyes and looked passed Mama. He was horrified to see that his house was on fire. The red flames engulfed the entire house reaching heights of about twenty feet. The dark black smoke had blanketed the once perfect blue sky. Folks that were once dumping pails of water on the flames had now lost hope and stood idly watching.

Donovan's stomach twisted with fear. "Sidney...Sage." He managed.

The tears flowed down Mama's dark round cheeks. "They rushed Sage to town. He hurt real bad. They gonna find him a doctor."

"Sidney?"

She paused. "She dead."

The words came to him like a dream. It came to him real slow, and her voice became very deep as it changed speed and dragged. "S h e   d e a d." The voice repeated in his head over and over. Sidney's dead.

He sobbed, and then he asked. "How?"

"The fire," Mama said. "We couldn't get her out."

Tracy was stunned by Donovan's story. She wondered how he was able to cope with such great loss and pain. As she thought about it, their backgrounds were similar. Both of her brothers were killed violently, her home was burned down, and her parents were run out of town in one horrible night.

She was surprised that Donovan revealed so much about his life to her. And yet there was still so much about him that she wanted to know. But to push for more information now could possibly shut him down. So she decided to instead ride by his side in silence. As they rode on toward town, now less than three miles away, she came to realize that she loved this man. And possibly he loved her as well.

Tracy had never been in love before, she found the idea strange. As she viewed it, one didn't get to choose the person he or she wanted to be in love with, it seemed more like this love chose them. If she had her preference of men to fall in love with, she would have never selected Donovan. Her choice would have been a man that was a professional like a doctor or teacher, like her father. She would have chosen a man that always carried a book in his hand and was knowledgeable about the world. She would have chosen a man that was peaceful and didn't feel the need to carry a pistol. Her choice would have been a man that easily talked and was open about his feelings. Donovan had none of these attributes, and yet she was in love with him?

She turned to Donovan and watched him as he continued to guide his horse forward. His head was bent slightly downward giving evidence of his humble demeanor. As fearless as Donovan appeared, she couldn't help but feel that he was very vulnerable.

As the horses moved on Tracy finally reached over and grabbed Donovan's hand. He responded by squeezing her hand, but he did not look in her direction. She studied him. More than a week ago she had witnessed Donovan confront two dangerously armed men without fear or hesitation. It was as if he didn't comprehend the risks involved or the value of his own life. And then in town a few days later he shot down the man that had attempted to assault her. Again he seemed to have no value of his own life, for he could have been captured by a posse and killed. After witnessing Donovan carry out these fearless acts, she found it odd that as she held his hand he seemed uncomfortable with their moment of intimacy.

Again she asked herself, why was she falling in love with this man? For sure he was unlike any man she had ever met. He seemed fearless, intense and dangerous, but he was also vulnerable, peaceful and humble. Normally she was not attracted to dangerous men, and yet she was attracted to Donovan. She reminded herself that she was not just attracted to him; she was in love with him.

She thought more about this as they rode on hand in hand. Did she really believe that Donovan was dangerous and fearless? She had watched him kill two men. And knew by the many wounds on his body that he had killed others as well. But did that necessarily mean that he was dangerous and fearless? That would all depend on his motives for killing. She felt that the two men that he killed last week were justified, for his motive was only to protect his father, even if it meant the loss of his own life. And when the drunk man had pulled Tracy off of the horse, Donovan immediately fired two rounds into him, but he had a motive then also, it was to prevent the man from inflicting further harm on her. Of course, Donovan didn't kill that man, probably because it wasn't necessary to do so.

If it weren't for Donovan his father would be dead now, and his mother, brother and all that knew him would be devastated with grief. Even Tracy would have been seriously injured or killed that night if Donovan hadn't stepped in.

In her mind, she wondered, with all the emotional baggage that Donovan carried, was it a mistake to fall in love with him? Probably, but in her twenty-eight years of life she had never experienced such a strong connection to a man before, and since she was already in love with him, it would be extremely difficult to walk away now.

Donovan guided his horse off the road into the grassy pasture. Still holding Tracy's hand he led her alongside him. When they were deep enough within the pasture Donovan climbed off and then helped Tracy down as well.

She was surprised that Donovan had gone off the road, she could have protested and insisted that Donovan stay on course and take her home. Or she could have even released herself from his grip and headed into town without him. But she did neither. Instead, she followed him eagerly, anticipating his intentions.

After he helped her off the horse he stood close to her. So close, that they shared each other's breath. Her heart thumped with excitement. He reached up and pulled on her lengthy hair.

She closed her eyes, so as to concentrate on each of his tender strokes. "What are you doing?" She panted.

Softly he answered. "I'm touching your hair."

"Why?" She asked.

"Because I'm going to kiss you." He said.

She opened her eyes and said almost in a whisper. "And why would you do that Donovan?"

Donovan slightly leaned forward so that their lips were almost touching. "Because I'm going to make love to you." He added.

Tracy took a step back to widen the gap between them. "Because I'm beautiful and you want another notch on your belt."

Donovan stepped forward to close the gap again. "No. Because you're beautiful and I'm in love with you."

And with that, she moved forward to meet his lips. Their first two kisses were short and delicate. It was as if they were trying to savor the moment of their first kiss. But then their unrestrained passions seeped in. Their lips locked, their tongues explored, and their heads turned this way and that. Their kissing was so drawn out and all-consuming that they could hear one another struggling to breathe.

As Donovan held her, his heavy pistols hidden within his long brown coat poked her. She ignored the slight discomfort. A breeze then carried Tracy's hair against Donovan's face; he stopped kissing her so as to take in the engaging scent. Then he reached for her shirt and unfastened the buttons until her breasts were exposed. Tracy watched as he stared at her beautiful breasts in amazement. His childlike innocence at that moment was pleasantly unexpected. This was the vulnerable side of Donovan that others would probably never experience. His face was so serious and focused, it was as if he was about to release all the pain and anger that he had been carrying with him for all these years.

She caressed his cheek and then kissed him. And as they kissed passionately, he found, squeezed and massaged her breasts. And as he reached down to unbutton her pants, she stopped him. He seemed puzzled, but again reached for her pants, and again she stopped him.

"No Donovan." She said delicately. "Not like this. I want to be a family first." "A family?" He questioned.

"Yes. You, Sage and me, a family."

Donovan seemed disappointed, and she felt hurt for him. She truly wanted to make love to him, but she would not do so unless he was committed to her. Men like Donovan traveled a lot and probably left women hurt all over the country. It wasn't that she was so innocent with her lovemaking, she had actually been romantic with two other men. Her issue was that she truly loved Donovan, and didn't want to entrust herself romantically to him just to be left behind later.

"I have many enemies. You wouldn't be safe with the likes of me." He said.

"I know what you are Donovan. That changes nothing for me." She admitted.

Donovan stepped back, and Tracy buttoned her shirt to cover her breasts.

Donovan sighed and then said. "I love you, Tracy. I guess I loved you when I first saw you in town that day. I haven't felt this way since Sidney. I didn't know I could feel this way. I wish that I couldn't. It just complicates things."

"What's so complicated Donovan? We're in love, and we should be together."

Donovan sighed again. "My time is running out. I'm amazed that I've survived this long. And I'm grateful that I got to see my son after being gone for so long. But I can't fight all of my enemies, there's too many. Sooner or later they're going to get me."

Tracy frowned and spoke through tight lips. "In this world, we're all in danger, not just you. Innocent people are hanged every day. Women raped at another man's whim. People are thrown in jail for crimes they didn't commit. Families burned out of their homes. In this unfair world, anything can happen. And there ain't a damn thing you can do about it. My brothers were killed; our house was burned down. My mother and father were run out of town." Tracy stopped and sobbed. "I don't even know where my folks are. I don't even know if they're alive. That's how cruel this world is. It's cruel to all of us, not just you." Donovan reached to comfort her as she sobbed into his coat. "If I have to live in this wicked world, I'd rather do it with someone I love than do it alone."

He held her as she continued to sob into his coat. Her emotions had been pent up for so long that she needed to get them out. Until this day she hadn't realized that she carried such a burden of grief from her own past. She was aware of the awful situations of her past, but she somehow managed to push down the sorrow in her subconscious. Maybe she did this to survive, she didn't know. As she continued to cry in his snug arms, she realized that she felt safe with him. This was probably why her emotions were coming to the surface now. She knew in her heart that Donovan would not hesitate to protect her, even if it meant the loss of his own life. He had already proven that. She stopped sobbing and reached around his waist and squeezed.

"Donovan listen to me." She said. "We have to be careful. No one can see us together. Do you understand?"

"Why?"

"Sheriff Landry is why."

"Why should I care about him?" Donovan asked.

"You should care because he'll kill you." She said bluntly. "He's been trying to court me for more than two years. And I've always refused him. But he's a very jealous man. If he finds out that me and you are together, he'll kill us both."

"Maybe I'll kill him," Donovan said coldly.

Tracy frowned. "You can't. No one can. I've seen many try. They're all dead. And if you try you'll be dead too."

"Dying don't scare me none Tracy."

She had to get through to him. "Donovan, if we're going to be together we have to be smart about this. We can still see each other, we just can't do it in public."

"When can I see you again?"

"Soon." She said.

"When?"

"Tomorrow."

"Where?"

"I'll meet you at Mama's house." Said Tracy.

Tracy released herself from his arms, grabbed his hand and led him onto the road while tugging the horses behind. When they were within a mile of the town, she stopped, kissed Donovan and told him that this was far enough and that she would be safe. Reluctantly he agreed. And though she didn't see or hear him within the darkness, she suspected that he had followed her for the rest of the way into town, and then watched her until she was safe inside her hotel.

Chapter 29

It was around eleven o'clock in the late evening when Tracy finally arrived in her hotel room. She was once again exhausted and emotionally drained. Though this time it wasn't from visiting all of her many patients throughout the day. Strangely enough, it was from spending just a few hours with the man that she loved, Donovan.

She worried greatly for his safety. Though Donovan appeared humble and low-key, she knew better. Behind his unassuming demeanor, he was dangerously intense. Not that she was afraid of him, for she knew without question that he would never harm her, but she was more afraid for him. Afraid that he would eventually get himself hurt or killed. Donovan had been injured many times, and hardly any of his wounds were minor. His injuries consisted of gunshots, knife cuts, and being whipped countless times. He could have died from any of his wounds.

Within the darkness of her room, she changed into her sleeping clothes and then snuggled herself into bed. She didn't light the lanterns on the wall for she did not want to alert sheriff Landry that she had arrived. On some nights when he saw the light in her window, he would soon afterward knock on her door, and she was not in the mood for a visit from him tonight. She closed her eyes.

Love.

The word floated in her mind. She was in love. It was so hard to believe but she was in love. Deep down she always thought it would never happen to her. And the reason being because she wasn't looking for love, nor did she care if she ever found it. Nonetheless, the feeling was amazing to her.

However, she didn't fool herself about Donovan. A relationship with him would not be an easy one, maybe even burdensome. Emotionally she wasn't sure if he could handle the companionship that she desired of him. He still seemed to mourn the death of his past wife some seven years ago. And there was so much that she didn't know about him. For example, where had he been these past few years? Why did he have so many enemies? Why was he so willing to put his life on the line for others? What became of the men that killed his late wife? And even more important, how did Donovan go from being a peaceful farmer to a gunslinger?

Not only was she in love with Donovan but he was very much in love with her. She knew this to be true for he had said as much. But it wasn't just his words that convinced her; it was the genuineness of his eyes when he looked at her. They were gentle, patient and loving. His eyes were focused and revealed so much, including his grief, his anger, his distrust and his fondness and love for Tracy. She knew by his transparent and illuminating eyes that he was in love with her. She believed Donovan's love for her was pure and unconditional, like a child that loved his mother. So many of the men that Tracy had encountered claimed wholeheartedly that they were in love with her. They tried to persuade her on how beautiful she was and how they desperately wanted to court her. They would surprise her with many gifts and sometimes promised on hands and knees that they would provide her with a happy and wealthy future. But even with all this, she didn't feel loved by these men. She always felt that their actions were forced and temporary. She suspected after a period of time, these men would grow tired of the gifts, tired of her and after a while forget about their promises. To Tracy this was not love; this was more of an infatuation. Not only could these men not live up to the high expectations that they set for themselves, but Tracy would never be able to live up to the expectation that they set for her as well. This was not love based on truth. This was not love at all.

Though Tracy was viewed by many men to be beautiful, she was still human. And only the man that could look beyond her beautiful outer shell and into her human inner shell, could ever truly love her. And because of the way that Donovan looked at her, the way he listened to her, and the way he respected her, without a doubt she was convinced that he truly loved her.

She found it interesting that his display of love was so low-key. He didn't go out of his way to give her great gifts. He didn't try to impress her with his great stories. He didn't make her promises of a rich and happy future. And he would only admit his love in a matter of fact way. He was the complete opposite of all the other men that tried to court her previously. This gave her the impression that his love for her was genuine and grounded. This led her to believe that unlike the others, Donovan didn't have any expectations about her or their possible relationship. But when he kissed her, he was not reserved at all, but instead extremely passionate and expressive.

As she dozed off she hoped Donovan would abide by her wishes and keep their relationship private, and not confront the sheriff or his deputy for any reason.

After sleeping for some time Tracy had opened her eyes for something had awakened her. She laid motionless in her bed listening. She heard the piano and voices from the saloon across the street, and the light wind drumming against her window. But nothing else, so she closed her eyes and before long was again asleep.

But not long afterward she once more opened her eyes. This time she sat up in her bed and looked around the room. Within the darkness, she was startled to hear movement in the corner. "Who's there?" She called out.

There was a pause before Landry answered. "Just me." He said. He then walked over the desk and set a match to the lantern. The small flame gave the room some visibility and she could now see Landry standing near the wall. Within the shadow of the small flame, his head was bent forward, giving the impression that he was in a low-spirited mood.

Tracy was shaken and didn't know quite what to say or do. She had known Landry to do some unexpected things, such as drag a prisoner through the streets naked, beat men almost to their deaths for displaying disrespect toward him or his brother, and shoot and kill men just because he didn't like them. But she never would have expected him to let himself into her room in the middle of the night without her consent.

As she watched him and he watched her, she could tell that something was troubling him. She had never seen him like this before. Though she wanted to know how he got into her room, and why, she felt for her own safety she would need to approach the subject delicately, if at all.

"Did something happen Landry?" She said trying to display a concerned tone.

He nodded.

"Is Gunther alright?" She asked knowing how much Landry cared for his brother, and only his brother could put him in such a gloomy state.

He sighed. "Gunther's fine."

Tracy then frowned knowing this was the moment to reveal her dissatisfaction, but only after first demonstrating that she was concerned for the sheriff's welfare and his brother. Only now could she intentionally say these next few words without a possible retaliation from the sheriff. "Then why are you in my room in the middle of the night without my knowledge?"

Landry smiled, which was a good sign to Tracy that this sometimes dangerous and volatile man was not offended by her question. Her purpose was not to offend but to instead accomplish two things. First, she wanted to find out what was so urgent that he felt he needed to let himself into her room in the middle of the night without her knowledge. And second, she wanted to make it clear to him that she did not appreciate him doing so, and that she did not want him to do so again. Though this was her room and she had every right to demand the sheriff respect her privacy, she could not convey these emotions in such a way for she could not enforce that he do so, or he would retaliate.

Through his grin Landry said. "I'm just looking out for my girl is all."

"How did you get in my room?" She asked cautiously.

"Paul downstairs let me in."

"Why would you need Paul? I would have let you in myself. I always have."

"I knocked but you didn't answer, I just wanted to be sure you was alright."

"I didn't hear the door because I was sleeping." Tracy pulled her knees to her chest. "This is not like you. Something's wrong. What is it?"

Landry leaned against the wall and sighed. "I've been thinking about us Tracy. I know I'm a white man and you're a colored girl, but you're special to me, and I want us to be together."

"White folks won't approve of us Landry."

Landry frowned. "I don't care what white folks approve. Besides they'll find themselves dead."

"You can't kill them all Landry."

"Yes, I can." He said with certainty, and she believed him.

Tracy was quiet for a moment before she finally said. "Landry, though I care for you deeply... I want to remain just friends."

Landry looked away with the pain of rejection displayed on his face. He abruptly stepped away from the wall and exited the front door, closing it after he had gone through.

After a moment of watching the door, she finally got up and locked it. What good would this do, he had a key now. She grabbed the chair from her desk and forced the back of the chair underneath the base of the doorknob. This may not hold Landry but it gave her some peace of mind knowing it was there.

She then sat on the edge of her bed and pondered for a moment. Landry was getting more desperate and bold in his attempts to court her. She was not interested in a relationship with Landry. It wasn't because he was a white man. It was more because she viewed him as malicious and unpredictable, like a wild dog with rabies. Like everyone else, she was afraid of him, and she was constantly on her guard when in his presence.

After tonight's episode, she was beginning to question how long she could avoid the sheriff's advances. If he wanted to force himself on her, she would be defenseless. As she thought about it, it was more important than ever that she and Donovan keep their relationship private. If Landry were to find out, he would kill them both.

Though she promised Donovan that she would visit with him the next day, she now found that she could not. Now the sheriff would be watching her, so she had to be visible in town so that he would not be suspicious of her whereabouts. She hoped Donovan was patient enough not to come looking for her.

Chapter 30

In his bed, Sage sat up and rubbed his eyes. He then turned to the spot on the floor where Donovan had slept and was disappointed to find that he was already gone. He walked over to the end table by the wall and washed his face in the ceramic bowl. When he stepped out into the main room he could smell bacon, eggs, and his favorite biscuits.

Mama and Donovan were seated at the table eating and chatting. Mama looked up and said. "Morning baby."

Sage nodded. "Morning Mama."

Donovan nodded his usual silent greeting, and Sage in return imitated him and nodded back.

"I made your favorite biscuits." Said Mama pointing to the pile of warm biscuits at the end of the table that was covered with a white towel.

"I've got to pee." Said Sage.

Mama frowned. "Go pee then."

There was a small shack out back about thirty yards or so from the house. As Sage approached the shack the smells of urine and shit filled his nostrils. Inside the shack, it was barely large enough for one person, which brought Sage to wonder how did someone as large as uncle Miles even fit in here.

One of Sage's chores was to empty the shack bucket each morning and night. There had been occasions that he had emptied the bucket just after Miles had relieved himself, and was sometimes caught off guard by the size and amount of Miles's load. Once he was so amazed by the size, that he actually brought the foul bucket into the house to show Mama. And when she saw what he brought in, she threw up, cursed him, and then threw up again.

After Sage had relieved himself he headed back toward the house and washed his hands inside the ceramic bowl next to the stove. Mama had insisted as long as he could remember, that he was to wash his hands before he sat down to each meal.

He reached for a warm biscuit as he excitably sat next to Donovan. The biscuit was as large as his hand and was so scrumptious that he finished it in three big bites. He then reached for two more and finished them in the same manner.

Mama warned. "Slow down Sage, you gonna find yourself choked."

Sage nodded and then turned to Donovan. "I'm going to the schoolhouse today. Haven't been since them boys beat on me. I'm scared of them."

These past few days Sage had gotten to know Donovan quite well. He was no longer uncomfortable around Donovan and looked forward to being in his presence. Though they were father and son, Donovan had said that he and Sage were friends. And as it was explained to Sage, friendship with Donovan was not to be taken lightly. Sage had never had a friend before and felt honored that a man like Donovan considered him worthy enough. However Sage was somewhat uncomfortable that Donovan seemed to trust him so freely. Sometimes when they were alone, Donovan would share some of his past experiences with him. However, when Donovan did so it was used more as a teaching tool for Sage than anything else. Nonetheless, he found that Donovan talked about his past with no one else. Not even Mama.

Donovan glanced down at his plate as he patiently chewed his food. "As you should be, them boys are dangerous." He answered. "But being afraid ain't got nothing to do with it. You have to make a choice without using fear to guide you."

"What if they beats me again?" Asked Sage.

"Just like before you'll survive." Said Donovan. "Maybe one day you'll figure out how not to get beat."

Mama frowned. "What if they beats him to death?"

"Dying ain't the worst of it." Said Donovan.

"Oh my Lord!" Said, Mama. "What are you telling this boy?"

"The truth." Said Donovan calmly. "The truth as I've experienced it. Dying is easy; living is what's hard. Some of these evil men prey on the weak and innocent. Surviving the aftermath of their destruction is impossible." Said Donovan still looking at his plate. "They take away what we cherish most, our loved ones. Those that are left behind are destroyed from their great losses. There's no end to the suffering and devastation that these wicked men can cause folks...Many times there's no justice either."

Mama was silent for she had never known Donovan to speak this openly before. She was however aware that he was referring to his previous experience with the men that killed his past wife Sidney. In the two weeks since he first arrived, she had not, until now, heard him make any reference about his past. However, she suspected that his statement was more for Sage's benefit than herself.

Sage leaned toward Donovan. "Have they ever beat you?" He asked.

Donovan nodded. "Some have."

"What did you do?" Asked Sage.

"I protected myself as best I could." He said.

"How?"

"I struck them with my fist and feet."

"Did that stop them?"

"Usually. But other times it did not."

"What did you do then?" Asked Sage.

Donovan paused as if he was thinking carefully about how to answer Sage's question. He placed his hand on Sage's shoulder. "I did what was needed to survive." He answered.

Mama interjected again. "What are you telling this child? Do you want him to be like you, and live the life that you lived?"

Donovan shook his head. "I don't want him to be nothing like me. The way I live is hard. I just want him to know who I am, and some of the choices that I've made. Maybe I can help ease him of some of his troubles."

Mama sighed. "It ain't my right to come between a boy and his father. I just don't want him hurt is all."

"We can't protect him from his hurt, he's got to protect himself." Said Donovan.

"He's just a child." Mama shot back.

"He's got to learn. If he don't he'll be somebody's victim his whole life. Is this what you wish for your grandson?" Donovan patiently watched his mother waiting for her to answer. But she gave none. So Donovan calmly continued. "He's been a victim long enough. It's not necessary for him to be in this world in such a way."

Mama raised her dark hands to her face and sighed. Then she turned to Sage who was watching her. "I can see the changes in him since you came back. He ain't even the same Sage no more. Before you came he didn't even talk. Now all he do is talk. He used to stay in the house all day, now he goes to the woods and don't come back for hours. He even walk different now. I've watched him, he tries to walk like you. That boy looks up to you Donovan. He wants to be like you. And that's what scares me." She swallowed and grabbed Donovan's hand. "You take the kind of risks that I ain't ever seen no one take before. It's like you ain't afraid of no man. If you wasn't my own son I would be scared to death of you. Sage gonna try to do something foolish thinking he's you. But he gonna find out he's not you, but then it'll be too late cause he'll be dead."

Sage left his chair and embraced Mama. He then looked her in the eyes. His expression was sympathetic. "Don't worry about me none Mama. I ain't gonna do nothing foolish."

She palmed his face with her hands. "You promise baby?"
Sage nodded.

Mama handed Sage his lunch, which was tightly wrapped in a tan cloth, then off to the schoolhouse he went. As he continued through the woods, he could hear the faint laughter and voices of the many students playing in the yard, which was just out of his view. He arrived at the yard as Mr. Bowmen was tugging on the bell that was hung just outside the front entrance of the schoolhouse.

The student's backs were turned to him as they raced to the doorway and squeezed in. Sage was the last one to enter, and he did so unnoticed by the other students. Mr. Bowmen, however, greeted him at the door. "Where have you been these past few days, Sage?" He asked.

"Been sick," Sage answered, and then made his way past Mr. Bowmen down the jammed aisles. As he walked he watched the students noisily rush to get to their seats. When some of them turned and spotted him, their pleasant smiles turned to frowns. Sage turned away from their unpleasantness and continued down the crowded aisles at what seemed like the pace of a turtle. When he reached his desk at the back of the room, he could see that Killeen was twisted within his seat three rows up, as he displayed an awful scowl.

At that moment Sage's stomach waved, like water hitting the walls of a bucket when walking down a hill. On either side of Killeen were his two buddies Billy and Danny, who were also twisted in their chairs glaring at Sage. However, their expressions were not nearly as dramatic and intense as Joshua Killeen.

As Sage guardedly watched the three boys, he thought about Donovan and felt somewhat upset with him. Though Donovan never suggested Sage to return to the school, he still believed Donovan was responsible, for if Donovan hadn't done all his talk Sage wouldn't be here now.

On many occasions, Donovan talked about not letting fear guide Sage with his choices, and made this course of action somehow seem effortless. His demeanor would be calm and self-assured when he suggested to Sage that there was no other alternative. It was easy for Sage to get pulled into Donovan's lectures; for he talked of great experience and so much conviction that it all made sense. After listening to Donovan he would walk away feeling and believe that he could accomplish all that Donovan claimed he could.

However, Sage now felt mislead by his counsel. This was not as easy as Donovan had presented it. At the moment he felt alone and afraid of

Killeen and his two buddies. He should have made another choice, such as stay home with Mama where it was safe. Mama tried to warn him, but Sage didn't listen. Now he wished that he had done so.

The more Sage thought about it the more he realized that Donovan didn't understand him at all. How could he? He had never been a part of Sage's life, except when he was very young, and that was a long time ago. In these many years since Donovan had been gone a lot had happened in Sage's life. Most of which brought upon memories of suffering and shame. A man like Donovan couldn't possibly comprehend the level of Sage's torment, a pain so great that at times it immobilized him.

"What you looking at Nigger?!" Shouted Killeen from his desk.

Sage blinked. Absorbed in his own thoughts he had not been aware that he had been looking at Killeen for quite some time.

Mr. Bowmen's back was to them for he had been writing the first lessons for the morning on the board. He recognized the voice and quickly turned. "Killeen! That is enough!"

Killeen pointed to Sage. "That Nigger is lookin at me."

Taking a step toward Killeen Mr. Bowmen responded. "So what."

For a moment Killeen seemed stunned by Mr. Bowmen's protective response, but he quickly recovered and then said. "My Pa says Niggers shouldn't be looking at folks."

Mr. Bowmen took another step toward Killeen. "There aren't any Niggers in this class. There are only students."

Again Killeen was taken aback by Mr. Bowmen's strong stance. This action from his teacher was unexpected. His face calmed for a moment, as he seemed defeated. "You're right." He admitted softly. "He's not a Nigger." Killeen raised his head and glanced around the classroom at his peers and then grinned wickedly. "He's just an ugly Nigger. And there ain't nothing worse than an ugly Nigger." This drew some snickers from his two buddies beside him, and light laughter was heard from one or two students in the class. However, the rest of the class was uncomfortably silent as they watched the scene unfold.

Sage was deeply wounded by Killeen's comments. Being called a Nigger in front of all the students was unbearable. And to listen to some of their snickers was even worse. As hurtful as the name Nigger was, there was also comfort in this hateful name. The name Nigger was reference to all blacks everywhere and anywhere. To be called a Nigger meant that Sage was part of a group and somehow he shared the burden with the group. This took some of the sting out of the word. It wasn't so much that Sage was being called Nigger, but that all blacks everywhere were being called

Nigger. But to be called an ugly Nigger was almost the death of him. Sage was alone with this reference. He did not know of any blacks that had scars on their faces. Therefore he didn't have the comfort of knowing that there were other blacks just like him to share this horrible reference with.

Snatching the yardstick off his desk, Mr. Bowmen stomped over to Killeen. He stopped just in front of him with the yardstick extended directly to his chest. "If I have to ask you again, you'll be sorry." He warned. And with that Killeen didn't say another word.

As Mr. Bowmen left his side to finish writing on the board, Killeen turned to Sage. Though his stomach trembled, Sage could not bring himself to look away. Instead, he watched Killeen as Killeen was staring at him. Although Sage was afraid, he was also angry. He was angry with Killeen for deliberately humiliating him in front of the other students. He was angry that Killeen brought attention to his scarred face, wounds that he had received from the very men that had killed his mother some seven years ago. He was angry that Killeen could cause Sage so much hurt and suffering.

He stared at Killeen not realizing that his fear was being replaced by his anger. For a moment a cold expression lingered on his face. Though Sage didn't intimidate Killeen in the slightest, he was however somewhat taken back at Sages assertive stance. Puzzled, Killeen finally looked away and faced forward.

Usually, the students worked out the problems on the board and Mr. Bowmen would turn to the remaining seated students and ask them if the answers were correct. If a student thought an answer was incorrect, then Mr. Bowmen would ask the student to come to the board and make the supposed correction next to the original problem. Mr. Bowmen would then ask the class to vote on which answer they thought was correct. Only after considerable class participation, would Mr. Bowmen finally reveal to them the correct answer.

Sometimes even Sage was directed to the board to work out the assignments. However, this didn't occur until nearly seven months after he had first joined the school. When Sage had first been called up to the board, the students mocked him. He had never been called to the board before and was completely caught off guard. As a matter of fact, Mr. Bowmen had to call out Sage's name twice just to get him to the board because Sage didn't believe that his name was actually called.

On his first attempt at the board, he tried to solve the answer but failed miserably. He could not concentrate just from the pressure alone and therefore stood at the board, chalk in hand, motionless. The students went crazy with laughter. Some of their voices blurted out that he was dumb.

Once it was decided that Sage could not solve the problem, Mr. Bowmen turned to the class and asked who wanted to come up and finish. Sage remembered that the entire class threw up their hands and every single student was grunting and yelling to be chosen. One of the boys up front that was finally picked charged the board colliding with Sage, knocking him into the far wall. The class roared with laughter. The student scratched the answer on the board and then turned to the class in triumph, and they all cheered for they knew the answer was correct.

On this day Mr. Bowmen was in odd form, for he had lectured nonstop until lunchtime. Not only did he lecture nonstop but he also went on lengthy tangents about matters that had nothing to do with the subject he was teaching. Usually Mr. Bowmen lectured for a bit, then he wrote the assignments on the board, and afterward, he would pick out several students at random to come to the board to work out each assignment side by side. But never before did he teach for such an extended time without some class participation to break up the time.

Mr. Bowmen pulled his watch out of his vest pocket. "Goodness." He exclaimed. "It's lunchtime already. The morning went by rather quickly didn't it?" And with that, he dismissed the class for their lunch break.

Sage watched as everyone reached under their desks for their lunches that were either tucked in a cloth wrap or a straw basket. He reached for his as well. He waited as each of the students made their way down the aisles. When the last of the students had exited, he then climbed out of his seat and made his way toward the front door. Over the tops of his wired framed glasses, Mr. Bowmen watched him. Sage turned to him. "Can I stay here with you?" He asked.

Mr. Bowmen shook his head. "No Sage, it's against the rules, you know that."

"They're your rules." Sage reasoned.

Mr. Bowmen smiled, for he seemed entertained by Sage's comments. "True, but if I were to break my rules for you, then I would need to break them for everyone. And I assure you it would not end there." He continued. "Students would then request of me to break other rules. And in fairness, I would be forced to abide them, only because I broke the rules for another. And after a while, I would lose the respect of the class. For a teacher to do his job well, he must have the respect of his students. A teacher that does not have respect cannot teach." He placed his hand on Sage's shoulder. "Do you understand?"

Sage nodded as he answered. "I understand."

"Good." Mr. Bowmen said. "Now run along."

Outside in the yard, the students were spread out in several small groups as they ate their lunches. Sage took his usual spot on a rotting log that was closer to the woods. He ate alone.

Not too far from Sage sat Killeen and his two buddies, Billy and Danny. Periodically they looked over their shoulders in the direction of Sage as they talked amongst each other. Though Sage was wary of the three boys, he couldn't help but feel some peace within himself about the situation. He had taken Donovan's advice. He did not let his fear of these three boys stop him from doing what he needed to do, which was to come to the schoolhouse today. As difficult and frightening choice that this was, Sage felt somewhat empowered knowing that he had defied his own fear and done so anyway. In an odd way, he was relieved and less fearful, which was a feeling that he had never realized before. He wondered if this was the emotion that Donovan felt on that day in town when he had faced and killed those two armed men.

The majority of the students had finished their meals and were involved in a game of chase. The object of this game was for one person, the chaser, to chase another, the runner, and to continue chasing the runner until they touched that person. Once the runner was touched the chaser would then yell YOU'RE IT! And then the runner that was touched became the chaser and that person at that juncture would then chase another in the same fashion. It was fun to watch as the folks scrambled to catch one another. Usually, there was only one chaser and everyone else in the yard was the runner.

Sage watched as one of the smaller girls chase the others for she was the chaser in this game. She unsuccessfully chased folks around the trees and across the yard. She frequently switched up on several runners but could not catch any of them. Finally, she grew tired and stopped in the middle of the yard. Some of the faster students taunted her as they moved within striking distance and then dashed just out of her reach when she tried to touch them. After numerous failed attempts the smaller girl became frustrated and stood idle in the middle of the yard. She looked around trying to decide who to chase next. Finally, she looked over in Sages direction. After careful consideration, she casually walked over to him. She reached out and touched him, and yelled, "You're it!" And then ran away screaming as if he were going to chase her.

Sage felt awkward, in the two years that he had been with this school, he had never before played the game of chase or any other game with these students. All he had ever done was watch them silently from this log. One boy ran up to Sage and taunted him. "You're it, dummy."

He reached for the boy but missed for the boy was quick. Sage stepped off the log and stood idle. Some of the girls took cover behind the trees yelling, "Sage is it!" Sage is it!" A few of the boys positioned themselves low to the ground so as to be able to dash if Sage came in their direction. Sage was apprehensive as he walked in the direction of the runners. They backed away with anticipation. After a while, another boy approached Sage and taunted him. Sage leaped for the boy, but again this one was quick and took off running untouched. Almost instinctively like a wild animal chasing its prey Sage went after him. Surprisingly Sage was closing the distance on the boy. The boy repeatedly glanced over his shoulder and his eyes were wide with disbelief when he realized how close Sage was getting. The boy made several zigzags in his attempt to lose the chaser, but Sage never let up and continued to gain ground. Some of the male students were cheering the boy who they called Johnny. "Run Johnny run!" They yelled.

Johnny managed some momentum from the cheers but Sage was still tight on his tail. In his final attempt to lose Sage, Johnny cut and headed toward the tree where some of the girls were partially hidden. His plan was to head toward the girls and use them as bait, hoping that Sage would lose interest in him, and go for the easier prey. However, when the girls realized that Johnny was leading Sage to them they started screaming and scattered in all directions. By the time Johnny reached the tree all the girls were long gone.

Johnny was out of options, he was exhausted and Sage was still gaining. It was just a matter of seconds before he would feel Sage's touch and would hear that horrifying yell. You're it! He cut sharply around the abandoned tree and Sage anticipating this move cut the opposite way so that they would be face to face on the other side. They nearly collided as Sage touched Johnny across the shoulder and said in a normal tone. "You're it." And then ran on toward his usual seating area the log, and then collapsed for he was exhausted as well.

The cheering from the boys had stopped. They were moving toward Johnny who was on his back with his knees up fighting for each breath. One of the boys started teasing. "You let that colored boy catch you like that? You ain't no better than him." Then all the boys chimed in, and Johnny did not respond.

Killeen and his two buddies had watched the wild chase from off to the side. When Sage made his way back to the log, Killeen and his buddies frowned at him.

Standing first was Killeen and then his buddies followed. They made their way toward Sage. He was leaning against the log when he saw the three boys coming in his direction. Sage realized another beating was coming. He wondered what Donovan would have him do at this moment. Though exhausted he pushed off the log and stood to his feet. Donovan would fight.

As Killeen and his two buddies were upon Sage, the bell rang several times, a signal that the lunch break was over. Gripping the bell chain Mr. Bowmen called. "All inside." He supervised as the students gathered their baskets and empty clothes and headed toward the entrance of the school. Begrudgingly Killeen and his buddies left Sage's side and headed toward the school as well. After giving them some distance Sage followed them. As usual, he was the last to enter the building. As he passed Mr. Bowmen just outside the door, he touched Sage's shoulder and guided him through the doorway.

Inside the schoolhouse, Killeen and his buddies scrutinized Sage while he was making his way to his desk. The little girl that had touched him earlier in the game of chase had been watching and smiled when he glanced in her direction. He tried to hold his impassive expression but could not for a partial grin had broken free.

After the lunch break, Mr. Bowmen had again lectured none stop without any class participation. He did so for the next few hours until it was time to dismiss the students for the day. Sage was entertained by this change of his lecturing style. His hands, body and facial expressions were very animated and exaggerated as he addressed the class. He somehow felt that he was watching a magnificent play and Mr. Bowmen was the star actor.

The students noisily climbed out of their seats after they were dismissed. Sage, however, remained at his desk until the last of them had exited the schoolhouse. He picked up his books and pretended to shuffle through them, giving himself distance between him and the other students. Killeen and his buddies were his main concern. Like before he knew that they would wait for him.

While he shuffled through his books, he tried to figure out how he was going to avoid the beating. Though he was anxious and fearful, he had resentment for the situation. He didn't like being the prey for the three boys, or that they could strike and injure him at their whim.

Mr. Bowmen cleared his throat from behind his desk. "You need to get going." He said.

Grabbing his books Sage walked past Mr. Bowmen toward the front door. In the doorway, he hesitated for a moment and then turned to Mr. Bowmen. "Killeen and his friends will be waiting for me." He said.

"Why?" Asked Mr. Bowmen.

Sage sighed. "They don't want me at this school. The last time they beat me so bad I laid in bed for three days."

Mr. Bowmen nodded sympathetically. "Why don't you take another way home? He suggested. "Instead of going your usual route go the opposite direction for a mile or two and then circle around so that you are heading toward your home, but on a different trail. Of course, this will take you much longer to get home, but at least you'll be safe."

Chapter 31

Sage was ecstatic as he stood in the schoolyard. The idea that Mr. Bowmen had was genius. He would take a different way home. He would start out north, then circle around and eventually head south in the direction of home. Sage smiled when he wondered how long Killeen and his buddies would wait before they grew tired and realized that he wasn't coming down his typical course. He figured they would even circle back to the school to see if he was still there. And to their surprise, they would find an empty school and no Sage.

After going north for some time, Sage cut west and then eventually was headed south toward his home. He had not taken this way before, so nothing seemed familiar. Because of the different surroundings, his pace was awkward and unsure. Even though he was certain that he was headed in the right direction, he still had some anxiety as he moved through the woods. Since Killeen and his crew were no longer a threat, he didn't feel the need to pace through the woods suspiciously. He was relieved that he didn't have to caution himself when he came across large trees or thick bushes, fearing that Killeen would leap out from hiding.

After walking for quite a distance Sage was comforted to finally recognize his surroundings. Not much further he thought. Even though he began to relax and felt out of harm's way, he still maintained his pace as his feet crunched on the dry leaves and brittle twigs below. The alternative route took longer than he anticipated and he knew that Mama would be worried.

Sage froze. He had heard something rustle behind him. Afraid, he turned. He saw nothing except the inner workings of the forest. He stood still searching for a small animal of some sort. Maybe a rabbit. But after a moment nothing had satisfied the movement that he thought he heard. After a while, Sage began to doubt that he had actually heard anything. Perhaps the isolation in the forest caused his imagination to inflate to the slightest sounds.

After a long moment of frightful silence, Sage again found himself relaxing. He had convinced himself from lack of evidence that nothing was out there. Once more he started out, but this time he was more cautious as he listened and watched the surroundings intently. But after he had taken only a few steps he was sure that he had heard another rustling noise from behind. He turned and to his amazement it was Killeen. He was partially hidden behind a thick bush. He was alone and all business displaying no emotion. Just blank. It was like it was someone else in Killeen's body.

Now that Killeen was discovered he stepped from behind the bush, and the two boys gazed at each other. Sage's face was distorted with disbelief and horror. His heart pounded so strongly that it ached. He grabbed his chest. He blinked often, for could not believe his own vision. Killeen was actually before him. How could this be when he had gone through such a great effort to avoid him?

Killeen eased a step forward, and Sage matched him as he took a step backward. By doing so Sage sustained the distance of thirty yards that was between them.

"What do you want?" Sage pleaded not taking his eyes off Killeen, bracing himself for an attack. "What do you want?" He repeated almost in tears.

"I didn't like you grinning at me. I didn't see what was so funny."

"Sorry," Sage responded. "So sorry."

"No…You're not sorry. Not yet, but you will be." Killeen took another step and Sage again matched him with a step backward.

"Leave me be," he cried. "I've done nothing. Just leave me be."

"No." Said Killeen. "You've done plenty. My Papa says that if a nigger grins, then he is as good as dead. That way he ain't got nothing to grin about no more." He looked about his feet, and when he spotted it he picked it up. It was a rock twice the size of his fist.

Sage didn't delay any longer, he turned and ran. While he ran he hollered. He yelled as loud as his voice would carry. His intention wasn't to gain the attention of others, for he realized that no one would be around to take notice. He screamed to hopefully relieve his own personal stress and fear that had built up within his chest.

Sage looked over his shoulder; Killeen was running and gaining fast. The only reason that he hadn't caught up with Sage by now was because he was juggling the large rock. Sage wasn't convinced that Killeen was alone, so when he came upon the wide trees and the thick bushes he avoided them and cut in a different direction. He didn't think his heart could take another surprise if one of Killeen's friends were to jump out of hiding.

Sage looked over his shoulder again; Killeen was much closer, still carrying the rock. Sage's voice became hoarse and he could no longer scream. He was coughing and choking, and his vocal chords itched badly. Sage continued to race ahead, he cut and dashed so many times that he lost track of the direction home. None of that mattered now for he was too far out, and Killeen was gaining with each step. Not only was Killeen closer, but Sage was exhausted as he gasped for air, and hacked from the yelling.

Again Sage glanced over his shoulder; Killeen was within three or four steps, almost within reach. He knew for certain that he was not going to make it home. This would be the end that Donovan had sometimes talked of.

He felt the tips of Killeen's fingers upon his shoulder and Sage dropped to the ground before they could take hold of him. Killeen wasn't expecting the sudden collapse and he plummeted head over as he toppled over Sage's back.

On the ground, Killeen laid moaning. During the fall he had managed to hit his face on the rock that he was carrying. There were some scratches and trickles of blood on his right cheek. Sage contemplated climbing to his feet and making another run for it, but he was exhausted barely breathing, still coughing, legs hurting. So instead he decided to rest. After a short time he peeked at Killeen, he was still moaning with his eyes shut. Sage closed his eyes for an instant and then promptly opened them again. Killeen was now faced the other way and the moaning had ceased. Sage closed his eyes again.

A familiar voice had awakened him. He looked up to see Killeen straddling him with his hands extended high above his head holding the rock that he had carried before. But oddly Killeen was frozen in this position as he looked intently at something just out of Sage's view.

"I said put that rock down boy, I won't be asking again."

Sage recognized the voice. It was Donovan. His tone was poised with authority. Sage wanted to look back at him but didn't dare take his eyes off Killeen and his rock.

Killeen was stunned as he finally stepped back. He was caught in the act and was self-conscious for what he was about to do.

"Who are you?" He asked with the rock still in hand, high above his head.

On top of Fletcher Donovan looked down at the boy. Under his large brown hat, he frowned. He then stepped off of Fletcher and as he did so his long brown coat moved in a way that exposed one of his holstered pistols.

When Killeen caught a glimpse of the Negro man's pistol, his eyes grew wide with terror. He dropped the rock and stepped back almost running. At that point, Sage rolled over and climbed to his feet, and stood slightly in front of Donovan.

Sage and Donovan observed Killeen as he looked back at them with eyes of apprehension. "He had it coming to him." Killeen blurted.

"And how is that?" Donovan asked.

Killeen decided not to answer and said this. "My Pa ain't gonna like this."

"Don't much care what your Pa likes." Responded Donovan.

Taken back by the Negro man's response, Killeen then said. "You don't know my Pa. He don't like niggers that don't know their place."

As Donovan spoke these next few words, he lifted his hand chest high and extended toward Killeen. With the extended hand, he clutched a fist and turned it violently as if he was snapping a chicken's neck. "This is my son." He said. "If you harm him in any way, I'm going to find you and wring your little neck like so." He said as he demonstrated how it would be done.

The forthright Negro man once more astonished Killeen. In his desperation, he attempted to taunt him by scowling, but the Negro man was not affected and evenly stared back.

"My Pa gonna come after you." Said Killeen in his final attempt to make the Negro man stand down.

Donovan removed the large brown hat so that his face was completely in view. He leaned forward so that he was closer to the boy. His face was tranquil with certainty. "For your Pa's sake, I hope that he doesn't." He watched as the boy thought this over and squirmed.

"Can I go now mister?" The boy asked.

Donovan nodded, and the boy hurriedly turned and ran into the woods. He was somewhat amused for as the boy sprinted, he periodically looked over his shoulder, like fearful dogs would do when their tails were tucked between their legs and they were in a scurry.

Donovan squeezed Sage's shoulder. "Let's get home, you're grandmas worried sick about you."

On Fletcher, Donovan climbed up front and Sage mounted on back. Donovan guided Fletcher around and they headed home. It was sometime in the late afternoon and the sun was falling to the west and the long grass swayed as the breezes teased. Sage was shaken up by what had just happened. If it weren't for Donovan, Killeen would have killed him.

"How did you find me?" Sage asked from the rear of the horse.

"I heard you screaming." He answered. "Your grandma was worried when you didn't show. So she sent me looking."

"His Pa gonna come looking for you." Said Sage. "He's as mean as they come. Folks around here know better than to cross him."

"I reckon so." Said Donovan.

"Some say he's killed before." Said Sage.

Donovan sighed. "I reckon so."

Sage was troubled with Donovan's unruffled mannerism. This was not a character to be taken lightly. Banther Killeen possessed an awful reputation. He was notorious and feared for his bullying tactics. Many of his clashes were in the saloon, and he relentlessly prevailed. Many times he would brawl two or three men altogether. He would toss those grown men around like bales of hay. He hurled them over tables, across the bar and sometimes through glass windows.

Sage had heard talk that on occasion he was known to kill men with his bare hands. When sheriff Landry and his deputy Gunther arrived on the scene, Banther would plead self-defense, and the many frightened witnesses would each time concur with his statements. As a result, Banther's numerous criminal acts went unpunished.

This truly troubled Sage. If any harm were to come of Donovan he would blame himself. It would be a great shame that after all these years of merciless endurance and dodging death, that somehow Sage had been responsible for Donovan's demise.

"I don't want nothing to happen to you," Sage admitted. "We's just getting to know each other. This is my fault. I brought you into this."

Donovan tugged on the reins and Fletcher stopped. He turned on his saddle and frowned. "Ain't nothing your fault boy. This is a cruel world that we live in. So much happens that is out of our control."

Under Donovan's gaze, Sage swallowed. "Joshua's papa gonna kill you."

Donovan sighed. "Sage, listen to me carefully, and never forget what I'm about to tell you."

Sage nodded.

"I have many enemies. There were a few times when I didn't think I would survive all the chaos." Donovan paused. "When I was laying in some of those streets shot up and bloody, folks close by would say he's as good as dead. And that's when I would manage to my feet. I had to keep going so that I could one day live to see you again. Because I live by the sword I'll die by the sword. That has nothing to do with you. That's a decision I made when your mother was killed many years ago. My time is running out, and one day soon my enemies will get to me. I'm grateful for this time that we've had together. When the time comes for me to leave this world, I will have no regrets, because I finally got to know my only son." Donovan turned forward and nudged Fletcher. "Never forget that." He said as they moved forward.

Sage wiped the tears from his cheek with the back of his hand. For all these years Sage had desperately wanted a father, and now he had Donovan.

When they departed the forest and arrive on the outskirts of the property, in the far off distance they could see that Mama was seated on the porch waiting anxiously for their return. As soon as she became aware of them she jumped to her feet and pointed. Donovan and Sage were not yet within hearing range, but they figured she had called out to Papa because a moment later he was out of the house and standing by her side. When they were close enough they stepped off the porch to meet them. While they were still seated high on Fletcher Mama glanced up with tears in her eyes. "Where's he been all this time?"

"He's alright Mama when I saw him he was on his way home." Said Donovan.

The two climbed off of Fletcher, and Donovan patted the horse's hind end and they all watched him trot back toward the woods.

"Why is you just now getting home?" Inquired Mama. "I was worried sick about you. I just knew something awful had happened this time."

"Sorry, Mama. Mr. Bowmen had me stay to clean the boards, and I lost track of time." Regrettably after this comment, Sage was genuinely ashamed of himself. This was the first time he had ever lied to his Grandma, and he felt that he had betrayed her. Unconditionally she had always been there for him. Not once could he remember her passing judgment on his unsightly appearance nor did she allow others to condemn him in her presence. His grandmother's friendship and devotional love was his only rationale for existing. Otherwise, he would not have had a reason to go on. There were countless nights that just the mere presence of her or the tone of her voice momentarily cured him of his immense loneliness. Occasionally she would just hum peaceful tones to help alleviate him of his troubles.

Now it was Sage's turn to alleviate his grandmother of some of her troubles. This was why he was not forthcoming about today's events. She had gone through enough anguish when he had not come home at his usual time. She was a woman now in her sixties, and he didn't know how much stress her heart could bear. And worse, he could not tolerate to witness her in such a worrisome state. He wanted to spare her of this torture.

He now understood why Donovan was so passionate and reckless when he protected those that he loved. It was a form of self-sacrifice.

Mama still suspicious turned to Donovan. "Is this true Donovan?"

Donovan nodded.

She sighed a long breath of relief. "You tell that fool teacher not to do that anymore."

"I will," Sage said.

Mama turned and headed toward the house. "Your supper is on the table."

Donovan placed his hand affectionately on Sage's shoulder. Without words, he was expressing to Sage that he agreed with his decision to keep the burden of the day's events to himself.

Once Mama was inside, Papa eyed them with suspicion. "You don't need to shelter me. What happened out there?"

Sage did most of the talking and explained to Papa about the classroom conflict with Killeen, the schoolyard after the game of chase, after school when he took another direction home to avoid Killeen, and finally when Donovan came about.

Papa was worrisome as he listened. "I'm glad Mama doesn't know of this." He said. "This would break her heart." Papa leaned on his cane. "Joshua Killeen has always been up to no good. That boy needs his ass whipped. But his Papa Banther is worse. He's protective of that boy of his. After what happened today he gonna come lookin for you. I suspect you'll see him no later than tomorrow, if not tonight."

"If I hadn't come along," said Donovan. "Sage wouldn't be with us now."

"I agree." Said Papa adjusting himself on the cane. "You had no choice on what you done. I would have done the same. But Banther won't see it that way." Papa gazed at the ground. It was obvious that he was overwhelmed by what he had just heard. "It's good Mama doesn't know of this." He said more to himself. "Me and Mama have been married for almost fifty years. We've had good and hard years. Mostly good years. From day one I promised to never keep anything from her. I've always kept that promise. A man is as good as his word. But today I'm gonna break that promise." He looked intently at Donovan. "I must admit since you've been back, this is the happiest that I've seen your Mama in a long while. I don't have the heart to steal her joy. The way I see it she has maybe a few more days with you. I'll let her do so without worry. Afterwards, when you're gone, her memories of you will be of joy only." He sighed. "That's why I must keep this news of what happened to Sage from her."

Donovan frowned. "Maybe I won't be leaving."

Papa nodded. "I already know this, and I don't understand this about you. Sheriff Landry and Deputy Gunther aren't men to go against. They've warned you days ago. Whether you know or not, at the end of these two weeks, you'll either leave of your own will or you'll be dead. Either way, you'll be gone. Knowing those lawmen like I do, if it were me, I would have long been gone by now."

Chapter 32

After about ten or so Sage and Donovan called it a day and turned into their room, they both were fatigued from the day's events. In the corner on the end table, the lantern was set to burn at a low dim. Sage was leaning over the edge of his bed as he watched Donovan, who was on the floor on top of his sleeping blankets near the wall. The reflection of the faint light danced around him, and Sage could barely see his outer silhouette.

"What if they come lookin for us while we sleep?" He asked.

"Who?" Said Donovan.

"Banther and Joshua Killeen."

Donovan was on his back and turned in his direction. Sage could barely see his face within the shadows. "That's not something you ought to be troubled with?" He said. "You need to get yourself some sleep."

"Papa said they'd be coming as soon as tonight."

"Your Papa is making too much of this." Said Donovan.

"What if he's right?" Said Sage.

Donovan sighed. "You're wearing me out with this talk of yours. Just go to sleep. Ain't nothing gonna happen tonight."

"You swear?"

"Swear." Said Donovan.

Complying with Donovan's request Sage rolled over and took his usual sleeping position facing the wall. He felt somewhat comforted knowing that Donovan was present with him. Though his eyes were closed, it was a long time before he was actually able to sleep. At one point Sage had awakened in the middle of the night long after the lantern had burned out. He called to Donovan within the darkness not expecting a response and was startled when he had answered back. His voice was clear and alert, which led Sage to believe that Donovan was not sleeping at all, nor did he intend to that night.

The next morning Sage had awakened only to discover that Donovan had managed to depart without his knowledge. All that was left were his empty sleeping blankets that were rolled up against the wall. Sage peeked under his bed and suspected Donovan not to have gone far, for most of his pistols were still concealed under his bed. Donovan would by no means leave the property without his weapons.

Sage noticed that two of the weapons were missing. One was a small two-shooter pistol the other was the knife. This was common, given that Mama had warned Donovan of carrying his shooting pistols in her home. She had explained that her faith in the LORD was all the protection that was needed in her house. So to appease his mother he carried the two weapons without her knowledge. The two-shooter was concealed within his boot, and the knife was tucked out of sight in the back of his britches. Weapons that Donovan had explained to Sage that could be used only for close range combat.

Sage stepped out of his room and approached the kitchen table where Donovan Papa and Mama sat. Everyone did their usual morning greetings, and then Sage sat next to Donovan across from Mama and Papa. On the table was a fresh plate of ham and biscuits. Mama instructed everyone to grab hands, and then she led them in grace, giving thanks to the LORD for the food that they were about to eat. During grace when Sage peeked he noticed that Donovan did not have his head bowed or his eyes closed.

After grace everyone reached for the food and heaped it onto their plates. On Sage's plate, he had a slice of ham and three large biscuits. Mama frowned. "You gonna eat all that?" She asked. Sage took his first bite, grinned and nodded earnestly in her direction. She couldn't help but smile and then said playfully. "You better."

Coming together for these mealtimes was one of Sages most gratifying moments. At these times everyone was relaxed and seemed to forget about their problems or worries for the time that it took to finish their meals. It was time for laughter, reminisces and stories. Usually, Papa told most the stories, but from time to time, Mama would share hers as well. Her stories were normally informative as compared to Papa's that were typically humorous. And when uncle Miles and his wife Maria were present they would also join in with stories and talk of their own. Donovan, however, was more serious, reserved and didn't speak much. He didn't tell stories and he would only nod occasionally and politely answer questions that came his way. But usually, he observed and said nothing.

After breakfast, Sage stepped onto the front porch and peered out. It was early morning, and the glowing sun was just coming into view. He was grateful that this day was Saturday and he was not expected to go off to the schoolhouse for two full days. After what had transpired yesterday with Joshua Killeen, he had strong reservations about actually returning to the schoolhouse ever again.

He could tell by the position of the sun that it was going to be another warm day. This pleased him. Across the way, Miles was already in the fields overturning the land to cover the seeds that Papa had planted the day before. In an attempt to find Fletcher, Sage took a minute to search abroad. He did not, however, see the horse, though he wondered, if he would whistle like Donovan, would the massive animal come running to him as well.

As Sage continued to gape toward the wooded area, he saw two folks on horses come into view. They were in the vicinity of the outer edge of the property and seemed to be headed this way. They were too far away to identify their faces but he had his suspicions. He took a deep breath and watched them as they moved onward. After they had trotted a few more paces closer, to his dismay he recognized one of the riders to be Joshua Killeen, and though he had never seen the other rider before, he knew this huge man next to him had to be his papa Banther.

Behind he had heard the front door creak open. Still watching the riders abroad, he listened as Donovan's boots tapped the wooden porch as he approached Sage's side.

Taking another deep tense breath Sage blurted. "That's them."

"Relax." Was Donovan's response, and this somehow was enough to somewhat calm Sage.

"What are we gonna do?" Sage asked, still watching the riders approaching.

"You can wait inside with Mama and Papa." Said Donovan.

Sage looked up, Donovan was composed with experience. This was not a situation that was new to him, and the unruffled expression on his face confirmed this. For that moment he thought about Donovan and the many scars that he had observed on his body previously. Hideous wounds from knives, whips, and bullets. Injuries that seem to have been unbearable in suffering, and in some instances nearly fatal. As Sage reflected on these injuries, surprisingly he became aware of the anger within himself mounting. In such a brief time he had grown to respect and love this man and was deeply distraught knowing that in his past someone had harmed him in the way that his marked body demonstrated. And now this Banther was emerging to inflict more injuries or even death upon Donovan. In his mind, Donovan had done nothing to deserve this. He did what any father would do, which was to protect his son from harm, or in Sage's situation, from death. If Donovan hadn't shown up when he did, Joshua Killeen would have killed him.

Sage turned from Donovan and watched the riders. He watched, as they were now half the distance from them. The longer he observed the more he came to understand the situation at hand. Once Banther immobilized Donovan, Sage would then be Joshua Killeen's next target. And Banther would oversee as his son beat Sage to his death.

Though Donovan had survived many battles Sage was certain, knowing of Banther's awful reputation, that he would not survive this one.

"I'm staying," Sage said decisively.

Donovan turned to Sage and studied him. He was not the same boy that he had first come across just a few weeks before. He was coming into his own. His stance was upright and defiant like a courageous soldier would do before combat. His expression was unwavering as he focused on the riders that were headed their way. He was so attentive in fact that he did not notice Donovan watching him.

"You best go inside." Said Donovan. "This is between me and that boy's papa. This is no place for a boy."

The concentration of Sage was broken as he gazed up at Donovan. "I'm almost a man." He pleaded. "I'll be staying with you."

After observing such conviction in the boy, at that moment Donovan couldn't help but have a high opinion of his son. Sage was transforming into a young man before his eyes. He was no longer the frail kid that was prey to all that crossed his path. He was making difficult choices to stand for himself. "You're more of a man than most men I've come across." He admitted. "But I can't guarantee your safety. You best go inside."

With tears down his face, Sage was still defiant. "Banther's gonna kill you, and then they'll come after me. I got no choice, I have to stay, otherwise, they'll come looking for me in the house. And then Mama and Papa gonna get hurt trying to look after me."

Donovan nodded for he understood this reasoning. "I reckon so." He said. "A man's got to make his own way. If your heart tells you so, I've got nothing against it. But don't leave this porch. I want you close to the door, so if things go bad for me, you can run inside and arm yourself."

Sage nodded, for he agreed.

Donovan turned his attention back to the riders. He concentrated on the large man. The man was as bulky and powerful looking as his brother Miles. On top of his head was a thick mound of unkempt black hair. His once white shirt was soiled and stained, and his dark brown pants were covered in dust. Around his waist, it appeared that he was weaponless. The only weapon that was visible was the hunting rifle holstered to his horse.

Briefly, Donovan turned his attention from the riders and scanned the woods on the outskirts of the property. He wanted to be sure that these riders had come alone, and that others weren't hiding within the safety of the trees. If it turned out there were others, he would then have no option but to go inside and arm himself.

Within the woods, he observed no one.

Side by side Donovan and Sage looked on as they continued to wait. When the riders were close enough to Miles, he turned and watched them as well, and as they strolled by, he tossed his shovel and followed them back in the direction of the house.

At that time Papa had stepped onto the porch and positioned himself just behind Donovan and Sage. "Mama's inside scared to death." He said.

As the riders gained ground Donovan was able to study the large man's face. The expression was malicious as he focused merely on Donovan. It was obvious that the man's intent was to inflict harm.

Donovan stepped off the porch and approached the riders who were still several yards out. His aim in doing so was to attempt to deter the likelihood of this confrontation. From his experience, he found that when the enemy realized that Donovan would not run or coward and that their lives were also in jeopardy, this would sometimes be enough to dispirit them to move on. As he marched toward them he stared at the large man, and the large man gawked back at him. When they were a few feet apart the riders and Donovan stopped and stared at one another.

Banther turned to Joshua and asked. "This him?"

Joshua nodded, but he didn't come across as confident and assured as his father. The sight of the fearless Negro man marching toward them was unsettling to him. Eyeing the Negro man, Banther stepped over the saddle and climbed down.

Donovan observed him attentively for if his fingers had merely brushed against the rifle, he would have pulled the two-shooter from his boot, and fired both bullets into the man's face.

The large man stepped away from the horse and rifle and approached the Negro man until they were within arm's length of one another. Donovan understood from the man's hostile expression that this conflict could not be avoided.

Off to the side Miles kept his distance, but gave the impression that if things didn't go right he would participate.

Banther was a half head taller than Donovan and glared down at him as he spoke. "My boy says you had words with him."

"That's right," Donovan said.

"He says you threatened him harm." Said Banther.

"I reckon so." Said Donovan. "He was looking to take my son's life."

Giving the impression of a bewildered dog, Banther turned his head sideways. He was in disbelief of the Negro man's forthright responses. He snorted like a crazed bull. "You don't know your place Nigger."

Donovan glared. "My place is with my son."

With powerful hands, Banther reached for Donovan's throat. But Donovan brought his hands up the middle and knocked Banther's hands off to either side. Then almost simultaneously he kneed Banther in his gut. Banther grunted and stumbled. And before Banther could catch his balance Donovan had stepped forward and front kicked him. Dazed, Banther fell on his back. Still, in motion, Donovan dropped down into Banther's chest with all his weight and force upon his knee. Banther's legs shot up and he rolled over as he gasped for the air that was forced out of him. Though he was somewhat incapacitated, Donovan was far from finished. While Banther struggled for his breath Donovan struck him several times in the face, then positioned himself so that he was behind Banther. He tucked his forearm around Banther's throat and then wrapped his legs around his torso. He pulled on Banther's neck and tightened his legs so that Banther was awkwardly stretched out. He struggled but Donovan held fast. His eyes bugged and his once pale complexion gradually turned dark purple, for he was not able to take in air. Behind him, on his horse, he heard Joshua Killeen bawling. Donovan held this position until Banther was no longer able to resist.

Donovan released his hold and pushed Banther over with his foot.

"Is my Papa dead?" Cried Joshua Killeen.

Donovan rolled to his feet and approached Banther's horse. He grabbed the rifle and brought it back. By this time Banther was sitting up as he hacked and choked in an attempt to breathe again, Donovan pointed the rifle to the back of his head.

"Don't kill my Papa." Joshua Killeen begged.

Banther turned to him. He tried to speak, but his voice was not audible from the prior choking.

Donovan forced the barrel into his mouth. "If I see you again, I'll kill you. You won't even know I'm around. All you'll feel is the bullet inside your head. And in that split second before it goes black forever, just know it was me."

Banther nodded, and Donovan pointed the barrel away. He managed to his feet, and like a drunkard, he stumbled to his horse. After a few attempts, he somehow got onto the saddle. He took one last look at the Negro man, and as he did so, Donovan raised the rifle with his finger on the trigger and pointed it at him. Banther turned, and he and his boy raced off the property.

Sage finally stepped off the porch and stood next to Donovan and watched the riders race away. As he focused on Joshua Killeen he couldn't help but feel sad for him. No boy should ever observe his own Papa getting beat almost to his death, as he had just witnessed. However, his sympathy didn't last long, for he realized that he could have instead easily been the one watching Donovan getting beat and eventually killed.

After the combat had gone underway, surprisingly it soon became obvious that Donovan was going to strangle this man to his death, but at what seemed like the last moment, Donovan had decided against it and released him. Maybe it was Joshua's cries that had changed his mind. Or maybe he had just realized that Sage was present and he didn't want his son to view such a scene. Either way Sage was grateful that Donovan didn't kill this man, especially in witness of his son. "What will you do if he brings back more men?" Asked Sage.

Donovan turned to him. His expression was heartfelt and his words rang of truth. "I reckon if I'm able, all that comes this way will be no more."

Sage knew that Donovan meant his words. Any man that attempted to do this family harm, he would do his best to kill them. But even so, Donovan was still merely flesh and blood, a human. And all humans were vulnerable to injury and death. The greater the numbers that Donovan faced the less of a chance that he would survive.

Mama finally stepped out of the house and stood next to Papa on the porch. She was visibly shaking. He reached and held her as they watched the riders race away. She shivered in his arms. From time to time they glanced at Donovan and were in great disbelief that he had for the moment managed to escape this conflict uninjured. But sadly their hearts were burdened for they felt that this conflict was not over. Banther would be back with help to take revenge against their son.

Chapter 33

"You say he just attacked you." Asked Deputy Gunther from behind his desk. Banther and Joshua Killeen were standing on the other side explaining to the lawmen what had happened earlier that day. Sheriff Landry stood across the room as he faced them and listened.

Banther's mug was swelled and bruised from the brawl that morning. There was dried blood mixed with dirt across the front of his white shirt. Landry and Gunther had never witnessed Banther in this condition before. They found it odd that Banther was even at the jailhouse attempting to file a complaint because usually, his victims were complaining about him.

"First he attacked my boy." Explained Banther. "Then he attacked me."

Gunther leaned back in his chair as he listened and then he and Landry exchanged glances. Usually, Gunther preferred to handle these types of complaints, and Landry would often stand off to the side observing and listening. They would often exchange unnoticed glances to one another to signal their thoughts of the situation at hand. In this particular situation, Gunther was signaling to Landry that he was skeptical of Banther's account of what had happened. And apparently, by Landry's slight nod he had felt the same.

Gunther leaned forward and rubbed his mustache. "Who attacked you?" He asked.

"I didn't get his name." Said Banther. "I haven't seen him around these parts before this."

Suspiciously Gunther glanced at Landry and then asked. "What did he look like?"

"He was a little shorter than me…a nigger." Banther finally admitted with his head down, ashamed.

Gunther laughed. "A nigger? You let a nigger beat you like this?"

"He ain't your usual nigger, Deputy. He ain't like no nigger I've ever come across."

"How's he different?" Asked Gunther.

"His eyes for one. He got strange eyes." Said Banther.

"Strange how?" Questioned Landry from across the room.

"His nigger eyes ain't got no fear in them."

Gunther and Landry exchanged glances again. This time Landry approached the desk; he had some questions of his own. "This boy you were talking of, the one that attacked your son. What's his name?"

Banther turned to his son. "What's the boy's name?"

Joshua Killeen was not responsive as he looked at the floor; he was still visibly shaken from the incident that morning. Finally, he glanced up to find that they all were watching him with anticipation. "Sage." He blurted under his breath.

"Sage?" Said Landry.

Joshua Killeen nodded.

"I'll be damned." Said Gunther.

"That man that you claimed attacked you and your son, his name is Donovan." Said Landry

"You know him?" Asked Banther.

"We know him." Said Gunther. "We've had a couple of run-ins with him. I almost killed that son of a bitch a few days back."

"You gonna arrest him?" Asked Banther.

"Nope." Answered Landry. "We ain't gonna do nothing with him."

A flabbergasted Banther turned to Landry. Gunther was also taken back but knew better than to oppose his brother until they were alone in private. However, his expression told his brother as much anyway.

"Look at my boy." Pleaded Banther. "He's scared to death of that nigger. You lawmen got to do something about this."

Landry approached Banther so that he stood before him face-to-face, eye-to-eye. He came to Banther in this manner so that there would be no misunderstanding about his meaning. He was somewhat taller than Banther but was not as large as him. "Your story is filled with half-truths. You've been beating on folks as long as I've known you. Most folks around here don't care two cents about you. Now I hear you got your boy beating on other younguns, giving them black eyes and bloody noses and such. Got him acting just like you." Banther swallowed, but he didn't say anything. Landry went on. "I know of this boy Sage. He ain't ever done nobody wrong. I figures your boy was beating on him. And his crazy papa didn't take a liking to this." Landry paused. "My guess is he probably had some words with your boy, or maybe even whipped his ass. And knowing you as I do, you didn't take a liking to this. So you decided you was gonna teach this Donovan fellow a lesson. But instead, you and your boy learned the lesson. Many of a decent folks have come to me about you. Most in this town are afraid of you." He said. "I've watched folks cross the street when they see you coming." Landry leaned in close to get his last point across. "I don't like to be made a fool of and I personally don't like you none. If that man beat you, then you had it coming. From what I've seen of him, you damn lucky he didn't kill you. There's nothing we can do for you." Landry pointed toward the door. "Now get."

After Landry said his last words, Gunther stood to his feet with his hand resting on his holstered pistol eagerly wanting to pull it out if needed.

Bewildered Banther tugged on Joshua and they left the jailhouse without further protest. Only after the front door had closed did Gunther speak out. "We need to get after this Donovan feller?"

"For what?" Asked Landry.

"For attacking Banther and scaring that boy half out of his wits." Said Gunther.

Landry glared as he said. "I don't give a damn about what happened to Banther. I'm not risking my life or yours on the likes of him. He's a liar. And I believe he did something to piss off that man and got what he had coming."

With his hands across his belly, Gunther sat back in his chair. "Donovan's still in town. We gonna have to do something about that."

"We will." Said Landry. "But not yet. He has a few more days. If he's in town after that, then we'll go after him."

"Why wait?" Asked Gunther.

"Because he hasn't been any trouble to us. And he may leave on his own accord." Said Landry.

"That nigger don't have a chance with us." Said Gunther.

"Maybe so." Said Landry. "But we can't take too lightly of this man. He could be as dangerous as we've seen. We'll need to be careful of that. Under no circumstances do you face him alone. Is that clear Gunther? If you see him, you fetch me at once."

Gunther frowned. "I can take him, Landry."

"I'm not doubting your skills brother. But these past few days I've seen this man do some odd things. And now he's got Banther afraid of him. Never thought I would see Banther afraid of anyone. So promise me, Gunther, that you won't face this man alone."

Gunther thought this over for a long moment and then he reluctantly nodded in agreement.

Satisfied Landry stepped away from the desk and approached the window again. He glared out. He watched as Banther and his son were just pulling away. He turned to the hotel across the street where Dr. Tracy resided. "You may be right about Tracy." He said. "She may not care for me as much as she puts on. The other night when I tried to kiss her, she turned from me and said she didn't want a relationship."

"I don't want to be right about her, but two years is a long time." Said Gunther. "If a woman ain't made up her mind about you by then, I reckon she never will."

Disappointed Landry nodded in agreement. "I trusted her, hoping one day we would be together. I told her things about me and you, that no one should know of." He paused for a long moment as he reflected on her and then said. "Thinking back, I don't think she's ever trusted me. After all this time, I find I don't know much about her. I don't know where she's from; I don't know nothing about her kin. She don't talk much, mostly she just listened to me go on and on."

"You talk as if you's in love with this woman." Said Gunther.

Landry turned from the window to face him. "I am in love with her."

"Why settle for a nigger winch?" Asked Gunther. "There's plenty of decent white women out there that would love to be with someone like you."

"Maybe." Said Landry. "But not one of them is as beautiful as Tracy. Nor are they as easy to talk with as she is. I could never love them the way I love her now. She has this amazing effect on people, especially with her patients. Whites and colored alike are somehow drawn to this woman."

Gunther nodded. "I reckon so."

"These past few weeks she's been different." Said Landry. "When I visit her she don't seem interested. Sometimes her thoughts wander while I'm talking with her. Lately, I've watched her come in late almost every night when just a few weeks before she came in late maybe one or two nights during the week." He paused for a long moment and then said. "I suspect she's courting someone."

Gunther frowned. "Folks know about you and Tracy, and they know that you would shoot down any man that tried to court her. There isn't a man in this town that would be foolish enough to risk you coming after them."

"They would if they figured me not to find out." Said Landry.

"Well, they figured wrong." Said Gunther. "We'll follow her. If she's courting someone, we'll know about it, and that'll be the end of both of them."

"We can't follow her, she'll find us out. We need someone she wouldn't suspect." Said Landry.

They both pondered this for a moment.

"How about Corwin?" Suggested Gunther.

Landry nodded. "He'll do fine."

Chapter 34

The Wagon pulled around to the side of the house. "Whoa!" Maria yelled as she pulled hard on the reins to bring the wagon to a halt.

High in the wagon seat, she glanced around the property. Her husband Miles was not too far away watching her. And not too far from him was Mama who was on the porch rocking in her chair. Maria fought the urge to wave and turned away. In the back of the wagon was her papa. She had tried to make him as comfortable as possible by packing the wagon bed with plenty of straw and covering him tightly with several blankets. She watched him for a moment. His eyes were closed, he had slept almost the whole three-hour trip back. He seemed so peaceful at this moment, as she observed his expressionless face. She then stepped off the wagon and headed across the field toward Miles.

It was late in the afternoon, and the sun was partially hidden behind the high tops of the trees. Miles was wet with sweat, and her nostrils were filled with his musty odor well before she had reached him. His muscular forearms bulged as he gripped the hoe. When she approached she could see by his expression that he was concerned. She didn't anticipate this reception, for she had expected him to be fuming about the incident that had occurred a few days back with the sheriff and his deputy.

"It's been days, Maria." He said. "Where have you been?"

Her demeanor was somewhat gloomy as she spoke. "I was with my papa. He's in a bad way. He's dying."

Miles nodded his understanding of her despair. "Sorry to hear of this. He's lived a good life. I'm sure he has no regrets."

She watched him for a long moment. Again this sympathetic reaction was unlike Miles. Usually, he was unfeeling to anything that she had to say. The only thing that Miles was emotional about was his work in the fields. As she thought about it, she found it odd that he had actually stopped working just to talk with her at this moment, ordinarily, Miles would never allow himself to be interrupted for almost any reason.

She wanted to reach for her husband and wrap her arms around his thick neck and cry out all of her grief, but decided against this, for she knew from experience that he would pull away and leave her disappointed. "I worked hard to make those biscuits for you." She said. "I was proud of what I'd done. That wasn't right you tossing them to the chickens and all. That hurt me."

As she gazed at him, Miles nodded again. For the first time since she had known him, she was witnessing his emotions. From his facial expressions and his open body stance, she felt that she knew what he was feeling, and was aware of what he was thinking.

"I missed you." He said softly. "Didn't think you was coming back."

At that moment she broke down and sobbed into his thick arms, and for a long moment, he held her. After a while, he winced in pain. She stepped back for she knew that his ribs were still tender from the deputy's beating.

"I'm sorry Miles." She said. "I was sore at you. I didn't think of anything else. I didn't want you to be hurt like this."

He firmly grabbed her shoulders and said. "I haven't been much of a husband to you, but I do what I can. What happens between us stays between us. We got to work out our own problems. We can't trust the sheriff and his deputy into our marriage. They don't mean us well."

She nodded and he released her.

Cautiously he eyed her. "How is it that you came by these lawmen?" He asked.

His question somewhat caught her off guard and she hesitated before she answered. "In town, I passed by the deputy. He stopped me and asked about my bruised face, and I told him. The next day he was at the house." She said. "Didn't even know he was coming." A complete lie.

"He could have killed me." He said.

"I'm sorry Miles. Didn't mean it to be this way. It won't happen again, I promise."

"What about the deputy?" He asked.

"The deputy?"

"Did you lay with him?" He asked.

The tears welled up in Maria's eyes as they looked intently at each other. She was stunned. "What makes you ask such things?"

"I know of him and his many women. I can't figure him coming all this way unless you was in his bed?"

She denied this and lied again as she had done so often in their short marriage. "No Miles. I didn't lay in his bed. Maybe he took a liking to me, but I've been true to our marriage vows."

After studying her for a moment, Miles decided that her answers were true.

Maria took an unnoticed sigh of relief and then said. "Miles I've got something to talk with you of. I brought my papa with me. He's in the wagon. I told him he could stay with us."

Facing the wagon Miles nodded. "He can't stay with us. We've got enough mouths to feed around here. Don't need another."

"He's my papa, he's dying. Can't take him back now." She pleaded. "He won't make the trip back."

"Your papa ain't never done nothing for us, we don't owe him a thing." Said Miles.

"I'm your wife, don't that count for something."

"You haven't been much of a wife to me either. You don't help around here. And you don't respect what I do."

The tears welled up in Maria's eyes. "I can't take him back now."

"You should have talked with me first." Said Miles. "You've got no choice on this."

"I can change Miles. I can be a good wife to you." She pleaded."

"It's too late for that. Your pa got to go." His words were final.

The tears finally overflowed down her cheeks. She didn't say another word, but instead turned on her heel and headed back toward the wagon. When she reached it, she stood for a long time looking in on her papa. He was awake and was looking right at her. He smiled and she forced a smile for him.

"Is we here?" He asked.

She nodded. "Yes papa, we is here."

She thought about what Miles had just said about her not respecting him. He misunderstood as usual. It wasn't that she didn't respect him, it was that she didn't like the way he treated her. Though he didn't beat her or wasn't abusive verbally, he often ignored and took her for granted. She was considered more than beautiful by most men's standards, and yet Miles hardly attempted to make love to her and never complimented her on her magnificent looks. He didn't even appreciate her when she attempted to do something special for him, such as cook his breakfast a few days back. But he worked hard. He worked harder than any man she had ever known. He even worked on Sundays.

Did she have the right to ask her husband to support her papa? Especially now that he was sick and dying?" She thought about the question as she looked down at her papa. He seemed so relaxed and stress-free now that they were away from the house. How much of a burden could he be? He wouldn't eat much and would spend most of his time in bed in the spare room. And most likely he wouldn't be with them but a few days longer. He would be no burden to Miles, she would see to that. She would feed him, bathe him and wash his clothes. Miles would hardly know that he was about. For the moment she hated Miles for putting her in this situation. She turned to Miles and cut her eyes at him. Even from the distance, she could see his surprised expression.

She then turned to her papa and reached for him. "Come, papa. I'll take you to your room."

Miles watched powerlessly as she struggled to pull the old man from the wagon, and led him into the house.

Chapter 35

Gunther climbed from his horse and loosely tied the reins to the rail of the porch. He had the famous grin on his face that he was known for. "How do?" He said to Corwin who had nervously pulled himself from the chair.

Corwin wiped his sweaty palms on his trousers. "Howdy Deputy." His voice quivered slightly.

Gunther waved him down. "Come on down here boy. I want to talk to you."

Corwin stepped off the porch and followed Gunther as he walked out about forty yards or so.

Corwin was considered somewhat well off for he owned sixty acres of land, consisting of corn, tomatoes, onions, and tobacco. He hardly did any work on the land he owned because his wife and three daughters in addition to one full-time hired hand did most of the work.

His wife was an Indian woman mixed with white blood. She was conceived when her Indian mother was raped by a white man. Corwin was told by the chief of her tribe that a child born from such an awful circumstance would never find an Indian man to take her as a wife. She was considered by the Indian men to be of bad luck. Therefore the chief offered to sell her to Corwin for a mere gold piece that he had on him at the time.

His wife was called Dark Moon. Which referred to the dreadful way she was conceived. It was felt by her tribe that she would never experience the true joys of life. Corwin affectionately called her Moon for short and immediately took her on as his wife. And a good wife she was. She worked constantly and rarely complained. She worked in the fields she cleaned the clothes, and she cooked the meals. And whenever he wanted to share pleasures in the night, she never refused him. Over the twenty years that they had been together, he had grown to love her, and she to love him. They had three beautiful daughters together. There first born Thelma was eighteen, their second born Brenda was sixteen, and their last born Melissa was four.

Though Corwin had named his daughters, their mother had dominantly raised the girls using the teaching and values of her Indian culture. She taught them her native tongue as well as English. She raised them to make their own clothes and to dress in colorful Indian attire, such as full leather dresses with various colored beads throughout for decoration.

Even the wonderful foods they prepared and ate were mostly of Moon's native culture.

Moon and her daughters had even made Corwin a pair of comfortable moccasin shoes, which he had on as he walked with the deputy away from the house.

"Me and the Sheriff want you to do us a favor." Said Gunther.

Even though Corwin was much taller than Gunther, the deputy's presence was intimidating. Corwin knew too well of the deputy's reputation. He had heard of some of the men that he had gunned down in the streets and the saloon. Some were justified, most were not. He also knew of the deputy's temper, and how he could become, without notice, like a dog with rabies.

"What kind of favor?" Asked Corwin.

Gunther stopped, frowned, and his eyes were mean and wild. "Does it matter boy?"

"No." Responded Corwin quickly.

Gunther calmed as he pulled on his mustache. "We need you to follow someone."

Corwin nodded. "Who?" He asked.

Gunther hesitated before he answered. "Dr. Tracy."

"Dr. Tracy?" Corwin repeated. "Why her?"

"You don't worry about that."

"Dr. Tracy's a fine woman. She ain't never done nobody wrong."

Gunther said. "That don't change nothing. We need you to follow her. If you don't want to do it just say so."

Corwin dropped his head with his fingers on his chin appearing to give this careful consideration. He then pulled the twig from his mouth and tossed it aside. "No, sir. I don't want nothing to do with this. You'll have to get someone else."

Gunther frowned as he said. "You refusing us this service."

"Yes, sir. I can't-do it." Said Corwin. "I ain't got nothing against Dr. Tracy, she's a mighty fine woman."

Gunther watched Corwin as he attempted to avoid his glaring eyes. Without notice, Gunther slugged him in the gut. Corwin let out a long drawn out grunt and then dropped to the ground clutching his midsection with both hands. Gunther then reached into his interior coat pocket and pulled out a bronze eyepiece. He tossed it to the ground beside Corwin's face.

"You'll need this." He said. "It's a looking glass. It'll keep you far enough away without being seen. You'll start tonight. And you'll stay with her until she comes home each night. After she returns home, then you'll come to the jailhouse and report your findings to me and the sheriff.

From the ground Corwin said. "How long do I do this?"

"You'll follow her each night until me or the sheriff say otherwise."

Corwin nodded and listened to the deputy's boots thud against the ground as he walked away toward his horse.

Chapter 36

Tracy watched out her hotel window toward the jailhouse. She knew Landry was there, but what she didn't know was if he was watching her from his window as well. Sometimes if she watched long enough she could see his shadow in the window, but this time she saw nothing. Maybe he was in bed asleep she thought.

She grabbed her coat from the wall and headed downstairs. When she reached the doorway in front of the hotel she observed the jailhouse once more. There was still no movement from within. She then went around the back and grabbed her horse. She hadn't seen Donovan for a couple of days and decided to visit him before he became impatient and came to town to visit her instead.

When she arrived at Mama's house she could see from the black windows that all were asleep. Of course, she didn't really expect to see otherwise. Still, she was greatly disappointed that she would not see Donovan on this night. Not wanting to turn away just yet, she continued to watch the house and its dark windows.

Tracy was somewhat embarrassed about coming to see Donovan in the middle of the night. This was not ladylike behavior. Usually, when she was out and about at such a late hour, she was either visiting or leaving a sick patient. But now her reason was only to see Donovan. To maybe tell him how much she loved him. But he wasn't around to do so, and she wasn't going to the house to fetch him. She felt disappointed as she pulled on the reins to guide her horse back the way she had come.

When she turned she stopped cold. "Donovan." She said in surprise. "What are you doing?"

"Watching you." He said. "I haven't seen you for a couple of days. I thought maybe you'd decided against us."

"I've thought about it." Said Tracy. "Us that is." She paused as she stared at him.

"Why are you here?" Asked Donovan.

She looked at him. "You know why." She said. "I'm here to see you."

He reached for Tracy. "Let's go for a walk." He said as he guided her toward the woods. She followed without a word, wondering where he was taking her. Their feet crunched the leaves as she followed Donovan through the woods. After about a hundred yards or so he stopped and turned to her. He caressed her hair. She closed her eyes to feel his gentle strokes.

"Donovan. What are we doing?"

"Were making love, Tracy."

She opened her eyes. "I want to get married."

"We will." He said as he kissed her softly on the mouth.

"When?" She said in between the gentle kisses.

"Soon."

"How soon?"

"When I get back."

"When are you leaving?"

"Tomorrow." He said.

"When will you return?"

"The month after next, after things calm a bit with the lawmen. Maybe by then, your folks would have come for you. Then you, me, Sage and your folks can ride out together and start a new life."

She pushed him back and eyed him. "You promise?"

His expression was sincere which left no doubt of his intentions. "I promise."

She then reached and kissed him. What did it matter now, they would be married soon, and she would spend her life with this man. He rubbed his fingers through her hair as they kissed, then he reached and fondled her breasts through the soft material of her blouse. Tracy caressed and rubbed the stubble on his face and squeezed his solid arms. He unbuttoned her blouse so that her breasts were exposed. He gazed at them for a long moment, before finally pulling the blouse off her shoulders. His strong hands caressed her bare shoulders, and then slowly worked down to the sides of her breasts and then around to her lower back. With each of his tender caresses, her breathing was fast and irregular. She then unbuttoned his shirt as well and tossed it aside. With bare chests, they both absorbed within one another as they kissed passionately.

She rubbed her fingers about the raised scars on his back. There were so many she thought. And she silently mourned for him as she guided her fingers over each wound. As they continued to embrace, his rough mangled skin pressed against her soft smooth skin. At that moment when their bodies touched Tracy imagined that his horrible injuries were somehow transferred to her body, and for that instant, she imagined that his previous pain and suffering were now her burden as well.

Donovan eased her to the ground so that she was lying on her back facing him. He then pulled off her boots and socks. After which he unbuttoned her pants and eased them off as well. He gazed at her body for a long time with amazement.

He then slid out of his pants, and they then reached for one another, and as one the made love with great passion and tenderness. When Tracy finally climaxed she cried for she had just given her whole self to the man that she loved.

Afterwards, they laid intertwined within each other's arms listening to each other breathe, and the wind swirling in the air. Tracy rolled over and kissed Donovan. "I love you, Donovan." She said.

Donovan turned to her. "I love you to Tracy."

Tracy rolled over and gathered her clothes, and began to dress. Donovan laid on the ground watching her. "Does anyone know you'll be leaving tomorrow?" Said Tracy.

"Just Sage." He said. "I thought he should know."

"What about your folks?"

"I'll tell them first thing in the morning." He said.

She frowned. "When were you going to tell me, Donovan?"

"I told Sage to tell you." He said.

Tracy reached down and kissed him once more. "This is good you leaving two days early." She said. "This way there won't be any trouble with Landry and his brother."

"I reckon so." Agreed Donovan. "Though I would like to spend more time with Sage and you. It's not worth the trouble it'll bring with those lawmen, besides I'll be back for you and Sage soon enough."

She kissed him again. "I'm so proud of you Donovan. I know you want to stay and fight those men, but this is the best way to assure that you Sage and me can be a family." She climbed to her feet. "I won't see you off tomorrow. I don't want to take a chance of being seen together." With that, she headed back through the woods toward her horse, climbed on and rode away. She suspected Donovan would follow her into town. But she hoped that he wouldn't, for Landry and Gunther could be anywhere.

Tracy was ecstatic on her ride back to town. She was in love and it felt wonderful. However, she couldn't help but feel somewhat disappointed. She wished that she didn't have to leave Donovan alone on their first night together as lovers. Tracy wished that their bodies could cuddle together throughout the night. She wished she could wake up the next morning by his side. Maybe they would converse over their shared breakfast together. She sighed. When they're married things will be different, but until then she would need to be patient. Now she understood why some of her women friends made such an issue of love and marriage. It was so wonderful to be in love, and she was so happy to know and love a man such as Donovan.

The ride into town was different. Usually, she was afraid and heard every sound that echoed throughout the dark woods. However, on this night she felt safe for she knew that Donovan was somehow close by and would protect her from any harm. But it wasn't Donovan that was following her. From within the dark shadows of the woods, at a far enough distance not to be seen or heard was Corwin. He had been watching and following her for several hours undetected.

Chapter 37

"Did you follow her?" Asked Landry from behind his desk.

It was just past 2 A.M. and Landry was dressed in a long white sleeping shirt that went just past his knees. Gunther was in the corner barefoot, shirtless and wearing long tan underwear. Across the desk from Landry was a nervous Corwin. His visit was late in the night and he had awakened both of the lawmen.

"Yes, sir. I did." Answered Corwin.

"Did she see you?" Asked Gunther from across the room.

Corwin nodded. "No. I don't reckon she did."

"Good." Said Gunther. "Is she just now getting back?"

Corwin nodded.

Landry and Gunther eyed each other. "It's after two," said Landry. "Where's she coming from this late?"

Corwin hesitated and took a deep breath. "Well, most of the night she was in her room. After a while, I thought she was sleep. I was just about to go home when she came out the hotel."

"What time was that?" Asked Gunther.

"About nine or so."

"Go on," said Landry. "Don't leave nothing out."

Corwin took another breath. "Well like I said, I saw her come out the hotel…"

"Quit stalling." Interrupted Gunther. "Where did she go?"

Corwin took another breath. "She went to Mama's house."

"Mama's house?" Questioned Landry. "At this hour. Why so late?"

"She went to see a fella." Said Corwin.

The room was quiet with sorrow as if a word had just been given that someone had died.

Gunther stepped away from the wall and approached Corwin. "What did you say?"

Corwin stepped back so as to avoid a possible retaliation by Gunther. "She went to see a fella." He repeated slowly.

"Ah be damned." Said Gunther.

"Hold on Gunther." Instructed Landry. "Let's hear him out." He turned to Corwin and nodded. "Go on."

Corwin watched Gunther hesitantly and then went on. "Well...they talked for a bit, then they disappeared into the woods for awhile. I didn't see much after that."

"You didn't see much." Snapped Gunther. "You were right there."

"I didn't want to be seen." Said Corwin.

Landry rose from his chair and Corwin flinched. "You telling us the truth?" Asked Landry.

"I am," Corwin said quickly.

Landry walked over to the dark window and looked out. He looked upward toward Tracy's hotel window. The window was black. She was sleep he thought. "How long were they in the woods?"

"I'd say an hour."

"That's a long time. What do you think they were doing?"

"Not sure. I couldn't get close enough."

"That's not what I asked you." Landry's sharp remark cut through the air. "I asked what you thought they were doing in the woods for that hour?"

Corwin shifted on his feet nervously. "I suspect they was lovers."

The sheriff's face tightened. "Lovers." He repeated. "Why do you think that?"

Corwin gave the question careful consideration before he answered. "The sounds that they made in the dark were sounds of such."

"This fella she was with, did you see his face?" Asked Landry.

"I did." He said.

Landry turned from the window and approached him. He stood directly in front of Corwin. The Sheriff was so tall that Corwin's face only came to the top of his chest. "Do you know him?"

Corwin nodded.

"What's his name?" Landry said firmly."

"Donovan." Said Corwin.

"Donovan," Landry repeated. "Donovan." He said again and then he turned and walked over to the window. He was quiet for a long time before he finally said. "I suspected as much. When you said Tracy was at Mama's house. I figured this fella to be Donovan. Now thinking back, it all makes sense."

Corwin shifted uncomfortably as his eyes shifted frequently from the sheriff and then the deputy.

The mood in the room had changed dramatically to gloominess and Corwin wished that he had not shared any of this information. But he figured not to have much of a choice in the matter. Now he was just waiting to be dismissed by the sheriff or the deputy.

"You did good, Corwin. We won't need you anymore." Said Gunther.

Corwin nodded and walked out.

Gunther waited until Corwin had closed the door. "What now, Landry."

"What now," Landry repeated still seemingly in a slight daze. "I've had enough of this Donovan. Get plenty of rest tonight, Gunther. Tomorrow we're gonna pay Donovan a visit."

Gunther smiled. "It's about time. What about Tracy?"

"I'll be paying Tracy a visit tonight." Said Landry.

Chapter 38

Tracy shifted in her bed; for she felt at peace as she thought about the special night she and Donovan had just shared. However, she greatly wished that Donovan were now in her bed beside her. She couldn't help but wonder what Donovan was like when he slept. Was he a motionless sleeper or did he twist and turn throughout the night? Did he snore or was he silent in his slumber. She smiled, questions she would answer soon enough once they were married.

Even though she hated to see him go, she was glad that he was leaving in the morning. This would be two days before the sheriff's deadline, which meant that he would be safe from harm.

Tracy was sound asleep when she was abruptly awakened by something. Did she hear something, was she dreaming, or was she restless and just happening to awake at this moment. Her bed was in the corner and she faced the wall. She lay still within the darkness listening but hearing nothing. However, she was still alarmed and certain that something had awakened her.

After a few unnerving moments, she finally called out. "Who's there?"

And yet she wasn't surprised to hear some movement within the corner across the room. "It's me." Said Landry. The tone of his voice was cold.

Tracy hesitated a long time before she mustered up the courage to turn in her bed to face him. "Landry, why are you here?" Her voice trembled and cracked as she spoke.

Within the darkness, Landry's vague shadow approached the bed and looked down at her. "We need to talk." He said firmly.

Her voice still trembled. "About what?"

"About us." He said.

"We talked of this before. There is no us."

"I've told you I don't like to be made a fool of."

"What are you talking about, Landry?"

"I trusted you. But now I realize you've never trusted me."

"What do you mean?" She said.

There was a long uncomfortable silence between them. "For two years I've tried to court you, and you've given me nothing but excuses, and I believed you. But it turns out you were lying all along."

"I wasn't." She said quickly.

Landry's voice was tense with anger but controlled to a low tone. "What is Donovan to you, then?"

Tracy felt her chest tighten, and her heart rate and breathing rapidly increased. However, within the darkness of the room, she was able to conceal her distorted facial expression. Even her hands raised to her chest went unnoticed within the shadowy room. How Landry knew about her and Donovan she did not know. Maybe he followed her. But she was careful when she left, and even if he had followed her surely she would have seen him. Nonetheless, he knew, and she had no choice but to come forward about her relationship with Donovan. If she were to deny it now, this would only enrage the sheriff and the consequences for herself and Donovan would be great.

She pleaded. "Landry I didn't want to hurt you. I was just trying to protect you is all."

"Protect me?" He questioned. "What is Donovan to you?"

She hesitated in an attempt to think of a way out of this. From what she could figure she was trapped. In her frustration, she started to cry. She didn't know what else to do but to cry. "I'm sorry, Landry." She sobbed. "I really do care for you."

"You're lying." Snapped the sheriff.

"I do care Landry." She blurted

"You've known him a few days, and you've already laid with him. I've known you for two years, and you won't so much as kiss me. You made a fool of me and I warned you of that."

"What are you gonna do to me, Landry?" She asked.

Landry turned and approached the window and viewed out into the night. He sighed loudly. "I'm not gonna harm you Tracy. I'm disappointed, but I would not harm you because I love you."

Tracy couldn't believe her ears. Maybe she had misjudged Landry's character. Maybe she should have been honest with him all along about not being interested in him romantically. All that time she was not completely honest because she felt the sheriff was a dangerous man and would bring her harm. But at this moment she felt ashamed and questioned her judgment of him. Even with her feelings of shame, she still felt overwhelming relieved that she and Donovan were no longer in danger.

She climbed from her bed and approached Landry by the window. "Thank you, Landry." She said.

"For what?"

"For being so understanding." She said.

His voice was tense with anger. "I'm not understanding any of this. I trusted you. Now I find I can't trust you at all. You made a fool of me. And I'm no fool."

"I'm sorry." She said.

"Your apology is empty Tracy."

"What do you mean?"

"I said I wouldn't hurt you. And I won't. But Donovan is a different matter." He said.

Her voice was panicked. "What does that mean Landry?" She said.

Landry turned to her and scowled. "He's as good as dead."

"No Landry please, it's not his fault," Tracy begged.

"And whose fault is it?" Said Landry.

"Mine." She said. "He didn't know about us. He still doesn't. But it's over now. He's leaving town. You don't have to worry about him anymore."

"That don't change nothing." He said. "I'm the fool now, only one thing gonna change that." He turned on his heel and headed for the front door.

She grabbed his arm. "Please, Landry don't harm him. He's no danger to you. He's leaving town because of you."

"How do you know this?" Asked Landry.

"I just do."

"You've seen quite a bit of him haven't you?"

She didn't reply.

"Are you in love with him?" He asked.

"Yes." She said slowly.

He stared at her for a long moment and she refused to turn away.

"I don't want you hurt Tracy. But you've made a fool of me. You could have given us a chance. I would have been good to you." He paused in thought. "I will spare him under two conditions."

Tracy was somewhat relieved and apprehensive as she released her grip from his arm. "What conditions Landry?"

"He's leaving town you say?"

"Yes. He doesn't want to face you." She said.

"He's afraid of me?" Asked Landry.

"Yes, very much so." She said. However, in truth, she doubted that Donovan was afraid of Landry or any man for that matter. And even if he were afraid he would not hesitate to face the lawman if the situation presented itself.

"I've seen many a men afraid, and Donovan don't seem much afraid to me." Said Landry.

"He conceals his emotions, but he's afraid nonetheless." Said Tracy.

He continued to stare at her as if he were distrusting of her. "My first condition is this." He said. "I want Donovan out of town, and he is never to return. If I see him again I'll kill him on the spot."

Tracy nodded in agreement, for in two months she and Donovan would be married and traveling hundreds of miles away from Landry and this town. This first request unknowingly to Landry was already set in motion.

Landry stepped closer and stooped down so that they were face to face. He was close enough so that she smelled the tang on his breath. "My second condition is this." He said.

With an uncomfortable anticipation, Tracy shifted while listening closely.

Landry continued. "I want you as my lover."

She gasped. She attempted to respond, but the words didn't come. She was speechless. She could not believe what the sheriff was requesting of her. Her breathing was irregular. "Landry...Landry." Was all she could muster in between her shortness of breath. "I can't-do that, I won't do that." She finally got out.

"I've waited a long time for you." His tone was bitter. "It was all for nothing." He bent down further and kissed her on the mouth and with his large hand grabbed hold of her breast.

Tracy stood motionless and stiff, as Landry kissed her lips and fondled her. She thought of what was at stake. She could give herself to Landry and Donovan would possibly live being that the sheriff was true to his word, or she could refuse Landry and Donovan would surely be killed. She loved Donovan deeply and so desperately wanted him to live. But then what? If Donovan found out about this arrangement it would be the end of their relationship. He would see her as unfaithful and a common whore, and would not marry her. It was difficult enough convincing Donovan to take her as his wife, considering his concerns of his many enemies constantly pursuing him.

Or worse, he would see this arrangement as rape, as it had occurred with his late wife Sidney, and then Donovan would come after the sheriff with a vengeance to only be killed by him. In any case, Donovan would not survive.

Tracy stepped back. "You bastard!" She said through gritted teeth. "You have no right to do this. I will not be your lover. Is that the only way you can have a woman, is to force her?"

The sheriff grabbed her by the shoulders and lifted her off the ground so that she was face to face with him. She yelled out and then froze. He had never touched her before in such an aggressive manner.

"Who the hell do you think you're talking to? I've been the perfect gentleman with you. And you misled me. If I wanted you, you could do nothing to stop me. I gave you a choice. I don't know too many white men that would give such a choice." He said. "You remember that." Landry then tossed her onto the bed and headed for the front door.

He pulled the door open and turned in the doorway. "Tomorrow your Donovan is dead unless you agree to my condition." He waited for a response. She gave none. "Fine," he added. "Don't try to warn him. Paul downstairs will be watching for you." He left the door open as he ducked under.

She listened to his heavy boots move down the hall, then down the stairs. She quickly climbed from her bed, closed and locked the door. She then dragged the small writing desk from the wall to the door. Afterwards, she grabbed the chair and placed it on top of the desk.

At this moment she truly did not know what to do. All seemed ruined and her life was falling apart. She couldn't imagine her life now without the companionship of Donovan a man that she loved so much. She hadn't felt such confusion since a few years back when her parent's house was burned down and she was forced to separate from them.

Tracy felt the timing was the key to all of this. This situation would depend on when Donovan was to leave town, and when the sheriff and the deputy left to pursue him. With some luck maybe they would miss each other. But even as she thought about it, she knew she didn't believe in luck. Luck had never been much on her side. If Donovan and the sheriff came face to face, Donovan would not survive, and therefore he would be out of her life forever.

She sighed in despair. Perhaps she should lay in the sheriff's bed and delay him for a few hours so that Donovan would have time to leave without incident. But how often afterward would she be expected to lay in the sheriff's bed? On the other hand, what did it matter for she would be saving Donovan's life? But the question in her mind, which caused her to hesitate, would she really be saving his life? Would the sheriff keep his word, or would he betray her out of spite and revenge?

Even after she and Donovan were married could she possibly keep such a terrible secret like this from him. A good marriage was based on trust and honesty, and from the beginning, she would be betraying that sacred trust. Of course, her reasoning was valid for she did what she felt was necessary to save her future husband's life. But would Donovan share her point of view of the situation and forgive her? Or would he instead not understand and leave her forever?   From what she knew and had witnessed of Donovan's previous actions, he would most likely seek revenge on the sheriff only to be killed by him in the process.

Tracy pulled up a chair and seated herself next to the window. She looked down at the jailhouse. There was still time to make a decision. She would watch the jailhouse until the sheriff and the deputy came out. Then at that time depending on the time of day she would make her decision about what to do about the sheriff's proposition.

Tracy was exhausted and fought desperately to keep her eyes open as she watched the jailhouse below. After some time had passed she leaned forward placing her chin on the window seal. Unknowingly Tracy was soon sound asleep.

Chapter 39

Donovan climbed onto his horse and then turned to his family as they stood and watched from the porch. Mama held Papa tight as the tears flowed down her face. Sage stood silently on the other side of Miles and Maria.

Donovan nodded to Sage. "Remember what I've learned you. Remember everything."

"I will." Answered Sage.

"I'll be back after things calm a bit." Said Donovan.

Sage nodded.

Donovan guided his horse around and trotted away. He rode for a few yards before he tugged on the reins to motion Fletcher to stop. Up a ways on the outskirts of the forest was the sheriff and his deputy on horseback.

Papa limped off the porch with his cane in hand and approached Donovan. "Can't be sure why they're coming," said Papa.

Donovan was silent. He knew that the lawmen were coming for him.

"I know things about you, Donovan." Said Papa.

Donovan turned to him, but he remained silent.

"That's right. I know about you." Said Papa once again. "I've suspected all along that you did in those men that killed your wife," Papa spoke quickly trying to get out all that he could before the sheriff and deputy arrived. "I've known that you killed others too." Said Papa. "I ain't judging you. There's some men out there that I'd like to see dead myself. But I ain't got the courage you do."

"I brought justice to those men." Donovan finally said. "I did what the law wouldn't do."

"Maybe so." Said Papa. "But these men coming our way, can't be killed by them pistols of yours. There have been many of men that tried and failed."

Donovan glanced at the lawmen who were now half the distance away but still three or four minutes out. He turned to Papa. "How can you be so sure?" He said. "I've killed many men. Some of them lawmen with reputations. What makes them different?"

"They may not be different. But I suspect they is. I've heard story after story of all the bandits that they killed. One dead body after another. And they ain't ever got so much as a scratch on them." He paused. "But you Donovan. You got one horrible scar after another."

Donovan nodded toward the approaching lawmen across the way. "Maybe so, but I don't see how as I've got any options."

Papa thought this over for a brief moment. "Sage has had enough bad memories, with his mama and all. He still has the nightmares. He don't need memories of his papa being shot up too. And it wouldn't be good for ya mama to see either."

"I don't see as I have a choice." Said Donovan.

Papa glanced across the field. The lawmen were much closer, and soon they would be upon them. He turned to the porch to stare at the uncertain faces that were staring at him. "Look at them." He said.

Donovan slowly turned toward the porch. As he suspected their expressions were of fear and anxiety. "This don't change nothing, I've got no options." Said Donovan.

"Unless you is sure you can kill them, lawmen, don't put your family through this." Said Papa.

Papa's suggestion was a fair one. Was Donovan absolutely sure he could kill these lawmen? His answer was no he was not sure. In truth, he was never certain if he would survive or not in these types of situations. In most violent situations he came to terms with the fact that he would not survive, and in some cases, he almost didn't. He did not know much about the sheriff or the deputy, nor did know the level of weaponry skill that they possessed. All he had to go on was what his papa was telling him.

The sheriff and the deputy were only a few yards away; Papa patted Donovan on the leg and then limped back to the porch.

The two men stopped their horses a few feet out from Donovan. Gunther was grinning as usual, and Landry was all business. Gunther's hand was resting on his side holster ready for a quick draw. Landry, on the other hand, took a more relaxed position with both hands resting loosely on his horse's reins.

"How do?" Said Gunther with his trademark grin.

Donovan nodded.

"You going somewhere?" Asked Landry.

Donovan nodded again.

"Maybe you should of left a few days sooner." Said Landry.

"And why is that?"

Gunther Laughed. "Cause time has just run out on you."

Donovan turned to Gunther but chose not to respond.

"What he means," said Landry. "You're not going anywhere, except jail."

"If you resist," added Gunther. "You'll be laying in a fresh grave before nightfall." Gunther patted his side pistol to give his threat an extra effect.

Donovan sat evenly on his horse. He let what the lawmen had said sink in. Even with the situation as it were, Donovan still had choices. In this encounter with the lawmen, he was fully armed. He had his two six shooters on his waist hidden by his long brown coat. He had a small gun in his boot, and a long knife in the small of his back. And holstered to the saddle of his horse was his rifle.

Calmly Donovan spoke. "I'm leaving as you requested."

"You're too late." Said Gunther. "You took your sweet time, now you're too late."

Donovan watched Gunther as he rubbed his holstered six-shooter. He was annoyed by the deputy's actions. It was meant to be a threat toward Donovan. Or maybe even to prompt Donovan to reach for his pistol.

The sheriff, on the other hand, was a different matter. The sheriff appeared awkward on the saddle for he seemed somewhat oversized for his horse. The sheriff was extremely self-assured and most likely had a solid reason for being so. Donovan figured it to be true what his family had said about him. The sheriff was a skilled gunman and killer.

Donovan thought back to the many gunfights that he had witnessed and been involved. In all those confrontations he could not recall ever having observed anyone that appeared as awkward and relaxed as the sheriff was at this moment.

What seemed even stranger to Donovan was that the sheriff's hands were nowhere near his weapons. Either he was that skilled with his armory, or he had that much confidence in his deputy's ability.

"Why jail?" Asked Donovan.

"You broke the law." Answered the sheriff.

"I have broken no laws." Said Donovan.

"You have," said sheriff. "You beat Banther one of our law bidding white men."

"Banther?" Questioned Donovan. "He had it coming."

Donovan's response caught the sheriff by surprise. "It don't matter what you think he's got coming. He's a white man. You can't beat a white man for any reason. And for that, you're going to jail."

Donovan still remained composed, which was beginning to annoy the deputy, so he rubbed his pistol more frequently to send a threatening message to Donovan, but Donovan seemed unaffected. "How long would I be in jail for this crime as you call it?"

"You ain't getting out." Snapped Gunther. "I'll guarantee you that."

"I figured as much." Said Donovan.

"You figured right," said the sheriff. His tone was serious and direct. "Now put your hands up, and don't make any jerky movements."

Donovan didn't move.

"You've got two seconds, boy. Or you're dead." Instructed the deputy.

Donovan slowly moved his hands up, even with his face.

"Good." Said the sheriff. "Now lift your right leg over that saddle and hop off. If you drop your hands, you'll be dead before you hit the ground."

Donovan did what he was told and climbed off the horse.

"Good. Now turn and face your horse."

With his hands in the air, he turned and faced his horse. Donovan clicked his lips and the horse whined and quickly galloped away leaving a trail of dust behind.

"That's a smart horse you got there." Said the sheriff.

Donovan didn't answer.

"You armed?" Asked the sheriff. "In a moment I'm gonna find out anyway, but if you lie to me, and I find out different, I'll kill you."

Donovan nodded, and the instant he did so the deputy quickly pulled out his pistol and pointed it at him.

The sheriff spoke again. "Listen closely. I want you to very slowly take your coat off and drop it on the ground, and then put your hands back in the air."

Donovan once again did what he was told, and dropped his coat off his shoulders and then place his hands back in the air. The sheriff and deputy eyed the two pistols on either side of his waist and the knife handle tucked in the rear of his belt.

"This son of a bitch thinks he's a gunfighter." Said Gunther.

"Maybe." Said Landry. He then spoke directly to Donovan. "Listen to me closely. I want you to use one hand, and one hand only to unbuckle your belt and let it fall to your feet. If I even think you're going for your pistol." Landry paused for a moment. "Then you know what'll happen to you."

Donovan stood with his palms even with his face. He turned his head slightly so that he could view his family on the porch. They were watching him closely. His mama had a distorted expression that revealed her great anguish. Papa and Miles's expressions were heartfelt as well. Papa nodded to him as he looked in his direction. Sage, however, displayed a unique expression, and Donovan could not help but to focus on him. Sage appeared unusually composed and peaceful. He seemed completely at ease given the situation.

Donovan had talked to Sage a few days earlier and explained to him of the men that he had killed to avenge his mother's death. He told him of the numerous times he had come close to dying, and of the many people, he had killed over the years. He had explained to Sage that he was at peace with dying and that if he were to die, even if it were in a horrible way, it was meant to be, it was his time. Donovan also explained to Sage that he didn't feel that he had much time left, but wanted Sage to know that he loved him very much. He had told Sage since he had seen his son, he could die with peace in his heart when the time came.

As Sage stared back at him with his calm demeanor he wondered what Donovan's thoughts were. Unknowingly Donovan smiled as he observed his brave son. And then Sage smiled as well. It was a slight smile, but a smile nonetheless. Then it came to Donovan that his son was imitating him. Sage was calm and relaxed because that's the way Donovan appeared. Sage had smiled slightly because his father smiled in the same manner.

Mama and Papa glanced at Sage and seem puzzled by his composed reactions.

Gunther interrupted. "What you grinning about boy?"

Donovan turned to the deputy. There was still time if he chose to kill the deputy. There was no guarantee that he would survive. And even so, he would be blindsided by the sheriff.

Any other time Donovan would have easily taken the risk and had done so at least two other times in the past. But now his family was watching him in this impossible situation. He didn't want his young son to witness him dying in such a way. The experience would haunt Sage for the rest of his life.

"What you grinning for boy?" Repeated Gunther. Donovan did not realize that he was still smiling. However, he did not answer the deputy.

Landry spoke. "I'm not telling you again. Take that gun belt off."

Begrudgingly Donovan had made his decision not to fight for he did not want to blemish his family's final memories of him. If his Papa had not spoken to him earlier, Donovan would have pulled his pistols and his family might have witnessed his brutal death.

Donovan turned to Sage once more, as he dropped one hand slowly to release his gun belt and felt it drop to his feet. Sage's expression was still composed, and Donovan knew that this was how he appeared to his son at this moment. Donovan again turned to the lawmen.

"Kick it to me." Said Landry referring to the gun belt.

Donovan stepped over the belt and walked away from it. As Donovan moved Gunther was pivoting as he pointed his gun at him. The sheriff's expression was of irritation.

"I said kick it to me," Landry repeated.

Donovan glared at him. "I'm too far away." Then he dropped his hands causally by his side.

"Put those hands up." Ordered the sheriff.

"There's no need, I'm not armed." Said Donovan.

As Gunther continued to point his pistol, his hand was red from squeezing so tightly. "You nigger son of a bitch put up those hands or die!" His voice cracked from the strain.

Donovan grinned at Gunther and then raised his hands to his face.

Gunther stepped forward. "What you grinning at boy?"

Donovan hesitated for a moment then blurted. "You're a scary little fellow aren't you? You're smart not to face me alone."

Gunther yelled and then fired off three loud shots that echoed in the sky. Donovan did not flinch, as all three shots missed, for they were only meant as a warning.

Gunther grunted loudly as he yelled. "I'm gonna kill this son of a bitch!"

"Calm down, Gunther. He's playing with you." Said Landry. He then turned to Donovan; his face was tense with anger. "You like to play games?"

"You're playing games, not me." Said Donovan. "Making up reasons to jail me."

The sheriff turned to Gunther. "Put your gun away. Don't shoot him unless I tell you so."

Gunther was confused. "Landry what are you doing?"

"He wants to play games. We'll play games." Said Landry. He then climbed off his horse with handcuffs in hand and carried them over to Donovan. He stood directly in front of Donovan.

"I'm not into games much, we can do this easy or hard. It's up to you." Suggested Landry.

Donovan appeared to be giving the sheriff's suggestion some thought. After a moment he spoke. "I'm no fool sheriff, I figure you gonna kill me. Your deputy told me as much already. That being the case, let's just do it the hard way." Then he smiled at the sheriff.

The smile infuriated Landry, and he took a powerful wild swing at Donovan's head. Donovan ducked, and Landry's mighty fist swung over his head. Donovan came back up, releasing two quick blows to Landry's chest and one to his face. The blows knocked Landry back a couple steps but he didn't go down. Donovan found this to be troubling. All the men in the past that he hit that many times and that hard, went down like stiff boards.

Landry shook off the blows and stepped toward Donovan with a determined expression. Donovan found his fighting style to be odd. As a matter of fact, he had no fighting style. His hands rested comfortably by his side as if he were going for a stroll. However, his eyes told a different story, they concentrated as he approached Donovan.

Once again Donovan waited for Landry to make his move. He stood his ground as Landry approached and stood before him. Then Landry swung two wild punches switching with either hand. Donovan ducked and swayed avoiding both punches then quickly countered with a punch to Landry's face, and a hard front kick to his chest. The sheriff grunted as he absorbed the blows and again stumbled a few steps back. He clutched his chest as if to squeeze the pain out. Then yet again Landry walked toward Donovan.

Once more Donovan was concerned that the sheriff didn't go down. Once again he delivered some powerful punches and this time one of his best kicks. He was still standing and moving toward Donovan once again. That last kick to the chest should have knocked the sheriff out cold. Donovan had never fought a man like this before. Usually, his fights were over in a few short minutes, and he always prevailed, unless he was going up against several men. But Donovan had the feeling that he was going to be fighting this sheriff for a long time.

The sheriff approached again, and Donovan stood his ground. Donovan was surprised how unruffled the sheriff was. Usually, men that Donovan hit would be in a rage at this point and then they would charge trying to overpower Donovan with many punches. Then they would tire themselves out and Donovan would then finish them off with a punch or two. However, the sheriff was different. He was poised and focused. Even though Donovan hit him with several solid punches, the sheriff was still in control of his emotions and concentrated as he approached Donovan. When the sheriff was close enough he faked a swing, and as Donovan moved to avoid the fake punch, the sheriff quickly stepped forward and kicked Donovan in the thigh. Donovan's leg gave away and he fell to the ground. He rolled to his feet limped a step and then went down again. His leg was completely numb, and Donovan wondered if it were broken. But as he saw the sheriff approach, he managed to climb to his feet putting most of his weight on the other leg.

Gunther yelled. "Beat his ass, Landry!"

When the sheriff was close enough he swung another wild punch, this connecting on Donovan's shoulder, which spun him around and sent him on the ground landing face down. Donovan had never been hit that hard before. The pain was unbearable. Before Donovan could climb to his feet, the sheriff kicked him in the side, which caused him to moan. The thud from the kick was so loud that Papa yelled from the porch. "Got dammit!"

Even after the powerful kick somehow Donovan managed to his feet. He could tell by the surprised expression on the sheriff's face that he didn't expect Donovan to get up. And before Donovan was fully balanced on his feet, he charged forward punching the sheriff in the gut. When the sheriff turned around clutching his midsection, Donovan hit him several times in either kidney and finally, the sheriff yelled out and went down like a tree.

Donovan then stepped back, bracing himself and then charged forward kicking the sheriff in the face. But because his leg was numb, the impact of the kick was weak. The sheriff shook it off and climbed to his feet, massaging his kidneys on the way up.

The two men glared at each other, no anger or hostility just concentration. Neither man underestimated the other and stood at a respectful distance.

Donovan limped forward swinging a punch, which the sheriff absorbed in the face, but quickly grabbed Donovan before he could pull back. The two struggled in the standing position grabbing and pulling at one another. The sheriff was much larger and stronger than Donovan so he was slowly overpowering Donovan to the ground. Once on the ground, the sheriff maneuvered himself so that he was on top straddling Donovan. Donovan never stopped struggling and tried to force the sheriff to sway this way and that. A couple of times it seemed that Donovan was going to overpower the sheriff and rock him over, but the sheriff managed to gain control and force Donovan onto his back.

Once Landry had control of Donovan on the ground, he began periodically throwing solid punches to his face. Each punch smacked loudly as it made impact. Donovan moaned. After several punches in the face, Donovan was soon unconscious. Only then did the sheriff roll off, collapse on his back and fought to get back his air.

Landry's face at this point was beginning to swell, and his chest and ribs ached. He had never been in a fight such as this, and he hoped to never be in one again. Even though his brother was behind him with a gun in hand, he had the feeling after awhile the battle with Donovan was a fight to the death, and for the first time in his life, he wasn't sure if he was going to win this one. He had told Gunther not to face Donovan alone and he was glad Gunther never did so, he was also grateful that at this moment he was not facing Donovan alone himself. He continued to lay on his back breathing hard.

Oddly Landry was thinking about Banther's situation. He understood why Banther came to them for help. He was lucky Donovan didn't kill him.

Gunther climbed off his horse and approached Landry. "Landry," he called out. "You okay?"

"I'm fine," he said in a low voice. "That son of a bitch wore me out."

"What now? Should I shoot him?"

"Not yet. We're not through with him. There's plenty of time for that. He's gonna pay for this little fight we just had." Said Landry. He waved his hand. "Bring me the cuffs."

Gunther grabbed the handcuffs off the ground and handed them to Landry. Landry then sat up and turned to Donovan next to him. He was still unconscious. He then grabbed Donovan's hands and cuffed them together. Once Donovan was cuffed he then grabbed the chains of the cuffs and dragged Donovan back to his horse. He pulled the rope off his saddle, and tied one end to the saddle and then tied the other end to the chains on the cuffs.

When Landry finished with the ropes, he looked up to see his brother watching him. "What's the matter with you?" Asked Landry.

"Your face. He hurt you real bad didn't he?" Said Gunther.

"It's probably not as bad as it looks. But either way, he's gonna pay for it. It's gonna be a long night for Donovan."

Mama, Papa, Miles, Maria, and Sage had never seen a fight like this before, and they were surprised and thankful that Donovan was still alive. But they knew it wasn't for much longer. The sheriff didn't kill Donovan at that moment because he was saving him for a more dramatic public killing later. That was his style. They watched as they dragged Donovan away by the rope on the end of the horse.

Chapter 40

When Tracy awoke in her room with her head on the windowsill, she became aware that she had fallen asleep. She looked down at the jailhouse. From her window, she could not tell if the sheriff or the deputy were present. How could she have been so careless?

She glanced down at the street. It was becoming crowded, as horses and wagons were beginning to come through, looking for parking spaces at the partly filled shops and saloons. Piano music, loud voices, and laughter were coming from the saloon across the way. Tracy figured it to be late morning and turned her attention back to the jailhouse. Again there wasn't any movement that she could see within the jail. Maybe the lawmen were already in transit in search of Donovan. Her heart pounded fast as she thought of what they would do to him. She tried to calm herself, maybe Donovan was well on his way.

She raced through the hall and headed down the hotel stairs; she had to know for certain if the lawmen were present. When she passed Paul at the front desk, he made no attempts to stop her, or even to warn her about the sheriff's previous threat. This astonished her.

When she arrived at the jailhouse she knocked twice, there was no answer. She tried to open the door, it was locked. Her heart painfully pounded again, they never locked the door unless they were both absent. She had to be sure, so she stepped around to the front and peeked into the window. She saw nothing. The jailhouse appeared to be empty. I'm too late she thought, hopefully, Donovan had left before they reached him. She was upset with herself. She loved Donovan so much and should have agreed to become the sheriff's lover to protect him.

There was a commotion of some sort behind her. When she turned she could see people running out of local shops and into the streets. People everywhere were talking loudly and some were pointing at something down the street as they spoke excitedly. Tracy ignored them, her only focus was Donovan, and whether or not he was safe.

She ran to the stable and grabbed her horse. When she came around on horseback she saw for the first time why the crowd was so ecstatic, and the astonishment of the scene nearly forced her from the saddle. At the edge of town, Landry and Gunther were on horseback, dragging Donovan at the end of a rope. Donovan was on his feet but had just collapsed onto the dirt road when she spotted them. He was a bloody mess from head to toe, and half his clothes were torn off. Gunther turned and smiled at the gathering crowd as if he were on stage in a play. The crowd quieted. "This here son of a bitch broke the law. So me and the sheriff had to break him." Said Gunther.

There was some laughter from the crowd. Someone yelled. "What did that son of bitch do, deputy?" This was followed by more laughter.

"He beat one of our good white citizens." Said Gunther.

The crowd spoke loudly amongst each other. Another yelled out. "We can't have niggers beating on our good white folks. What you gonna do with him."

Landry spoke. "We gonna kill him."

"He looks dead already." Yelled someone, and then the crowd broke out again in laughter.

"Which one of our law bidding white man did this son of a bitch beat?" Yelled another.

"Banther." Said Gunther.

The crowd went silent. They all had confused expressions. Most of the people within the crowd had either had unpleasant confrontations with Banther or knew of someone who did. He was a bully and most of them feared or disliked him. The few that were brave enough to take him on, suffered consequences that were sometimes fatal. Often times the victims that survived Banthers wrath complained to the sheriff and the deputy, but nothing was ever done. Now, these lawmen wanted to punish and kill the man who was finally able to stop Banther. This made no sense, so they stood in silence and disbelief.

Landry and Gunther noticed the change within the crowd, but this made no difference to them. Landry stepped forward and inspected Donovan. He laid slumped forward. Landry nudged him with his foot, and Donovan moaned but did not move. Landry glanced over the crowd as they watched him. He was all business as usual. He grabbed Donovan by the back of his collar and dragged him to the nearby post in front of the saloon. The crowd watched as he leaned the Negro man up against the post.

He turned to Gunther. "Bring me your pistol."

Gunther reached into his holster and pulled out his pistol.

Landry turned to Donovan. "Donovan!" He called.

Donovan opened his eyes. He was nauseous and dizzy. He felt as if his body was tumbling head over heels. He looked down at himself, his clothes were ripped and there was blood all about him. The pain he could deal with and sometimes control, but this feeling of sickness he could not manage. It took him a moment before he remembered where he was and what had happened to him.

"Donovan." The sheriff called again.

This time Donovan looked up, but he did not answer.

He waved the pistol in front of Donovan's face. "I'm gonna give you a chance to get back at me." He said.

He dropped the gun at Donovan's feet. "If you can get to the pistol before I shoot you." The sheriff said. "Then I guess you'd be free to go." He paused. "If you don't, I guess you're a dead man."

Donovan stared at the gun between his feet for a long time. The pistol was out of reach. He would never be able to reach that gun before the sheriff reached for his. Even on his best day if he were healthy and uninjured he still wouldn't have been able to reach for it.

Finally, he looked up from the gun and stared at the sheriff. He tried to focus on him, but it was hard with the dizziness. But from what he could make out, the sheriff's face was swelled and bruised, and this pleased him, however this time he could not smile. He looked past the sheriff and tried to focus on the deputy standing by the horses. His hands were at his sides in a ready to draw position. At that moment Donovan figured he would have to kill both of them. And that wasn't likely from this position. Donovan looked down at his boots. His two-shooter pistol was inside his right boot, but he would never be able to get to it in time. Donovan tried to think back on all the gun battles and difficult situations over the past seven years, wondering if he had ever been in a situation as hopeless as this one. He could not think of one. He was relieved at the moment that his family wasn't around to witness his final demise.

"I'll pass." Donovan managed.

Sheriff became visibly angry. "You don't have a choice."

Donovan nodded. "No." He barely got out.

The sheriff reached for his gun and fired one shot into Donovan's chest near the left shoulder. The impact knocked Donovan back into the post. The sheriff watched him for a moment and then stuffed his gun back into his holster. "Now reach for that gun." He demanded.

Donovan nodded. "It's too far away."

The sheriff pulled out his gun again, this time firing into Donovan's thigh. Donovan clutched his leg as he yelled. This time the blood squirted out toward the sheriff's boots.

The sheriff stuffed his gun back into his holster. Donovan was completely surprised on how quick the tall awkward man could draw his side gun. Donovan didn't think that he had ever seen a gunman as quick before. Even if he was healthy and able to draw from his own side holster, he wasn't completely sure that he could overcome the sheriff. His family and Tracy were right about this man. But it was too late now.

"The next one's going to your face." Said Landry.

Donovan tried to stare at Landry defiantly but the dizziness finally got to him, and he toppled over.

This made no difference to the sheriff; he was going to draw again.

As Tracy moved toward them no one in the crowd seemed to take notice of her, they were all caught up in what was happening to the Negro man against the post. The crowd seemed afraid to move or attract attention to themselves.

Tracy pulled her horse between Landry and Donovan. She hopped off and stared at the bloody Donovan. She couldn't believe her eyes. She wept.

"You killed him," said Tracy. "You've killed him." She finished in a whisper.

Some of the crowd appeared to be confused and began talking to one another.

"He's still breathing." Said the sheriff.

Tracy approached him. "It doesn't matter. I'm a doctor, and after what you did to him he'll be dead soon. Let him die in peace Landry."

"Can't do that." He said.

Tracy began to sob again. "Please Landry. You've done enough. Let him die in peace."

"No. You see my face. He did this."

She walked forward and whispered into his ear. "I will lay in your bed. If you do me this favor."

"Look at him, Tracy. He's gonna die anyway. Have you thought this through?"

"I have."

"Why do you care so much?"

"I love him Landry, and I want him to die in peace. After which it doesn't matter if I'm faithful to him or not."

Landry spoke firmly. "Don't make a fool of me Tracy. Or you will end up like him."

"I won't make a fool of you." She turned and approached Donovan. The sight of him with the blood and his torn clothes caused her to break out in tears before she reached him.

"Donovan." She called, but he didn't answer. She watched his chest move up and down, but he would not be alive for much longer. He would be lucky to make it through the night.

Tracy turned to the crowd whose eyes were on her. "Someone help me get this man on my horse!" No one moved, for they were afraid to. "Please!" She said. "I need to get this man to his family." There was some uncomfortable movement amongst the crowd, but no one moved forward. "Please help me!" She yelled. "This man doesn't have much longer! He needs to be with his family!"

On the opposite end of town, Tracy saw a wagon heading her way. The crowd in the street parted to make room for the fast approaching wagon. The wheels crunched on the hard dry dirt road as it came upon Tracy. Papa and Miles sat up front; Mama and Sage were seated in the back. They all displayed anxious expressions. Mama broke out in tears when she saw Donovan. "Oh GOD! Oh GOD!" She said.

"Put him in the wagon." Said Tracy.

They avoided the curious eyes of the sheriff and his deputy who were watching the scene closely. Miles leaped off first. He then helped Papa, Mama, and Sage climb down. It took all of them to carefully load Donovan into the bed of the wagon. They finally covered him with blankets.

Tracy watched the wagon do a u-turn and then race away. From the bed of the wagon, Sage watched Tracy as they gained momentum down the street. She reached for her horse and climbed on. Landry grabbed the reins.

"Where are you going?" Landry demanded.

She jerked the reins out of his hands. "I'm going to bury the man I love. Don't worry. I won't make a fool of you. I'll keep my promise to you." The horse nickered as she galloped away.

Gunther came up behind Landry. "Why did you let him go?" He asked.

Landry said as he watched Tracy ride away. "You saw him. He won't make it through the night."

Without another word, Landry turned and headed for the jailhouse, and Gunther hung back to do what he did best, entertain the crowd.

Tracy had her horse sprint to catch up to the wagon. Mama and Sage were huddled over Donovan, both crying. When Miles saw Tracy coming alongside, he stopped the wagon. Tracy tied her horse to the end of the wagon bed, then climbed aboard and waved Miles to continue on. Tearfully she inspected Donovan's wounds. First the gunshot wounds, one in the chest toward the shoulder, the other to his thigh. Then she looked over the other wounds that were caused by the dragging.

The wagon rocked back and forth as it moved along the bumpy road. Tracy, Mama, and Sage often swayed into one another.

Mama said. "Sage, when we get to the house go fetch Reverend Jolly. We gonna need him to bury Donovan."

Sage nodded tearfully.

"That won't be necessary." Said Tracy.

Mama looked at Tracy stunned. "Why not child?"

"Because we're going to help Donovan through the night." Said Tracy. "He's in a bad way, but he's been through worse. His previous wounds tell me as much. But if the sheriff finds out we've kept him alive, he'll kill us all."

"Then we'll pray he don't find out." Said, Mama.

Chapter 41

Back at the house, Donovan laid in the bed. He was often in and out of consciousness, and as he did so he moaned.

"What's wrong with him?" Asked Mama.

Tracy rubbed her fingers through his scalp as she examined his head. She then pulled on both eyelids and inspected his eyes.

Turning to Mama she said. "He's got a head injury. I've seen it a few times. My father called it a concussion. He needs plenty of rest, and to be kept cool. Keep a damp cloth on his head at all times. When he wakes again, give him water. He may be awake for only a few moments, so make sure you give him water immediately." She said.

"What about the bullets in him?" Asked Mama.

Tracy pulled the blanket back and examined his wounded chest. His upper torso was wet with blood. The bullet hole was a small dark red puddle. She placed her hands on his chest, as it moved up and down. She lowered her head and placed her ear to his lungs and listened to him as he breathes. After a few moments, she reached for his pants.

Tracy said. "Help me get his pants off."

Mama and Tracy pulled off his blood-soaked pants. Even his tan underwear was soaked. Tracy examined his thigh. She could see the blood oozing out of the bullet hole.

"This is his worst injury." Said Tracy. "He's losing blood here."

Tracy then ripped off a section of his pants and tied it tightly around his thigh. She watched as the blood finally clotted.

"Keep this around his leg for a couple of days. Make sure it's tight. He'll need a few days rest before I take the bullets out."

Tracy turned and headed out the room.

"You leaving us Dr. Tracy?" asked Mama.

Tracy turned to her. "I'll be back tomorrow. Donovan should be fine. Just do as I say."

"Can't you stay? He might need you."

"No." She said abruptly. "The sheriff will come looking for me here. Then he'll find Donovan alive, and kill us all."

Disappointed, Mama nodded and Tracy turned and left.

It was just turning dark before Tracy returned to town. She dreaded leaving Donovan's side but she had no choice, for the sheriff would come looking for her there. But she did all that she could do, and the instructions she had left with Mama would be enough. Tomorrow she would make another trip to look after him, and the day after that she would remove the bullets if he were strong enough.

She passed the noisy saloon, listening to the loud voices and laughter. As she passed the window she could see a crowd of seven or eight men gathered around Gunther listening to him tell one of his famous stories. Tracy figured he was probably telling them how they captured, dragged and killed Donovan. Her face became tight with anger. Then she looked up at the jailhouse. The window was dark as usual, and she wondered if Landry was watching her at this moment. There was no movement in the window that she could see, but she knew that he would be visiting her soon to make due on their agreement.

Tracy felt sick to her stomach at the thought of being Landry's lover. But from what she could figure there was no way around it. She would almost rather die than be his lover, but it wasn't just her life at stake. Donovan's life was at stake, and she wanted him to live. She was going to marry him, and start a family. When Donovan was well enough they would go so far away that Landry would never find and harm them again.

Tracy entered her hotel room. She leaned forward on the door letting out a long sigh of relief. She thought about lighting the lanterns but she didn't want Landry to know that she was home. However, considering the circumstances with Donovan it was crucial that Landry knew of her whereabouts so that he didn't go looking for her at Mama's house.

Begrudgingly she lit the lantern on the wall nearest the front door. When she turned she was horrified to find Landry against the far wall near the front window watching her.

"I've been waiting a long time." He said. "Where have you been?"

Tracy had her hands to her chest attempting to catch her breath. "I was burying Donovan." She said. "You didn't have to kill him." Tracy had to come across believable so that he would not go looking for Donovan later.

"You could have stopped me." Said Landry. "But you were too late." He paused. "It's all for the best. I didn't trust him with my brother." Landry stepped toward Tracy. "No matter. You and me have an agreement."

Tracy spoke with bitterness. "For tonight only?"

"For as long as I wish it." He snapped. "I want folks to see us together. I want them to think we're a couple."

"I will not!" Said Tracy abruptly. "I will not be seen with the likes of you!"

She was surprised that Landry seemed hurt by this. He didn't seem to understand Tracy's hostility.

"We're a couple now." He said, more of a question than a statement.

"We're not a couple. We have an arrangement." She said.

His expression was first confused and then angry. "Fine," he said. "Take off your clothes."

Tracy blew out the lantern and removed her clothing.

On her back Tracy laid with her arms limp by her sides, legs spread apart, no emotion. The sheriff was on top of her, thrusting and panting. At times the bed rocked and bounced from the floor. Landry moaned as he reached his orgasm

His large body collapsed on top of hers squishing her down low within the mattress. Tracy made no attempts to move.

The next afternoon back at the house Tracy carefully inspected Donovan. He was in the bed asleep, or maybe unconscious. She reached over and pulled back his eyelids inspecting both eyes. His pupils did not respond. He was still unconscious. Tracy wasn't her usual friendly self, in fact, she was very moody, and Mama sensed this.

"Has he awakened since last night?" Asked Tracy.

"Yes," Mama said softly.

"Did you give him water?"

"I tried," Mama said. "He wouldn't take it."

Tracy quickly turned to Mama. "No! No! No!" She yelled. "He must have water! He needs strength so that I can operate on him. We don't get a second chance at this. If he doesn't get water he'll die."

Mama cupped her hands over her mouth. "I'm sorry." She gave no excuses, just a sad humble apology.

Tracy felt bad for her outburst. She had never yelled at Mama before, but the pressure was overwhelming. There was too much at stake. Not only was Donovan's life on the line, but she was the sheriff's lover. And this thought made her sick to her stomach. If she weren't certain that Donovan was going to live, she would have never ended up in bed with the sheriff. She would have left town leaving all possessions and friends behind.

Tracy knew when she left Donovan the night before, that his chances of survival were better than good, as long as he had proper care. No excuses, his life was on the line, otherwise, she would have sacrificed her body for nothing.

Tracy turned away from Mama and pulled back the blanket to see Donovan's thigh. It had a fresh wrapping and it was secured tightly. The wound was completely clotted. At least Mama did this correctly. If Donovan had lost any more blood he definitely would have died.

Tracy thought about it, maybe she was too harsh on Mama. She wanted to apologize but the words wouldn't come. Tracy was a different person. She felt as if she were walking in a daze as if nothing were real. She thought about the sheriff and how he plunged inside of her. It didn't seem real, and yet her pain and sense of insecurity and deteriorating self-worth were very real.

Tracy watched Donovan in silence as he laid unconscious. It didn't seem real watching him either, and yet it was very real. The more she watched his blank face, the more she wondered if he would come out of this. It was so bizarre seeing Donovan so vulnerable, so helpless, possibly on the brink of death. What would she do if he died?

"No!" Tracy blurted. "Donovan will live!" She turned to Mama embarrassed that she had spoken out. "The dressing on his leg looks good. Make sure you keep a watch on that, we don't want him losing more blood." Tracy added.

Mama nodded.

"So far he seems alright, just need to make sure he gets water when he comes to."

Mama nodded. "I'll do that Dr. Tracy."

Tracy stared at Mama. Her round dark face was sad, but it was also strong. As Tracy watched Mama, she came to the conclusion that Mama had already come to terms with Donovan's death if it were to occur. What a strong-willed woman Tracy thought. This was her son on this bed possibly dying, and Tracy was selfishly acting as if she were the only one suffering a loss. Tracy had known Mama for more than two years, and in that time Mama had practically taken Tracy in as her own daughter. Because of Mama Tracy felt as if she were part of a family. So much so that she made a point to visit Mama at least once a week. In all those visits she had never said a harsh word or raised her voice to this woman who everyone called Mama.

Tracy walked over to Mama, grabbed her hands and squeezed them firmly. "Please forgive me, Mama. Donovan is your son, you must be in terrible pain right now."

Mama nodded. "I am Dr. Tracy. All that has happened to him, I don't understand. His wife was killed, his son almost killed. Him being gone all those years, and us thinking him dead. Then he comes back. But when he came back, he wasn't the same Donovan that I knew. Sometimes when I'm with him, I feel like I'm with a stranger." Mama paused. "It must be God's will."

"Was it God's will for his wife to be killed, for Donovan to be out of Sage's life for all that time?" Tracy asked sympathetically.

Mama answered. "Oh yes, child. It was God's will."

Mama's quick response caught Tracy by surprise. "How can you be so sure?"

"Because all that happens is God's will. Good or bad. It's his will. There are no accidents. Everything happens as God wants it."

"Why does God want these awful things to happen?" Tracy asked thinking about her own painful experiences.

"He does it this way to teach us and to help us."

Tracy was quiet for a moment as she took in what Mama had said. They had had many conversations like this over the years about God and life in general. Even though Mama was not educated and could barely read and write she was very wise to the ways that life seemed to work. Even though Tracy could not prove the validity of Mama's thoughts, her words seemed to make perfect sense.

"What does God want to teach Donovan?" Asked Tracy?

"I don't know. Can't be sure of what God's plan is for him. That's between God and Donovan."

"Do you think Donovan knows?"

Mama thought about this for a long time. "Yes. Donovan knows." Mama paused again. "I don't think he's listening. Not everyone will listen. I pray he listens to what God is teaching him."

Tracy turned to Donovan and placed her hand on his forehead. "He still has a fever." She turned to Mama. "We need a wet towel on his head. Keep it on until his fever goes down." Mama nodded. Tracy gently grabbed Mama's hands again. "I have to go. I'll be back tomorrow. If you do all that I said, Donovan will live." Mama nodded again.

Tracy grabbed her coat and headed for the front door, Mama followed. "Dr. Tracy." She called.

Tracy turned in the doorway. "Yes, Mama."

"Donovan don't look so good to me. How can you be so sure he gonna live?" She asked.

Tracy thought about it, and then walked over to Mama and placed her hands on her face. "He's gonna live because I've sacrificed everything to make sure of it."

Mama wasn't sure what Dr. Tracy meant by this, but she felt more certain about Donovan's situation.

Chapter 42

The Sun shined brightly on Sheriff Landry as he gazed out the window of the jailhouse. His hand was elevated to protect his eyes from the sun's rays. A pleasant smile lingered on his face, for he often liked to stare out the window at the many people who he protected. He wondered how much the people appreciated him and his brother as the lawmen of this town. He at least felt some pride knowing that if he or his brother were to walk down the street folks would eagerly approach them, and often shake their hands.

The day before was another prime example how efficient he and his brother were at bringing down troublemakers or gunfighters. He was however surprised that they brought down the Negro gunfighter so easily. From his experience with other gunfighters, he figured this Donovan to put up the most fight. Perhaps this Donovan realized that he would not stand much of a chance against him and his brother, both of which were very experienced gunfighters themselves.

Landry felt a great sense of relief knowing that Donovan was not only apprehended but was now dead. As Landry thought about it, he came to realize that Donovan had several opportunities to pull out his pistols, but never did so. The thought lingered in Landry's mind. Maybe the Negro gunfighter was caught off guard and wasn't sure what to do. Not likely, though Landry, an experienced gunman like Donovan would be difficult to catch off guard, and even if he were caught off guard he would be that more dangerous.

Maybe he was afraid, Landry reasoned, like most men that had come across him and his brother. However, the more Landry thought about it, the more he realized that this was not the case either. He had come across many men and women that were frightened of he and his brother, and they all shared similar characteristics of fear. Most folks would sometimes stutter when speaking, avoided eye contact, moved about quickly when they were given an order or had a high build up of perspiration on their faces.

Donovan displayed none of these characteristics. When Landry commanded an order of Donovan, he often hesitated and moved about coolly at his will. As far as the eye contact, he looked at Landry and Gunther directly in their eyes, often with hostility. And finally, there was not a drop of sweat on his brow. Not only was he not afraid, but at times he was extremely bold. And yet the most puzzling question in Landry's mind was why then did the Negro man not reach for his pistols. Just a few weeks back Donovan had gunned down two men that were threatening his folks. Not only did he gun them down, but the odds were greatly against him because both men had their pistols pointed at him, while his pistols were still holstered. And yet the Negro man managed to kill both men, while he himself only suffered a shoulder injury. This was beyond fearless behavior for any man let alone a Negro. When Landry questioned the Negro about the shooting, he had the feeling that Donovan was prepared to pull his pistols on he and his brother as well. In Landry's mind, this type of behavior made him extremely dangerous.

Not only was he not afraid of the lawmen, but it became obvious to Landry that the Negro man was toying with them. The thought of this angered Landry. He didn't like to be made a fool of and somehow he felt that Donovan had made fools of he and his brother. For the moment he wished Donovan were alive so that he could kill him again. Except for this time, he would shoot the Negro off his horse when they first arrived at the house. Yet it didn't matter now because Donovan was dead.

The front door opened and in stepped Gunther. He watched Landry as he closed the door. He approached the desk and seated himself. He leaned back with his hands behind his head and said. "Is that a smile on your face, Landry?"

Turning from the window Landry faced his brother briefly and then turned back to the window. "Maybe." He answered emotionless.

"I've known you my whole life, and I've never seen you smile more than three times. To what do we owe this special occasion?"

With his eyes still focused outside the window, Landry spoke. "You're my brother, and I'm glad you're still with me." He turned from the window to face his brother again. "We did right by killing Donovan. He was a dangerous man. I believe he was looking to do you in."

Gunther leaned further in his chair. "That nigger couldn't have done me in. There ain't too many men that can do that."

Landry frowned. "Don't be so cocky, Gunther. There's always one that can. In life and death, all it takes is one."

"I'm not cocky," said Gunther. "I just know how good I am."

Landry nodded. "Your good there's no denying that. All I'm saying is you're all I've got. I don't want nothing to happen to you. All it takes is one bullet, and just like that you're dead." Landry gazed at his brother to see if he was getting through to him. Gunther was none responsive. Landry continued. "That's why Donovan had to die. I had a bad feeling about him. I think he was gonna kill you."

"I could have handled him, Landry. I've shot and killed maybe twenty men like him" Said, Gunther.

"Not like him." Said Landry. "This Donovan was different. He was more dangerous than those men that me and you had come across."

"He's a nigger, Landry. How dangerous could he be?"

"Don't know. But he didn't seem right to me." Landry paused in thought. "Why did he give his pistols so easily?"

"Because he was afraid and he knew better." Said Gunther.

"He wasn't afraid. That I know. And by the way, he handled himself with those two men a few weeks back, I'm sure he's killed others in the same manner."

"What does it matter? He's dead." Said Gunther.

Landry nodded in agreement. "Thought he would be more trouble to us is all."

"Enough about the dead nigger." Said Gunther. "Why are you all smiles today? What happened with you?"

Landry grinned wide with embarrassment and felt awkward as if he were a child. "Me and Tracy are lovers, we're a couple now."

Gunther laughed as he slapped his palm on the desk. "It's about time you fucked that black winch! I would of done her myself, but that's your girl."

"She's wonderful." Said Landry. "I feel closer to her. I love her so much."

"You can't love her, Landry. She's a black winch. You can fuck her all you wants. But you can't love her." Said Gunther.

Landry blinked at his brother. "I love who I wants to love. Ain't nobody gonna change that."

"You can't trust her. Besides she don't feel the same about you."

Landry had a slight reaction for he was taken aback by his brother's comments. "What do you mean Gunther?" He said.

Sensing Landry's wounded ego Gunther tried to approach the situation more delicately. "All I'm saying is black winches don't know how to love a white man. She don't love you, Landry."

His brother's words snapped him to attention like someone throwing a bucket of cold water in his face. Landry tried to conceal his pain and disappointment but his face gave away his emotions. He knew that Tracy wasn't in love with him, but what he didn't understand was why she didn't love him. He had given her so many reasons to love him. He was nice and respectful to her, most white men didn't give Negro women such good treatment. He had proven over and over that he could protect her for she had witnessed on many occasions first hand Landry bravely facing and gunning down armed men in these very streets under her window. Not only that he had the most important job in town, he was the sheriff, and his job was to protect all within his town. Didn't she know how important he was, and hadn't she often seen how the people showed their gratitude to him daily, with pats on the back, and hardy handshakes? Why wasn't this enough for Tracy to love him? Yet instead she admitted to loving Donovan, a man that she barely knew. She loved him so much that she was willing to lay down with Landry so that she could extend Donovan's life just for a few moments more before his death. He should have shot him in the head like he had done with all the bandits and gunslingers that previously wandered through his town. He should of killed Donovan on the first day that he had seen him, which was right after he had witnessed him gun down those two men.

Landry walked to his brother and pulled him out of the chair by his shirt, and lifted him to his face. His lips were tight and his complexion was red with fury. A surprised Gunther reached for his side pistol but did not pull it out of the holster. Calm and unafraid Gunther was, for he knew all too well that his older brother would never bring harm upon him. However, he was somewhat troubled for this was the first time that Landry had put his hands on him in such a manner.

"Landry, what the hell are you doing?" Said Gunther.

Landry spoke through tight lips. "Don't you understand? I love her. I love her Gunther."

"Put me down." Was all Gunther would say.

Landry lowered him back to his seat. The redness in his face was soon replaced with his pale complexion. Landry stared at his brother ashamed for what he had done.

"I never thought me and you would be fighting over no woman." Said Gunther.

After which Gunther pulled out both of his six-shooters, opened the chambers and released the bullets on top of the desk. He watched the bullets roll around until they hit one another. He turned to Landry with a scowl. "I'm getting rid of these bullets in case I decide in the middle of the night to shoot you for putting your hands on me."

"You think you can?" Said Landry quietly. It was more of a question than a threat.

Gunther was stunned. "What's that?"

Again Landry asked more in the form of a question than a threat. "Do you think you're as good as me with those pistols?"

With self-assurance, Gunther answered. "I am."

"Then you're a fool little brother. And that's why I watch you so closely. That type of thinking will get you killed."

"Who's gonna kill me, you?" Snapped Gunther.

"Not me Gunther. Never me. You ain't as good with them pistols as you think you are. I've saved your hide more than once. If it weren't for me, you'd be dead now." Said Landry.

"If you let me handle my own affairs you just may find out how good I am." Said Gunther.

"You're reckless and you take too many chances." Said Landry. "If you was to handle your own affairs you would be dead."

This type of behavior was strange for the brothers, for they usually didn't fight to this extreme. Gunther headed for the backroom, and the sheets rustled as he climbed into bed. Landry felt awful for what he had said to his younger brother, but in truth, his brother needed to know this for a long time coming. Maybe it would save his life; maybe this would prevent him from being so reckless with his pistols. He didn't say these things to hurt his brother, but instead, his intentions were only to protect him.

Many times Gunther would get himself into situations that he was in no way skilled enough with his pistols to get himself out of. And luckily Landry was always in the area to help him out.

What came to mind was one time, in particular, was when Gunther had picked a gunfight with five men in the saloon over a whore. When Landry arrived on the scene, the men were about to draw their pistols. If he had arrived a few seconds later, he would have witnessed his brother's execution. Luckily he arrived in time and he and his brother together killed the five men.

Landry walked over to the window and again looked out. He watched in the direction of the hotel where Tracy stayed. He wondered if she was home.

Chapter 43

Inside the hotel room, Tracy lit the lamp on the wall nearest to the front door. She hesitated for a moment before she did so, she was afraid that she would find the sheriff waiting in the darkness of her room again. When the lamp was lit she was relieved to find that he wasn't about. However, the light within her room would notify the sheriff that she was home, and it wouldn't be long afterward before he would be knocking on her door, or letting himself in with his private key. Just thinking about the situation that she would again find herself in on this night made her extremely noxious and sick to her stomach. She so much desired to be at Donovan's bedside so as to give him the proper care that he needed but was fearful that the sheriff would come looking for her if she stayed too long. So her only reasoning for coming back to the hotel was to make an appearance so that the sheriff would not suspect Donovan to still be alive.

She sat on the edge of her bed for a long time watching and waiting for the sheriff either to knock or let himself in. Maybe he wasn't coming she thought. Tracy finally blew out the lantern and changed into her long white gown. Her uncovered feet hardly made a sound as she approached her bed. Climbing into the bed she faced the front door and continued to watch and wait for Landry to enter. The unknown of whether or not he was coming created such anxiety that Tracy was certain she would not sleep at all that night. As she waited she could hear the muffled sounds of the neighbors down the hall talking and moving about. She could also hear the planked floor creak as folks walked past her door. She was relieved that the walking sounds never stopped at her door but instead went past until she could hardly hear them at all.

It was after midnight when she finally heard his heavy boots moving down the hall toward her door. She was extremely disappointed because by then she had convinced herself that on this night he wasn't coming. She sat up helplessly and waited for him. The heavy steps stopped at her door, and the key twisted in the lock. The sheriff pushed the door open and ducked under, and then closed it behind him.

"Landry?" Tracy asked.

"It's me." He answered.

"It's very late, I'm tired."

Landry's tone was firm. "We have an agreement."

"It's late, Landry." She pleaded.

Landry ignored her, as he sat on the edge of the bed and removed his heavy boots. They clunked as they dropped to the floor.

"It's late Landry, don't you even care how I feel?"

"We have an agreement." Was all Landry said.

On this visit, the sheriff didn't depart Tracy's hotel room until well after the sun was up, which was nearly noon. On her back, she watched him at the edge of the bed as he slipped into his boots. He avoided eye contact as he dressed as if he were ashamed of what he had done. He slid off the bed and headed for the door. Before he reached the doorknob he turned to Tracy and said. "I'll be back tonight." He then opened the door wide, and left it as such, as he entered the hallway.

Tracy listened to the sheriff's heavy boots move down the passage. As she did so, she also heard the men's voices as they made conversation with the sheriff as he passed them by. She stared at the open door not wanting to move until the voices had stopped. She wanted to be sure that the sheriff was gone before she got up to close the door. At this point, she hated him so much that she did not want any contact with him, and was deathly sickened that he had access to her treasured womanhood. A prize only worthy for the man she loved, Donovan. If Donovan survived and was to find out about the arrangement with the sheriff, as unpredictable as Donovan was, GOD only knows what he would do. Even after they were married Tracy would have to carry this secret to her grave.

When the conversations stopped and she was sure that the sheriff was gone, she climbed out of bed and approached the door. Before she reached it her neighbor appeared in the doorway. He looked at her, and she looked back at him. It was seconds before she realized that she was not clothed. She slammed the door in his face, then fell against the door and sobbed.

How much more of this could she take? He was again coming tonight. How much more of herself and spirit could she give to this evil man? She thought of leaving town, but what would become of Donovan? He was too injured to travel with her. She had to stay and endure for she couldn't leave without Donovan. She dropped to the floor and once again cried, for she realized even if Donovan survived he wouldn't be fit to travel for weeks to come.

After finally gaining some composer Tracy managed to her feet. She grabbed a towel and some clean clothes. She had to rid herself of the sheriff's aftermath. She went into the room at the end of the hall and washed in the bucket. Once she felt she was clean enough, she put on her clothes and headed down the stairs. When she passed Paul at the front desk, he smirked at her. Humiliated, she continued on and exited through the front door.

She went to the barn around the back, grabbed her horse and headed down the dirt road. As she guided her horse along the road, she noticed that several people had their eyes fixed on her. She ignored them and moved on.

When she came by the saloon she saw the deputy on the walkway visiting with three other men. When the deputy saw her he beamed, and then said something to the three men, and they then turned to her and laughed. She kept her composure until her back was to them, and then the tears spilled out of her eyes. She then reminded herself that she could endure all the agony, torture and public humiliation for the man that she loved so much, Donovan.

Chapter 44

Mama was leaning over Donovan and feeding him water. He had just awoken and in her rush, she practically knocked the bowl of water off the bedside table in her attempt to get it to him. She had not forgotten Dr. Tracy's urgent instructions for when Donovan was awake. She lifted his head and put the bowl of water to his lips. At first, he gulped and choked spitting some water onto her dress.

"Not so fast," she said. "Take your time, it's not going anywhere."

She poured the water into his mouth again. This time he gulped it down.

"My, you must be thirsty." Said, Mama, as she laid the empty bowl on the floor.

Donovan tried to focus. His eyes darted around the room. "I'm alive?" He questioned. His voice raspy. The last thing he remembered was the sheriff threatening to kill him. He pulled up the sheets to inspect his tightly bandaged thigh. "It really happened?" He said almost in disbelief.

Mama watched him sympathetically. "Yes, child. You is alive."

Donovan tried to sit up, but the pain in his head, shoulder and most of his body forced him to stay put. His entire body felt raw from being dragged behind the horse. "How could this be?" Donovan said wincing in pain. "I was sure he was gonna kill me."

"He was," Mama said. "Dr. Tracy stopped him."

Donovan rubbed the back of his head, and his eyes squinted with pain. "Tracy was there?"

Mama nodded. "She told the sheriff you was as good as dead. Now we all praying to GOD that he don't find out about you. Dr. Tracy said he'll kill us all."

"He'll try." Said Donovan. "But this time I won't be so willing."

Mama put her hands to her mouth. "What do you mean?"

Donovan studied her face, she was afraid for him. He didn't' want to put her through any more grief than she had already been through. "I mean nothing."

Mama dropped her hands and sighed with relief.

"How long have I been here?"

"Two nights and two days. Dr. Tracy has been looking out for you. She's the reason you still alive. She comes during the day, but she don't stay long, on account of she don't want the sheriff to know about you. She usually gets here early afternoon or so. When you get strong enough she said she gonna take them bullets out of you."

Donovan frowned from the agony of his wounds. "Where's Sage?"

"He's in the yard with Papa. He's checked in on you a few times. I'll go fetch him for you."

Mama not only brought back Sage but in came Papa, Miles, and Maria. They all crowded in his room and gathered around his bed.

"I'll be damned." Said Papa leaning over the bed. "You son of a bitch. I think you gonna live through this too."

Donovan forced a painful smile.

Miles stepped forward and placed his large hands on Donovan's arm. "I'm glad you're still with us little brother." Was all he could say before he left the room and headed back to the fields. Maria followed him, her arms intertwined with his.

Sage stood by the far wall staring at the floor not saying a word as he nervously rocked from foot to foot. Donovan watched him, and Mama noticed. She grabbed Papa's arm and led him out of the room so Donovan and Sage could be alone. Mama closed the door behind them.

"Sage," Donovan called from his bed. Sage looked up at him. "Come over. We need to talk."

He hesitated and then approached Donovan at his bedside.

"Have a seat."

Sage looked around for a place to sit. "Where?"

Donovan nodded toward the edge of the bed. "Sit there."

Sage hesitated as he looked at Donovan's painful state.

"It's okay, Sage."

Sage nodded and as gently as he could he sat on the edge of the bed.

Donovan adjusted himself so that he could face Sage. However, the pain on his face showed as he made the effort to do so. Sage leaned forward awkwardly as if he wanted to help his father, but by then Donovan was adjusted.

"Let's talk." Said Donovan.

"About what?" Asked Sage.

"It doesn't matter. Let's just talk."

Sage's bottom lip began to quiver as if he were going to cry. "Are you gonna be alright?" He asked.

Donovan nodded. "I'm afraid so. I'll be in some pain, but I'll be fine."

Sage watched the floor as if he were building up the courage to ask his next question. "Why did they do this to you?"

Donovan thought it over. "I don't know, Sage. But it don't matter none now."

"Are you going after them for what they done?"

"No," Donovan said calmly. "Revenge is a waste of time. Revenge took me away from you for over seven years. If I had it to do over again, I would have done different."

Sage let what his father had said sink in. "Then what are you gonna do?" He asked.

Donovan thought it over, for he felt it was important to be completely honest with his son. Even though he was alive now, and would most likely survive his new injuries, he still wasn't sure how much longer he could survive. He still had many enemies wandering about. And now he had to be more careful than ever with the sheriff. Every precious second of life counted more than ever now. There was still much he wanted to teach his son, maybe he would use this time to do so.

"We must be careful. No one must know I'm here. No one must know I'm alive."

Sage nodded. He understood his father's life was in danger, especially from the sheriff and the deputy.

Donovan continued. "Tracy and me are getting married. She's special like your mama was."

Sage was pleasantly surprised. "You and Dr. Tracy?"

"Yes me and Tracy. When I heal some we're moving away." Donovan paused to watch Sage's reaction. "And we won't be coming back."

"What about Mama and them?"

"They're old and established here. Don't make sense for them to follow us across the country."

Sage bowed his head. "What about me?"

"I want you to come, but the choice is yours. Just know we can't come back."

Pondering he asked. "When will you need to know?"

"As soon as I'm healed and able to travel. Maybe four weeks at the most."

"Do you have to leave?" Asked Sage.

"I can't give the lawmen another chance at me." Said Donovan. "If they find me alive they'll harm everyone that helped me."

It wasn't that long ago when Donovan thought differently on these matters. Instead of figuring a way to safely leave town without incident, he would have instead been contemplating on how to march through town and assassinate the sheriff and his deputy. But things were different now. He had to look after his son, his folks and his future wife. He couldn't recklessly put himself in dangerous situations where he could be killed and taken away from them.

Sage nodded in agreement. "Don't know if I can leave Mama."

Donovan nodded. "I understand, Sage. It's a difficult decision. You go with your heart. You have plenty of time to decide." Sage nodded and then Donovan asked. "How's my horse?"

Beaming Sage answered. "He's fine, I've been watching out for him. When I whistle he comes running to me now. I ain't scared of him no more. I just can't get on him on account he might buck me."

Donovan smiled. "He won't buck you. But he might run off with you."

Mama reentered the room. "Sage," she whispered. "Let your daddy be. He needs to get his rest so Dr. Tracy can get them bullets out of him when she comes."

Sage turned to Donovan one last time. "You gonna be okay?"

Donovan nodded, and then Sage gently hopped off the bed and left the room, and Mama again closed the door.

Exhaustion swept over him like a thundercloud on a bright summer afternoon. He turned his head and closed his eyes, and within minutes he was asleep.

When he awoke nearly two hours later Tracy was at his bedside watching him. Her expression was serious and focused. He rubbed the sleep from his eyes. To him, she seemed tense, or maybe even angry.

"What's wrong?" He asked.

"I told you to stay away from him." Her voice was low with tension and anger. He stared back at her with no emotion. "You could have been killed." She added. "Do you know what I've been through the last few days?" She paused waiting for his answer. But all she got was Donovan's blank expression. "Do you know what I had to do to save your pathetic life?" She snapped.

Donovan was surprised by her outburst. He never expected Tracy to react this way about anything. He slowly nodded his head.

She stepped forward and pointed her finger. "Do you even care, Donovan!?"

His face tensed and his lips tightened for he did not understand the source of this anger. If it weren't for his injuries he would have left the room, but unfortunately, he was trapped with her. "I didn't ask for help." He said. "And I don't need your help now."

"What?" She responded caught off guard. "What did you say to me?"

"I didn't ask for your help, and I'm not asking now." He said coolly.

Her eyes squinted with rage, and then she leaped at Donovan slapping him across the face. Donovan's face showed no emotion as his head turned from the impact. She screamed and slapped him again. He grabbed her wrist with his uninjured hand and held it. She tried to jerk away, but he wouldn't loosen his grip.

"Let go of me!" She yelled. "You're hurting me!"

Donovan didn't respond, but she clearly saw the anger on his face as he frowned at her.

"Let go of me Donovan, you're hurting me!"

She jerked back, and at that moment Donovan released her, and she fell back by her own force onto the floor. She laid still and was in disbelief that she had ended up on her back. Her breathing was fast as she sat up. He wasn't even looking at her. His head was turned in the opposite direction.

From the floor, she yelled. "Don't you even want to know if I'm okay?"

"You're fine." He said from the bed, his voice still had a hint of anger.

"And how would you know?"

He didn't answer.

After a long moment of silence, she finally climbed to her feet and approached his bed. His eyes were closed, so she nudged him. He didn't respond. She nudged him again. This time he opened his eyes.

She eyed the red marks across his face and felt ashamed for what she had just done. She had never reacted in such a way before.

Tracy felt as if she didn't have control of her own actions let alone her life since she had been giving herself to the sheriff every night. She was lost and helpless. Even though she struck out against Donovan, she wasn't angry with him. She loved him and was only venting on him, for she didn't know how else to rid herself of some of this burden.

As she watched him with those marks on his face that she had caused she wanted to jump into his arms and tell him everything about her and the sheriff. But her instincts were strong against this, for she wasn't certain how Donovan would respond to such information.

She could tell by Donovan's face that he was still angry.

"I'm sorry." She heard herself say.

Donovan did not respond.

She glared at him, and then she touched his forehead. His temperature seemed normal.

"Your fever is down." She said.

Donovan said nothing. She wished that she had never reacted the way that she had done. But strangely enough, she felt some relief afterward. But the thought of receiving another visit from the sheriff on yet another night drained her again.

Her anger began to mount again as she watched Donovan's none responsiveness.

"I said I was sorry, Damn you!" She blurted.

Donovan turned to her. This time his expression was not angry but blank. He seemed to be studying her demeanor.

"What!?" She snapped.

"What's wrong with you Tracy?" He asked.

"I just told you, you almost got yourself killed."

"Something else is bothering you. What is it?" He said.

This last comment caught her by surprise and for a moment she wasn't sure what to tell him. Maybe this was her chance to come clean and tell all that had happened between her and the sheriff.

In a calm voice, she responded. "I'm just worried about you, is all."

Donovan watched her as if he was waiting for her to say more, but she said nothing else. He seemed not to believe her. Because Donovan rarely showed his emotions he was sometimes hard to read, and at this juncture, he was again emotionless.

"If something else is going on. I need to know Tracy." He said firmly.

Tracy gazed at him peculiarly. Were her thoughts written across her face? He had only known her for a few weeks and he could already sense that she was holding back. "You know nothing about me." She said softly.

"I know enough." He said. "Your behavior is odd for you. You wouldn't be like this unless you had a reason."

Tracy was calm now. Listening to Donovan's voice was soothing to her even though she wasn't comfortable with the topic. She just wanted him to keep talking. His voice was confident and self-assured. She felt safe in his presence, even though he was bedridden with two bullet wounds.

Sadness engulfed her again, she loved this man so much, and she could not imagine living the rest of her life without him. The agreement with the sheriff was the right thing to do. It kept Donovan alive.

Tracy moved forward and grabbed Donovan's hands and cuffed them within her own. "Do you love me, Donovan?"

"I do." He said.

"Are you going to marry me?"

"Of course Tracy."

She paused for a long moment. "You're right. Something else is bothering me. But I'm not ready to talk of it. I may never be ready."

Donovan nodded in understanding. "Most of the time I don't feel like talking myself." Though Donovan was usually serious, at this moment he was the most serious that she had ever seen him. "Tracy." He continued. "My past wife Sidney kept secrets from me, mainly to protect me. Looking back it was the wrong thing for her to do. There was nothing she could do to protect me. If someone is hurting you, I need to know."

"No one's hurting me, Donovan."

He sighed. "Alright, Tracy." He paused in frustration and then said. "Mama said you stopped the sheriff from killing me. How did you do it?"

"The sheriff thought you was dead."

"Why would he think that?"

"Because I told him so." She said.

"And he believed you?"

"Not at first," she said. "But after he looked you over, he figured you would be dead soon enough."

"Why would he think that?"

She avoided his eyes. "Because that's what I told him."

"And if he finds me alive?"

"He'll kill us all." Said Tracy.

He frowned slightly. "Then we'll make sure he don't find out."

Tracy inspected Donovan, first checking his eyes, then his head, and finally the wounds. She asked him a question about the pain from his injuries. And he responded by saying his pain was bearable. After a lengthy examination, she concluded that he was in good enough health to remove the bullets from his shoulder and thigh.

She instructed Mama to bring a bottle of whiskey for Donovan. She wanted him drunk enough so that he would pass out so as to minimize his pain while Tracy removed the bullets.

It took Donovan over an hour before he finished the bottle. Tracy watched him curiously, for she had never seen Donovan in a drunken state before and her guess was that she would most likely not see him in this way again.

On the bed, his head was turned to the side facing Tracy. He was very playful, which Tracy found odd for Donovan's usually serious and none emotional character. She enjoyed this side of him. He smiled at her drunkenly, and she returned the smile.

"Are you drunk, Donovan?" She teased.

"Nope." He said with a slur. "I'm not…drunk." He tried to wave his hand to express himself, but it was a limp drunk hand.

Tracy couldn't help but laugh at him. Grabbing her tools from her black medicine bag she walked to the front room and placed them in the fire. It was late afternoon and Papa was seated in his chair just in front of the hearth. Mama was in the kitchen area washing up the dishes that were from dinner.

"How's my boy?" Asked Papa from his chair.

She turned to him and smiled. "He's drunk."

With the scorching instruments in hand, Tracy headed back to the room with Donovan.

She placed the hot instruments on a white towel on top of the bedside table. Standing beside Donovan she massaged his head. "Do you love me?" She asked.

Slightly his eyes drooped and he seemed as if he would pass out at any second.

"Donovan." She called. He opened his eyes to her. "Do you love me?"

"Yesss." He answered. His speech was slow and drawn out.

"Do you know why the sheriff wanted to kill you?" She asked.

"Yesss." He said.

"Why?" She asked.

He smacked his lips in an attempt to get his words together. "Banther." He said.

"You think it was because of Banther?"

"Noooo." He said slowly and drawn out. His eyes were now closed as he spoke. "They… wanted me… to think… Banther."

"You don't believe them?"

"Noooo." He said.

"Then what do you believe, Donovan?"

He did not answer.

"Donovan." She called once more. His eyes opened for only a moment and then closed again. "Why do you think he came after you?" She asked again.

With closed eyes, his response was barely audible. His voice was so low that she had to lean forward pressing her ear close to his lips to understand.

"Because of you." He mumbled, and then he passed out.

Tracy was stunned.

Chapter 45

Her papa's eyes were closed and wet, as he struggled with his breathing. Maria watched as his chest heaved up and down. He had been getting much worse. When Dr. Tracy had stopped by earlier she had said. "There's nothing she could do for him. Just make him as comfortable as possible." It was hard to believe that her father was dying. When she was a child he seemed always to have strength and a lot of energy. It was as if he would live forever. Even as a child, Maria figured that she would probably die before her father. But that didn't seem to be the case now.

When her mother died she was too young to really understand what death meant. Somehow she thought her mother's death was temporary and that she would return soon. Even when she saw her father crying over her mother's body, she still didn't understand how permanent death was. It was odd to her that her father would dig a hole in the back of the house, and place her mother wrapped in an old blanket into the opening. When he started placing the dirt on top of her mother she realized that her mother wasn't coming back. Then the tears came. She never really got over her mother's death. Even at the young age of seven, Maria had a very loving relationship with her mother. She could remember them taking long walks in the woods, making dolls from leftover cloth and stuffing them with hay. She had nothing but fond memories of her mother.

But her father was different. He didn't know how to raise a little girl, or at least it seemed that he didn't put forth much of an effort. They didn't talk much, and never went for long walks in the woods. Never was she disciplined by her father. He let her do as she wanted when she wanted. There were never any talks about boys or how her friends treated her badly, which was quite often. Being with her father was lonely, and sometimes she hated him for this. But as she grew older she learned to adjust to him and accept him for how he was. A lot of the time she pretended that she lived by herself. Often she wondered what type of relationship did her father have with her mother. Was her mother happy with her father, or was she unhappy like she was.

Young boys helped her fill in the gap that her father left her. The young boys were usually affectionate to her, hugging, touching and kissing, and eventually sex. Sex was a good escape from her present state. It was a method of getting away, and she used the young boys as much as they seemed to use her. However, she found that the young boys her age could not provide the pleasure that an adult man could. Being with an adult man for the first time was an incredible experience. They were so much in control, knew how to pleasure her just right, and seemed to enjoy having sex with her much more so than the boys her age. Not only did the adult men enjoy her more, but she found that she could more easily manipulate them to do almost whatever she pleased. After a while, it became a game for her. She would ask the adult men to do things such as fight another man whom she claimed had mistreated her. Or she would ask them for money, or she would have the man go into town to buy her a dress.

Her father moaned and opened his wet eyes. Raising his hand he tried to speak, but nothing came out. Sitting beside him she rocked him in her arms, calling his name over and over in a soft whisper. "It's gonna be okay daddy." She said. "Everything gonna be alright."

Nothing came from his lips as he tried again to speak. His chest heaved as he tried to suck in air. His eyes became wide with fear.

Rubbing his head and rocking slowly back and forth. "It's okay daddy. Don't fight it. You're going to a better place. You gonna be with mama now. She gonna be waiting for you."

His eyes were wide, and he was fighting for his breath. As Maria watched him she couldn't help but sob. She had never seen a man struggle to take his last breath, let alone her father. Leaning forward to get closer to him her tears slid off her face and onto his. He was doing so well when she brought him home a couple of days ago. She figured that she was going to have a chance to spend a lot of time with him. But now it was obvious that this was not possible.

Where was Miles, she needed him now. She can't-do this alone. Mama. Where's Mama? No one's here to help, she's all alone. Maria wanted to call out to Miles, but she didn't want to disturb her father in his last moments. The tears came harder and she squeezed him tighter. Then she felt him go still when she looked at him his eyes were lifeless. There was no longer an expression of struggle on his face. It was peaceful, content, no burdens. Holding him she sobbed.

Stepping out onto the porch, her wet eyes searched the field for Miles. Miles was in the middle of the field with his hoe in hand. Sobbing she stepped off the porch moving in his direction. Her steps were unsure as she moved toward him. He turned to her when she was halfway to him. She cried harder when their eyes met. Miles dropped the hoe and headed to her.

When he reached her she said. "He's dead. My daddy's dead." She collapsed into his arms, sobbing into his sweat-soaked shirt. Miles held her tight not saying a word. He seemed to understand the pain that she was in, for he would feel the same if he were to lose his father.

He swept her up and carried her back to the house. When he reached the porch he sat her in the chair just outside the front window. She watched him go inside the house. When he came out his eyes were also wet, and he sat in the chair next to hers. They sat in silence. Miles did not go back to work that evening. He instead stayed silently by Maria's side for he knew that she needed him, and hopefully, she would do the same for him, when his father passed on as well.

Chapter 46

Mama pulled back the curtains. Donovan covered his eyes with his forearm. "Too much sun." He said.

"Too much sun?" She questioned. "It's morning, the sun ain't even out yet."

"It hurts my eyes." Said Donovan.

Mama watched his distorted expression and his arm that was raised to shield his face. Reaching up she snapped the curtains closed. Only then did Donovan's expression return to normal as his arm dropped to his side.

"I think Dr. Tracy gave you too much whiskey, but at least she got them bullets out of you." Said, Mama.

"Where is she?" He asked.

"She went home, I guess. She stayed pretty late looking after you. It seems you two was doing some talking."

Donovan squinted in an attempt to recall the events of the night before. He remembered when Tracy had handed him the bottle of whiskey to help ease his pain during the surgery. Thinking back the last thing that he remembered was Tracy silently watching him as he drank the whiskey. He did not recall doing much talking. However, it troubled him to think of what they may have talked about. He hoped in his drunken state that he did not reveal information about his past.

"What were we talking about?" He asked.

Mama seemed puzzled. "Don't know child, I wasn't in the room with yall, and besides the door was closed. But I knows you was drunk. Never seen a man more drunk than you was last night."

It was rare to catch Donovan with a drink in his hand and even rarer to catch him drunk. Walking about drunk was dangerous. If an enemy were to confront him while he was inebriated, he would be defenseless. On one occasion Donovan watched as a drunken man accidentally brushed up against a sober man causing him to spill his drink over himself. A fierce argument broke out between the two men. Then both men reached for their holstered pistols. The sober man got his pistol out long before the drunken man could even find his. It was at first a comical situation, for those in the saloon were laughing as the drunken man struggled to get his pistol from his holster. The sober man waited patiently for the drunken man to finally pull out his pistol and then shot him in the face.

Donovan watched the scene and nodded in disgust. The sober gunman got a glimpse of Donovan's loathing and turned his pistol on him some twenty feet or so away. "What you looking at Nigger? Maybe you want to end up like him." He said referring to the dead drunk man on the floor.

Donovan's guns were well hidden behind his long brown coat, giving the appearance that he was unarmed. He turned his gaze to the dead man that was on the floor as if thinking over the question that was just asked of him. His intention in doing so was to briefly distract the gunman. The sober man grinned at this and glanced over the crowd seeking their many nods of approval. But this action was a mistake because when he turned to again face the Negro man, he mistakenly found that Donovan had his gun drawn and had just fired off two shots that hit him in the chest. He was dead before he hit the ground. From within the deafly quiet bar, he whistled and then cautiously exited the saloon. When the horse fast approached, Donovan climbed on and raced out of town.

It was two more days before Donovan could get himself out of bed. He was tender from the surgery, particularly from the wound on his thigh. Papa had carved him a cane out of a long dead stick that he had found somewhere in the woods. At first, Donovan hobbled on the stick just within the privacy of his room. But after a day of practice, he managed to hobble to the front porch where Mama presided. She was pleased to see him.

She said. "You're doing so good Donovan. Dr. Tracy sure knows what she's doing."

Donovan nodded as he sat in the chair next to her. He grunted as he came down in the seat. After experiencing such pain just from sitting, he was certain that he would need help getting back to his feet.

"It's been three days. Where's Tracy?" He asked.

Leaning back in her chair and giving it some thought Mama said. "Don't know. It's not like her to be gone this many days."

"You think something happened to her?"

"Oh no, she's just fine. I think she's just being careful on account of the sheriff and all. She probably knows the worst for you is over."

He turned his attention toward the fields. He watched Miles to the far east of the land. He was in a rhythmic motion as he hoed the land, making a trail for the seeds that they would soon plant. Sage was on the west side and had just spotted Donovan on the porch. Even from this distance, Donovan could see the wide grin on his face. Sage raised his hand and waved long and wide. From the porch, Donovan returned the wave. Sage said something to his grandpa whom was next to him and then started in Donovan's direction.

"I should have killed them." He said as he watched his son approaching.

"Who?" Mama asked.

"The Sheriff and his deputy. I should have killed them."

Mama watched him. It was as if she was looking at a stranger and not her son. "Do you think you could have?" She asked.

"I don't know." He said. "But it wouldn't have mattered much because they was coming to kill me anyway."

Mama didn't know what to say to this, and by then Sage had stepped onto the porch.

"Looks like you gonna be okay." Said Sage.

Donovan nodded. "I reckon so."

Another day had gone by and again no sign of Tracy. Donovan was still fairly sore from the surgeries, but less sore than the day before. However, the cane was still needed for him to walk about. On this day he went a little further than the porch, with Sage right by his side. They decided to walk around the back of the house along the dirt trail up the steep hill and rest at the top. From this view, they could see the top of the house with streams of black smoke coming out the chimney. They could also see a much smaller looking Miles digging small trenches. Papa could be seen in the pigpen, moving the pigs about, getting one ready to be slaughtered. The front of Miles's house was quiet and gave the impression that it was empty, but Donovan knew that Maria was inside, still mourning her papa's death. Mama had told him last night that he had died the night before, and they had buried him behind the house. They marked his grave with a cross that Papa had made. The words GOD BLESS HIS SOUL was scratched deep into the wood.

Donovan felt sad for her, for he knew all too well what it was like to lose a loved one. At least her papa didn't die a violent death. At least she didn't have to carry the massive burden of feeling responsible for his death.

From the view above they could only see the back of the house, and could not see the front porch where Mama was probably sitting at the moment. Behind them for about one hundred yards was a flat field with long green and yellow grass. And just beyond the field was the thick forest.

After a while Donovan came to realize that in every direction he was staring, his son was doing the same. He smiled.

"You like it up here, Sage?"

Sage looked around wide-eyed. "Never been up here before."

"Why not?"

"Mama likes me to stay close to the house."

This made sense; Mama was protective, maybe too protective. All these years Donovan had been doing just fine without their help, now all of a sudden he was letting his folks dictate his actions in troubled situations. For example, with the sheriff and his deputy, on two occasions he let his folks talk him into not confronting the lawmen. He was disappointed in himself for letting them persuade him otherwise.

Donovan turned to Sage who was watching Papa and the pigs. "Sage, do you know where my pistols are?"

After some hesitation, he nodded. "I grabbed them after the sheriff and the deputy took you away. I hid them in the barn, under the hay."

Donovan looked down toward the barn. It was small from this height, but about three times as big as Miles's house, which was some fifty yards across from it. "Sage, tonight I want you to get those guns, and bring them to the room."

"You gonna kill them, lawmen?" Sage asked.

"No Sage, I'm not looking to kill anyone. Those days are over for me. This is not about revenge. I would leave today if I could ride far enough. But like I am now, I can't ride anywhere."

"Then why the pistols?" He asked.

"For protection." He said. "The lawmen think I'm dead. But if they happen to show up here and find me alive, then we'll all be in danger."

Sage nodded in understanding of the situation. "What about Papa and Mama?"

"What about them?"

"They don't like those pistols in the house." He said.

"It don't matter to me what they like, them guns is our only chance for survival if them lawmen find out about me."

"Are you scared?" Sage asked.

Donovan turned his gaze to the bottom of the hill. Papa had finally separated one of the pigs and was leading it around to a small shack at the end of the pig yard. "Why do you ask that?" He said.

"You don't seem scared of nothing. The other day with them lawmen, I was afraid for you, but you didn't seem afraid to me. And you don't seem afraid now."

Donovan didn't want to mislead his son. Their time together was short, and he wanted his son to know the truth about him. Even though he was uneasy about sharing his fears with his son, he did feel it was necessary for Sage to understand that his father had fears. Many fears in fact. Perhaps this information would help the young boy deal with his own personal fears. "Sometimes I'm more afraid than others. I'm somewhat afraid now." He admitted. "But over time, I become less and less afraid."

Sage seemed almost not to believe his father. "How do you hide it like that?"

Donovan signed. "I don't hide it. I understand it and accept it, and then do what I have to do."

Sage was quiet for a long time and then asked. "Will you teach me to fight as you do, to use the pistols as you can?"

"No." Answered Donovan abruptly. "It's not necessary for you to know such things."

"I'm not looking to be a gunfighter. I just want to be able to protect myself when the time arises."

Leaning against his cane, Donovan stared off into the woods. Sages reasoning for wanting to learn to fight and to use the pistols was valid. At times life was unpredictable and his son as an adult may be forced to defend himself more than once. "I will teach you." He finally said. "But I warn you I won't be easy on you."

Sage had excitement in his voice. "When?" He asked.

"In the morning, after breakfast. We'll start up here." Donovan then headed down the hill as he leaned on his cane for support. Remaining on the hill, Sage watched him in silence.

Donovan watched the reflection of the bright moon that shined through his window. As he laid calmly on his bed he thought of Tracy. Her actions were unexpected on her last visit, and he couldn't help but to wonder about her unusual demeanor on that night. It had now been three days since she had last shown herself. Of course, the circumstances were risky, and Tracy was wise not to come to the property at all. For the more she came, the greater the chance that the lawmen would find out about Donovan. When Donovan was first injured, she had no choice but to come to the house for his life depended on her. But now that he was well on his way to recovery, it wasn't necessary for her to come at all.

Donovan didn't like these feelings of vulnerability, not being able to do anything but wait. He sat up and rolled out of bed. He shifted his weight from side to side to test his balance without the cane. He winced, for the pain was still present and he could not walk without the use of the cane.

He walked over to the window using the edge of the bed to brace himself. As he stared out, he saw that the land was blanketed with yellow rays from the bright moon. Even the shapes of the trees at the edge of the forest were visible.

Donovan turned his gaze to the pile of guns that were sitting in the corner next to his bed. Inside the holsters of his gun belt, there were two pistols, his knife, and a brown saddlebag. Sage had brought them in earlier when Mama and Papa were asleep.

He stared at the pile for a moment focusing on the brown saddlebag. He had almost forgotten about it. The saddlebag was on his horse when the sheriff and his deputy surprised him a few days back. He wondered why Sage brought this in. Maybe he knew that there was just over $6200 in cash and gold pieces. Money that he had collected during his travels.

He moved toward the bed. His leg felt weak and unstable. He wondered if he would ever have full use of his leg again.

"Again," Donovan said as he watched Sage pull the gun from the holster.

Sage and Donovan were on top of the hill, and they had been up there for quite some time. Sage had Donovan's pistols strapped to his waist. And he was drawing empty guns and pointing them at an imaginary figure. The holster belt was too long for Sage, so Donovan doubled tied it in the front. Now it gave the appearance of being wrapped too tightly, but it served its purpose for now.

"Again," Donovan said, commanding Sage to draw the pistol from the holster.

Sage's face was flustered for he was exhausted. But he did as he was told and again pulled out the gun, pointed it and then stuffed it back into the holster.

"That's sloppy," Donovan said. "Do it again, and concentrate."

Sage sighed. "How long do I have to do this?"

Donovan stepped forward and stood before him. "You will do it for as long as it takes. You said you wanted to learn; well this is how you learn. Now draw."

Sage gaped at Donovan, and almost without thinking he pulled out the empty gun and pointed it at Donovan's chest. Then he dropped the gun by his side ashamed for what he had done.

"Good," Donovan said, and then he stepped away and took his original position. "Again." He commanded.

After a while, Donovan finally instructed Sage to take a break.

Sage sighed as he untied the gun belt. He then headed down the hill for some water. As Donovan watched him he wondered if he was being too hard on him. He wondered if he should ease up on him some, or even if Sage could withstand such a grueling training schedule. The type of training that Sage was performing now was the same training ritual that Donovan had put himself through just after his wife's death. And over the years he had trained often during his downtime when he was in search of his wife's killers. It was his constant training and practice that had kept Donovan alive for all these years.

As Donovan watched Sage come back up the hill, he came to the conclusion that he would not be doing Sage any good if he were to train him easy. His training would make the difference between life and death. Hard was the only way.

Sage pickup the gun belt and tied it around his waist. He looked at Donovan and held up his arms. Donovan grabbed the belt up front and pulled hard.

Donovan stepped back taking his position. "Now use your other arm, and draw."

Sage looked forward concentrating. He reached for the gun with his other hand and dropped it.

He decided not to pick up the gun and instead stared at it. He then turned to Donovan and said. "Why do I have to use my other hand? I'm not good at it."

Donovan responded by saying. "Sage, you're not good with either hand." Sage frowned, and Donovan found Sage's expression amusing. He had never seen Sage convey frustrations or anger before. He didn't think it was possible for him to do so. However, Donovan's face was neutral and Sage had no idea that his father was amused. "But with some practice, you'll probably be good." He said.

Sage picked up the gun stuffed it in the holster, and stared straight ahead.

"Draw," Donovan commanded.

He reached with his left hand and again the gun dropped to the ground. This time Sage didn't wait. He immediately picked it up and stuffed it into his holster and stood at attention waiting for Donovan's command. Again this pleased Donovan, and at this moment Donovan knew that Sage would make it through the difficult training and would not quit.

"Good." He said. "Draw!" He yelled.

And again Sage pulled the gun, and even though he was sloppy and odd looking, this time he did not drop the gun.

"Good," Donovan said. "Again."

This went on for about an hour, and Sage finally got to the point where he could draw his pistol with his left hand without dropping it. However, it still felt awkward and he was nowhere close to being as skillful as he was with his right hand.

Sage sat next to Donovan on the hill in silence as he rested. At that moment he resented his father, but he was pleased that he was learning how to handle a pistol. They had been training for several hours, and he hadn't expected the session to go on nearly this long. He instead figured Donovan to take a few moments to teach him some things, and then leave Sage alone to practice at his own pace. Now hours into the session, Sage realized that they were only halfway through the first lesson. And the worst part was that the lessons were not just for this one day. This type of grueling training would proceed daily. Sage dropped his head to his knees and signed. When he looked up, Donovan was watching him. Sage frowned at his father and then turned his attention down the hill.

Small birds were chirping, and flying wildly from tree to tree. He smiled as he watched some of them chase each other in small circles and then disappear into the thickly leafed trees. Sage's head tilted upward as he watched the birds in action.

Down the hill, uncle Miles was in the fields as usual. He was always the first to start his work in the fields, usually, before the sun came out, and was always last to leave the fields, which was usually just after the sun had gone down. As he watched Miles he tried to think of how often and hard Miles worked. As he thought about it, it seemed that Miles was always working. Even on Saturday and Sunday, he was in the fields working. Sage wondered why did he work so hard. Not only did he work hard but he never complained. Sometimes he would be sitting at the table at dinner bobbing back and forth as if he was going to fall over into his plate from exhaustion. And even then he didn't complain, never saying how tired he was. Or that he worked harder than the rest of them. Nothing.

"I'm ready," Sage said under his breath cutting his break short. "What's next?"

Again Donovan was pleased, but his expression was neutral. "You're gonna learn to fight."

This pleased Sage, but like his father, he didn't show it either.

Donovan placed his cane on the ground and stood just in front of Sage with his hand raised to face as if he was going to fight. "Stand like this, Sage. Make a fist and put them close to your face. Good. Now put your feet apart. No, that's too far. Look at me and do like I do. Good." Donovan stepped forward and grabbed Sage turning him slightly. "Just like that."

Donovan stepped back looking him over. "Now punch."

Sage hesitated, and then punched at the air, then waited for his father's critique, for he always criticized him after a command.

"Don't just punch with your arms. Put your body into it."

Sage stood in his fight stance and punched again at the air, this time trying to swing his body. It felt very awkward, and he guessed that he looked silly as well.

"Like this Sage." Donovan stood in his fight stance, and then he swung a right cross, turning his body slightly into the punch. Donovan's punch was smooth and very quick. To Sage, it gave the appearance of being very powerful. He would have hated to be at the end of that punch. "Now you do it." He instructed.

Once again Sage stood in his fighting stance. He concentrated, then threw a right cross. His punch was much slower, and his body turned more so than Donovan's, which caused him to lose his balance, but nonetheless, it was a punch, and his father nodded his approval and said "Good," which was always a good sign.

The fighting went on for two more hours, taking short breaks here and there. During the two-hour period, Donovan taught Sage the importance of putting your body into the punch. "This is how you get your power." He told him. "If you punch with just your arms, you have no power and can't possibly defend yourself." They practiced punching, jabs, and blocks with either hand. By the time they had finished it was noon and lunchtime.

They walked down the hillside by side. Donovan had the gun belt resting over his shoulder, and Sage's face was wet with sweat. Even his shirt was soaked with perspiration.

"Are we done, now?" Sage asked almost relieved.

"No. We're just beginning." Said Donovan.

Sage yelled. "What else do we gotta do?!" He said almost crying.

"Some kicks." Said Donovan. "After lunch, you'll learn the different ways to kick, like a Chinaman once taught me."

That night Sage slept in the same room as Donovan. Before since Donovan was injured Mama had felt that Sage should sleep with her and Papa.

Donovan slept on the bed, and Sage slept on the floor next to the wall. Once again Mama had provided him with several soft blankets and a pillow. Sage was exhausted from the practically all day work out with his father. He didn't think he would be able to go through another day of this grueling training, but he didn't know how to get out of it. He was hoping at dinner that Mama would persuade Donovan to stop the training. And at one point he was thrilled when she brought it up. She had told Donovan that she didn't think it was right for him to teach Sage how to use those guns and to fight with his fists. But Donovan said that Sage wanted to learn these things and that it was his idea. And when both Donovan and Mama turned to him waiting for his response, he had to admit that it was true.

Sage made himself comfortable within the bedding on the floor. Looking over his shoulder, he could see the bed, but from being at such a low angle he could not see Donovan. "Are you awake." He called.

He heard Donovan sigh. "Yes, Sage."

"What are you doing?"

"I'm thinking."

"About what?"

"Go to sleep Sage. We have a long day tomorrow."

Sage rolled over making an attempt to again get comfortable. He was regretting ever telling Donovan that he wanted to learn to fight and use guns. He had no idea that it would be this hard of work. His regrets were, short-lived, for within a few minutes he was snoring softly. Donovan rolled over and peaked at him. A gentle smile lingered on his face, for he was proud of his son's efforts.

Chapter 47

"Did she see you?" Asked Sheriff Landry who was seated behind his desk. Corwin rubbed his hands nervously across his trousers, for he was once again inside the jailhouse at the lawmen's request. Gunther was across the room as he leaned against the wall facing them. He displayed a playful grin as he turned the chambers of his pistol. Corwin uneasily eyed the weapon.

"No sir, Dr. Tracy didn't see me," Corwin said.

"How many days did you follow her?" Asked Gunther

Corwin rolled his eyes as he gave the question some thought. "Since Tuesday, three days I'd say."

"Three days," Landry repeated. "And where did she go in that three days?"

Corwin rolled his eyes in his head again. "From what I could see she was tending to her patients."

"Patients!" Gunther snarled. The clicking of the turning chambers stopped. "That's not what we asked you. We want to know who did she see? Where did she go? We want names and places."

Corwin bowed respectfully and apologized. He then gave them all the names and places that he had seen Dr. Tracy visit in the last few days.

"Did she go to Mama's house?" Landry asked.

Corwin rolled his eyes in his head. "No, sir. I didn't see her go there."

"Are you sure about that?" Landry repeated.

"Yes, sir. I is sure on that."

Landry and Gunther exchanged glances, while Corwin stood quietly waiting for his next instructions.

Landry asked. "Aren't you and Papa good friends?"

Corwin shrugged. "We know each other, but we ain't what you call friends."

Landry eyed him suspiciously. "I heard different." He said. "I heard you two go way back."

"No." Corwin lied. "We know each other because we're neighbors. But that's all. We ain't friends."

"We need you to do us another favor." Said Landry waiting for Corwin's answer.

Corwin nodded. "Yes sah." But the tone of his voice said otherwise.

"I want you to go to your neighbor's house, and talk to him for a bit. See what you can find out. Then come back and tell us what you know or what you've seen." Said Landry.

"What am I suppose to find out?" Asked Corwin.

"You never mind that. Just go talk with him, like a good neighbor, then come back here and tell me and Gunther what you know and we'll take care of the rest."

This request was the oddest of all of their request so far, but Corwin nodded nonetheless.

From the front porch Papa was leaning forward in his chair with a cup of whiskey in hand, and alongside him in Mama's rocking chair was Corwin. He too had a cup of whiskey in hand and a twig that dangled from his lips. It was mid-afternoon and the sun was high to the west.

In the center of the field, Miles had taken a short break because Maria had brought him water to quench his thirst. They talked for a moment and then affectionately hugged before Maria carried the empty cup back to the house so that Miles could continue with his work.

Corwin pointed his cup toward Miles. "Is that all he do is work?"

Papa nodded. "I reckon so," he said. "I'm glad to see him and his woman getting along so fine."

Sometime of silence went by as they stared off into the fields. Finally, Papa asked. "You alright, Corwin? You don't seem yourself."

As the twig dangled from his lips, Corwin raised his cup and took a mouthful of whiskey. "We've been friends a long time." He said after he swallowed.

"We is best of friends." Added Papa.

Corwin nodded. "That wasn't right what the sheriff did to your son and all." Papa nodded humbly. Leaning back into his chair Corwin took another swig from his cup. "Black folks and white folks alike don't care for me much. Black folks won't so much as look at me, and white folks always wanting special favors from me. They make me do things that I don't wants to do." Corwin turned to Papa. "Besides my wife and kids, you's my only friend."

Papa nodded and then took a sip from his cup.

Corwin glanced around to the dark windows behind. "Where's everybody?" He asked.

"Mama's at Miles's house, she gonna show Maria how to cook some things, not sure where Sage is." Said Papa.

Corwin sighed to himself. "I came to warn you about something." He then turned the cup over to finish the remaining whiskey. Papa watched him closely. "The sheriff and the deputy have been on me for a time. They're making me do things that I don't much like."

"Like what?" Asked Papa.

"Like follow Dr. Tracy." Said Corwin. "At first I refused. I told the deputy that Dr. Tracy was a fine woman and I wanted no part of this. So the deputy beat on me some and told me I had no choice in the matter. So I followed her for a few days. I didn't understand why, but I did what I was told." He paused to collect his thoughts. "Then one night I followed her over here and watched her and your son go off into the woods. I told the lawmen what I saw. And the next day your Donovan was killed."

"Why would the lawmen kill Donovan over Dr. Tracy?" Asked Papa.

"I reckon the sheriff got feelings for Dr. Tracy."

"How do you know this?" Asked Papa.

"The other night in the saloon the deputy was so drunk that he could barely stand on his own. He was telling to no one in particular about his brother and Dr. Tracy."

"That don't explain why you need to warn me." Said Papa.

Corwin uneasily stood from his chair and approached the edge of the porch. "Now the sheriff and his deputy got me coming over here for something. I'm not sure of what. They wanted me to visit you and then come back and tell them what I seen, or what we talked about. Make no sense to me." He turned to Papa. "Maybe it do to you?"

Papa shook his head. "Have no idea." He said.

Corwin stared off into the distance for a while. Finally, he said. "There's one other thing. Dr. Tracy and the sheriff have been carrying on."

Papa seemed stunned by this. "What you mean carrying on?"

Corwin turned to Papa. "Folks say he stays in her room all night. I've known Dr. Tracy for some time now, and I didn't figure her to take a liking to the sheriff. Folks say that he's forcing himself on her. That's what I figures too." He turned away and stepped off the porch and headed home.

After a while, the front door squeaked open and Donovan stepped out onto the porch as he leaned on his cane.

"How much did you hear?" Asked Papa.

"Everything." Said Donovan softly.

Chapter 48

Donovan stepped into the dark house and Papa remained on the porch. Sage was behind the front door as Donovan came through. He then followed Donovan to the back bedroom.

In the bedroom, Donovan stared out the window for a long time, and Sage sat in silence on the floor. The half-moon wasn't as bright on this night, so Donovan stood almost in total darkness at the window's ledge.

Donovan thought about Tracy and what she had meant to him. He had only known her for a few weeks and was already in love with her. He wondered if such a short time span was enough to commit to marriage. He had known his previous wife Sidney for six months before they were married. However, he had known from his first glance of Sidney that he was in love with her. And they were happily married for several years before her death. In fact, those years with Sidney were by far the happiest years of his life. He wondered if he would be as joyful with Tracy.

After Sidney's death, relationships were near impossible for Donovan. He could not allow himself to become attached to anyone, only to later be devastated with intense pain because this person could possibly be murdered or raped as Sidney was. This type of torment he would not tolerate again. And avoiding relationships was the only way to evade this overwhelming agony. And yet after years of avoidance, he had allowed himself to fall in love with Tracy. His emotions at this moment were intense as he thought about Tracy and the sheriff together.

Over the years on his travels, he had come across several women. All of which had an understanding that Donovan was not interested in a long-term relationship, and before long he would be traveling again, alone. Nonetheless, some foolishly pursued a commitment from Donovan only to find that they were disappointed when he later left town without so much as a goodbye.

Donovan continued to silently stare out the dark window. It all made sense now. This would explain why Tracy was so oddly upset a few nights before when she struck him across the face. This would explain why she screamed. "Do you know what I had to go through to keep you alive?" Tracy was distracting the sheriff by sacrificing herself, her body so that

Donovan could live without the lawmen's knowledge. The old man on the porch had said that the two had been together each night since the shooting.

Donovan slid to the floor and placed his head between his knees. He loved Tracy so much that the thought of her with another man under such harsh circumstances were excruciating. What he knew about Tracy was this. She was very protective about her body, and only a man whom she loved could even touch, or view her body in an intimate manner. In fact on the very night when Donovan and Tracy had finally made love, she would not do so until he told her that he loved her and promised to commitment to marriage.

Though Donovan should have been grateful for Tracy's sacrifice to save his life, he was not. Instead, he felt disappointed, hurt and betrayed by her actions. She should have instead let the sheriff kill him.

The question now was what would Donovan do about this situation? A few months earlier Donovan would have marched through town and attempted to kill the lawmen out of vengeance. But he had since learned that revenge was not necessarily the best solution. However, his thoughts concentrated on the sheriff for he wanted him dead for his acts on Tracy. But Donovan was still injured and would be so for weeks to come. His injuries were not his only reason for hesitation. He had to also consider his family and Tracy. If Donovan were to be killed by the lawmen while going after them, the lawmen in retaliation would then go after his family and Tracy for harboring him. Though he did not know of what action he would take with the lawmen if any, he was very clear on what action would be taken with Tracy. He wished that he had never allowed himself to get involved with her.

"Are you gonna kill the sheriff, for what he done?" Asked Sage from the other side of the dark room.

"No, Sage. I'm not gonna kill anyone."

"What are you gonna do?"

There was a long silence within the darkness before he spoke. "I'm not gonna do anything." He said.

"What about Dr. Tracy?"

"Tracy can take care of herself."

"What if she can't?" Asked Sage.

"There's nothing I can do for her." Said Donovan with finality in his tone.

It wasn't that Sage wanted to put his father's life at risk, for he knew all too well that it was a tremendous risk. His plan was to stand by his father's side and help him fight. Sage dropped his head in disappointment for he greatly loved Dr. Tracy. She was one of the few people that treated Sage like a normal person, versus the others that displayed contempt of his scarred face.

Sage continued to watch Donovan unnoticed. Though Sage was young at the time, he remembered when the five men tied Donovan to a tree and beat him with the whip almost to his death. He could recall in his mind the awful sound that the whip made as it sliced through the air and cracked onto Donovan's bareback. He remembered his mother begging for the men to stop. He remembered after the endless beating Donovan's body hanging limp against the tree.

One of the men picked up a nearby log and struck Sage in the face. The pain was horrific. He fell to the ground nearly unconscious. After the blow to his face, he heard his mother's hysterical screams. A gunshot was fired and his mother's screams were abruptly silenced.

Sage walked over to Donovan and sat next to him on the floor. He wanted to put his arms around his father to comfort him, but he felt that Donovan would be uneasy with this display of affection so he chose against it. They sat in silence for a long time.

Finally Sage asked. "You sure you killed those men that killed my mama?"

Donovan nodded. "Yeah, Sage."

"How did it feel?"

Donovan turned to Sage trying to read him, maybe trying to understand why he was asking such a question. He even hesitated as if he would not answer, but he did finally answer. "It was disappointing. I thought it would take away all my pain, all my bad memories, but it didn't."

"Then why did you kill all of them?"

"I was trying to get justice for what they did to your mama."

"Justice?" Sage asked.

"Yeah, Sage, Justice. I was trying to make things right again for what they did. But killing them didn't make it right."

"Why not?" Sage asked.

"Because killing them didn't change nothing. It didn't bring your mama back, it didn't take away my pain. It did nothing." Donovan paused for a moment. "And it took me away from you, and that was wrong."

To Sage that sounded sort of like an apology. Maybe for Donovan, this was as close as he would get to an apology. Of course Sage didn't feel that an apology was needed. He felt his father was right in what he had done. As a matter of fact, he admired him for taking the time, and effort to find and kill those men. They deserved it. Like Donovan said it was justice, and if it weren't for Donovan those men would have probably raped and killed more women. Those men would have probably taken some other small boy's mama from him. Maybe killed someone's father. If it weren't for Donovan those men would be still walking around unpunished for their crimes against innocent people. As Donovan said, justice was served on those men.

As he continued to sit next to Donovan in silence, he thought back on all the years that had passed that he had greatly envied all the boys that he had witnessed with their fathers but knew his desires to have a father would never come true. It was still difficult to conceive that a man such as Donovan was his father. Sage wondered often if Donovan was perhaps a ghost of some sort and had come back to his human form. Or maybe Sage was just stuck in a dream, and that he would soon awake to find everything as it was just before Donovan had come back into their lives. As he thought it over, it made sense that maybe Donovan was a ghost, or that he was dreaming, for no man could survive what Donovan had survived over these last few weeks. Maybe he so desperately wanted a father that his mind was somehow playing tricks on him, convincing him that Donovan was real when in fact he was not.

After considering for a long moment, Sage finally asked. "Are you a ghost? Or am I just dreaming and I'll wake up soon?"

He was surprised by Donovan's expression. Typically he could not read his father because his face was usually neutral. However, at this moment Donovan had a slight change in his expression as he turned to face Sage. It was so slight that it was hardly noticeable, but Sage did notice that his father was surprised by his question.

Donovan then sighed. "I'm not a ghost Sage, and you're not dreaming."

Sage leaned against the bed and was relieved. "Good," he responded.

Moments later when Sage looked up, he found that Donovan was still watching him with a puzzled expression on his face. Sage concealed his satisfaction for apparently, his question had taken Donovan off his guard. From Donovan's expression, Sage was utterly convinced that Donovan was not a ghost, nor was he dreaming, which pleased Sage.

Chapter 49

When Donovan had awoken the next morning, he glanced over only to find that Sage was already gone. Donovan figured him to once again be on top of the hill practicing self-defense. Donovan found it puzzling that Sage did this on his own. He would arise well before Donovan to practice drawing his shooting pistols and shadow fighting. Then he would continue to practice long after dark when Donovan and Sage had finished their extensive training session together.

In the beginning, Donovan admitted to himself that he was worried that Sage wouldn't be able to cope with his grueling training sessions and that before long he would quit. However now Donovan's concern was that Sage practiced too hard. He couldn't help but wondered what drove him to work so hard. Donovan himself had practiced his grueling schedule so that he would be prepared to one day face and take the lives of all of the men that had taken part in his past wife's murder.

After getting himself dressed Donovan exited the house and made his way up the hill. He had a slight limp, but he no longer required the use of his cane. His leg seemed to be getting stronger each day. He hoped before long that he wouldn't be limping at all.

As Donovan approached, Sage pulled out his pistol and pointed it at an imaginary villain, and then stuffed it back into his holster. He had much improved since they had first practiced two weeks prior thought Donovan. As he continued to approach, Sage didn't seem to notice him, for he was concentrating so hard on his imaginary villain. He quickly pulled out his pistol and pointed. His expression was tense with concentration. Watching him Donovan figured him to be quicker than half the men that he had come across in his many battles. His improvement was very good considering that he had only been handling pistols for such a short period of time. It was as if Sage was born to handle a gun.

When Donovan finally reached Sage's side on top of the hill, he lost sight of his imaginary villain and waited patiently for Donovan's instructions. On this day Donovan wanted Sage to feel as if he was in a real-life situation, so he instructed Sage to face him, and to draw his pistol when he felt he was ready. As usual, Sage didn't' hesitate and eagerly did what he was told. He faced Donovan and as he did so Donovan took his gun holster off his shoulder and tied it around his waist. As soon as he finished buckling his belt, he quickly pulled out his empty gun and pointed it at Sage. He held the gun for a long moment in Sage's direction. Sage wasn't expecting this and never made the attempt to reach for his gun.

"Always be alert." Said Donovan angrily, as he pointed the gun at his son. "Never be caught off guard. I've seen many men die because they were caught off guard. You only have one life…stay alert." He turned the gun away from Sage and stuffed it back into his holster. But as he did so Sage quickly reached for his pistol in an attempt to catch his father off guard. Expecting this, Donovan had with his other hand pulled out his gun well in advance of Sage even getting his pistol out of its holster.

Sage was disappointed, but he said nothing and displayed no emotion. He instead quietly stuffed the half-drawn pistol back into the holster. Donovan was pleased that Sage tried to catch him off guard. Very pleased at how aggressive Sage was becoming. He was definitely not the same Sage that he had come across when he first arrived just a few weeks before. He was much more confident and bolder now. Even when he walked his head was higher, shoulders were straighter. When you talked with him, he looked you straight in the eye, unafraid.

They continued to draw their empty pistols against one another until Mama announced lunch. After lunch, they made their way back up the hill to practice hand-to-hand fighting. This time Donovan wanted to see how Sage would handle himself in a real life like situation.

Again Donovan was pleased that Sage was eager to do so. They stood across from each other with their fists balled. They circled one another, and as they did so, Donovan would instruct Sage to punch high, punch low, front kick, sidekick, faster, harder, and so on. Donovan would move side to side to avoid the punches, or he would throw up his arms to block an incoming punch. Sometimes when Sage slowed down or got sloppy with his punches or kicks, Donovan would swing a solid punch and connect in the center of Sage's chest. Usually, the blow would knock the wind out of Sage, and he would be down for a few minutes. However, Donovan was always thrilled to see Sage get up from the blow without complaint and then come after Donovan even more aggressively with his strikes. As Donovan watched Sage's aggressive attacks, he was pleased by the power his son now displayed.

Donovan held up his hand and Sage stopped in mid punch. Donovan stepped past Sage and moved toward the edge of the hill. Someone was riding toward the house on horseback.

"It's Dr. Tracy," Sage said.

"I figured." Said Donovan.

Sage turned to him. "Can I take my break?"

Donovan paused for a moment and then nodded his approval.

Sage made his way down the hill.

Donovan sat down and watched as Tracy guided her horse across the field toward the house. He watched as Miles took the time to wave as she passed him by, and she in return waved back. Then he watched Mama eagerly go out into the field to greet her. Tracy climbed from her horse and they embraced. Papa came from around the barn and greeted her as well. Then Sage reached them, and she hugged him. They all talked for a moment, then he saw Sage point in his direction, and they all looked up toward Donovan who was sitting and watching from the hilltop.

She talked to them for a bit longer, and then she left them to head toward the trail that led up to Donovan.

He watched her and waited patiently as she climbed the hill. He wasn't sure what he was going to say to her, and he wasn't all that happy to see her. She looked up at him and smiled as she made her way up the hill.

"What are you doing way up here?" She yelled playfully as she moved forward.

Donovan didn't answer. He just watched her.

When she reached him she sat next to him, trying to catch her breath. "I understand you're doing quite well. They say you don't even need the cane anymore." She said staring down below.

"It's been two weeks Tracy. Why haven't you come around?" He said.

"Someone's been following me. I didn't want to take chances. Sometimes I would hear a horse close by, but when I called out, no one answered. Sometimes there would be other noises like limbs breaking or dry leaves cracking. Sometimes they made so much noise that I think they wanted me to know that they was following me." She turned to Donovan. "It wasn't you was it?"

"No…It wasn't me. I haven't left this place since my injuries." Said Donovan.

Tracy smiled, as she reached to touch his face. Donovan was none responsive. "Do you think you're well enough to ride away? We can get married now. And move away, and never come back."

Donovan didn't answer.

Tracy seemed concerned as she watched him. "What's wrong?"

He turned to her. "You shouldn't have done what you did."

She was puzzled. "Done what Donovan?"

There was bitterness in his voice. "I'm talking about you and the sheriff."

"What about me and the sheriff?" Her voice was calm, too calm. For a moment Donovan wondered if it was even true about them.

"You laid in his bed." Even as he said the words, it was hard to believe. He was hoping she would deny it, and if she did he would believe her. He wanted to believe her.

She turned and looked down the hill. Mama had gone back to the porch, but from this angle, she couldn't be sure. Papa was back in the barn. And Sage was standing close to the house punching at air.

She said referring to Sage. "What's he doing down there?"

He ignored her. "Did you lay in his bed?"

Tracy was not surprised by Donovan's question about her and the sheriff. She knew it was only a matter of time before he found out about them, however, she didn't think it would be this soon. Countless times in her mind she played various scenarios of how she would feel once Donovan found out about her relationship with the sheriff. Relieved is how she felt at the moment. She was relieved that he finally knew, she was relieved that she didn't have to tell him and that he found out on his own.

Turning to face him, she found his demeanor calm. From past history of what she had seen and heard of him, she figured he would be in a rage. But he wasn't. It was as if two friends were sitting next to each other talking about nothing of importance.

"I was protecting you." She said.

"By staying in his bed. How is that protecting me?"

"If I didn't he would have killed you."

Donovan turned away. "Then you should have let him kill me." He said coldly.

"He had come to me the night before he came to you. He had me followed and found out about me and you being lovers. Landry was upset and asked me to be his lover that night. I refused him. Then he asked me, why have I never been his lover in all the years of knowing him, but I became your lover after only knowing you a few days."

"What did you tell him?" Asked Donovan.

"I told him that I was in love with you. I told him that we are going to be married."

"And what did he say?" Asked Donovan.

"He was angry. And he said that if I didn't become his lover he was going to kill you...I was torn of what to do. I knew his words were true. He would kill you. He's killed many. Even so, I refused him. I was hoping you would be gone before he reached you. I wanted to warn you, but he had Charlie watching me, so I couldn't. The next day I saw you after he dragged you into town. I couldn't believe my eyes. Then when he pointed his gun to your head. I gave in and told him that I would be his lover. I couldn't watch you die like that."

"What will he do if he finds me alive?"

"He will kill you, then me."

"Why, if your agreement was to keep me alive?"

"My agreement with the sheriff was not to keep you alive. My agreement was to let you die in peace. I told him that you were going to die. If he had thought you were going to live, he would have shot you in the head."

"You should have let him do so," Donovan said.

She watched as his face turned from calm to tense with anger. The change in his face frightened her.

"When was you going to tell me about you and the sheriff?" His voice was tense with anger.

"I didn't think you could handle it. Now I see I was wrong. I'll never keep anything from you again." She promised.

"But you did keep this from me. I've been honest with you. I've told you about my past. What other secrets do you have?"

Surprised by his question she answered. "I haven't kept any secrets from you. I was protecting you."

Bitterly he said. "I don't need your protection. You easily lay in another man's bed. Perhaps you are a whore. A prostitute." He stared at her waiting for an answer. She came to realize that he was serious. He wanted an answer; he thought that she might be a town whore or a prostitute.

She snapped at him. "I'm a doctor, Donovan. I'm not a whore."

"You're no doctor." He said. "You're pretending to be a doctor."

Her mouth dropped open as she stared at him. She couldn't believe that he was saying this to her. He sincerely did not trust her now. After all, she had done for him, saving his life twice, he didn't believe she was a doctor. Even now she was laying down with the sheriff every night, so as to again save his life. He calls her a whore and tells her that she isn't a doctor. Yes, it was true that she wasn't a doctor. She didn't go to medical school, didn't have a degree. But her father was a doctor, and she had spent a lot of time with him when he was with his patients. He taught her a lot of what he knew. She was a better doctor than some doctors that were doctors. And many Negroes were ignored by many of the white doctors, so in most cases, she was all they had. And if a black doctor was really good, then in some cases, the poor whites would use them as their doctors as well.

"I'm a doctor!" She yelled. "I saved your life more than once. No one else around here would have done so."

"You're no more than a whore to me, and I don't trust you." He said.

Tracy stood to her feet and pointed a finger in his face. "Don't you ever call me that again!" She was so upset that she was in tears. "I'm not a whore. I did what I had to do to save the man that I love. I did what I needed to do to save your life, so Sage can see his daddy for another day. If you ever call me a whore again you'll never see me again."

He didn't even hesitate. "You whore." His voice was cold.

She buried her face in her hands. He did not want to be with her anymore. He did not trust her, and he thought she was a whore. All because she had agreed to lay down with the sheriff. Maybe she should have never made the agreement, but if she hadn't, Donovan would have been killed.

Sleeping with the sheriff was the only way. Why couldn't he understand this?

Tracy turned from him and headed down the hill. It was obvious now that she and Donovan would not be married, and that they would not spend their lives together as a family. She was angry with Donovan for not understanding why she did what she did, and she hated the sheriff for forcing her in this situation that now cost her this relationship with Donovan.

She wondered how Donovan found out. It didn't matter now. What Donovan had said felt so true to her. But she told herself that she was not a whore. She was only saving the life of the man she loved.

Chapter 50

On this night she waited for the sheriff to arrive as he had done each night for the past several weeks. All of the lanterns within her room were lit, for she wanted as much light as possible so as to see his dangerous reaction when she refused him. On their other nights together she refused to perform with any light present, for she did not want to view the sheriff's face as he climbed on top and pleasured himself inside of her. Nor did she want him to see her body in such intimate positions. And lastly, the darkness concealed her pain, humiliation, and her self-sacrifice for being with a man whom she hated.

It was extremely difficult to let a man whom she hated so much touch her body in an intimate manner, for he didn't just perform the sex act, but he also touched her breasts and the inside of her thighs. And after he climaxed inside of her, he moaned a pleasure that she did not share.

If Donovan understood what she had gone through physically and emotionally just to keep him alive, maybe he would change his mind and marry her. But she knew that this would never happen. He would not change his mind, and he would not marry her. And worse, since Donovan was almost completely recovered from his injuries, he would soon be leaving this town forever, without her. She wiped her eyes. At least she had given him a second chance with his son. At least the man that she loved so much was still alive.

She heard the familiar footsteps of Landry as he moved down the hall toward her room. She had a feeling of calmness and peace for regardless of the outcome, her decision was made.

When she heard him stop at her door, she opened it before he could get his key in. He seemed surprised.

"We need to talk." She said.

He stood in the doorway, for a moment not knowing what to do. She waved him in. "Come in Landry."

He ducked under the doorway and stepped in. "I didn't come to talk." He said as he sat on the bed. He took off his large boots and they banged as they dropped to the floor.

Tracy closed the door and sat in the chair across from him against the wall. She glared at him, but he never met her eyes. Instead, he stood and pulled off his pants and then sat his bare ass on her bed.

"Come over here, girl." He said.

"Landry we need to talk." She said.

"I didn't come over here for talking. I told you that."

"I'm not doing this anymore. I've kept my word with you, now I owe you nothing."

His face puzzled as he stared at her. "What do you mean?"

Tracy was still calm and relaxed, for her voice never changed its pitch. "I mean, Landry I'm not laying down with you anymore. I'm not a whore."

He stood to his feet, and Tracy did not so much as flinch. She would stand by her decision no matter what the consequences.

He stepped forward and towered over her. His voice was panicked. "We have an agreement."

"Yes," Tracy said. "And I have kept my promise. I owe you nothing now." She watched him waiting.

"You stop when I say stop." He demanded.

Tracy's voice was tense but her face was calm. "I've laid down with you like a common whore, every day for the past three weeks. In the bed, I have done everything that you asked of me. Everything!" She yelled. "Now I will do no more for you. I am not a whore. I am not your whore." She again watched and waited for his reaction.

He then raised his large hand in an attempt to slap her and was taken aback when she didn't attempt to protect herself.

"You're gonna have to kill me." She said firmly.

Landry then slapped her across the face. She fell off the chair and onto the floor face down. She looked up at him then slowly climbed back into the chair. He pointed. "Get on that bed."

"I'm not a whore. You're gonna have to kill me."

Landry raised his hand and slapped her again, knocking her to the floor again. Naked from the waist down, he towered over her.

She managed to look over her shoulder and say. "You're gonna have to kill me. I'm not your whore."

Landry grunted as he grabbed and tossed her on the bed. By the time she recovered Landry was on top of her. His large hands pulled and ripped at her clothes.

"Just kill me! Just kill me!" She screamed.

He stepped back and stared at her for a long time. He seemed hurt by her reaction.

"Just kill me." She said softly. "Just kill me. I don't want to spend another night with you. I hate you. Don't you understand? I hate you."

He continued to watch as she sobbed. He then reached for his trousers and boots and exited the room.

She rolled over and cried into her pillow. Was it over? Would he now leave her alone, or would he come back for her again at another time? Donovan was wrong about her, she was not a whore.

Landry charged through the jailhouse door and slammed it shut. He paced the room as he mumbled to himself. He was then surprised to see his younger brother peeking from around the corner. He had figured him to be at the bar since it was only just after eleven.

With a grin on his face, Gunther leaned in the doorway. His playful expression told Landry that his brother had a woman with him.

"What's got you all upset?" Gunther asked.

"Are you alone?" Asked Landry.

Gunther turned his head to the darkness behind him. He then turned to Landry and smiled. "Hell no. I've got me a sweet little lady back here."

"When is she leaving?"

"Now I guess," Gunther said with a smile. He then went in the back for a moment, and Landry could hear them whispering. Then Gunther came out of the room with a beautiful woman on his arm. She had long brown hair, very pale skin, and was slightly taller than Gunther. Her smile was polite as she nodded to Landry. Gunther walked her to the door, they kissed and she was gone.

Landry envied how his younger brother could so easily meet so many women. Sometimes he wished he had his brother's outgoing personality so that he could become acquainted with women as easily as his brother. Landry was ashamed of himself, for he could not even get a beautiful black woman such as Tracy to want him. He instead had to force her against her will to do so.

Landry turned to his brother. "How do you do it, Gunther?"

"Do what?"

"How do you meet so many women?" Landry asked.

"Well, I just do." Gunther started with his usual cocky voice. But after a moment he came to realize how serious his brother was about this question. He then changed his tone. "I don't let them push me around." He said seriously. "I know what I want, and they know what I want. I make it clear if they gonna be with me I will get what I want. I don't let them women waste my time. If they play games with me, then there will be consequences for them."

Landry nodded. "What type of consequences?"

Gunther smiled. "Maybe I'll pull out my pistol and point it at their heads." He laughed. "I wouldn't kill them, but they don't know that. Maybe I just grab them and shake em up a little. Mostly I don't even have to do that. Mostly I just look at them like I ain't got no sense, and that will usually straighten them up." He grinned at his brother. "That would work for you, Landry."

Landry nodded again, and there was a moment of silence between them. "You was right about Tracy. She don't care nothing for me. She never has."

"She's a nigger, Landry. What did you expect? They don't know what's good for them. I suppose I've never known a nigger that was smart enough to know what's good for them."

"I suppose you're right." Said Landry.

"There's plenty of women in this town that want a man like you. I'll introduce you to some."

"What kind of man do these women see me as?" Asked Landry.

The question surprised Gunther. "Got damn, Landry. What's happened to you? You let a black winch bring you down like this."

"Just answer my question, Gunther. How do you think women see me?"

The two men stared at each other. Finally, Gunther answered. "They see you as I see you. Someone they can count on, someone that is strong and will always fight for them. Someone who is loyal and would never leave their side. They see you as a man that's brave and fearless. That's how I see you anyway, and I'm sure they see you the same."

"What about Tracy?" Asked Landry.

"Tracy don't like you because you is white." Said Gunther. "She wants to be with her own kind, nothing you can do about that. She'll never be with a white man."

Landry nodded for this made sense to him, Tracy didn't want to be with him because he was white. It didn't matter how good of a man he was, she would never want to be with him. Coloreds are hard to figure out.

Landry turned and smiled at his brother, and Gunther laughed.

"Women come and go." Said Gunther. "But me and you will always be."

"You damn right." Said Landry.

They moved to the window and stared out. They could hear the piano from the saloon, mixed with some laughter and loud voices. The light from the saloon window lit the sidewalk just out front.

"I don't trust what Corwin said last week." Said Landry.

"What did he say that you don't trust?" He asked

Landry said. "Corwin said he didn't know Papa very well, and yet they've been neighbors since we came here five years ago. I've heard through folks in town that them two are good friends and that Papa is Corwin's only friend. When we sent him to see Papa, he claims they didn't talk about nothing, and he didn't see nothing."

"Why would he lie about that?"

"That's what I'm not sure of. It's been on my mind for a few days. Maybe he was just scared, or maybe he got something to hide."

Said Gunther. "But what would he have to hide?"

"Don't know, maybe nothing. I sent him to the house because I wanted to find out about Donovan."

"About, Donovan?" Said Gunter. "He's dead."

"I know. But I wanted to find out where they buried him. I wanted to know how the family took his death."

Gunther was puzzled. "Why do you care?"

"I just want closure. When I kill a man I want closure. Donovan was alive when they carried him off, so we didn't see him die. I need to see him dead to get closure."

"Well, they've buried him by now."

"Then I need to see a grave."

Gunther paused. "Do you think he may be alive?"

"He could have never survived what we put him through. He's dead. I just want to see his grave." Said Landry. "Tomorrow morning, we'll go by the house and look over Donovan's grave."

Gunther thought about it. "I'll go, Landry. It's just a grave. I can handle this."

Landry put his hand firmly on Gunther's shoulder. "You sure about this?"

He nodded. "I'm sure."

Landry's tone was serious. "You're all I've got Gunther, ain't nothing gonna take you from me. Nothing."

"I know, big brother. I ain't going nowhere." Said Gunther.

Chapter 51

These past few mornings he had been getting up as early as Uncle Miles. He stood on the porch and watched Miles make his way out to the fields and begin his long day's work. Sage smiled for he had some satisfaction knowing that he and Miles were up at the same time. Sage then chuckled for Donovan the supposedly light sleeper who was awakened by all sounds, did not awaken this morning when Sage had snuck out of their room.

Sage stepped off the porch and eyed the area. He searched the forest on the edge of the property. Since Donovan's injury a few weeks before, each morning Sage would look for Fletcher and then call to him. He would place his fingers to his lips and whistle. And though Sage's whistle was nowhere near as ear piercing as Donovan's, it was still loud enough for the large horse to respond.

The horse whined from beyond the thick trees. Then the pounding of the hooves was heard as they thumped within the forest. Soon the powerful horse jumped into view as he headed full speed across the field.

Sage laughed. "Here I am boy." He said to himself.

When the horse reached him, Sage did not move, instead, he laughed as the horse circled him and then stood in front of him bobbing his head up and down, snorting and whining for affection. As the horse lowered his head to Sage's level, he reached up and scratched the horse's long snout just between his eyes.

"Good boy!" He said. "Good boy!"

Sage then worked around to the body as he continued to rub and scratch the horse's side. Fletcher craned his long neck around so as to watch Sage as he did so. After some time had passed Sage pulled his coat back and extracted his pistol from his belt. He stared at it for a moment. He then pulled some bullets out of his pocket and loaded them into the gun, and then placed the gun back into his belt and closed his coat. He did this only because; in the last few days Donovan had been teaching Sage how to safely handle a loaded gun. Each morning Donovan had been watching as Sage loaded and unloaded the pistol numerous times. After which he would instruct Sage to fire live rounds into the trees.

As Sage moved around Fletcher he was surprised to see the deputy on horseback approaching. He felt panicked and headed for the porch so as to warn Donovan. However before he could reach the porch, the deputy yelled out, and Sage knew that he was talking to him.

"Hold on there!" Yelled the deputy. "Where do you think you're going?"

Sage froze in mid-step, as he faced forward afraid to move.

After an extended period of time, he waited with his back to the deputy as the sound of his horse's hooves approached.

"Turn around boy. I'm talking to you." Said Gunther.

Warily Sage turned to face the grinning deputy who was just stepping down from his horse at that time. He felt some comfort knowing that Miles was watching them in the background.

"Where you going youngster?" Gunther asked.

"Inside." Sage barely got out.

Gunther waved him down. "Come on down here, I want to talk with you some."

Sage hesitated, for he knew of the deputy's awful reputation and could not think of a single reason why the deputy would want to talk with him.

The deputy waved him down again. "Come on down here boy. Don't make me ask you again."

Sage swallowed and stepped away from the porch, and headed toward the deputy. He stood before him but said nothing.

The deputy looked him over. "You're little Sage, aren't you?"

Sage nodded. However, he found that he wasn't so little compared to the deputy. In fact, he and the deputy were about the same height.

Gunther touched Sage's shoulder. "Sorry about your papa and all."

To Sage, the deputy's apology seemed more like he was boasting.

"Where did they bury him?" Asked the deputy.

The question had taken Sage aback, but he tried his best to conceal his astonishment. He didn't have an answer for the deputy. So instead he awkwardly stood before the deputy in silence.

Firmly Gunther squeezed Sage's shoulder. "Answer my question boy. I don't like to repeat myself."

At that moment Sage saw Miles drop his hoe and walk toward them. The deputy pointed an angry finger. "Hold it right there! Don't you come any closer!"

Miles froze about forty yards or so out. He yelled out. "What can we do for you, deputy?"

"You can shut your mouth, and go back to your business, is what you can do!" Yelled Gunther to Miles. He then turned his attention back to Sage and continued to squeeze his shoulder as he asked again. "Where's he buried? I ain't gonna ask again?"

Sage squirmed from the pressure on his shoulder but said nothing.

At that moment the front door creaked open, and the deputy pulled out his pistol. "Come on out." He said.

Papa cautiously stepped out leaning on his cane. He walked to the edge of the porch. His face was concerned and afraid, but he kept walking as he stared at the deputy and his pistol.

"You almost got yourself killed old man." Said Gunther.

Papa nodded. "I see that."

Gunther laughed and stuffed his gun back into his holster. "You see how quick I am?"

"I do." Said Papa. To Sage he said. "Go in the house and help Mama."

The deputy cut his eyes at Papa. "He ain't going nowhere until he tells me what I wants to know."

Papa swallowed and rubbed his free hand nervously on his trousers. He pointed to Miles's house. "He's behind the house."

For a long moment, Gunther continued to stare in the direction of Miles's house. Finally, he turned to Papa and said. "Let's take a look."

Sage watched as the deputy and Papa walked side by side. From the fields, Miles watched also, but he didn't move, as was previously ordered by the deputy. From the front window, Sage could see Mama's worried face as she looked on at Papa and the deputy. From her porch, Maria had just stepped out and watched as the deputy and Papa passed her by as they continued on toward the back of the house. The deputy smiled as he went by her, she turned away.

As they approached the back of the house the deputy cautiously pulled out both of his side pistols. One was pointed forward; the other was pointed at Papa.

When Papa turned to him, he smiled and said. "We can't be too careful, can we?"

Papa nervously nodded and continued to lead the deputy around the back of the house. They stopped at the cross. 'GOD BLESS HIS SOUL' was scratched on its surface.

Gunther stared at it for a moment. "Is that him?"

"That's him," Papa said.

"Why don't it have his name on it?" Asked the deputy.

Papa shrugged. "Don't have a reason, just don't."

Gunther stared at him for a moment, then stared back at the grave. "All right, I've seen enough." He said and then headed back as Papa followed while leaning on his cane.

Sage was relieved as he watched the deputy and Papa come from around the house. When he witnessed the deputy pull out his pistols, he was anticipating hearing gunshots afterwards. Then he remembered that Maria's papa had died a few days before, and was buried at the back of their house. Papa had probably shown the deputy his grave and passed it on as Donovan's.

As they approached the deputy nodded to Sage. "Is that Donovan's horse?"

"It's mine." Sage's response was soft and unsure.

Gunther eyed him suspiciously. "Where did you get him?"

"My papa gave him to me." Said Sage.

"Well, your papa is dead."

"It's my horse," Sage said firmly, he was surprised by the tone of his own voice.

"Your papa was killed by the law, and anything he owned now goes to the law. That horse belongs to the law." He reached out his hand. "Hand him over."

Sage pulled the horse reins tight so that the horse stepped in closer to him. The horse snorted. "You can't have em." His voice was again firm.

The deputy frowned and then stepped forward to retrieve the horse, at which time Sage simultaneously guided Fletcher back until they were a few feet away.

Gripping hold of the reins, Sage then leaped and pulled himself upon the bare back of the horse. "You can't have him." He said defiantly.

The deputy stopped and glared. "You really are stupid, aren't you boy?"

Papa yelled. "Sage, get off that horse and give it to him!"

"It ain't his horse!" Sage yelled back.

"Give it to him now!" Papa demanded.

Sage ignored him and stared at the deputy. The deputy eyed him for a moment before taking a step forward in another attempt to approach the horse. But as he did so Sage guided the horse backward matching the deputy's step. The deputy stopped again as he watched with disbelief of the boy's boldness.

Then Papa took a step forward, once again demanding Sage to get off the horse. But Sage matched his steps as well and guided Fletcher back yet a few more steps.

Gunther looked away and eyed the rifle that was holstered to his horse. He then grinned as he faced Sage and said. "That's alright boy. If I can't have that horse, neither can you." After which he turned on his heel and headed for his horse.

Without hesitation, Sage kicked the sides of the horse and yelled. "Haww!" The horse whined and snorted and started in a full sprint. Sage had ridden the horse many times since Donovan's last injury, but he had never ridden Fletcher in a full sprint. He had been fearful that he could not hold on at the speed that Fletcher traveled. This time he had no choice, for he knew the deputy was going for his rifle.

As the horse dashed out into a sprint, Sage wrapped himself around the horse's neck and held on. The horse took off so quickly that for a moment he thought he was going to slide off the back.

Gunther smiled as he walked over to his horse and grabbed the rifle from the side pouch. He cocked it, then raised it to his eye and aimed.

Papa begged. "Don't hurt the boy."

"I'll deal with the boy after I deal with the horse." He said as he moved his rifle in motion with Sage and the horse. "That boy has no respect for the law."

Sage and Fletcher were racing full speed across the fields. At such a swift speed the horse's legs moved and kicked so furiously that they were blurred and gave Sage the impression that he and Fletcher were somehow floating across the land. Surprisingly as the mighty horse's head bobbed dramatically and the powerful legs kicked underneath him, the movement from Fletcher's saddle position was at a minimum.

From the distance, a loud thunderous boom echoed the sky, and Sage knew immediately that the deputy had gotten off his first round. However at the speed that he and Fletcher were traveling, he doubted that the deputy's bullet would find its mark, for they were now too far away for the accuracy of his rifle.

But the horse stopped suddenly as he reared his head upward and whined loudly as Sage soared over the top and landed on the earth several feet out. While laying face down he looked over his shoulder. The great horse was limping as if his hind leg was injured. Then Sage turned to the forest some 100 or so yards out. They were almost there he thought. Maybe he had pushed the horse too fast and somehow had broken a leg.

Sage glanced at the deputy who was aiming the rifle from his shoulder as he moved in their direction. On hands and knees, Sage made his way toward Fletcher. The horse continued to whine loudly and was struggling to support his massive body weight on one of its rear legs. In its agony, the horse began to spin, and Sage was horrified to see blood draining from the left side of the horses rear end.

Another loud rifle shot echoed throughout the sky, and Sage saw the blood burst from the side of the horse just before he went down. Fletcher squirmed and squealed while he laid helpless on his side.

On his hands and knees, Sage finally made his way to Fletcher. He tried to avoid the horse's bloody wounds as he laid upon his neck to comfort him. He cried as he held onto the horse for after a while Fletcher no longer squirmed but laid still in death. Sage called out his name over and over.

Again he glanced over his shoulder, to witness the deputy strolling in their direction with his rifle now pointed downward some two hundred yards away. Papa was not far behind as he struggled with his cane in hand to keep pace with the deputy. Miles was following Papa, and Mama was on the porches edge watching the scene in horror.

Sage eyed the deputy as he stood to his feet and yelled. "You son of a bitch! You son of a bitch!" He then turned to the dead horse and said to himself. "Son of a bitch." He then turned to face the deputy who was about one hundred seventy yards away. Papa's leg was hurting him too badly and could no longer keep pace with the deputy. He had stopped and was leaning on his cane. Miles caught up to Papa and stood by his side.

Leaving the horse Sage stalked toward the deputy. His pace was fast and his face was tight with anger. He thought of what Donovan had mentioned before about staying calm in threatening circumstances and thinking through the situation at hand. But he felt anxious, and rushed, as he marched forward in a hurried fashion. His only thoughts were of how he was going to kill this deputy. As he moved the front of his coat blew open exposing the pistol inside the buckle of his belt.

Gunther caught a glimpse of Sage's pistol and stopped in mid-stride. He frowned and then tossed his rifle to the ground and pulled back his coat exposing his pistol as well. "This boy is dumber than I thought." He said just under his breath.

Sage finally stopped marching when he was twenty yards from the deputy. The two stared at one another for a long moment. The deputy was taken aback by the boy's outrageous and combative behavior. The longer they stared at one another the more furious the deputy became of this boy's obvious lack of fear and respect for his badge.

"I'm gonna have to kill you boy." Said the deputy.

Through tears, Sage remained silent for Donovan had taught him on their daily trainings not to engage in conversation during battle, for this would only distract him and get him killed. Sage, however, was not concentrating so much on the deputy before him, as he was on the dead horse that he had left behind. As he faced the deputy he continued to sob and mourn Fletcher's death.

Across the way, within his peripheral vision, Sage saw Donovan charge out of the front door of the house and quickly head their way. Sage was disappointed for this was his fight and he didn't want Donovan involved. Without moving his head without shifting his eyes, he focused on the deputy again. He did not want the deputy to be aware of Donovan's presence.

"I don't want to, but I'm gonna have to kill you." Said the deputy. "You ain't got no respect for the law."

"There was no need for shootin that horse." Said Sage.

The deputy smiled. "I reckon you is planning on killing me now, huh boy?"

"You reckon right." Said Sage. The self-assured tone of the boy's voice was once again unexpected to the deputy.

Sage saw that Donovan was moving fast toward them, he was now about Sixty yards away. He had his rifle in hand and his shooting pistols on either side of his waist. His expression was tense with concentration. It was clear that Donovan was once again risking all to come to his son's aid. Hopefully Sage could kill this deputy before Donovan got to him.

Donovan passed Papa and Miles and nudged them both to step to the side out of harm's way. And they both did so.

"Reach for your gun, boy." Said Gunther. "Let's get this over with."

As Sage stared at the deputy, again he thought about Fletcher's demise and the tears filled his eyes and crawled down his cheek. His face tightened with anger. He then took the stance that Donovan had taught him to take just before one were to draw a pistol.

As Sage took his stance Donovan stopped some twenty yards out and raised his rifle in the direction of the deputy. He then dramatically nodded his head off to the side, which was a gesture for Sage to leave the scene.

Sage was disappointed but did as he was instructed and attempted to walk off in retreat of the situation.

Gunther yelled out. "Hold it right there, boy! You ain't going nowhere!"

Sage turned to him.

"There ain't no getting out of this." The deputy continued. "You pull your pistol, or I'll pull mine. Don't make no difference to me."

Sage watched as Donovan pointed to the opposite end of the field where Papa and Miles were standing. This was where he wanted Sage to go as well. Ignoring the Deputy's warning, Sage moved in that direction.

The deputy pivoted in an attempt to follow Sage, and then he caught a glimpse of Donovan and his rifle. His face was red with disbelief. He took a step back as if he were to run, but then got back his composure. But his face remained red, and his surprised expression never faded. "You're not dead." He said as if he didn't believe his own eyes.

"I reckon not." Said, Donovan, as he moved in closer with his rifle aimed at the deputy's chest. When he was about fifteen feet from the deputy he finally stopped and said. "That horse had been with me for many years. You had no right doing what you did." Said Donovan through tight lips. "A few months ago, I would have killed you for what you just done. But I've changed some since then." Donovan cut his eyes. "But my son is another matter altogether." He clinched the rifle tightly and raised it to the deputy's face. "If my son had been harmed. I would have turned this town upside down to get to you." Donovan paused for a long moment as if he were undecided about squeezing the trigger on the rifle. "I don't understand deputy. Why you would slay a horse and challenge a fourteen-year-old boy?" Said Donovan. "I need a reason to go against myself and not blow your head off."

"I'm the law." Was all the deputy could say with some apprehension.

"The hell with you and your law!" Yelled Donovan in disgust. "I've come across many a lawmen like you and they're all cowards. They prey upon the innocent and the weak. Your kind of law means nothing to me."

Fearful of the Negro man and that he was just moments from his death the deputy said nothing else. For the first time in his adult life, he felt extremely vulnerable and wished that his older brother was at his side to help him. He knew that if Landry were present this situation would be different. Donovan would be dead, along with his family for harboring him.

Much to the deputy's surprise the Negro man lowered his rifle and said. "It's over. Leave and don't come back." He warned. "If you come back I'll kill you and whoever is accompanying you."

Donovan had decided against killing the Deputy for two reasons. To kill this deputy would send a ripple through this town and start a mini-war. Not that Donovan was afraid of a mini-war, for he had been in several and had managed to survive. But this time his family would be dragged into the conflict. And this he could not let happen.

The other reason was that he wanted to set an example for Sage. Though Donovan was highly distressed that his horse of fifteen years had been senselessly killed, he wanted Sage to understand that even in this horrific circumstance, vengeance would not heal the suffering of such a great loss. A lesson that had taken Donovan years to realize, only after killing the last of his past wife's killers.

The threat of the Negro man irritated the deputy. A Negro man should never be giving a white man orders let alone a lawman. Now that the rifle was pointed down, the deputy felt that he had the advantage. He reached for his pistol, but Donovan was expecting this and with his free hand he had already pulled out his pistol and fired an explosive shot to the deputy's torso. The deputy went down clutching his chest. Before he fell he had managed to get off one shot. Donovan continued to aim his pistol at the deputy. While on the ground the deputy looked down at his bloodied chest. "I'm shot?" He questioned. He was in disbelief that he had been shot by the Negro man. He moaned in agony. "Help me." He said. "I need a doctor."

Sage found the deputy's pleas to be awkward. During his time as the deputy, he had managed to shoot and kill many. Sage had heard numerous stories about some who had begged for their lives only to be left in the streets to die.

Though the deputy was on his back, he was still holding his pistol. Donovan moved his pistol toward the deputy's face. "Let go of that pistol, or die."

For a moment the deputy ignored Donovan's command and laid still. Unexpectantly Sage opened his coat, pulled out his pistol and marched over and pointed his weapon at the deputy. The deputy took notice as Sage approached. "You gonna kill me, boy?" Asked the deputy.

"Not if I don't have to." Said Sage.

The deputy found Sage amusing and laughed.

Though Donovan didn't take his eyes off of the deputy, he frowned at Sage's actions. He did not want his son involved. But now was not the time to confront him.

"Drop the pistol deputy. If I wanted to kill you, you'd be dead already." Said Donovan.

"What you gonna do with me?" Gunther asked.

"We're going to get you to a doctor."

Gunther was skeptical. "After all, I've done, why would you help me?"

"Personally I don't give a damn about you and what you need." Said Donovan. "I'll only help you for my family's sake. Killing you won't help their situation none." Donovan cocked the handle of his pistol. "But if you force me to, I'll kill you, and let whatever comes after that come."

The deputy finally opened his fingers and released the pistol. Donovan kicked the weapon out of the deputy's reach. He then reached around the deputy's waist and pulled out the other pistol. After which Donovan patted the deputy down for other weapons.

Donovan turned to Sage who was apprehensive as he continued to point his gun. "Put your gun away, Sage. It's over now."

"You sure?" Sage asked.

"Yes. It's over." Said Donovan.

He then brought the pistol down, so that it rested against his thigh.

Miles and Papa finally made their way to the scene. Papa shook his head with regret. "The sheriff is gonna kill us for this." He said.

Donovan nodded. "It was unavoidable. It was either him or Sage. I gave him a chance to walk, and he didn't take it."

Papa nodded. "Not gonna make no difference to the sheriff."

Donovan turned to Miles. "I need a wagon and a horse. I gotta get him back to town." Miles nodded and headed to the barn.

Mama was approaching slowly toward them. Donovan could see the tears streaming down her face. When she reached Donovan she reached out her arms and hugged him tightly. Her expression was uneasy as she pulled back. "Oh Donovan, what have you done?"

"I did the only thing that could be done. I saved my son's life." He said.

She turned to Sage and smiled. "Yes, and I'm grateful to that. What are we gonna do now? The sheriff is gonna be powerful angry at us."

"I've spared his brother's life. Maybe he will spare ours." Said Donovan.

"What if that don't matter to him none." Said, Mama.

"If it don't matter to him. Then I reckon I'm gonna have to kill him." Said Donovan.

After Miles had brought the wagon around, he and Donovan lifted the deputy into the back. Mama and Maria had grabbed some blankets from the house and wrapped them around the deputy. Afterwards, Mama and Maria held each other for they both knew their situation was unsure.

Sage was standing across the way where Fletcher laid. He swatted at some of the flies that had landed on the horse's unseeing eyes. Donovan joined his side and stared. When Sage turned to him, he saw tears streaming down Donovan's face. Over the years he and the horse had been through a lot. He could not have survived this many years without Fletchers swift speed and extensive endurance. Partly if it weren't for Fletcher he wouldn't be at his son's side right now.

"I tried to save him." Said Sage.

"I know." Said Donovan. "It was his time, there's nothing you could have done."

Donovan made his way back to his family and Sage followed.

"The way I see it, we only have one choice." Said Donovan. "I'll take him into town myself, find him a doctor, and face the sheriff alone. I'll try to reason with him, if he doesn't reason, then I'll kill him."

"The sheriff is very protective of his brother." Said Papa. "The deputy has never been shot before now. He gonna take one look at his brother in that wagon with all that blood, and then he gonna kill you."

"We have no choice." Said Donovan.

"And if he kills you?" Papa asked. "Then what about us?"

Donovan nodded. "You'll need to be ready. Gather enough food for several days, stay in the house, and wait for him. When you see him coming wait until he gets close to the house, then you all stick your guns out the window and shoot him. He won't be expecting it. But don't shoot until he's close."

"I don't know if I can do that," Mama said.

"You have no choice," Donovan said. "You either kill him, or he'll kill you."

"I'll go with you." Said Sage. "You'll need some help."

Donovan placed his hand on Sage's shoulder. "No, Sage. Your family will need you here, more than I'll need you with me."

Though he was disappointed Sage seemed to understand.

Mama stepped forward to Donovan and placed her thick hands on his face. "Donovan answer me one question." He nodded. "Do you believe in GOD?"

When Donovan was younger he was raised to believe in GOD, and he did believe in GOD. But after his wife Sidney was raped and killed, he didn't believe that GOD existed, or he hated GOD for letting this horrible incident happen, for allowing him to have to live with such anguish. Even long after his wife was killed and he had traveled the country searching for the killers, he saw men do many things to each other that turned his stomach and caused him to lose faith in GOD. But now thinking back maybe it wasn't GOD that let these horrible things happen, maybe it was just the choices of man. Of course, Donovan couldn't just blame man, he had to blame himself as well. It was he who chose to travel across the country to find the killers of his past wife. And once he came about the killers it was he who chose to kill them for their crimes. There seemed to always be choices. Even now he chose to face the sheriff alone, so as to protect his family from harm. As he thought about it he came to realize that even Tracy had made some difficult choices. She chose to lay in the sheriff's bed to save Donovan's life. As a result of that choice, Donovan was able to spend more valuable time with his son, and teach him how to defend himself. Though Donovan thought he hated GOD for a time, he did not. Deep down he knew that GOD was always with him. Always guiding him.

"Yes, mama. I believe in GOD." Said Donovan.

Mama smiled. "Then pray with me, son."

And for the first time in years, Donovan bowed his head in prayer.

Mama spoke softly. "Lord, please forgive Donovan for all his past sins, and for the sin that he will attempt today." Mama paused for a long time. When she spoke it was through her tears. "Thank you, Lord, for helping him to find his way...Ah man."

Chapter 52

Donovan was perched high on the seat of the wagon. The deputy moaned from its bed. The deputy's horse was tied to the back gate. The family stood alongside the wagon with apprehensive expressions. "There's no other way." Said Donovan.

Sage stepped forward. "Will you be back?"

Donovan turned to his son. Sage had come a long way since their first encounter just a few weeks before. Donovan was especially proud of Sages transformation from a weak, unsure, scared little boy to the confident, courageous, poised young man that he had become. He reckoned Sage would be fine in the world now. He reckoned Sage was somewhat fortified from some of the wicked acts of man. "You remember everything I've taught you." Said Donovan. "These past few weeks have been a lifetime for me."

Donovan jerked the reins, and the wagon moved forward. Running alongside Sage yelled. "Will you be back?"

Donovan wouldn't answer as he looked on and guided the wagon toward the main road.

Deep down within himself, Sage knew that Donovan would not return. The sheriff was a dangerous and a skilled killer. Though Sage was afraid for his father and was certain that he would be killed, at the same time he had overwhelming emotions of pride and admiration for his father's bravery. His father was sacrificing himself by taking the battle to the sheriff, in order to protect his family from harm.

Sage turned to Mama and buried his face within her bosom. He and Donovan were so close now; he couldn't imagine the rest of his days without him. "I should go with him. He's gonna need help." Said Sage.

She caressed his head and said. "You know he won't let you do that. He won't take a chance on you getting hurt. He don't want any of us getting hurt, that's why he going alone."

Donovan guided the wagon along the dirt road and when he was about a half mile from town, he turned to the deputy. He was coughing and had blood on his lips and chin. He figured from the deputy's pale appearance that he wouldn't survive the night. Thus a conflict with the sheriff was inevitable, and therefore so was his death. Though Donovan was certain that this would be his final battle, he was intending to kill the sheriff as well. There was no other option, the sheriff had to die, or he would kill his family. Looking back on his numerous battles, he had never been in such a desperate situation as he was in now. This sheriff had to die.

Donovan thought on. This deputy was lucky to be alive now. If he had confronted Donovan just a few months before, Donovan would have killed him. However, since coming in contact with his son, he found that his need to settle conflicts with death and violence had subsided. He no longer needed the violence to ratify his anger, his personal misery or his thirst for vengeance.

Though violence was sometimes necessary for protection, it was often not the only option. For the first time ever, all the faces of the men that he had killed raced through his mind. He had not given those men much thought until now. As he thought of them he felt sad for them and their loved ones that they had left behind. So much pain their deaths must have caused to the left behind family members such as mothers, fathers, daughters, sons, and wives. Donovan never thought of this before now, because he was caught up in his own anguish from losing Sidney. For years he couldn't see past his own pain.

Thinking about his own emotions, Donovan found that he was no longer angry at the world when he had been angry for many years before. For the first time since Sidney was alive, he felt peace within himself. Even now in this moment when he was going to confront the sheriff, his insides were filled with harmony. Though the lawmen had done him and his family wrong and had grossly violated Tracy, his motivation for killing the sheriff was not revenge. His only and final purpose was to stop the sheriff, for if he didn't all that he ever cared about, including Tracy would be dead. This type of reasoning was a much stronger motivator than revenge alone could ever be.

When they reached the edge of the town, he pulled the reins back to signal to the team of two horses to halt. On this afternoon, the town's population was somewhat active, but not as great in numbers as it would have been if it were the weekend.

Donovan reached for the pistols that were holstered to his waist. He opened the chambers and did his customary inspection that was often done before he entered a known battle. Afterwards, he inspected his gun belt, making sure that a bullet was encased in each of the small loops that encircled the belt. He then reached behind and felt for the knife that was in the small of his back. Finally, he grabbed his rifle that was leaning up front and opened it, to ensure that it was loaded to its max with ammo.

He snapped the reins and guided the wagon forward. The wheels grinded as they rolled over the dirt road. The hooves of the horses clunked rhythmically with each step forward. He held the reins loosely in one hand as his other hand was down low near his side pistol. Tilted forward was his brown hat, just over his eyes. Across the way, at the end of the town's main road, he zeroed in on the jailhouse.

Oddly to Donovan, people seemed to recognize him right away. There was a commotion at the side of the road as someone pointed and announced. "It's him! He's alive!"

After a while the commotion spread along both sides of Donovan like a fuse on a stick of dynamite. Folks stared in astonishment and disbelief. Many appeared afraid as if they were watching a ghost. Donovan felt awkward when he saw a small group of women pull out their crosses from around their necks, and point them in his direction as they prayed amongst one another.

Finally, someone peaked into the wagon's bed and saw the injured deputy. And then all hell broke loose. "Oh, Shit!" Yelled the bystander. "He's got the deputy and he don't look good!"

After that people went into a panic. "Oh God no!" A man close by yelled. Donovan saw a couple of women huddled together crying. The noise level of the crowd was loud, as people talked and yelled about the scene before them.

To the left just beyond the crowd, he saw Tracy race out of the hotel entrance. She stood on her tiptoes to see him over the crowd. He pulled the reins and the wagon stopped in the middle of the street. Her long wavy black hair rested on the back of her shoulders, and her beautiful dark face was barely noticeable from this distance. She was more beautiful than ever he thought, and at that moment he realized how much he had missed her.

She squeezed through the crowd and ran to him. She looked inside the wagon, then burst into tears. "What have you done, Donovan?"

"He was going to kill my son," Donovan said.

Tracy grabbed Donovan's arm. "Landry's going to kill you." She said defeated.

Gradually the roaring crowd quieted until they were completely silent. Donovan and Tracy noticed that the people were staring toward the jailhouse. When they turned in that direction they saw Landry within the doorway watching them. He could see that the sheriff was not armed, a perfect opportunity for Donavan to kill him. Donovan reached for the rifle. And as he did so the sheriff disappeared inside the jailhouse.

Donovan figured the sheriff had gone inside to arm himself. He stepped off the wagon in anticipation of the sheriff's reappearance. Hurriedly the silent crowd scattered off the road to make room for the inevitable gunfight.

Tracy grabbed his arm. "Come Donovan. He's going to kill you."

He turned to Tracy. "I can't leave, Tracy. He'll kill my family, and he'll kill you."

She tugged on his arm again. "When he sees his brother in that wagon, he'll go into a rage. Give him a chance to calm some. When he's calm you'll have a better chance of getting him."

He continued to watch the jailhouse as he thought over what Tracy had just said. The sheriff reappeared in the doorway. This time he was armed with pistols on his waist, and a rifle in hand.

She pointed to the restaurant a few doors down. "We'll go there, and wait for him."

"He'll follow us." Said Donovan. "I need to face him now."

"He won't follow. He'll want to spend time with his brother. As long as you're out of sight, he won't come after you."

She didn't wait for him to answer, she pulled and he followed. Arm and arm they raced for the restaurant. Donovan looked over his shoulder as they entered the doorway; the sheriff eyed them as he moved toward the wagon. As he looked into the bed his legs buckled, his rifle dropped and he fell against the wagon's side.

A short Spanish man with a white apron stood by the front window. He stared at them with scared eyes. He had a receding dark hairline that climbed back to his ears. He had been watching them through the window.

Now he stepped away and rubbed his hands nervously through his bald scalp. "Don't want no trouble, mister." He said with a thick Spanish accent.

"Neither do I." Said, Donovan, as he approached the side window. The bald man scattered away so fast that he knocked over a couple of chairs, and then finally fell over a table toppling head over heels. Donovan stared at him blankly then turned to the window. He could see that the sheriff was yelling something to the crowd, and then a man with a black suit carrying a small black bag approached the wagon.

Tracy walked over to the bald man who was laying on his back moaning in pain. He spoke quickly running his words together. "I want no trouble, Dr. Tracy."

She approached the Spanish man and said. "He wasn't going to hurt you, Alfred. He was just trying to get to the window."

Alfred struggled to his feet. "Why you come here. I not want trouble."

"Don't worry, Alfred. We won't involve you. Why don't you take your family out for a few hours." Said Tracy.

Said, Alfred. "Why I need to go? This is my restaurant. You leave."

"We're not going anywhere." Said Donovan from the window.

Alfred frowned at him. But when Donovan turned to face him, he quickly looked away.

"Alfred what are you worried about?" Said Tracy. "It'll all be over soon, then you can come back."

Alfred snorted. "Me and family like you, Dr. Tracy. You've helped family many times when other Doctor wouldn't." He looked down at his feet. "I owe you. But I not want anything to happen to family."

Tracy frowned. "Then leave. Take your family with you. Donovan and I are staying."

"I don't want blood...or dead bodies in restaurant," Alfred said as he cut his eyes toward Donovan.

Donovan frowned at him and then turned his attention back to the window. "The blood will be in the street. When I see him coming, I will meet him there."

Alfred thought it over. "What sheriff say if I let you stay here?"

"Tell him that Donovan forced you." Said Tracy. "He'll understand that."

Alfred agreed and smiled. "Yes, this is what I tell him." He turned to Tracy. "You may stay." He stared at Donovan. "Whatever food you eat, you pay for. I don't want no trouble from you. When sheriff comes, you go outside. I don't want any blood or dead bodies in restaurant. Not good for business." He turned and headed for the kitchen.

Tracy walked over to the window and stood by Donovan's side.

"Who is that man with the sheriff, in the black suit?" Asked Donovan.

"That's Dr. Solimen. Dr. Jack Solimen. He's been around for years. His patients are mostly rich folks. They pay him well. He has a large office nearby."

Dr. Solimen was looking over the deputy in the back of the wagon. They watched as the sheriff waved over a group of men. The group of four climbed into the back of the wagon and pulled out the deputy. His face was white, with blood coming down his chin. The front of his white shirt was covered with wet blood. The men carried the deputy to the jailhouse, the sheriff and the doctor led the way.

"You think Dr. Solimen can save him?"

"Nothing can be done for him." Said Tracy.

"How long does he have?"

"Not long." Said Tracy.

After watching the men carry the deputy through the entrance of the jailhouse, Donovan pulled a table against the wall underneath the window, and then grabbed a chair and seated himself as he continued to watch the jailhouse. Tracy grabbed a chair and seated herself across from him.

A loud argument broke out from the kitchen. One of the voices was Alfred the other was a woman's voice. The argument was in Spanish and went on for about three minutes before a pot hit the wall, and clanked into what seemed like the floor. Then again the woman's loud voice was heard, and then Alfred spoke, and another pot hit the wall and then the floor, then there was silence.

Alfred came out slowly and a very attractive Spanish woman in her early forties came strolling behind him. She stared at the ground humbly.

Alfred forced a pleasant smile. "This is my wife, Sofia." He introduced her, stepping back like one would do in a stage play after introducing the actors. She looked up briefly to smile.

Tracy smiled but Donovan did not.

"Sofia is…how do you say…uh…yes, modest woman. She's afraid of trouble, and doesn't want you here." Alfred forced a laugh. "I tell her, that this Donovan is maybe killer, but she claims me to be a coward. I'm no coward." He said. "So you must leave. I don't want this, you understand. But I must prove to my lovely Sofia, I'm no coward. So please go."

Silently Donovan dismissed them and gazed out the window once again. Suddenly a loud battle cry filled the room, and Sofia charged Donovan pointing a slender finger. She cursed him in Spanish as she pointed at him violently. Unfazed by her outburst Donovan continued to stare out the window.

Alfred grabbed her. "No, Sofia." He said, and then he spoke to her in Spanish and led her into the kitchen. As she was led away she glared at Donovan over her shoulder.

Donovan and Tracy sat in silence as he continued to stare out the window. His face was serious. Tracy reached across the table and grabbed his hands. Only then did he turn to her. She smiled gently. "I'm sorry that I hurt you, Donovan. I just wanted you to be around a little longer. I know now that I was wrong." She paused for a moment as if fighting back tears. "I broke my agreement with the sheriff. We are no longer together."

Donovan watched her as she stared back at him. He was ashamed of himself. She did nothing wrong. She saved his life more than once, and by doing so he was able to spend more time with his son. He was able to teach him how to defend himself in this often cruel world. She didn't just save his life, but she sacrificed herself to do so. Now she was sitting across from him apologizing as if she had done something wrong.

As Donovan watched her he came to realize how in love he was with her. He truly loved her. But now it was too late for them. Before the day was over, he would be dead. And even if it wasn't so, how could she ever forgive him for what he put her through. "I wish things were different between us." He said.

His comments caught her by surprise. "Different how?"

Donovan glanced out the window again and then turned back to Tracy. He gently squeezed her hand. "I should have thanked you, Tracy. You saved my life; you gave me and Sage more time together. You did nothing wrong. It was me who owes you an apology." He paused for a moment. "I've done you wrong. I hope you will forgive me."

Tears slid down Tracy's cheeks. "It was awful, Donovan. I hated being with him. The only reason I could do it was because I loved you so much. That's the only reason I could do it." She paused. "I'm not a whore."

"I know, Tracy. I didn't mean that."

"But you said it."

"I was hurt by what I found. I didn't know how to handle it." He said.

"You were hurt." She questioned angrily. "I was sleeping with him to save you. He had been trying for years to get me to lay in his bed. And I have always refused him until I saw him pointing that pistol at your head. I knew it was the only way I could save you."

Donovan stared out the window again in the direction of the jailhouse, anticipating the sheriff to come out at any moment. Then he turned back to Tracy. "I wish we could start over." He said.

"Start over how?" She asked.

"I would have married you. Maybe taken you away from here."

She thought it over. "You still can."

He nodded. "It's too late. I'll be dead soon."

"You don't know that. You may live through this, like all the others that you somehow survived. Then we can get married, have a family." She said.

Donovan nodded. "If I live through this, I would like you to be my wife, and to have my children."

Tracy laughed. "Yes, Donovan I will marry you. You know I will marry you." Tracy said.

"Let's get married tomorrow." He said.

Tracy thought it over with a grin. "Yes, tomorrow will be fine."

Donovan felt awkward talking of marriage, but listening to Tracy and watching her excitement about the subject almost convinced Donovan that they would be married. For the moment, he had forgotten about the sheriff and was excited about marrying Tracy. She would be such a beautiful bride. He wondered what she would wear. Would she wear a dress? He had never seen her in a dress before. He smiled. She would make a wonderful wife and a wonderful mother. He imagined that they would be married for years to come, and have at least ten kids. They would grow their family on a large farm and they would all be so happy together.

Donovan stared out the window again and then stared at Tracy. As he watched her the reality began to set back in. Donovan forced a smile, but he had seen how quick the sheriff was with his pistols, and Donovan didn't recall when he had seen anyone faster. Not only that but if his brother died, the sheriff would be even more motivated to kill Donovan.

Unfortunately, they would not be married, and he would not live past this day. He laid his rifle upon the table. As he did so her expression became sad as the reality of their situation came upon her as well.

"I want you to keep this with you," Donovan said. "If I don't kill him, he's gonna come after you, then my family. You'll have to stop him."

Tracy stared at the rifle; she hated guns and didn't like to handle them. She didn't like the weight of them and didn't like the loud explosion that they made when fired. But worse she didn't like the hideous injuries that these weapons caused on people. As a doctor she had witnessed many gun wounds, and she doubted that she herself could inflict such wounds on another human being.

"Pick it up," Donovan said.

"I can't."

"This is the only way you can protect yourself if the sheriff gets past me."

She stared at the rifle for a moment longer, trying to decide what to do. "I can't-do it Donovan."

"Tracy, he's gonna kill you. And if he kills you, he'll kill my family, my son. I'll need you to stop him." Said Donovan.

Tracy continued to watch him. She knew his words were true. Landry would kill everyone. She awkwardly grabbed the rifle.

Donovan reached over and carefully gripped the rifle. "Hold it like this, put your finger on the trigger, point and pull. Don't shoot until he's right upon you."

"If you don't kill him, how can I?" She asked.

"He'll be injured. I'll get a bullet in him. I promise you that. I'll get a bullet in him. But if he's alive, he'll be hurt which will give you an edge. He'll come in the restaurant looking for you. Just wait for him. When he opens the door, shoot him. He won't be expecting this."

Tracy nodded. "Okay, Donovan. I'll shoot him."

She watched Donovan sigh with relief. He appeared calm as far as his movements and breathing, but there was something uneasy about him. It was almost undetectable.

She pulled her chair around next to him. She grabbed his hand and held it tight. His hand trembled inside of hers. He was afraid. How ignorant of her, she never figured Donovan to be afraid of anything. And by looking at his demeanor one would never know of his fear. But the tremble of his hand told her different. "Are you afraid, Donovan?" She asked, wondering if he would answer her truthfully.

He turned to her and smiled. It was awkward watching him smile at this moment.

"I've been afraid most of my life. But that don't change nothing." He said. "Fear gets in the way, so it's best to pretend it's not there. Otherwise, it will overtake you, and you won't be able to do a thing."

"I'm afraid Donovan. I'm afraid for you, and I'm afraid for me. I'm afraid of what I got to do if you don't make it."

Donovan put his arm around her shoulder and leaned into her. This was unexpected, being that Donovan wasn't the affectionate type. "Not much I can do about that, Tracy. I just hope I kill him, so you don't have to."

They sat in silence and snuggled as they continued to watch the jailhouse. After less than an hour the front door of the jailhouse opened and out came Dr. Solimen. His head was bowed. He spoke to a couple of ladies standing on the sidewalk. One lady put her hands on her face and appeared to be crying.

"The deputy's dead." Said Donovan.

They watched as Dr. Solimen stopped and talked to several people as he headed down the street. Most of the people had the same sad expression. Donovan figured that the doctor was telling bystanders that the deputy had just died. It is a sad situation to have one of your family members die, Donovan knew all too well about that feeling.

As they watched Dr. Solimen making his way down the street, it soon became apparent that he was headed toward the restaurant.

"He's coming this way." Said Tracy.

"Why?"

"I don't know, maybe Landry sent him."

As Dr. Solimen came closer to the restaurant Donovan climbed out of his chair and approached the door, and waited. There was a light knock, and then the front door pulled open, and Dr. Solimen peaked his head in. He was surprised to see Donovan standing there, and jerked back, and then once again peaked his head in.

"I have a message from the Sheriff." Said Dr. Solimen.

"What is it?" Donovan said.

Dr. Solimen swallowed. "His brother is dead, the sheriff will meet you out front after he makes the burial arrangements. An hour at the most."

"I'll be waiting," Donovan said.

In the doorway Dr. Solimen turned until he found Tracy sitting at the table. "The sheriff also has a message for you Tracy." She did not respond. Dr. Solimen grinned. "The sheriff said that you betrayed him, like no other. He said he'll forgive you if you promise him something." He paused and stared at Tracy, but she said nothing. "He wants you to be his wife. Only then will he forgive you for what you have done."

Tracy stood to her feet, walked over and stood behind Donovan. She put her arm around him, and they both stared at Dr. Solimen. "I will not." Said Tracy.

Dr. Solimen frowned. "Then you will die with him." He then closed the door and headed toward the jailhouse. This time when folks tried to talk with him, he ignored them. Donovan and Tracy watched him disappear into the jailhouse.

Donovan and Tracy seated themselves back at the table. They both stared out the window in as they continued to watch for the sheriff's departure.

Finally, the sheriff appeared in the doorway. Donovan thought it was odd that the people standing close by didn't say a word to him. They seemed to be afraid of him. Dr. Solimen stepped out behind the sheriff. They said a few words to one another before Dr. Solimen went back into the jailhouse.

Landry started walking down the center of the main road. Donovan could see his six-shooters resting against either side of his legs.

Donovan stood to his feet, and Tracy stood with him. He stared at her for a long moment. She was so beautiful in every way. This would be the last time he would see her, so he wanted to get one last look. He smiled. His smile caught her by surprise. She could not, however, return his smile; instead, the tears flowed over her face.

With his hands he wiped away her tears and kissed her. Afterwards, he said. "I love you, Tracy."

She embraced him and said. "I love you too, Donovan."

Finally, Donovan eased past her and headed to the front door. When he reached the door he stood frozen with his back to her.

"Donovan." She called.

He turned once more to face her.

"I'll be waiting for you. Don't be long." Tracy said.

He nodded and then pulled the door open and headed out.

Tracy ran to the window and watched. Landry was across the street facing the restaurant waiting for Donovan. Donovan walked in his seemingly normal relaxed and calm manner toward the sheriff. He kept walking until he was about an arm's length away. Tracy found this action by Donovan to be unusual, for, in the gunfights that she had witnessed in the past, the men always stood as far from each other as possible.

As Donovan approached the large man he could see that his eyes were bloodshot red, giving the appearance that he had been sobbing, and mourning his brother's death. The sheriff's expression was gloomy and exhausted. He looked as if he would break down at any moment. But Donovan knew that he wouldn't, not in front of Donovan anyway.

He found the sheriff's gun stance odd. His arms were resting comfortably by his sides, his shoulders were slouched forward, and even though his eyes were focused on Donovan, his head was bowed downward. It gave the impression that the lawman was defeated. But Donovan knew all too well that this sheriff wasn't even close to being defeated.

Donovan looked at the sheriff's eyes, they were focused and alert. However, his body posture gave the impression that he was not alert and could be very slow to the draw. If Donovan hadn't seen firsthand how quick the sheriff was with his pistols, he too might be fooled by his casual posture.

He and the sheriff continued to stand at about an arm's length from each other. Donovan wanted to break the sheriff's concentration, so he walked right up to him, but truthfully he didn't expect to get this close to the large man. Donovan was expecting him to pull out his gun before he reached him, but he didn't. Maybe he was waiting for Donovan to pull out his gun first.

"My brother's dead." Said Landry.

Donovan was calm and relaxed for he had come to terms with what was going to happen to him. He knew he would not live, but he wanted to make sure the sheriff would not live as well. "I didn't want him to die." He said breaking one of his longtime rules of never talking during a potential gunfight. But this time he was buying time to maybe catch the pathetic looking sheriff off his guard. "He was going to kill my son, I had to stop him." Donovan finished.

"Your son?" Landry questioned. "Gunther said nothing of your son." He paused for a moment and swallowed. "I can't believe you're alive. I saw you on that day. You were so close to death. I don't see how you survived."

He looked for a moment as if he was going to break down. Donovan was surprised by the sheriff's demeanor. Because of what happened to his brother, he had expected him to come out in a complete rage, but instead, he came out defeated and exhausted from grief. Donovan decided to keep him talking. He seemed to want to talk about his brother.

"What did he say happened?" Asked Donovan

At that moment the sheriff's eyes changed. His eyes became more attentive, maybe angry. It was as if he had yawned and was now fully awake. He stared at Donovan for a moment, and Donovan stared back, anticipating the big man's next move. But none was made. "Gunther said you was looking to shoot him in the back."

"No," Donovan said. "I wasn't looking to shoot him at all. But he pulled his pistol and left me with no choice."

Landry nodded. "That's how I figured it. He knew I would be angry with him if he told me the truth. I told him to stay away from you. Not to face you alone. But he didn't listen. He never listened." He sighed. "But that don't change nothing. He's dead now. And he's dead because of you. I hold you responsible, and I hold anyone that helped you responsible. When I'm done with you, I'm going after Tracy, your brother, papa, mama." He paused for a moment. "And your son."

He barely got the word out before Donovan reached for his pistol, there was an explosion, then Donovan found himself on his back. He couldn't see, and he felt the pain in his chest where he figured the bullet had struck him. He could feel his gun within his hand but he could not lift it. He thought he had gotten a shot off, but he heard only one shot, and he was now laying on the ground with a bullet in his chest. He opened his eyes, to only see blackness. Then he felt nauseated, and before long everything started spinning. The world was spinning from head to toe. Faster and faster it went, he stretched his hands out, pressing them hard against the dirt road where he laid, trying to balance himself against the spinning. This must be what it is like to die he thought. He hoped he had got a shot off and killed the big man. He didn't remember seeing the sheriff pulling out his pistol.

Tracy pressed her face against the window of the restaurant. Watching Donovan and Landry standing so close together was tense. She wondered what on earth were they talking about. She expected them to start shooting immediately after Donovan had stepped out of the restaurant. But was surprised when Donovan walked right up to Landry, standing almost close enough to touch him.

When Donovan first walked out of the restaurant she wanted to follow him with the rifle that he had left her, but she knew he would refuse her, and she didn't want to break his concentration. But at least they would face the sheriff together, and if need be die together side by side. But as Donovan explained someone had to stay back and kill the sheriff. Which made sense. If the sheriff had killed Donovan he would have easily killed Tracy out in the open, and she had never fired a rifle before. So she would have to get very close to shoot Landry, and he would not have let her get that close.

It was more advantageous for her to wait for him within the restaurant and catch him by surprise when he entered. The thought of this act terrified her. She would at that time be facing the sheriff alone. And if she didn't catch him by surprise or get close enough she would be dead also.

She saw Donovan reach for his gun, he was very quick, but even quicker was the sheriff. Even though Donovan seemed to reach for his gun first, both men pointed and fired simultaneously. Their shots were timed so close together that their pistols sounded as if one shot was fired between them. Donovan took a bullet to the chest and dropped to the ground. There was movement in his arms and legs as he laid helpless on his back.

The sheriff also took a bullet to the chest and was still on his feet, but he swayed awkwardly as if he was drunk. He had one hand on his chest that covering the wound, and in his other hand the pistol was gripped tightly as he rested it against his thigh. He was astonished as he stared at his bloody wound. This was the first time he had ever been wounded by another man's pistol, and he wondered if he would survive the injury. He turned his attention to Donovan who was on the ground. He had greatly underestimated this man's ability. He knew now that the story about the encounter between his brother and Donovan's son was probably true. Judging from the Negro man's skills, he could have easily killed his brother if he had wanted him dead. But instead, the Negro man attempted to bring his brother to town so that a doctor could aid him.

Landry raised his pistol and pointed it at the Negro man's head. Even though Donovan appeared half dead, he would this time make sure of it.

By this time Tracy had stepped out of the restaurant entryway with her rifle in hand. She called out Landry's name, and he turned to her. The rifle blared as she fired it. However, she was too far away for accuracy and the bullet missed its mark completely. Landry turned his pistol in her direction, she dropped the rifle in admitted defeat. As he swayed and pointed, she closed her eyes and waited for the inevitable. Her death.

Two shots were fired, and she opened her eyes in time to witness the sheriff stumbling back and fall dead. From the ground Donovan's arm was raised with his pistol extended. Fresh smoke came from its barrel. Afterwards, his extended arm went limp and dropped to his side.

She ran to him and dropped to her knees. His eyes were open but glazed as he stared at her. "Is he dead?" He asked.

She nodded. "Yes, Donovan. He's dead."

He sighed with relief. "You should have waited until he came to the restaurant."

Tearfully she nodded. "If I had waited you'd be dead now."

He sighed again. "Now you're all safe."

She nodded again. "Yes, Donovan, we're safe now."

Donovan briefly closed his eyes and then opened them again. He stared blankly at Tracy. "Tell my son it was my time. He'll understand."

She raised her head and whispered. "It's not your time Donovan." She said tearfully. "It's not your time."

Hello Reader. If you enjoyed the book, I would greatly appreciate your feedback by rating this book. Hopefully, your feedback will help draw others to the book as well.

To leave a review, please go here: **Thou Son's Keeper**: *He thought he could leave his violent past behind and go home to his son...he was wrong*

Thank you again!

Rod Cole